ESMER

Deception in Miami is the ..... book in The Esmeralda King Collection by Kathryn Louise.
Esmeralda King is a crime investigator who solves cases on behalf of the rich and famous.
Kathryn Louise was one of the most anticipated fiction authors to hit the literary scene in 2022.

"Exciting and thrilling, I couldn't put the book down!"
- Becky Meakin

"Such a clever plot twist, I had no idea what was coming next."
- Mark Jefferies

"Loved it! Can't wait for the next Esmeralda King case."
- David Cousens

KATHRYN LOUISE

A CIP catalogue record for this book is available from the British
Library.
Printed and bound in Great Britain by KLA Books.
978-1-7391309-6-1 (paperback)
978-1-7391309-7-8 (eBook)
978-1-7391309-8-5 (hardback)

Dedicated to Oliver.
Without you, the plot wouldn't have been written...

DECEPTION IN MIAMI

ESMERALDA KING

KATHRYN LOUISE

Prologue

My name is Esmeralda King, but my friends and family call me 'Esme'. Born in 1992, I am the daughter of Lynda and James King and the sister of Hunter. I grew up in a small village called Windlesham, Surrey in England until 2010, which is when I moved to study at The University College London.

It was at this point that I met my lifelong friends— Casey Hughes, Mollie Frith, Amie Stone and Tilly Baker. We lived, studied and partied together. We also made a pact that we would die for each other, but I will leave that explanation for a little later in the book. Each one of us are smart, gifted and highly intelligent, all in our own specific areas of expertise.

Casey studied Law; Mollie studied Medicine; Amie studied Psychology, and Tilly studied Business.

Hunter, being four years my senior, joined the police force straight after sixth form and moved into the forensics team for the Metropolitan Police. I adore him, he is my protector, my big brother and my bodyguard. I think that was why, historically, a lot of men feared dating me. No one was ever good enough, not in Hunter's eyes anyway.

I had inherited my mother's dark brown eyes and hair, olive skin and stunning smile. People often referred to her good looks as that of a Mediterranean beauty, but my drive to work and learn meant that my appearance, more often than not, was somewhat dishevelled, and in my opinion, men just weren't a priority.

Three years after starting university, I gained a first-class degree in Computer Science, where my love of technology took me to my first job in Central London for an IT company. That was my first insight into the world of Cyber Security Forensics and ethical hacking. It gave me the opportunity to work on several top-secret and high-security projects for the British Government.

At 26 years old, my work colleagues and senior management soon realised my potential as a forensic analyst. I became security cleared, passed several professional qualifications and learned how to solve complex investigations. I was quickly promoted to a senior specialist. A further five years later, extensive travelling and a lot of learning and experience led me to where I am today.

It was not until I started working for the government in association with the intelligence agencies that I started to realise... sometimes things aren't quite what they seem, but you keep your eyes and ears open, your back to the wall and your mouth firmly shut. A mixture of complex situations, a lot of money and political circumstances can either make you look like a superstar or get you into a lot of trouble.

I had been approached on numerous occasions to solve outside cases but declined due to work conflicts.

The rich and famous want answers but undercover and under wrap for fear of it leaking into the media and public domain. They are willing to pay to solve their complicated situations, but they want someone who is highly intelligent, quick to solve cases, and can keep a secret. I guess that person is me—Esmeralda Sophia King.

With a little help from my nearest and dearest, I have access to highly sensitive files, records and information that most people can't reach.

I soon realised that working for myself, on my own cases, may be a better option. Giving me the freedom to work as and when I please, the financial security to live a more than comfortable life and a career that I know I am good at. Of course, it is completely and highly illegal and I'm walking a very thin line with every case I take on, but I just can't beat the adrenaline or the curiosity.

High-profile individuals approach me with their unsolved crimes and situations that the police can't or don't want to get involved in, hence why I'm offered danger money.

I'm the one willing to go a step further, to delve a little deeper into people's backgrounds and confidential files.

What I hadn't quite worked out yet was whether the money is worth the danger.

I guess I am about to find out...

Chapter 1
The Funeral

Would it be inappropriate for me to light a cigarette right now, right here, amongst everyone? I thought to myself as I watched the coffin slowly lower into its final resting place. Smoking was the only way to settle my nerves, but I knew deep down that it wasn't the right moment.

I stood as far back as I could from the most stunning silver metal casket I'd ever seen. Sprawled with white calla lilies and the image of a man I had never met before. Now, I'm no expert on coffins but it looked extremely expensive. In fact, I knew it was expensive—this was the funeral of Michael Richardson, the son of Arthur, a multi-millionaire.

The sound of distraught tears, heart-wrenching emotion, and sobbing filled the air like a painful storm was brewing. Usually, funerals meant closure, an end to any pain and suffering, but in this instance, it wasn't the end, not by a long stretch. This was just the beginning of a complicated and dramatic family feud.

So, is this what a millionaire's funeral really looks like? Michael was only 50 years old—far too young to be lying in a metal box, about to be buried under six feet of earth. I still couldn't quite get my head around death, especially when they were taken too soon.

Why had I been called to solve the mystery behind someone's supposedly innocent death? Why did someone think it was under suspicious circumstances?

I counted the amount of Rolex's peering out from the sleeves of most of the men's suits, and the Gucci, Prada and Versace sunglasses on every woman's face, even though the sun wasn't shining. Limousines and fancy cars lined the side of the road next to the graveyard like a prestigious car showroom.

I had only ever been to a cremation before and not a burial, so this was new to me. I began wondering how many people would show up to my funeral. Would I be missed? Would the attendees be sad? I had spent so much time working recently that I had lost contact with a lot of friends and rarely saw my family, so maybe I wouldn't be missed that much after all.

The sky was dark and cloudy, the rain was heavy and falling in such a way that my black umbrella was doing very little to keep me dry. My dark tights and mid-length skirt were damp and stuck to the back of my legs. There was a chilling feeling that lingered in the air as if something was wrong.

The hairs on my arms and down my back stood on end. I could feel the tension lingering like a bad smell.

Edging slowly towards the large shadowing oak tree to the side, I stood, watching patiently for the service to finish.

Despite me not knowing anyone there and attending a stranger's funeral, something felt oddly familiar. I glanced around at the gathering of people, all there to say their last goodbye, hoping something or someone would stand out. One by one, I studied the faces of his nearest and dearest. I had so many questions swirling through my mind.

Are they genuinely mourning? Are some of them glad to see the last of him? Did he have any enemies? Is anyone missing? Was there really anything peculiar in the way he had died? These were all the pieces of the puzzle I had to pull together.

I watched every movement like a hawk. I studied the eye contact between the mourners and their body language, piecing together relationships between the small crowd as the funeral celebrant finished reading the Lord's prayer. He paused, hung his head out of respect to the deceased, and closed his eyes, leaving an eerie silence. The only sound that could be heard were the two large crows perched above me, squawking to each other. They had flown in mid-way through the service, out of the pouring rain, and sat like two old men looking on, occasionally putting the world to right.

A small speaker balanced precariously on a stand next to the coffin began playing 'Have I Told You Lately That I Love You' by Rod Stewart, the steady beat and his soothing monotone voice caused yet another wave of tears and emotion from those around me.

There was something about funerals, even if you didn't know the person being buried, that brought back a flurry of sadness from memories of other funerals you had been to. Remembering those that I had lost, I felt a lump in my throat and my eyes started to water.

Snap out of it, Esmeralda, I thought to myself. *You can't be a blubbering fool today, you need to be alert and aware of your surroundings. After all, you are here on official business.* But, at the same time, I didn't want to stand out from the crowd.

Diving into my pocket, I reached for a tissue that I had strategically placed there that morning and wiped my eyes, being careful not to smear mascara and blinking to reset my feelings. I pushed my glasses back up into place from the bridge of my nose and took a deep breath.

Now that the casket was firmly inside the burial hole in the ground, the music began to fade. One by one, the mourners threw dark red roses on top of the casket before turning and making their way back to their cars, clutching nothing but the order of service cards that had been handed out at the beginning. A few hugs were given but it felt like emotion was fairly distant from them as a family.

I did the same, making my way back to my car that I had parked in the most askew way, in the only space I could find. I couldn't have cared less—I was late and the only thing that mattered was getting to the funeral without drawing attention to myself. Immediately after I got in, the windows began to steam up, so I launched my soaking wet umbrella into the footwell of the passenger side and turned the heaters on full.

'Ugh! This weather sucks,' I said to myself, looking in the rear-view mirror to check my appearance. 'I need some sunshine.' My pale face was staring back at me. 'Well, there is no chance of that, not now I have taken on this case... any type of holiday will have to wait until further notice.'

Reading the address for the wake venue from the order of service, I quickly entered 'London Road, GU19 5EU' into the satnav, flicking the car into drive as quickly as I could as I didn't want to be left behind. Setting off along the small track between two curtains of graveyards on either side of me, I couldn't help but notice the beauty of this place.

Brookwood Cemetery was stunning, set in what looked like acres of beautifully landscaped gardens and memorials. I would never be able to afford a burial of this scale and magnitude—I wasn't important enough—but what would it matter if you were dead anyway? I guess it all boiled down to status for some people.

I followed the winding driveway along to the large iron gates that stood at the entrance, the last car in a long line of vehicles belonging to the Richardson family and friends. We all drove slowly for about seven miles through the beautiful Surrey countryside, taking in the rolling scenery as we went while the cars on the other side of the road slowed to watch the procession passing in the opposite direction. I must admit, it was quite impressive, similar to what I imagine it would be like to follow someone famous.

Finally, we reached a turning in the road—a curved ten-foot-high brick wall and another set of iron gates, just as majestic as the last. A large black sign with elegant white and gold letters read 'Pennyhill Park – Hotel, Restaurant and Spa'. I had never been to the venue before, but I could see why they chose it. The impressive winding driveway and main house with its elegant grandeur came into full view as I pulled into the main car park, lined with the tallest fir trees swaying gently in the breeze. This was the type of place you would hold a royal wedding.

Pulling in alongside a brand-new black Bentley Continental GT, I tried to play it calm. I needed to fit in amongst the wealth of the guests arriving. My white sports coupe didn't stand out like a sore thumb, but it wasn't at the same level as some of the cars there.

Scrabbling for my handbag on the seat next to me, I pulled out a compact mirror and pretended to adjust my hair and glasses. I couldn't see through the black-tinted windows of the Bentley, but I kept one eye on my reflection and the other on the car next to me.

The Bentley car door swung open. At first, I saw a finely tailored black leather shoe step onto the tarmac, followed by a suited leg. Then a muscular and well-manicured hand grabbed the outside of the door as he got out of the car. I tried not to look but I couldn't avoid making eye contact with him. I almost dropped the compact down the side of the chair in a panic. Trying to regain all my composure, I flipped it shut, stuffed it back in my bag and rustled around for a lipstick instead.

He was attractive... he was *very* attractive, but who was he? I had to find out. His short black hair was combed back into a male model-type style, and his dark luscious eyes were alluring and matched his well-groomed facial hair. As he looked briefly into my car, our eyes met, and he smiled cautiously. I tried to return the smile but no sooner had I placed the lipstick back in my bag and unclipped my seatbelt, he had already shut the car door and was making his way across the vast parking area, down the steep steps to the grand walkway and out of sight.

My heart was pumping and the nervousness was kicking in as I thought of the awkwardness ahead of me. Attending a funeral wake where I needed to be hidden, conspicuous and blend in, but at the same time, ask as many questions as I could. I was on my own. Maybe I should have come with Amie or Casey or one of the others, but there wasn't time.

I switched off the engine and opened the door, hurling my handbag over my shoulder. It wasn't easy walking in high heels, but I did my best to lock the car and look elegant as I did so, walking in the same direction as everyone else.

The main entrance of the venue took me to a sloping archway. A series of paved steps to one side made it easier for me to keep up the pace of the others. A large oak-built pergola stood above me, vines and pretty climbers swirled around and clung to the timbers as I looked up, admiring its beauty like something out of a secret garden, before passing underneath and out the other side. I did my best to keep walking, but I couldn't help stopping occasionally to appreciate the quaintness of the hotel as I approached a large, cobbled courtyard.

Emily Carter was the previous legal advisor to Arthur Richardson and his business until he passed late last year, then when his son, Michael Richardson, took over the company, she began working for him instead. I was told that Michael had drowned whilst at sea, sailing with his son, Oscar. His body was recovered hours later.

Oscar was the last one to see him before he died but there was nothing on the police report to say that there was any connection to his death or anything that would relate to foul play. Just as I was about to ask more questions, I caught a quick glimpse of the man who stepped out of the Bentley next to me about half an hour earlier. He passed us in the corridor, walking in the opposite direction. I followed his casual, swaggering walk to the gents' toilets, but he stopped, looked back, slyly smiled, then turned and continued.

Who on earth is he? It was almost as if he wanted to draw attention to himself. The smile, the stop and turn and the way his eyes almost had a message in them to follow him. I blinked, trying to bring myself back to the conversation with Emily, instead of watching this stranger and being drawn in.

'Poor Michael, devastating it was, and at such a young age. We became so close after Arthur... you know...' Her voice trailed off.

'I'm sorry... I.' I shook my head at her as if to apologise for not really listening. 'Were you very close to Arthur and Michael?' I asked but maybe I shouldn't have. I was prying just a little too much, but I needed to know. I had to find out as much as I could before leaving.

'I loved Arthur so very much. I know everyone in the family talked about us. They disagreed with our relationship and there being such an age gap, but to us, it didn't matter. He was so young and adventurous at heart.' Her eyes looked genuinely pained as tears began to swell, giving them an almost glass-like appearance. She held up a silk handkerchief, sniffed and gently dabbed the corner of her eyes in turn.

'I'm so sorry for your loss, I didn't re—' She stopped me instantly before I could ask another question.

'And not to mention the trauma of having to leave our home without anywhere else to go. It was humiliating to say the least. I lost everything when I lost him. After Lillian passed away, I think he was lonely, he wanted company just as much as I did. I don't think people understood our needs. We...' No sooner had she started to pour her heart out to me—a complete stranger, might I add—the extremely attractive man appeared from behind, placing his hands on the shoulders of her elegant satin blouse and startled her. She stopped instantly and froze.

'I do apologise, Miss... er...' He stopped, waiting for me to add my name.

'King. Esmeralda King,' I replied.

'Nice to meet you, Miss King, however, Miss Carter gets a little too overwhelmed from time to time and we are just about to raise a toast to my late father in the dining room if you would care to join us.' He walked around to join Emily on her side and looked at her out of the corner of his eye. She quickly blinked a couple of times as if to acknowledge his hushing commands and briefly nodded.

'Yes, that's right, we need to raise a toast to Michael. Lovely talking to you, Esmeralda.' She smiled but I could see there was more to her story. More than he was prepared for her to divulge.

'Likewise, lovely to meet you both.' I smiled back as they began following the crowds of others, leaving the main reception and heading to the dining room. There must have been over one hundred people at the wake.

Some of the pieces of the puzzle were beginning to present themselves to me, one by one. If his late father was Michael, then the most attractive man I had seen in a long time must be Oscar. Why did I not notice the resemblance between him and the picture of the man from the coffin? He must take after his mother, who I was yet to meet. But what was the relationship between Oscar and Emily, or maybe there wasn't a connection at all, she was just the legal representative of the business and that was that.

If she had been asked to vacate their family home, where was she living now and who was in the family home? Maybe it had been sold after he died. I guessed that Lillian was Arthur's wife.

Mental note—Emily Carter, the legal representative for the Richardsons' corporate empire, was in a relationship with Arthur, the head of the family, and they didn't like it. Oscar was the son of Michael, whose funeral I was at. I had to meet more of the family and piece this all together.

I followed the sound of 'Canon' by Johann Pachelbel being played as I joined the gathering of people in the main dining room. In the corner, to the side of the glass-walled bar, was a shiny black grand piano and a well-dressed man in a black suit and bow tie perched on the edge of a matching stool. The way he played the piano was breathtaking. The chords echoed around the walls as everyone stood watching him. Three young barmaids dressed in white shirts and short, tight black skirts weaved in and out of the guests, carrying silver trays full of champagne.

'Chink, chink.' The sound of a metal knife rapped against the side of a glass and suddenly stopped the quiet chatter as well as the piano. It instantly grabbed everyone's attention as all eyes became locked on Oscar Richardson. He stood above us all on a wooden stage, placed in the corner of the room.

There was silence. He cleared his throat as he scanned the audience of the room.

'Firstly, I want to thank you all for coming today.' Again, he stopped and breathed. Oscar appeared to be choked, struggling to say the words he wanted to. His eyes seemed to pause as soon as they reached mine, just as they had done in the car park. I looked around, hoping that it was just a focus point for him, but I couldn't help but feel awkward. I shifted from one foot to the other, my high heels were already making my feet throb from standing up for too long, but I kept calm, hoping he would move on to his next victim. He didn't. His dark, empty stare, locked on me.

'Secondly, I want to raise a toast to my beloved father.' There was a slight pause as he held up the slim, sparkling glass in his hand and continued. 'Who I will miss dearly. He was loved by everyone... it's endearing seeing so many of you here today. He inspired me to be a better man, to love, to care, and most importantly, to be the person I am today. I will be forever in his debt.'

Although I wanted to believe Oscar and his sad, short words as a grieving son, there was something that wasn't sitting right.

'To Michael.' Oscar lifted his glass even further into the air before drawing it to his lips and taking a sip. The whole room did the same.

'To Michael,' echoed around the walls and was followed by the sound of people sipping, then applause. I copied, trying to blend into the others like a shadow on the wall.

'To Michael,' I murmured under my breath while carefully watching everyone around me.

'You must be Esmeralda King.' I felt a hand on my shoulder that made me jump. Turning around to find the owner of the hand was a middle-aged, greying man.

'Sorry, I didn't mean to make you jump. I just thought I would introduce myself to you as you were standing here all alone.' He smiled politely at me, waiting for my response.

'Er... yes, I am Esmeralda King. How did you know?' My eyes narrowed. 'And you are?'

'Samuel. Samuel Richardson. Michael's brother.' He held out his hand for me to formally shake. I accepted, noting that his hands were large and warm, wrapping around mine and almost twice in size.

A very expensive-looking wedding ring was embedded tightly around his fourth finger. It was a thick and shiny metal band that appeared to have a hole in the middle, almost as if something was missing—a diamond perhaps, or a gem of some description. I quickly moved my eyes back to his.

'Oh, I am so very sorry for your loss. My thoughts are with you and your family.' I gave my condolences as our handshake was still in progress.

'Yes, it was a big shock to the whole family. We all knew he had taken on such a responsibility... it obviously became too much for him. He will be sorely missed.' I retracted my hand and left it hanging awkwardly by my side.

'Too much for him?' I questioned.

'Yes, you honestly believe he drowned on his own sailing boat? Michael was a competent sailor. He won multiple competitions and was used to the conditions of the open sea. He...' Samuel gave me a puzzled look.

'I can't imagine the grief your family are going through right now, especially after losing your father less than a year ago too.' My lips pursed together. I didn't want to say too much but I was hoping he would give me a little more information on the family history than he was currently providing.

'May I ask how you were acquainted with my brother?' He wasn't giving anything away, instead, he fired another question at me.

'I... um... worked for your brother for a short while.' My quick response was an attempt to shut him down, but he wanted more.

'Oh, really? What do you do?' His head tilted as he looked interested.

'A project manager. I was in the acquisitions team. Poor Oscar, to have found his father in such a way and then be able to take care of the speeches at his wake. He must be a very strong man.' I wanted to know more.

'I wouldn't worry about Oscar... he is more than capable of looking after himself. They weren't overly close. He is more like his mother in that sense.' Samuel seemed to change his tone.

'Ah, that's a shame, but at least he has his mother's support, I guess, especially on a day like today.' I edged a little closer to him, hoping he would continue the conversation, but instead, he lifted his chin and let out a loud laugh into the air as though I had said something amusing.

'You must be joking. She's where she needs to be today, and if Oscar isn't careful, he will end up the same way,' Samuel said in a matter-of-fact tone. 'Anyway, it was nice to meet you. The acquisitions team, you say. Maybe I will see you around?' He patted me on the shoulder and walked away, leaving me standing on my own once again.

The smartly dressed young waitresses began walking around with silver trays full of hors d'oeuvres, offering them to anyone along their route. A young and petite, pretty brown-haired girl with the warmest of complexions started to head in my direction until she stopped just in front of me.

'Would you care to take one?' she asked.

The miniature menu card on the tray read, 'Rosemary polenta bites with peperonata, truffle arancini balls and sticky shallot, fig and almond filo parcels.' I glanced at the selection before making my choice and delicately placed the food in my mouth, savouring its exquisite taste.

I held up my hand, signalling to the waitress that I had finished, but she still stood there smiling rather than moving on to the next group of people. She nodded towards the tray.

'Oh no, I'm all good, thank you. Lovely, but I couldn't possibly eat anymore,' I apologised.

'Madam, the menu is for you.' She nodded again as both her hands were carefully holding the tray.

'No, honestly, I really couldn't. I...' Before I had a chance to finish, she moved a little closer to me and winked before whispering.

'The menu, Madam... you really need to pick it up and read the other side.' She extended the tray up so that I could pick it up as smoothly as possible. I was confused but did as she prompted.

Picking up the card and flipping it over as normally as I could, I found a handwritten message on the reverse.

'Meet me in the car park at 15:15hrs, behind the third three. Come alone.' I quickly looked up and around the room, hoping that someone was looking at me, waiting for me to read it and give me a signal, but no one was.

'Who wrote this?' I asked the waitress.

'I don't know,' she replied quietly. 'My manager gave me the card, pointed to you in the hall and told me to hand it to you but without anyone seeing. I'm just doing as I'm told he...' She turned to find him, but something seemed to catch her attention and she looked nervous. 'I must go.'

'Okay, thank you,' I replied, nodding my head in appreciation. She smiled and quickly walked away. I tried to see where she went but she disappeared into one of the doors and was gone.

Raising my arm to read the time on my watch, it was already 15:10. I needed to make my way back to the car park and meet my mystery message writer.

Making my apologies through the small gathering of people and out of the main entrance, I started back to the car park. Saying the words over and over in my head as I went, 'Behind the third tree, come alone.'

Who is it? Who wants to see me? I was half-expecting it to be Oscar, but why would he want to speak to me?

I counted the large trees as I approached the row of them. *One, two, three. That one. I* headed in that direction and slowed down to look all around me. Was anyone else in the car park? No, I was alone, completely alone. I didn't feel safe, not one little bit. My heart was pounding in my chest and the wind was swirling around me, blowing my hair into my face.

As I reached the gap in the trees, I ducked under one of the lower branches and once again looked all around. I couldn't see anyone, maybe it was because I was a few minutes early. Maybe the note wasn't for me after all.

Suddenly, there she was as if out of nowhere, appearing from behind the tree next to me.

'Esmeralda? We meet at last,' she said, walking towards me and holding out a petite hand to shake mine. It was cold but soft and tanned. She had a healthy glow about her.

'Sarah Richardson. Thanks for coming today, Esmeralda.'

'You're welcome,' I replied. 'How did you—' I had so many questions, but she cut me off instantly.

'I must be quick. If anyone sees the two of us talking, it will blow our cover. I take it you have met Oscar and Emily?' she asked, tilting her head to one side.

'Yes, I—'

'Great, then you have met the man himself.' Her gentle eyes seemed to narrow before continuing. 'As I said in our conversation, my father died suddenly last year from kidney failure, the majority shareholding of the family business was left to my brother, Michael, who apparently hung himself at home and was found by Oscar in the early hours of the morning three weeks ago.'

'What do you mean apparently?' I challenged her.

'Esmeralda, if there is one thing you should know, it's that Oscar is a spoiled child and always has been. Michael had a real handful with that one growing up. I know that Michael was under pressure as the business was getting on top of him, but not enough for him to end it all. I wouldn't be surprised if... well, let's just say I think there is foul play involved in Michael's death. I don't know exactly what, and more to the point, I believe there is still more going on. That's why I need your help.' Sarah clutched at my sleeve as if it was her last lifeline.

This case fascinated me, but I had very little to go on, other than the fact that a sister had a hunch that her nephew was involved in the death of her brother.

'That's why I'm paying you £1 million to figure out this whole mess, Esmeralda. I can't go to the police as they aren't interested, and I can't afford for this to be in the public domain since it will devalue the shares of the business. As promised, I will transfer 50% now and 50% when you can unravel the truth.' There was a rustle in the trees as if someone was there and listening to us—it startled both of us as we stepped back, our bodies against the tree trunk in silence. Watching, waiting and listening.

'No one in the family knows I am working this case, right?' I whispered gently to her.

'No, and no one must know. They will block us both out and we will never get to the truth. For the sake of my father, who will be turning in his grave if he knew, I need to get the answers and without the media finding out.' She held up her hand and placed it softly on my shoulder, her voice faint.

'How can I get in contact with you?' I asked.

'I'll be in touch.' She handed me a white business card —no name, no address, just an international telephone number. There it was again, the rustling in the trees. I held my breath, expecting someone to confront me, but as I was about to speak, a small bird came hopping out of the undergrowth, clutching at a small stick in its beak. Turning towards Sarah and almost laughing with relief, I found that she had gone, vanished almost into thin air. I was standing below the trees, in the car park, completely on my own. Letting out a big deep breath, I threw my head backwards, resting it on the rough bark behind me and contemplating for a second what I was getting myself into.

Chapter 2
The Richardsons

Two weeks earlier, my phone buzzed angrily on the kitchen surface. Someone was calling with a blocked caller ID.

Even though it was 2:15 in the afternoon, I was just in the middle of eating my favourite sandwich—chicken, bacon and cheese with added mayonnaise and cracked black pepper on thick and crusty doorstep bread. I had been so engrossed in a case that the government asked me to quickly review, that stopping for lunch or any type of food hadn't been a priority. About ten cups of coffee was all that had kept me going since the early hours of the morning.

I was sitting at the kitchen bar in my cosy London apartment, one leg curled up to my body, my chin resting on my knee and the other loose and swinging. If anyone knocked on my front door right now, they would find me casually dressed in a loose-fitting t-shirt, the faded image of a woman's face on the front, washed-out grey jogging bottoms that had seen better days and thermal socks that were about three sizes too large for my feet. My hair piled high in a messy bun, reading glasses at the end of my nose, and a small amount of mayonnaise residue at the corners of my mouth.

I really didn't want to answer the call, but it was distracting my attention and there was something inside prompting me to pick it up. Before it vibrated across the side for the last time, I finished my mouthful, placed my sandwich back down neatly on its plate and wiped my mouth on the back of my hand, pressing the answer button.

'Esmeralda King,' I said in a polite but efficient tone, trying to disguise the sound of me finishing the mouthful of sandwich. I waited for the caller to speak.

'Miss King, my name is Sarah Richardson. I understand you may be able to help me with a personal matter. It is quite sensitive, so I would appreciate your confidentiality in this instance.' She stopped and paused.

'Can I ask where you got my number from?' I replied. I had to be careful when someone new called me for the first time—they could be anyone. The last thing I wanted to do was divulge information to the police or government agencies. I almost expected her to hang up as she took a while to answer.

'Erm...' she finally spoke. 'My father, Arthur Richardson, was a close friend of David Roberts. I believe you were close to Mr Roberts. They met the night before he died and the last voicemail he had was from David, giving him your name and number... it said you would be able to help him.'

None of this made any sense to me other than the fact that David Roberts had been my manager for several years, he also spent his youth working for various UK intelligence agencies. He became my mentor not long after I joined the British government. David taught me almost everything I know and more. I owed him so much but there was more to this story.

'I didn't think much of his voicemail as it was almost a year ago that we lost my father, but then when my brother passed away last week, I had this horrible feeling that something wasn't quite right. I knew there was a reason why I kept your number and had to speak to you.' There was a chill in her voice, she seemed pained and needed help. I continued to listen, eager to find out why David had given her father my number and said I could help.

'Esmeralda, are you still there?' she asked.

'Sorry, yes, I am. Did you say that your father met with David the night before he died?'

'Yes. He did,' Sarah confirmed.

'And his voicemail said that I could help?' I wanted to check I had heard everything correctly.

'It did, yes, he was very clear.' I could sense the fear in her voice.

'The thing is, Sarah... I am a private investigator. People normally call me because they have a situation that they need me to solve, or they need me to find answers to questions that they can't get themselves. It sounds like your father was concerned about something and reached out to David. Why else would he give him my number? But I'm not sure...' I began questioning what she wanted from me and whether I would have the time to spare working on this case.

'I do need your help. I knew there was something wrong when my father died but I chose to ignore it. He and my brother, Michael, had such a close relationship until the last few weeks before he was found. Michael was the eldest of us, so I guess my father confided in him, and he was the first person in line to take over the business, but I thought things were strange when I caught them arguing in the office last time I was in London. I tried to find out what was going on but neither one would tell me what it was about.' Her voice sounded solemn as if it was about to break. The line went quiet.

'Sarah, are you okay? Please take your time, I know this must be hard for you.'

'Yes, I'm just I... something isn't right, Esmeralda, and I need answers. I know he is my nephew, but Oscar is definitely up to no good.' She paused.

'Oscar? Your nephew? Why do you think he is up to something?' I asked.

'My father's business, ATR & Partners, was established in 1990. He had built it up over the years to a successful empire. One by one, we all joined as a family to help run it. Last year, it was valued at £50 million. Michael became a large shareholder and director, I was asked by my father to run the American office, and Samuel, my younger brother, ran the entire legal team and sub-divisions. We both hold shares but not as much as Michael did. We were passed the two estates he owned to make it fair,' she explained.

'So, I am guessing that Michael's shares have passed to yourself and Samuel now that he is gone?' I was scrambling around the side for a pen and paper so that I could note all this down.

'No, that's what you would have thought... but the shares have all transferred to Oscar. He now holds the majority shares. Samuel was fuming but Emily had all the paperwork tied up and there was nothing he could do.' I could hear Sarah's sighs as she exhaled disapprovingly.

'Hmmmm,' I was thinking out loud. 'So, Emily is who?'

'She was my father's partner and legal advisor. Despite us all not agreeing with her relationship with my father because of the age gap, she's been the only constant in this whole mess and a pillar of strength to all of us.' Sarah sniffled as if she was holding back tears.

My mind was whirring like a sports car on a racetrack. The more Sarah spoke, the more interesting this case was becoming, and I loved an exciting case to get stuck into.

'The trouble is, I'm only here in the UK for my brother's funeral, then I'm back in Miami.' Sarah stopped again.

'I can help you, Sarah, but I will need a lot more information, and I will possibly need to ask some sensitive questions along the way. Would you be able to get me access to your corporate network?' I asked. If I could gain entry to their business systems, it may give me answers from within emails, files, folders and all sorts of details that people store electronically. You would be surprised to see what information people send to one another because they believe it is confidential.

'Yes, I can get you set up on our work systems, security passes and access, but the family can't know that I have spoken to you. I need to be sure of what is going on before I make any accusations, it could go horribly wrong for me if you know what I mean?'

Sarah seemed worried about her own family finding out.

But why? Is she scared of them or scared of what she would find out?

'Of course, I can be more than confidential. I can work undercover for the business, gathering and collecting information. No one will ever know.' I wanted to reassure her that she could rely on me to work on this case. 'But it will cost as I need to rely on other third parties to give me access to areas such as public and medical files, government documents, etc.'

'I have money, Esmeralda, it's not a problem. My father made sure we would all be comfortable for the rest of our lives.' It sounded like Arthur was fair in dividing his property between the three siblings, but there also seemed to be a lot of resentment. I sensed a cold chill in her voice as if there was more to this case but she wasn't ready to divulge. 'It may be worth you attending my brother's funeral. That way, you will get to meet all the family members, friends and acquaintances. It may make you draw your own conclusions?' I could hear her occasional sighs.

'When is it?' I asked, pen in hand to make a note.

'5th November. 11.30 am. Um...' She paused. 'Let me quickly check something for you.' She sounded like she was rustling papers. 'Brookwood Cemetery, Surrey, followed by the wake at Primrose Park in Bagshot,' Sarah confirmed.

I had no idea what was going on behind the scenes for the Richardson family. I didn't know them at all, but if Sarah seemed to think something wasn't right and she was going to pay me to investigate, then it was worth picking up.

'Sure, I'll be there. I can't promise how long it will take to get to the bottom of this, Sarah, but I will try to be as quick as I possibly can. I will break down my fees and send them to you, but as I mentioned earlier, I may have to delve into matters that might not be pleasant, and I have to go to extreme means to get information that isn't always legitimate, are you sure you want to proceed?' I needed to check that she was behind me.

'Esmeralda, I have no choice. This is my last chance for the sake of my father.' I could almost feel her pleading with me. 'Esme...'

'Yes?'

'I think someone killed my father, there is something peculiar about my brother's death and I don't think this is the end of it.' Sarah's words instantly sent a wave through my body like an electric current. 'I need justice once and for all.'

'What do you mean that's not the end of it?' I asked.

'I think whoever was involved in my families' deaths had an ulterior motive and I have a bad feeling that they haven't got what they wanted just yet. I just can't prove it, that's all.' I could hear whispering in the background but couldn't quite make out what was being said.

Is she having a side conversation with someone?

'Okay, on that basis, I will take on your case. I will need you to be honest with me and tell me everything you know. I have an account that I will need you to transfer the money to—it is offline and untraceable. You must not share this with anyone else. I require a deposit upfront and the remainder on completion. As soon as this has been done, I will start the investigation. I'm sending you a message now with all the details.' I waited for it to send and for Sarah to acknowledge receipt.

'Thank you, Esmeralda. I must be quick... someone is coming and I can't have them overhear this conversation.' She suddenly sounded flustered and in a panic.

'One last question, Sarah... what about Oscar's mother? Was she and Michael married? Did she not gain any inheritance from Michael when he died? Where is she now?' I asked.

'Ha, no. Not in her condition, she wouldn't know what to do with it and...' Her voice lowered to a whisper. 'Oh,

I must go...' The call went completely dead. I looked at the screen, but it was black.

'Sarah, are you still there?' I quickly tried to get a response, but she was gone.

What did she mean by 'in her condition'?

David instantly popped into my head. I needed to speak to him about what he had to do with this family. He clearly knew the father, but how? Maybe he could give me some information that would help. I was reluctant to call him after so many years and especially how it ended, but I needed some answers and he may be the key to this whole scenario.

I quickly searched my contacts for David Roberts, finding two mobile numbers.

Let's try this one first... if he doesn't answer, I will try the other.

This time, I stood up. The sunshine was beaming through my large, rooftop apartment windows, showcasing all the dust in the air like a beautiful sandstorm. I always felt the need to pace back and forth whilst on calls as it helped me focus.

For anyone in the building opposite looking in, they must have thought I was weird, step after step along the creaky wooden floorboards, my head down, looking at the imperfections like an agitated lion in its cage. I would pace till I reached the opposite wall, twist on my toes, and then back again.

I could hear the ringing in my ear. *What should I leave as a voicemail after all this time?* It must have been at least three years since we had last spoken and it gave me goosebumps to think of hearing his voice again.

Although David was my mentor and we worked together, he meant so much more to me than just that. We knew it wasn't allowed and he was in a position of trust, but it was all my fault. I was the instigator—I was the one who couldn't control my emotions and how I felt for him. I was 26 at the time, he was 40, divorced and had children but I saw the way he looked at me. We both felt the same way. We had a connection that I had never felt with anyone before.

The last time I saw him, we spent the night together. It was late, we were working on a case, just the two of us at my apartment after a few drinks. One thing led to another and I leant in to kiss him. David and I had spent many nights together over the months—our relationship was deep and meaningful... or so I thought.

That last night I saw him, he felt distant as if something was playing on his mind. He was more attentive than ever. The way he stared into my eyes, it was as if he was trying to tell me something, but I was too lost in the moment to read the tell-tale signs. That was the most incredible night I'd ever had with anyone and probably will have again, but the following morning when I woke, I found the bed bare next to me. David had left without saying goodbye, just a note on the table that read:

'Esme, you deserve someone so much more than I. Never have I met a more beautiful and intelligent woman. Last night was a night that I will remember forever but I will hold you back in more ways than you will ever know. D. Roberts.'

He signed his name in such a formal way, it was like a quote from a book, not someone who had just made love to me and then left. I arrived at work to find that he had resigned. Human resources said they couldn't give me an address and his phone number didn't work. It wasn't until a whole year later that I found an email address and a number for him on a case that had been handed to us from another department. I didn't have the courage to call it or even check if it was him or not as I was still hurt that he had left like that. *If he really liked me, why did he leave?*

I don't think I have ever found a man more caring, passionate or as clever as he was. He broke my heart.

The last ring rang out. It switched to answer phone. There he was... his voice. I stopped pacing and froze just to listen to his calm and soothing deep tones. As it finished, the beep sounded and I closed my eyes, took a deep breath and said the words with my heart racing in my ears.

'David. Esmeralda King. Please can you call me?' I hung up. So formal and straight to the point. I was cold and scorned.

Oh, dear Lord, I thought to myself. He *won't call me back. What if he doesn't even remember me?*

I stood for a moment in a daydream, contemplating how my life could have turned out if he hadn't left when he did.

My phone suddenly rang, making me jump. I held it up and looked at the vibrating display. It was David. My heart was pounding in my chest. What on earth was I going to say? I went for it, swallowing hard and answering before it went to my voicemail.

'David?' I finally said.

'Esmeralda,' he said quietly, then stopped. 'How are you?' He seemed surprised to hear from me.

What do I reply to that? How about 'Great since the last time you slept with me, then disappeared leaving a cryptic message on my bedside table, never to be seen again.'

'Great, you?' I said instead, swiftly moving the conversation back to him.

'Are you sure you're okay? I was worried when I saw I had missed your call.'

Was he really concerned or was it just something to say?

'I'm fine, I had a question I wanted to ask you about an Arthur Richardson,' I cut straight to the point but he went quiet. *Did I say something wrong?* I paused for a moment, giving him a chance to reply but nothing. I looked at the phone to check he was still there. 'David?' I prompted him again.

'Sorry. I... you caught me off guard there. Why do you need to know who Arthur is? I went to his funeral nearly a year ago.'

'So, you know who he is then?' Why was he being cagey about this man?

'How did you get my number, Esmeralda?' he asked.

'You taught me well, didn't you? I can find out information on anyone and break any system. Your number wasn't hard to find—it was on a case file from head office, so you clearly weren't hiding your identity as well as you thought you were.' I was a little abrupt, but who could blame me? I was hurt.

'Esme, I am sorry... I... I should have explained but there were no words...' I wasn't sure what he was trying to say.

'It doesn't matter anymore, I'm over it.' I acted like I didn't care but I was desperate to know what he wanted to explain.

'Over it or over me?' David asked. I wasn't about to tell him how I really felt.

'Listen, I need to know about Arthur. I've been contacted by Sarah Richardson, his daughter. She says that you gave him my number and said I could help but it was on his voicemail the night he died. Why did he reach out to you, David, and how do you know him?' Now was the time for him to tell me everything he knew about the family and how he was connected.

'I don't think you should get involved with the Richardson family. It has trouble written all over it. Sarah is lovely but I'm not sure she can handle the truth either. Some things are better left buried,' he replied cryptically, still not answering my original question.

'I'm not sure I...' My eyebrows frowned as I tried replaying David's words again in my head.

'You do know who the Richardson family are, don't you?' I could hear a busy background noise like he was walking along a main road.

'I don't. I... I got a call this afternoon. I immediately called you. This is the first time I have heard of Sarah or Arthur or the Richardson family. Who are they?' I felt a cold shiver run down my spine. David and I had been involved in solving some of the government's darkest crimes, so for him to be wary of working on this case, it made the hairs on my neck stand on end.

'Now is not the right time. I can meet you, but not right now. In the meantime, search for their name on the internet. You will find lots of articles about the Richardson family in the media. I can then piece together what I know. Let's meet tomorrow if you are free. The coffee shop on Curtain Road at noon.' He hung up before I had a chance to respond. He knew I would be there.

I was used to the secrecy after working for the government for so long but not normally coming from David. If he was so concerned about the family, why on earth did he give Arthur my number? I needed to gather as much information as possible before our meeting tomorrow—I wanted to be armed with questions to ask.

I lifted the lid on my laptop and opened the search bar. While that was connecting to the internet, I got a small glass from the kitchen cupboard and poured myself a water from the dispenser on my large American fridge and took a well-deserved sip. It felt refreshing, but what wasn't refreshing was the notion that I would be seeing David again tomorrow, albeit in a professional capacity.

Sitting back down at the kitchen bar, I typed into the search engine 'Richardson family' and pressed enter, waiting for the listings to return. Despite me earning quite a substantial amount of money from my career, I still hadn't invested in an up-to-date laptop. It was like an old friend, some of the keyboard letters were worn from my typing and the screen was scratched and dented but I had all my files and quick search tabs configured exactly as I wanted them. I would wait until it broke before I traded it in.

I found a mixture of 'Richardson Gang' and 'Richardson family' articles. *Surely, they can't be related to the Richardson Gangs of London, can they?*

Two brothers—Charlie and Eddie Richardson—were involved in turf wars with the Kray twins back in the 1960s. They didn't seem like nice people at all and had been jailed several times for various convictions, but they had wealth, properties and a gang behind them to maintain presence in central London.

The other Richardson family that had multiple articles featuring them was Arthur and Lillian Richardson at the head of the family. Sons, Michael and Samuel, daughter, Sarah, and grandson, Oscar. That was clearly them but what I did find interesting were several articles such as:

'The Richardson family in court battle over money laundering accusations'

'Turmoil as the Richardson family lose uncle in severe car accident'

'Arthur Richardson arrested for affray and grievous bodily harm to public house landlord'

'The Richardson family business accused of drug trafficking offences'

It looked like none of the above had been held up in court. Either through the lack of evidence or conspiracy theories seemed to make these cases disappear as quickly as they had emerged. So, what exactly did Sarah want my help with? Did she think that someone had killed her father as well as her brother or was there a lot more to it?

I spent most of the afternoon gaining evidence on the Richardson family. Noting the connections, the history, background and, more importantly, who everyone was. Every time I started a case, I created a timeline and a map of people with pictures, notes and information. My apartment looked like a crime scene with printed article titles, photographs and scribbles of writing that only I could understand.

I couldn't leave it all out on display, so each time I spent working on a case, I would take pictures, store them in a secure drive and permanently destroy my evidence. That way, I could keep everything away from the risk of being found.

The following morning, I was up early. I had been tossing and turning all night thinking about the

Richardson family case and an embedded list of questions in my mind that I wanted to ask David.

Grouping together the most important documents that I had gathered from the night before, I neatly inserted them into a card folder and placed them into my leather bag. Making myself a cup of coffee and pouring it into a thermal flask, I grabbed my jacket from the back of the front door and made my way to the train station on the corner of my road. I could have walked but I thought it would be easier to get the tube from Covent Garden to Shoreditch. One change, four stops and a short walk would get me there.

Dressed in tight dark blue jeans, a cute sweater and black leather ankle boots, I had made a little effort but not so much that I wanted David to think I was trying to impress him. An attempt to style my hair resulted in it flowing gently over my shoulders, the front held back firmly behind my ears, and contact lenses rather than my ugly, semi-broken glasses. It was the first time I had left my apartment in over a week and had worn the same pair of jogging bottoms for six consecutive days. A step out in the fresh air would be good for me and a great way to clear my head before meeting him.

The tube was busy for a Friday. Normally, the hustle and bustle of office workers frantically moving about the city was on a Thursday, but for some unknown reason, the carriages were packed with smart-casually dressed men and women. The train whirred into position along the platform, a fair distance between the pavement and the doors as they bleeped and opened.

Everyone's eyes were firmly on me as I cautiously stepped over the gap and into the standing area. I clutched onto the handrail to steady myself while the train was in transit, then the doors aggressively slammed closed again. I looked around slowly as the tube rattled and shook along its journey, a cold, fresh wind gust down the carriage from the semi-open window at the end. A mixture of people reading, looking at their phones and the occasional person flicking through the daily news of the Metro newspaper.

I looked at my reflection in the window, taking a moment to reflect on where I was in life. Was I a bad person for taking money from the rich and famous to solve their precious problems? If their cases were above board, then they would get the police or lawyers to handle them, but here I was, getting paid a fair amount for the risks I was taking to get them the answers they wanted.

Now wasn't the time to take the moral high ground. I had done some things in my past that I wasn't proud of, so I wasn't innocent by any stretch of the imagination, but from time to time, it got me thinking if the money was worth the danger and the hassle. It was better than any drug though—the adrenaline, the curiosity, and the desire to reach a conclusion kept me wanting more.

The tube shunted to a halt. I did my best to stay standing and waited for the doors to open. I must have daydreamed for the last couple of minutes as it only felt like seconds. I looked up as the sign outside the doors read Holborn and it was time for me to get off and make my way to the central line.

I always loved the underground in the winter, it felt warm and cosy as opposed to the summer when it was hot, humid and claustrophobic. I didn't need to look at the maps or signs... I knew exactly what tunnel to follow, which line and how many stops. I got off at Liverpool Street and walked the short, ten-minute journey to Curtain Road.

On the corner of the crossroads where Rivington Street and Curtain Road met, an old greying man in a long tan coat, dark jeans and smart trainers entered the quirky coffee shop where David and I used to meet frequently. I sped up to try and reach the door just after him, but as he turned to see if anyone was approaching and to hold the door open, I noticed it *was* David. He looked tired and worn like a once-loved childhood toy that had been cast aside. I gulped. So many memories came flooding back of the dark-haired, mysterious and admired man that I once knew —and loved.

'Oh, Esmeralda,' he said, glancing back. 'You made me jump.'

'Hi, David, you're looking well,' I lied.

'I don't feel it but thank you.' He accepted my compliment with a warm smile. 'You're looking... well... just as beautiful as ever.' I blushed. As we moved through the entrance, leaving the door to gently close behind us, he stepped closer to me, almost to give me a hug but I quickly edged forwards to stand in the queue ahead of him. I couldn't bring myself to touch or smell him just yet, it would bring back too many painful memories that I didn't want to relive.

'What can I get you?' I asked, raising my shoulders and tilting my head to take a better look at him. His deep brown, comforting eyes hadn't changed.

'A vanilla latte, please. Here, I'll get these.' He rustled around in his coat pocket and pulled out a small black leather wallet, but as he opened it to get some cash out, I noticed a picture of his ex-wife and three children—all boys. It was quite an old photograph as his children looked a lot younger than I knew they would be now.

I noted it but quickly transferred my attention back to his eyes.

Why would he still carry around a picture of his ex-wife? Maybe I was wrong to think that he ever liked me at all. Maybe I was just a one-night stand and he missed her and the family life he once had. Perhaps they were back together again and that's why he left...

I ordered both our drinks whilst we spoke about pleasantries—how cold the weather was, how busy life and work always is and, more importantly, how long it had been since we last saw each other. Despite my animosity towards him, I missed him and our chats so much. I didn't just lose a lover... I lost a close friend.

Carrying our mugs back to the table and sitting uncomfortably opposite each other in comfy armchairs, we both smiled politely, sighed and sat in silence. Fidgeting. Both of us nervously thinking of what to say but neither knowing what to say or how to say it.

I guess I was going to have to go first if I wanted answers.

'So, how did you and Arthur know each other?' I jumped straight in, my ears standing to attention, waiting for him to tell me everything. I felt like I was interviewing him as a chief suspect in a case.

'Did you do your research?' he asked.

'If you mean, am I aware of all the cases against the Richardson family yet none have been followed through, then yes. If you were referring to the amount of assets, property, estates and investments totalling more than £100 million then, yes, I am also aware. Even though their business doesn't account for the substantial amounts of money they have, there is clearly a side hustle. What I'm not completely sure of is whether they are related to the Richardson Gang from London and if someone did, in fact, kill her father or brother or both.' If I was standing up at this point, I would have had my hands on my hips, demanding David to reveal all, but I remained seated.

'Esmeralda, you need to keep your voice down,' he whispered, leaning into me and the table, almost with a warning. 'I brought you here because I thought we could have a quiet coffee without anyone following and being able to see all around us.' David looked out the large windows around the coffee shop, checking for familiar faces.

'Follow us?' I repeated, narrowing my eyebrows at him. 'Why would anyone follow us?' I was more confused now than I had been when Sarah first called me.

'Yes, the Richardson family are loosely connected to the Richardson Gang... but a cousin of a second cousin, if you know what I mean?' His eyes widened. I hadn't a clue as to what he meant but I leaned in towards him.

'Go on,' I quietly prompted.

'Arthur and I met many years ago. We were at private school together. His father died during an altercation whilst in prison. His mother had more sense than money and tried leading an affluent socialite life. A young boy got in the way, so she sent him off to school. He spent many summers with me and my family. He was intelligent, but not just smart... he was extremely business savvy.' David appeared sad, recalling memories from his past when sharing them with me.

'Okay,' I said, pairing my lips together to cool my coffee down before taking a sip and attentively listening like a child following a storyteller.

'He was like a brother to me, Esmeralda, but he got himself in multiple scrapes and with some very dangerous people. It was hard keeping him on the right side of the law.' David did the same and blew the steam from his latte before sipping and gently clearing his throat.

'You must understand that I had to clear a lot of files.' He looked up at me sheepishly.

I wasn't sure quite what David was getting at. Was he admitting to being responsible for all of Arthur's cover-ups? What did that have to do with why he needed my help?

'Enough was enough. Everything happened all at once and I couldn't be a part of it anymore.' David seemed to be justifying his actions as he looked at me with lost emotion.

'What was enough? I don't understand. What did that have to—' David cut me short and tried to hold my free hand. The other was wrapped snugly around the warm coffee mug.

'One of his investments had gone horribly wrong. His share price was about to hit rock bottom and he was set to lose the business. His health was deteriorating, and he thought that someone was deliberately sabotaging him. Arthur needed help investigating files and I thought you may be able to help him. I had no idea that it was the last time I would speak to him. A week later, I got a call from Sarah saying he had passed away and gave me the date of the funeral. I just assumed that it was his poor health.' David's eyes looked sad but there was a part of me that was angry.

Angry that he wanted to pass the buck over to me rather than deal with it himself.

'So, you decided to just give him my number instead, rather than dealing with it yourself? Why get me involved in your and Arthur's dirty work? Now I have Sarah on my radar, bringing me into everything. It could drag up a lot of the past. Is that wise?' I was fuming, how dare he!

David sat there in silence, leaning back in the chair. He wasn't telling me everything. I knew there was more.

'Don't I deserve an explanation? You disappeared and now you're throwing all this at me. What is the matter with you?' I wanted to raise my voice and shout but now was not the right time. Not in the middle of a coffee shop. 'David! I'm giving you one more chance before I leave and walk away.'

He sat back up but looked down in shame. He seemed to swallow as if he was looking for the courage to start the next sentence.

'I lost Jane, Esmeralda.' His eyes filled with tears and I instantly felt bad.

'As in your ex-wife Jane?'

'Yes. The last night we spent together, I got a call from my son, he was distraught. Jane had been diagnosed with stage four cancer and there was nothing we could do—it was just a matter of time. I felt bad that I left you in the way that I did, and God only knows how much I only wanted to be with you, but it wasn't fair bringing you into our family problems. Jane and I weren't together, but she was still the mother of our children, and someone needed to care for her. To see that she got the treatment she needed. It gave us that extra time together as a family.' I shuffled my chair closer to David, but he seemed to back away. 'I owed her that much.'

I checked all around me to see whether anyone else was listening into our conversation.

'I wanted to help Arthur but I also wanted to be with you. I had things I needed to do. Being there for the boys was my biggest priority, my needs came last. Arthur called me not long after she passed away. I was there for his wife and Lillian's funeral. That's how we got talking again but I never told him how ill Jane really was.' I could see David holding back his emotions.

'I'm so sorry, David. I didn't realise. I...' I had no words. No wonder he looked tired and broken, he had been through so much. I wanted to comfort him. All the anger and resentment I had towards him diminished now. I was the selfish one after all, thinking about my own feelings and not what he was going through. I could have helped him. I could have been there for him.

'Why didn't you tell me?' I shrugged with consolation.

'It wasn't fair. You were young... you didn't need that pain in your life. You needed to find a man who was a similar age that you could be happy with. I wanted the best for you, Esme. I still do.' He looked at me in the same way that he did all those years ago.

Don't let your heart be broken again, Esmeralda, I said to myself. *Don't be drawn in.* I kicked myself under the table.

He quickly switched the subject back to the case.

'So, Sarah called you. Why now, almost a year later?' He shrugged and wiped his watery eyes on the napkin from the table and placed it back down in a crumpled heap.

'It looks like the business was handed down to his eldest son, Michael. His other son, Samuel, and Sarah were given an estate each and shares in the business. Michael appeared to be running the company until last month when he passed away. Sarah seemed to think that something was suspicious although she wasn't sure what. She mentioned the grandson... Oscar?' I fiddled in my bag to get the papers out, but David grabbed my wrist quickly and stopped me in my tracks.

'Not here, Esme. We can go through the papers another time. You don't want anything related to the Richardson family getting into the hands of anyone other than us.' He looked worried.

'You really think something has happened to Arthur and possibly Michael?' I asked.

'I can't be certain, but I wouldn't be surprised. Did she mention someone by the name of Emily Carter?' David looked up, frowning.

'Yes... but briefly. Why?'

'She was Arthur's legal representative. A very clever woman but I never trusted her. I could never seem to get close to Arthur when she was around. I think she was burrowing her way into Arthur's fortune, especially after Lillian died, and he fell for it. It was as if she appeared out of nowhere. Although he made sure that there was a signed prenuptial agreement, hence why she was left out of the will, the business and the estates, much to the surprise of Michael, Sarah and Samuel.' He smiled wickedly.

'This definitely wasn't on the internet.' I raised my eyebrows towards David.

'Nor would Arthur have wanted it to be in the public domain. He tried so hard to keep things private, but his illegitimate dealings and business agreements were hard to keep under wraps. He was a character, Esme. You would have liked him despite his shenanigans.' David seemed to brighten his mood slightly. 'They were a very troubled family and I don't think they ever recovered from...'

'From what?'

He paused and looked as though he had said something he shouldn't.

'So, what are the next steps?' He turned to me, pushing his coffee cup to the middle of the table, changing the subject and wrapping up our meeting.

'Sarah has asked me to attend Michael's funeral—undercover, of course—to meet the family and try to piece things together. It is in two weeks. If anyone asks, I am employed by the firm and working in the acquisitions team. From there, I can work my way through emails, files and confidential material.' I had a glint in my eye and he knew what that meant.

'Nice. Are you sure you want to take on this case? I had all the time in the world for Arthur, but I don't believe his family had his best interests at heart. Samuel was harmless, but Michael and his son, Oscar, were... let's just say more like the Richardson Gang. As for his wife... that's another story.' David started to bring his belongings together as if he was ready to leave but I wasn't.

'Michael's wife? Where is she?'

'Where she belongs. In a mental institution. That one was a bad egg from the start. Nothing but trouble for everyone.' David stood up quickly. He seemed agitated and didn't want to talk about her.

'Wait. What?' Just as I stood to follow David, a couple approached me from the side and tapped me gently on the shoulder.

'Excuse me, are you leaving? Can we possibly take your table?' a young woman with a middle-aged man said as she moved her bag closer to the table. I glanced down at the two coffee cups and collected them in one hand.

'Yes, sure, we were just leaving anyway. I'll get these out of the way for you and you can...' I turned around to join David so we could leave together but he was gone. Nowhere to be seen.

'I... um... it is all yours.' Confused, I took the mugs to the counter, thanked the staff and left the coffee shop.

I stood on the street looking both ways but there was no sign of his tan-coloured coat or his silver fox hair. He had vanished into thin air once again. This time, there was no note, no apology... just his last comment running through my mind.

Chapter 3

Friends Forever

I needed a place to unwind, to have a clear state of mind and a fresh way of looking at the new case I had been offered by Sarah Richardson, and what better way to do that than to have a few drinks with the girls.

The five of us owned a cocktail bar in London together —Cinco Chicas (which meant five girls in Spanish). Each of us were equal investors and co-owners of the establishment.

We would often meet up there and discuss cases when I needed help. Even though I ran and managed them, pulling together the intelligence and solving the mysteries, we all joined forces as one collective, splitting the money between us, so we had a vested interest. It was a team effort. I wouldn't be able to delve into police reports without Hunter, or the medical history without Mollie, or receive legal advice without Casey.

We had a bar manager called Hugo, who we loved dearly and trusted to run it implicitly. He gave a real Spanish feel to the place. His close network of Albanian security specialists ran the safety of the venue. Despite these huge men towering above us all and looking very scary dotted around the club, we had all grown quite accustomed to them. In fact, it was quite nice to have protectors looking after us. It all came at a premium, but I was happier knowing that we had a team around us.

Cinco Chicas was vast and spread across two levels, including a dance floor that featured either a disco, band or entertainment of some description most nights. Two busy bars serving all varieties of cocktails and a spacious office, back room and comfort area. If we wanted to talk in private, we went in there. If we were looking more for atmosphere and a good time, we would all meet at the main bar.

The club was elegantly decorated. The concept was to attract an upper-class clientele, a place to go where you had to dress for the occasion. Authentic leather booths with cowhide seats that were for reservation only and came with the choice of champagne or spirit buckets on ice.

There was even a private area that you could hire for cocktail-making parties. It was always booked months in advance and the reviews from guests were outstanding. If nothing else, the five of us were proud of the venue we had built together.

It felt like a second home to me, but it also worked out as a great business asset. Our secure business lounge quite often turned into a crime case discussion area, accompanied by a few glasses of champagne and cigarettes.

The cash or private transfers that we received from our investigator clients were pulled through Cinco Chicas' accounts. You could call it a money laundering business or a way of washing cash—it was exactly that!

But how did five young women in their early 30s, you could say in standard professions, afford a top venue in the heart of central London, and how were we all so exclusively connected? Hunter was part of the club, but he couldn't be connected formally in any way to a money-laundering private club in London for fear of losing his career and access to police files that we needed. Of course, he was compensated, but it was off-record and untraceable. It would take an investigative specialist like me quite a while to really trace his assets and uncover it all. More importantly, they would have to know what they were looking for.

Casey, Mollie, Amie and Tilly were my best friends. The five of us together made a great team. We all met whilst studying at University College London. We were thrown together. Just like most university students, you never really knew someone until you began to live with them.

Neither one of us wanted to stay in the halls of residence, so our parents searched for private accommodation and found that a local landlord was renting out his five-bedroom house on the outskirts of London. It was perfect, a 30-minute journey into the city and as affordable as we could manage.

We hadn't met one another before, but the minute we were introduced, we hit it off instantly.

Casey was the wild one—blonde, tall, incredible long legs, amazing figure and the prettiest smile that turned men weak at the knees every time. Not only that, but she was also very smart, studying criminal law and judicial systems.

Mollie, on the other hand, was a little quieter. She was the sensible one of the group. Constantly making sure everyone was okay and, more often than not, sorting out our crap. She was the one that everyone turned to when they had screwed up. Mollie's parents were both from Italy, so she had inherited their gorgeous olive skin, chocolate eyes and the loveliest dark brown hair that she frequently died auburn.

Amie was our 'hot head', and boy did she have a rage inside her. The most gentle, calm individual until something rattled her cage. She then went from zero to ten in a matter of seconds. Her fiery long red hair and pale complexion gave us all a good run for our money. As a psychiatrist, she understood how others felt, but we put her tantrums to good use as Amie was always the one that would defend our corner, finish our arguments and be there to reason with us when we were being irrational. You could call her arrogant in most situations, but we loved her dearly.

Last but by no means least was Tilly—sweet, calm and completely scatty. She seemed to be in her own bubble where life was great and nothing much seemed to matter. A whizz at business studies though, she excelled at everything she did just because of who she was. She was adored by all who knew her. Her only problem was that she couldn't say no and always wanted to help. She was destined to be successful.

That was my team. Our parents dropped us on day one at our new home, our bags and belongings sprawled everywhere. We immediately bonded—inseparable and a force to be reckoned with.

Year one was an absolute blast and went quicker than we could have imagined. Year two was hard and we all felt the pressure. None of us were working, so the income was tight and any money our parents had given us was rapidly running out. By year three, we were broken, times were hard, the five of us exhausted and under more pressure to hit deadlines than we could have imagined. That's when it happened.

I had started my final module on advanced ethical hacking. In layman's terms, it means that you attempt to gain access to a computer system and test its security controls so that you can prevent an actual malicious hacker from gaining access and stealing data. Imagine you are testing the lock on your own front door works and then proceeding to gain access and noting all the entry routes so that you can prevent burglars getting in. You would be identifying any potential easy-access areas to lock down.

I found the subject fascinating. The top of my class in every component. I had been given harder and harder systems to try and break to test my ability, but I managed to successfully do it each and every time. So impressed with my speed and ability, my professor decided to put me forward for a university competition.

All the top Computer Science students from across the country attended a convention at Oxford University. I didn't think I had the slightest chance of coming anywhere other than last but we went for it anyway.

I found it so easy, I could have completed the task with my eyes closed. I surprised myself. The look on everyone's face that participated displayed the same look of shock as myself when I won. Even my parents who were watching from the auditorium were beaming with pride.

Standing on stage like a practice graduation ceremony, I was called out and given a large trophy for first place while the hall applauded in astonishment. I remember calling the girls and telling them what had happened. As supportive as they always were, they called a get-together and demanded that we have drinks to celebrate. It would have been nice to go to a club for drinks but none of us could afford it, so it meant a trip to the local off-license to purchase some cheap bottles of alcohol and some nibbles.

Winning that competition gave me the encouragement and the self-confidence in my ability to take cyber security to the next level.

We consumed drink after drink, but back then, the hangovers weren't as bad as they are now. We turned to shots and mixers to really get the evening going but the combination was toxic. All five of us were unable to string a sentence together or walk in a straight line.

'So, Esme... I've been thinking about it all afternoon. If you can hack into a computer system, why can't you hack into a bank's central system and steal us all some money? I'm in desperate need of a little cash right now,' Tilly said as she threw her body down on the sofa next to me and laughed.

'Because that would be highly illegal, of course,' Casey butted in. 'But I like your thinking, Tilly. We could all do with it, right?' She winked at me.

'It's so easy. I could break into someone's system in minutes.' My mind began to think about the processes I would need to go through and how I could do it.

'Go on then, show us what you're capable of, Esme!' That was Casey's wild side encouraging me to do things I shouldn't.

'And do what, show you that I can break in?' I laughed in retaliation.

'Go on. Steal us some money. You wouldn't dare!' Tilly gave a cheeky laugh and shoved Casey.

'Guys, that's really not a good idea. We could get into a lot of trouble and regret it in the morning.' Sensible Mollie interjected like the mother hen that she was, hiccupping as she did so.

'Then I'll put the money back. Simple.' I smirked. 'Besides, they wouldn't know it was me... I could leave their network without a trace.'

'Smart. I knew there was a reason why I loved you, Esme. You're so clever.' Amie sat in the large armchair opposite us with one leg folded over the other like an elegant doll. She was already so drunk that she was struggling to keep her eyes open and her head up.

I got to my feet and headed towards the corner desk. I pulled the chair backwards, took a seat in front of my laptop and the two monitors that were connected to it. The girls followed me and stood behind my chair, almost waiting for me like I was about to perform a magic trick. Casey brought the two bottles of wine and glasses over to us and proceeded to fill them all as I began typing in my password and credentials to access the system.

'So, girls, I have a few accounts on the dark web that are used for storing virtual money, I can place the funds in there, turn it into cryptocurrency to use and then transfer it back out again.' I interlocked my fingers and stretched them out as if warming up before exercise.

'If I am in stealth mode on the dark web, no one will be able to trace the funds anyway.' Not that they could comprehend anything, but I tried explaining what I was doing anyway and how they could access the funds in each of the accounts.

'I have no idea what you just said but it sounds super cool.' Tilly took another sip of wine and smiled. She must have seen double the monitors because she was swaying from side to side.

I picked up my glass, took another couple of large gulps of white wine and tapped away. First, accessing the accounts that I wanted the funds to enter, and then on the other screen, I started searching for investment firms that I knew had a strong financial position. I picked a couple of corporations that had a high share price, strong performance in their last quarter and were publicly traded.

'Right, okay, let's start with this one, girls.' They were all hooked, their eyes fixed on my screen.

'So, basically, a company should have a security system that acts as a layer of defence to protect their information. If I send a barrage of signals all at the same time to bombard it, their systems can't cope and will shut down. A bit like a dam trying to hold back water. It's called a DDOS attack.' You could tell they didn't have a clue, but their drunken eyes widened. I continued to tap away on the keyboard like a pianist playing at a concerto.

'Oooooh,' said Tilly, downing the rest of her wine. 'Smart.'

The signals were sent and I continued. Their systems failed one by one and started shutting down. Like a back gate, I was able to turn the handle and let myself in. I had access to everything. Their entire file system from their payroll to staff credentials, bank accounts, customer files... you name it.

As I headed straight for their banking system, I couldn't believe just how much was in their account. £120BN. Surely, they wouldn't miss a couple of thousand pounds, would they? Especially as I would be transferring it all back in. I glared at the screen, realising the seriousness of what I was about to do but the alcohol got the better of me and I continued anyway.

'Esme, maybe we shouldn't be doing this after all. My parents would be so pissed with me if I was kicked out of university, especially after three years.' For Casey to take the moral ground, I paused and looked back at them all one by one.

'If we are going to put it back, will they even notice?' Tilly replied before slowly sliding down the side of the desk and ending up in a pile on the floor beside us. Her head rested on the plant pot to the other side. That was her done for the night.

'She has got a point... I'll transfer it out and then put it straight back in again. It will just show as an anomaly, a banking error.' I looked back at the screen and began typing again. There was no stopping me.

This time, I loaded the transfer screen, entered in my undiscoverable credentials and then clicked on the amount section.

£150,000 *from a pot of £120BN—they won't even miss it*. I thought to myself.

I entered in the numbers and then hit submit. I watched as the screen almost counted the digits and then a symbol began spinning like it was thinking about the transaction. A green tick displayed, showing it was complete and my computer returned to the transfer screen.

'So, now what?' Amie's impatience started to present itself.

'The money should be in the central account but it's an account on the dark web that should be untraceable. To make it even more difficult to find, I can send it to five other accounts—one for each of us. Your access code will be your date of birth and an access key that only we will know.' This was the clever part, making my tracks completely vanish so that only a very clever hacker would be able to find it.

I opened the main account—the money was there. I split it into five equal amounts of £30,000 and sent it to five different accounts.

'Girls, if I enter your mobile number here, it will send you a code that will expire in 24 hours that you need to click on to access.' They all nodded simultaneously. One by one, their phones chimed to display a message from the system. Each one having to read out a 20-digit automatically-generated code that I needed to authenticate.

'Wow, that's like magic,' said Casey. 'It's genius.'

'Yes, it is genius, but it is also theft. I would go away for a long time,' I reiterated the seriousness of what I had just done.

'Six years minimum, in fact,' Casey confirmed.

'Exactly, that's why I now need to put it back!' Just as I returned to the screen to transfer it all back to the investment firm, there was a loud bang at the front door.

We all panicked, staring at each other and froze like musical statues.

'What the fuck, Esme!' Amie said in an angry whisper. 'That's probably the government's intelligence agency or an undercover spy... they have got wind of your transfer and come to arrest us.'

'Don't be ridiculous.' I laughed. 'How would they be so quick? Besides, they would probably break the door down, not bang on it,' I whispered so whoever it was couldn't hear our conversation.

Bang! Bang!

There it was again. It rudely awoke Tilly snoring on the floor. She responded by saying, 'Coming,' but mumbled and fell straight back to sleep again.

I raised my eyes, snapped the laptop closed so that the screens in turn shut off, and went to answer the door. I nervously looked through the peephole and my heart relaxed as I caught a glimpse of the person on the other side, unlocking the catch, and smiled as I opened the door to let him in.

'Hey, Esme, let us in... it's freezing outside.' My brother was standing before me, shivering, even though he was in a closed indoor corridor.

'Hunter, seriously? What are you doing here at this time of the night?' I shrugged my shoulders at him, opening the door wider for him to come in.

'I missed the last train home and I'm not paying for a cab all the way back. I'll just crash on your sofa for the night and be gone in the morning. You won't even know I'm here.' He shoved his way past me, slamming the door behind him and waltzed into the front room. He glanced around at all of us looking extremely guilty about something.

'Besides, you guys are all up so I might as well continue drinking with you. I'll have a glass of whatever she is having.' He held out an empty hand to Casey, motioning for her to get him a glass of wine.

I think Hunter and Casey had a little soft spot for each other because whenever we were out together, they were inseparable. The way they looked at one another, it was so obvious they had feelings, but nothing had ever happened. Well... nothing that I was aware of.

My brother had a way of being the life and soul of the party, just as Casey did. Over the next couple of hours, we drank way more than I care to remember. The cards came out and I lost, just as I always did. I put it all down to them cheating.

My memory of the night ends there—it all became a bit of a blur.

The following morning, I awoke with the most dreaded hangover. I struggled to piece together the broken memories from last night's antics. Several bottles of wine, prosecco and the unexpected arrival of my brother. I glanced at my side table on which there was still a half-full champagne flute, an empty packet of cigarettes and my reading glasses.

I could hear the clashing sound of saucepans, plates and cutlery as well as the noise of the kettle boiling but I had no idea whether that was my brother or one of the girls. Throwing both my arms above my head to stretch out whilst yawning as wide as I could, I noticed that the time on my watch was just about to reach 11 am.

Shit, I have overslept, I cursed. I wanted to get up early today as I had loads to do.

Time for me to get up, have a shower and get dressed, but the headache pounding above my eyes gave me the feeling of just wanting to sit in my pyjamas for the rest of the day, or at least until my head had a chance to catch up with the rest of my body.

That's when it hit me. The investment company hacking attempt from last night... did that actually happen or was it just a vivid dream? I tapped around the sheets on the bed trying to find my phone. If I could just check my secure account for activity, I would know for sure. I couldn't find it anywhere—it wasn't on my bedside table or under my pillows. I reluctantly looked beneath my bed and it was there, underneath a pile of old clothes that I had kicked under rather than putting in the washing bin. I grabbed it impatiently and tried to log in.

Password incorrect.

'For fuck's sake!' I muttered. 'This is all I need. Come on,' I mumbled again. Trying to enter the same combination again but hitting the screen harder as I did so and getting highly impatient and agitated in the meantime.

The screen shuddered and the device vibrated in my hand but then unlocked itself. Multiple messages flashed before my eyes as they popped into my private account, alerting me to several transactions.

USER NO. 36457 ACCOUNT ACTIVATION SUCCESSFUL

USER NO. 36457 YOU HAVE £1,500,000.00 NEW FUNDS AVAILABLE

USER NO. 36457 TRANSFER TO UNKNOWN ACCOUNT NO. 3142578 OF £300,000.00 SUCCESSFUL

USER NO. 36457 TRANSFER TO UNKNOWN ACCOUNT NO. 3158364 OF £300,000.00 SUCCESSFUL

USER NO. 36457 TRANSFER TO UNKNOWN ACCOUNT NO. 3198213 OF £300,000.00 SUCCESSFUL

USER NO. 36457 TRANSFER TO UNKNOWN ACCOUNT NO. 3421906 OF £300,000.00 SUCCESSFUL

USER NO. 36457 TRANSMISSION ENDED

'Oh no. Oh no, no, no! This is bad news, very bad news!' I repeated out loud to myself half-believing what I was reading. I banged and hopped about the room, frantically trying to slide on some underwear and the screwed-up jogging bottoms from beside my bed before rushing to the bedroom door. I stopped and paused, my left hand resting on the handle as if it had suddenly dawned on me.

Wait, just one little minute. I grabbed my phone from my pocket and once again logged in to check something. 'That can't be right?' I desperately scrolled through the list of alerts.

I transferred £150,000.00 not £1.5M, didn't I? I didn't put an extra zero on the transaction, did I? More to the point, I can't have stolen £1.5M... that is just ridiculous!' My shaking hand immediately attached itself to my mouth, covering my gasp.

I felt hot and extremely dizzy. The room was spinning and not in a good way. I*'m in so much trouble right now that I can't even comprehend it. I need to put that money back in and quickly before anyone finds out.*

I opened the door in a mad panic, sick with dread.

'Morning, morning, Esme,' Hunter called out before I had fully emerged from my room. 'Oh my, you don't look well. You look like you have seen a ghost.' He was busy helping himself to everything in my kitchen.

I shut the door behind me, leaning up against the frame, my hand still behind me grasping the handle. It was as much as I could do to steady myself and regain composure.

'Well, I think I'm about to meet one soon,' I replied in a trance.

'Huh?' Hunter seemed confused. Of course he was... he had no idea what I had done. After just starting with the police force, he would have had me arrested then and there, regardless of whether I was his sister or not. Only the girls knew, and half of them were so drunk that I don't think they would have even remembered this morning.

I had to log into my account first and then transfer back all the funds, deleting my tracks as I went so that no one could trace it. That seemed easy enough, just as easy as last night was.

I ignored Hunter bustling away in the kitchen and sat down at my desk, flipping open the laptop screen and turning on all the monitors.

'Straight back into university work with a hangover, you must be keen—either that or behind on a deadline. Fancy a coffee?' Hunter asked in the background of my focus.

'Uh huh.' I nodded, putting on my glasses and concentrating on what I had to do.

System loading...

The screen came up with the same login fields as last night. I entered my credentials, but instead of showing the same platform as yesterday, it came up with errors.

I tried again. Looking at the keyboard tiles as I typed to make sure I entered it correctly. S*hit!* I hit the desk in frustration with both hands, cursing under my breath.

'Hey, Esme, are you okay?' I could hear Hunter talking but I just ignored him and continued.

Last password attempt, the screen prompted. I needed to get this right or I was out.

Come on, Esme. I entered one more time before being locked out of the system, and as I glanced up, it loaded, bringing up all the details I needed.

I sat there, staring at the screen, unable to take in what I was seeing. It didn't add up. There sure was £300,000.00 in the master account that I set up. If that was true and I had transferred it four times to the girls and there was £300,000.00 then I did indeed move £1.5M from the firm. Oh, this was way worse than I thought.

I am officially a criminal—a cybercriminal—and I'm sitting in my apartment with a member of the Metropolitan police. What could be worse?

Oh, Esmeralda, what have you done? I sat back in my seat, my hand on my chin, thinking for a moment.

'There you go, sis.' I nearly leapt out of my chair as Hunter placed a steaming hot mug of coffee next to me on the table and squeezed my shoulder. 'I'm so proud of you, Esme. You seem like you are thoroughly engrossed in your degree. Good for you. If only Mum and Dad could see you now.' Hunter seemed proud. He was normally an irritating, annoying brother who would only wind me up in all situations. But here he was, proud of me because I had hacked into an investment firm and stolen a lot of money.

Yes, if only Mum and Dad could see their criminal daughter in action, I thought.

I hadn't even noticed him walk up behind me or if he had seen the contents of the screen that I was staring at. That was the least of my worries.

I had better check the other accounts and start moving it all back to the main one. Just as I started to click the mouse, a notification popped up in the top right-hand corner. I would normally have dismissed it, but I was drawn into reading it.

'BBC NEWS. TOP UK INVESTMENT FIRM SUFFERS CYBER BREACH AND LOSES OVER £1.5MILLION!'

I couldn't quite believe what I was reading. S*urely that can't be...*

As Hunter walked to the bathroom, I held my head in my hands.

Think, think, think Esmeralda, I whispered to myself.

Withdrawing my hands in panic mode, I clicked on the popup and began reading the article.

"In the late hours of this morning, Claydon and Hilder, a leading UK investment firm, has reported to the media that they have been the subject of a cyber-attack in which hackers have stolen more than £1.5 million. Their head of security, Derrick Caulder, has said they aren't sure exactly what or how it has happened, but they are conducting investigations and hope to get to the root cause as soon as possible."

I felt sick to my stomach and couldn't read anymore. That hacker, the cyber-attack that happened last night, was *me.*

How could I possibly transfer the money back now if they couldn't trace it leaving their account? Would I risk being caught returning it? I thought to myself.

Right, let's not panic. I'll go to the other accounts and transfer the money back to one central location. I'll figure out from there what I then need to do.

I needed to think about this in a calm and logical manner.

I entered in the digits for the first account, which was allocated to Casey.

I tapped away furiously locating the first one and hit enter. As my eyes widened, my pupils retracted in yet more shock. Yes, I transferred £300,000.00 yesterday but the balance now read £289,523.00.

'What on earth?' I whispered under my breath. 'How is this possible?'

I flipped open my phone and searched for Casey's number, clicked on her name and then began to text.

'CASEY, WE NEED TO TALK ABOUT LAST NIGHT!' I waited for her reply, then saw her typing.

'WE SURE DO, HAVE YOU SEEN THE NEWS?' she came straight back.

'I HAVE BUT I'M MORE CONCERNED ABOUT THE MONEY, THERE IS SOME MISSING?' The panic inside me was building.

'YEAH, ABOUT THAT... I NEEDED TO PAY MY CREDIT CARD.' I read her message with dread. Was she being serious? That money was not for her to pay her credit card bill. Now I needed to find over £10,000 to pay back. I didn't have that sort of money, neither did she.

'ARE YOU KIDDING ME?' I had no patience whatsoever at this point.

'I'M JUST AT MY MUM'S. WILL CALL YOU THIS AFTERNOON AS SOON AS I LEAVE.' That was that. Casey didn't seem concerned at all, yet there I was having a mild panic attack and featured across the BBC news morning headlines.

I thought I would try the other accounts to see if I could at least get the rest of it all into one central account and then work out what to do with it from there.

I proceeded to work away, entering the digits of the second account, which was Mollie's account. If I could rely on one of the girls, it would be her.

Hitting the enter button, the main transaction and balance summary page began to load. I waited tentatively for the figures to present themselves, tapping my pen patiently on the corner of the desk.

£295,000.00, the numbers appeared, staring at me like an angry overdraft.

'Jesus Christ,' I said quietly to myself. 'That's another £5,000.00. What on earth has Mollie spent that on and, more importantly, how have they figured out how to use the account and transfer the funds? I'm pretty sure they couldn't even string a sentence together let alone remember how to pay with crypto coins.' I felt sick to the stomach.

I had better check the others in that case...
£282,000.00 in Amie's and £289,000.00 in Tilly's. In total, £44,477.00 had gone from last night's balance of £1.5 million. I couldn't transfer the money back minus this amount. A second transaction would leave me more open to being traced.

I ran to the kitchen sink and was sick in the basin. It felt like my stomach had been ripped from inside of me. The people I investigated, learned and read about had no guilty consciences—those people weren't me. I was going to prison for a very long time, and I could kiss goodbye to any type of career in cyber security and ethical hacking. I could already imagine the judge's comments in court.

'This young lady has used her university training in ethical hacking for financial gain. You are ordered to pay back the full amount, plus damages and court costs as well as 10 years behind bars.'

The fact that my so-called friends had spent the money and didn't think to call me beforehand was ludicrous. *Perhaps if I go back to bed, go to sleep and wake up again, all this will go away, and it will all be just a horrible nightmare.*

I had hoped that the sound of the running shower Hunter was in would have damped down the sound of me being ill. It still didn't make me feel any better. If anything, I thought I needed to be sick again.

I picked up my phone and created a group chat between all five of us. I didn't call it anything to do with money so that if the police did recover our belongings, they wouldn't instantly pick it up.

'GIRLS, WE NEED A MEETING. WHAT TIME ARE YOU ALL BACK HOME?' I wasn't expecting a quick response, but I wanted them to know I meant business and it was important that we worked out what we were going to do next.

I spent the afternoon thinking about all the ways that I could cover up this mess, and the chaos that would come from doing such a thing. I thought about my career and what I would do if I couldn't pursue my dream of working with computers. I couldn't search it on the internet as I was too afraid of anyone looking at my browser history and anything I was searching for. That would be the perfect piece of evidence to attach to my theft.

Is there a way that we could get away with what I've done? How will we get back the money we have spent and stolen? Hackers did this sort of thing daily and for a lot more money than this and they were never caught. Maybe... *just maybe...* I contemplated.

It was just after 5 pm and I could hear keys in the front door and the sound of talking and laughing. The girls had returned. All four of them at the same time.

'Oh, hi, Esmeralda, aka the ultimate bank robber of all time.' Casey entered the room, multiple shopping bags hanging from her wrists. Not just any bags... I noted about five different designer names that were familiar to me and all of which were extremely expensive.

'I hope that's not...' She smiled and held up her hand towards me.

'I know what you are going to say, Esme, but seriously, these were all reduced, and I haven't spent it all. I even got you a little something as a thank you,' Casey said it like it was okay and that she had won the money from the lottery, all the others laughed in chorus with her. Mollie, Tilly, and Amie all carrying a similar number of bags.

'Casey, what the hell? That money is not for you to spend. We must put it back.' What did she not understand about the money not belonging to her?

Casey looked confused. 'Why not? Why can't we keep it? We have all been talking about it this afternoon over lunch and how they will never find it. You said that it was untraceable. The black web or something?' She waved her hand aimlessly trying to justify herself.

'The dark web,' I corrected her.

'That's it. So, if it's on the dark web, then it's hard to trace... right?' All four girls were standing before me with shrugged shoulders and nodding in agreement with Casey.

'Hard to trace, but it's not impossible.' They weren't going to take this without a fight.

We all sat down together to discuss the situation. It was four against one, and whilst I was the main culprit and mastermind behind this heist, the fact that they had been spending the money meant that they were as guilty as I was. We were in this together, forever.

I agreed not to transfer the money back, but they had to be discreet. We had to use the money sensibly and any large amounts needed to be discussed between us all so that it didn't look out of the ordinary and for fear of being caught. We used the funds as a type of overdraft. Only there if we needed them, and once university had finished, we agreed to put half of each of our funds into an investment—Cinco Chicas. The other half, we were all going to buy our own apartments with.

That was years ago now, and although we haven't been caught yet, we are still guilty of stealing and spending it and we are all in it together. No one else can know how we came into money—it would be a sworn secret for eternity. One thing we weren't sure of was the media coverage. Since that day, we hadn't seen any more press releases about the company's theft, but we were always looking over our shoulders in case they came to find us.

I thought about it every day for years. The crime that wouldn't go away and I could be arrested for it at any time, but our lives had to go on.

Fast forward and the five of us plus my brother now ran the investigations together. Each of us used our own expertise to solve the complex pieces of every investigation and split the money that we got from clients.

The Richardson family investigation would require a lot of searching and digging for confidential information to solve it.

All six of us, including Hunter, were sitting in the private room at the back of Cinco Chicas discussing the case. We weren't able to leave the information that we had gathered so far laying around as the room was frequented by security and cleaning staff. It had to be discussed, photographs taken and stored in a secure password-protected drive, any other critical evidence was kept in our minds to solve.

I explained all about their family history, the phone call from Sarah and the mysterious meeting with David. I left out the part about him and I having a relationship years earlier. I kept that secret, even at the time when it all happened. I recalled the events that took place when I attended Michael's funeral and the outside connections with people like Emily Carter, Samuel Richardson and the inheritance.

All the girls were leaning towards Oscar as the guilty party—all except me. I felt it was too early to make a judgement. Hunter wanted to know more about Emily Carter. In my eyes, everyone was guilty until proven innocent. Anyone who wanted to get their hands on the family estate and assets could have carried out the murders of both Arthur and Michael Richardson.

Only time would tell...

Chapter 4
Undercover

It was Monday morning and less than a week since I had been to Michael Richardson's funeral. Today was the day that I started at the Richardson firm—ATR & Partners. I was more nervous than I had been starting in my very first job all those years ago, young and inexperienced, not knowing what to expect.

I'm not sure why I felt so apprehensive. It wasn't that I was performing an actual function within the business. It was simply a route for me to hide at a desk, gather the office chit-chat, see if I could glean any confidential information and download any content that could be used as evidence for her father's murder case.

Sarah told me that I needed to report to the head of acquisitions, a man by the name of David Alsopp, who would greet me at reception and walk me to my desk. I had to tell him that I'd transferred from the US to the

UK office, and if there were any problems, he needed to speak to Sarah.

I had no prior experience or knowledge of the investment and business acquisitions industry, but I was to keep my head low, and if there was anything I really wasn't sure of, to send her a message. Most of my time would be spent figuring out what was really happening behind the scenes of the Richardson family and their empire.

I had Sarah's help in guiding me to some places, but most of the time, she didn't even know what she was looking for.

As it was the first morning and I didn't want to draw attention to myself, I thought I would grab a cab to the office rather than the underground. I could apply my makeup in the back and make sure I had everything I needed.

All dressed in a black pair of smart trousers, a white satin shirt that had a cute ribbon to one side of the neck and heels that were only a couple of inches in height. I packed my handbag simply with my phone, purse and a few cosmetics. I wasn't one for packing every essential item in case I needed it—a heavy handbag on the tube after work wasn't ideal.

One quick glance around the apartment to check I had shut all the windows, turned off the iron, my hair tongs and anything else that needed to be off, and I headed for the front door.

I loved my apartment dearly but sometimes my neighbours were a little loud and always wanted a chat when I was in a rush to get somewhere. I headed down the long-marbled corridor to the main staircase, quickly making my way down two flights of stone stairs and out of the main doors.

It was drizzling slightly, and the smell of damp, dirty streets filled the air, just as it always did in London.

It was a cold, grey and murky day to start the week. I felt the need to hail a cab quickly so that my hair didn't turn frizzy, so I held up my arm to the first black cab that approached. It indicated and pulled up to the side of the road for me to get in. His window lowered and a friendly middle-aged man with a flat cap on asked me, 'Where you off to, love?' in the cutest cockney accent.

'New Change, St Pauls, please.' I didn't wait for his reply. He nodded, so I reached for the handle, opening the big heavy door and climbed in, clunking it closed behind me.

'Good weekend?' There was always something about cab drivers in London, so friendly and talkative. Of course, you got the occasional miserable one, moaning about the traffic or the weather or people he had collected previously, but overall, they made the journey more pleasant. To be fair to them, if I was a cab driver in London, I would moan all the time... imagine the number of annoying back seat drivers they had to shuttle around all day, it would be enough to make anyone go insane.

'Yes, good thanks. Always seem to go so quickly. You?' I asked politely in return.

'Yeah, not too bad thanks. Worked Saturday but yesterday was nice with the family.' He winked into the rear-view mirror and then concentrated back on the road.

I wasn't much of a conversation starter, so I took the opportunity to make myself look presentable. A small tube of moisturiser was plucked from my bag, the tiniest squirt of liquid was applied to my cheeks, chin and forehead, making me feel more awake and refreshed. A few strokes of mascara, a dusting of foundation and a brush of my hair before I was good to go.

As I applied my makeup in the back of the cab, I listened to the early morning breakfast show that was playing in the background. Capital radio hosted by the charismatic Roman Kemp, Sian Welby and Chris Stark. The driver chuckled away as he listened to their humour and camaraderie. I frequently listened to the same show as they had a tendency to lift your spirits even on the gloomiest of mornings, just like today was.

We arrived 20 minutes later, which felt like 20 seconds.

'Okay if I drop you here, love?' The cab driver pointed to the right-hand side of the pavement. I nodded and looked up at the stunning view of St Paul's Cathedral and the towering glass building next to it. ATR & Partners with their logo was standing proud on the top floor of the building, so I knew I was in the right place.

'Great, thanks. Cash okay?' I looked at the counter above his inside mirror and read the numbers 18.35. I took a £20 note from my purse and passed it through the small gap in the Perspex between him and myself. 'Keep the change.' It wasn't much but I didn't want a pocket full of coins.

'Thanks, love, have a good day,' he said, handing me a small receipt in exchange.

I clicked the handle and yanked the door open again. It was always so difficult getting out of the cab and looking dignified all at the same time—the most awkward manoeuvre of the day. Slamming the door closed and giving him the thumbs up, I stood for a few moments straightening my trousers and taking a big deep breath before walking to the glass revolving doors in front of me.

The main area was impressive. Large expensive-looking artwork hung on one side and a beautiful marine fish tank, about seven-foot-high stood on the other. I walked towards the long concrete desk to speak to the two women perched on director seats behind it like robots. Both had black hair, neatly pulled straight back into a ponytail, thick, well-executed makeup and bright red lips. They both smiled, showcasing their white, immaculate teeth.

'How can we help you today?' they spoke in tandem and on cue.

'Erm, I am here to see David Alsopp.' I stopped just before the lady on the left.

'Which department is he in, please?' she said, tapping away at the keyboard in front of her and occasionally checking the screen.

'Acquisitions, I believe.'

'Okay great, and your name, please?'

'Esmeralda King.' I smiled nervously.

'Brilliant, I have sent him a message to let him know you are here. If you would like to take a seat, he will be down in a moment to collect you. Your badge number is 5, please wear this at all times. If you are permanent staff, David will organise another pass for you.' She pointed to the three bright red armchairs behind me, arranged around a small glass table, and handed me a security badge on the end of a lanyard.

'Thank you.' I took the badge and headed for the seats as I had been told to, but no sooner had I sat down and placed my handbag on my lap than I heard a deep voice say my name.

'Ms King?' he asked.

'Yes, that's me. I looked up to find a young gentleman holding out a hand for me to shake. He looked so young, yet he was the head of the acquisitions team.

'David Alsopp, but please call me Dave.' He gave me a strong handshake.

'Wow, so young,' I stupidly whispered out loud to myself before bending down to collect my handbag from the floor.

'I'm sorry, I didn't quite catch that.' He leaned into me, waiting for me to say it again.

Shit, Esmeralda, stop speaking your mind out loud. I could almost kick myself.

'Sorry, I said that was quick. You were quick at collecting me from reception. You...' I shook my head in disbelief. He didn't really seem to care what I was saying, I think he heard me the first time but was just playing with me.

'Right, let's get you up with the rest of the team and settled in. Good journey this morning?' He began quickly walking towards the lifts, so I followed. Before I had a chance to reply, he continued.

There was an awkward silence as we entered the lift to the first floor. Three other people stood in the same close vicinity as us, all waiting for our own floors but just stood with our bodies facing the doors, arms folded in front of us and staring up at the numbers on the display. I felt awkward and rude.

Just as the doors opened, I froze. Directly across the other side of the office, I saw a familiar face. I also recognised the man that he was talking to, both were at the funeral—Oscar and Samuel. They were deep in discussion, neither looked happy with one another and I didn't want them to see me. Now was not the right time to bump into them. I needed more time to think of a story and a conversation starter. I wasn't ready, not on day one.

I hit the button to hold the doors open, turned right towards the lift mirror and began adjusting the silk bow to the side of my neck, undoing it and doing it back up again. I was hoping that they would have finished and I could continue my business.

'Come on, Ms King, this is our floor,' Dave ushered for me to get out. The rest of the people in the lift looked on impatiently and watched as I carried out my strange behaviour. After a few moments, I looked up, noticing that they were finishing their conversation and Samuel was walking away in the opposite direction. Oscar looked angry and glanced towards me just as I stepped outside the sliding metal doors and took a double take. He didn't smile or move. As I followed Dave through the office, trying not to look back up at him, I could feel his stare following me.

What is he thinking? Is he suspicious?

I had to just keep my head down and continue to my desk. One by one, all the workers lifted their heads from their desks and sat in an apathetic manner as I passed by. Dave continued to talk as we made our way between the desks placed in rows throughout the open plan office.

'So, there are 30 of us in the acquisitions team. I am one of five team leaders, and we report into the head of legal, Samuel Richardson. Any escalations thereafter go up to Oscar and the board of directors.' I listened carefully to his words.

'To be honest, most things get resolved by Samuel as Oscar is fairly new to the position, but it must be quite a serious escalation in the first place to reach Samuel. Always come to me first. Do you have any questions?' Dave stopped and turned around, checking to make sure that I was still behind him and listening to what he was saying.

'Erm... nope.' I shook my head, so Dave continued walking.

Samuel reports to Oscar... that can't be easy for him. After working for the family business, he's now reporting to his nephew? Surely that was reason in itself not to kill your brother? Or maybe he was thinking that if he killed his brother, the position would go to him and not his nephew. I was so busy contemplating a variety of scenarios in my head that I didn't notice Dave had stopped at an empty desk and was looking at me.

'Ms King. This is your desk. You will need to log on to your phone to use it for all external calls, but they must not be personal. That is what your own mobile phone is for. Employees caught making external personal calls except in an emergency will have the amount deducted from their salary. I believe that Sarah has transferred your access and account logins to the UK office and has sent these all to you. Is that correct?' He looked at me quizzically.

'It is correct.' I had one eye on Dave and one eye on everything around me.

'Then I shall leave you here. All desks and floors are numbered. I am located on 1.12, which is floor one, desk 12.' He pointed to the sticker on the screen behind my desk, mine was 1.34. 'The ladies' toilets are at the end of the corridor, second door on the right and the kitchen area is at the end of the corridor. If you need anything, email me and I will come straight back to you.'

I nodded, feeling overwhelmed.

He gave me a whistle stop tour of the office, provided me with the facilities and then walked off. If that was what they called an induction, then anyone working here would feel extremely lonely and be left to settle in on their own.

Thank goodness this was not a lifetime career for me and I was here to get what I needed and leave. Let's hope it was days rather than weeks.

The office seemed lonely—it wasn't a loud buzzing atmosphere as I recalled my office once was, in fact, it had no atmosphere at all. In a way, I missed the days when I had a team around me, screens with forensic data running checks, the sound of people talking about controls, meetings around case progression and charts of data for as far as you could see. It's funny what you miss in hindsight.

'Hey, my name is Amber. Dave can be a bit of a bore sometimes—a real know-it-all. If there is anything I can help with, just let me know.' A young girl popped her head around the side of the screen and smiled, shuffling forwards on her chair to make me feel welcome.

'Ah, thank you. I'm Esmeralda. Esmeralda King.' I smiled back. 'Have you worked here long?' I asked.

'Far too long. I joined as part of their internship program. I only have six months left and then I'm hoping to go travelling and perhaps work abroad for a few years.' She seemed lovely and would be a great ally to help me find out what I needed.

'Nice. I bet you can't wait. Great to meet you,' I quickly said before her head disappeared back behind the screen and I was left to figure out access to my computer.

The thought of not taking the opportunity to speak to Amber whilst I had the chance was scratching away inside my mind. She had no loyalties to the business or the Richardson family if her plan was to start travelling. What did I have to lose?

Let's find out what she has heard and what the consensus is here in the office. I thought to myself.

I pushed my chair backwards and started the conversation.

'Amber?' I quietly called out.

'Uh huh,' she answered and then swung her head back around.

I spun the wheels of the chair around so that I could get to my feet and peered over the screen instead of her cranking her neck to one side.

'Sorry to bother you, I know you are busy, but I couldn't help hearing about one of the directors earlier, and as I am new, I just wondered what had happened or if you knew what...' I carefully whispered it in such a way that I was hoping it would open a discussion. I didn't need to finish my sentence—she was already eager to gossip.

'So, you are talking about Michael, right?' She stopped what she was doing, sat back in her chair and looked up at me. She was a petite girl and had kicked off her shoes, sitting cross-legged. Amber folded her arms in seriousness. Her bobbed brown hair framed her blue eyes and cute features.

'I am, yes. I don't know if it is true, but I heard a rumour and...' Once again, before I could finish, there she was again.

'So... we all thought there was something going on.' Her eyes filled with excitement as she leaned forwards and spoke.

'Who's we?' I quickly asked.

'All the office girls.' She shuffled around. 'Michael was normally very flirty. Quite a lady's man, confident and threw his weight around the office. All the women loved him, and he knew it. I found him quite an insecure man... as if he was making up for something else.' Amber giggled quietly to herself.

I listened, captivated.

'Then, suddenly, things changed. His light-hearted attitude changed to arrogance and he seemed to be irritated by everyone. You could sense the tension in the air when Emily and Oscar were in the same vicinity.

The glares, the exchange of pleasantries between them. Everyone could tell there was something going on. Michael turned from a well-kept, physically fit man to a leaner, more troubled physique.' Amber's face changed from excited to one of confusion.

I had my head resting peacefully on my propped-up hand, waiting for her to continue.

'One morning, we arrived at the office to chaos. Everyone was walking around chatting to one another in little huddles. No one wanted to be caught talking about Michael's disappearance, but everyone blatantly was.' She shook her head in disbelief.

'You said disappearance? He died, didn't he?' I knew the answer, but I wanted it to come from her.

'Ask anyone in the office. No one believes he has gone. We all think it is an insurance scam. It doesn't make sense, does it?' Amber seemed to be asking me for clarification. 'The arguments between his son and him. Michael's father unexpectedly passed away a year earlier and all the affairs he was having in the office, not to mention the business cover-ups. I think he disappeared deliberately if you ask me.' She shrugged her shoulders with disinterest.

Business cover-ups? What on earth does she mean?

My eyes studied her expression furthermore.

'Business cover-ups. What do you mean?' I asked.

'Oh, I'm sure I have already said far too much.' Amber seemed to switch into professional mode. Her feet dropped to the floor, she unfolded her arms and set back to her screen, tapping away at the keyboard. 'I'm so sorry, I need to get this report done and finished before my client chases me again. I'm sorry, will you excuse me.'

And that was that. I took her actions as cue that our conversation was over, and she had fed me enough information.

'Yes, sure. I'm sorry, I know you are busy. Nice talking to you, Amber.' I shuffled nervously away from her screen and back to my own desk.

I knew that it was always interesting listening to the rumour mill at an office. Everyone will put their own opinion on what they think is the truth and add a layer of gossip, of course, but on the odd occasion, there was a little something worth knowing.

Chapter 5
Psychosis

I opened my phone and began to compile a message to David as I lay in bed staring at the ceiling, unable to sleep. I knew it was a bad move to pick up my phone but there was no way I was even close to being tired. 'I'M GOING TO START CALLING YOU CINDERELLA.'

The text dots began moving—he was typing. I waited in anticipation as to what he would reply with.

'???'

Really? Is that all he can reply with? I said angrily under my breath.

'FIRST, YOU DISAPPEAR JUST AFTER MIDNIGHT. SECOND, YOU VANISH INTO THIN AIR. I NEED TO SPEAK TO YOU. I HAVE MORE QUESTIONS.' Once again, I waited for his response.

'NOW?'

'ITS 10 PM? I'M IN BED!' I answered.

'PERFECT. I'LL BE AT YOURS IN 15.' My eyes widened. Was he being serious? I had 15 minutes to get out of bed, freshen up and change my clothes into something more appropriate. Given the relationship we had before, I didn't want any excuses to give him mixed messages this time. David turning up whilst I was in my pyjamas was not a good idea.

I ran around the apartment in lightning speed, throwing on a pair of tight jeans, a baggy jumper and quickly throwing the dirty saucepans and plates into the dishwasher before he arrived. I lit a candle to disguise any smells and kicked a few out of place items underneath the sofa, never to be seen again. By the time he arrived, I looked like a hot, sweaty mess and my face was all flushed.

He didn't ring the doorbell—he didn't need to. I heard the lift chime and his heavy footsteps approaching my door, I opened it and sighed, standing in the doorway to greet him.

'Good evening, Esme,' he said in a calm and collected tone.

'Evening, David.' I moved out of the way and held my arm up to show him in.

'Couldn't sleep?' he asked.

'No. I have too many unanswered questions to sleep.' I rubbed my forehead as if the case was hurting my brain. I was tired, confused and frustrated all at the same time.

'About what exactly?' He moved in and made himself comfortable in my armchair as if it was his own home. I smiled... I missed him sitting there, waiting for me to get ready before an evening out.

'About everything. Emily, Oscar's mother, Michael's death, the business. The whole thing is just whirring around aimlessly in my head, and I have so much missing.' I paused, standing beside him. 'Coffee?'

'Hmm, do you have anything stronger?'

'Of course. Whisky, rum, gin?' I knew he was more of a rum man, but I gave him the option in case he had changed his preferences since it had been so long.

'Come on, Esme, you know me. Rum with ice please, just a small one.' He smiled at me with his tired eyes. Hunter's favourite tipple was rum, so I always had a bottle for when he was over.

I reached across to the small side cabinet that was standing in the corner next to the sofa and opened the black wooden doors. Inside was a shelf of my special thick glass tumblers and a variety of spirits. I picked up the almost full bottle of rum and filled the bottom a couple of inches off the glass, replacing the bottle and gently closing the doors with the glass in my hand.

I could feel David looking at me, burning a hole in my back. Two small, silver stainless steel ice balls were in the kitchen freezer, chilled and ready to be placed in his glass. I had bought them especially for David and they had been there for three years, ever since he left. I noticed them every time I opened the freezer but refused to throw them away. They hissed from the warmth of the rum as I dropped them into the bottom of the glass and handed it to David.

'Thanks, Esme, you have no idea how good this is going to taste.' He smiled like he was back home, but I had to shake myself out of thinking it was going to be the way it was before. Three years was a long time ago and a lot had changed. I had changed.

'So, why did you leave? Again.' I sat down on the sofa opposite him, my legs up on the seat next to me in a comfortable position. I had all the time in the world to listen to his excuses, but more importantly than anything else, I needed answers to the case.

'Esme, do you know how difficult it is, staring someone in the face that you want so much but can't have? It's torture. I've missed you every day since the last time we were together. Even being here with you in this apartment brings back so much to me.' He leaned back into the chair and looked up at the ceiling, exhaling with release.

'You were the one that left—twice. I could have helped you, supported you, been by your side. Each time you leave, I feel like I have done something wrong. So, why are you really here? Tonight, of all nights? Why not meet me tomorrow in a coffee shop?' I felt the emotion building up inside me like a combustion engine waiting to blow.

'You want answers. I want to help you. I think this case is bigger than you realise and there are some things that you can't find in files or emails or the internet.' He sat up resting his elbows on his knees. I felt like I should be paying attention.

'Like what?' I inquisitively asked.

'Like Oscar's parents.' His eyebrows were raised as though he was trying to tell me something.

'Go on...'

'Oscar's parents, Michael and Laura, met whilst she was working at a local hospital in her placement year of university. Michael was taken into the Accident and Emergency department as a result of a sporting injury, followed by a series of sports rehabilitation sessions.'

'Laura was extremely intelligent—the only daughter of two very wealthy and highly successful medical consultants. She had only dreamed of following in their footsteps since she was a little girl. Despite her IQ being classed as exceptionally gifted, in the high 170s range, her mental health seemed to hold her back at times. She flew through college and university, achieving a first-class honours, but it had taken a toll on her wellbeing.' David told me about the history of the couple like it was a love story.

'During her final examinations, she experienced hallucinations, delusions and multiple changes in emotions as well as other signs and symptoms. Her lecturers had noticed the change in her behaviour but were hoping it was down to stress. However, her parents, being in the medical profession and knowing their daughter only too well, knew it was more than just final year pressures.'

'How do you know all this, David?' I asked.

'Arthur would tell me everything. He was worried about Michael at the time and what he was getting himself into. I know it's not quite right, but we searched all her medical records too.' He looked solemn and I could tell there was more than he was admitting to.

'Did he ask you to check her background?'

'Of course, he did. Don't forget that I was very close to the family at the time. I was like an uncle to those children, so I felt obliged.' David took a sip of rum and swallowed heavily, then continued.

'Several examinations later, and as her health took a turn for the worse, she was diagnosed with schizophrenia. On orders from her parents, she was admitted to one of the top hospitals in the UK, prescribed medication and had the best medical treatment plans there were.'

'Whilst schizophrenia can't be cured, Laura knew when these bouts were about to hit, what the signs were and how to quickly get on top of things before it caused too many problems. The older she got, the better she managed to control it with the help of medication.'

'Laura enjoyed working in accident and emergency as it was fast-paced, she enjoyed the adrenaline rush of helping patients in their critical conditions, but the stressful situations and her inability to switch off at the end of a shift meant that she had to take a different route if she was going to be able to hold down a successful career. Her father had warned her of her options, especially as she wanted children so desperately.'

'After only a few months, Laura moved to the sports rehabilitation clinic at the hospital and trained as a physiotherapist. It was there that she met Michael—a young, masculine, very good-looking man in his early 20s. The son of a wealthy businessman and the gentlest of characters.'

'He was playing rugby at the time and had just managed to gain sponsorship at an international club when he was tackled and had torn several ligaments, including his tibiofibular, talofibular and calcaneofibular. I remember Arthur being so proud and delighted with what Michael had achieved to then have both their dreams shattered. Minor surgery and physiotherapy enabled Michael to slowly walk and then run but it dashed any hopes he had of playing professional rugby again.'

'Although Michael had a fiancé, the minute they laid eyes on each other, they instantly bonded. Anyone could see it—they were inseparable way before they became a couple. She saw him as a comfort blanket, and he wasn't put off by her condition. He was a soft and easily led man. Laura was smart, driven and knew what she wanted—Michael, the money and the lifestyle.'

'They would meet in secret, only the two of them knowing about their relationship until Michael couldn't take it anymore and confided in his father, asking what he should do. He decided to break it off with his fiancé, Emma. She didn't take it too well and initially caused a lot of friction for the new couple. She would follow them to his home or hers and wait outside for several hours. She also sent threatening letters. It didn't faze Laura one little bit—she wanted to kill Emma but Michael got scared. Eventually, they had to get the police involved so she stopped.'

'I think there was a lot more to that scenario, but I will leave it there for the time being. All I know is that they never heard from her again.' David raised his eyebrows and looked down at his almost empty glass, swirling the remnants of rum and the cold steel balls around.

'Do you want a top up?' I asked, getting ready to reach for the cabinet next to me.

'No, I mustn't. I should be heading off soon so you can go to bed. I won't keep you long.' He took the last sip and placed the glass on the table between both of us, pushing it forwards and out of his way.

'What do you mean more to it?' I was intrigued.

'Laura had a name for herself, most people called her evil. To pay Emma back for stalking them, she got her fired from work, she spread rumours around the village that even made her friends turn their backs on her and threatened to burn her family house down while she slept.' I was shocked but, in a way, I was expecting something like this to be revealed. Not one single member of the Richardson family that I had spoken to so far had a good word to say about her, and now I was beginning to realise why.

'The Richardson family weren't too sure about Laura. In their eyes, she was broken and needed fixing. They felt that Michael was an easy target and all she wanted was money, but the more they tried to persuade him against her, the more he dug his heels in, bringing them closer together. Even Lillian, who was adorable, had warned Michael, but he clearly saw something in her that no one else did.'

'Michael chose to focus on business instead of sport and began working at the family business for his father, Arthur, and Laura continued her profession in physiotherapy until they welcomed their son, Oscar, into the world when they were both 24. My understanding, but this hasn't been confirmed, was that they were having difficulties conceiving—you might want to check her medical records. I only have the ones I investigated prior to them having Oscar.' I made short notes regarding the key points from David on my phone, I will add them to my master case file and send them to you tomorrow.

'If I stand any chance of solving this case, I need to speak to Laura Richardson. Maybe she is the key to this?' David nodded to agree with me.

'The only trouble is that Laura has been detained under section 3 of the mental health act 1983 and is currently residing in Pashen Hospital, London and has been there for the past six months. To get any time at all with her, you would need to tell the hospital that you are a close family friend and have come to see how she is doing rather than a private investigator.' David leaned back in his chair. He appeared to be thinking about the situation.

'Wow, what did she do? Would you come with me?' I asked. 'At least you know her and have connections to the family. If they ask any questions, you will probably know the answers. I wouldn't have a clue.'

'We are treading on thin ice here, Esme. I don't know exactly what happened and why she was admitted but I heard her mental health had deteriorated rapidly. I would do it sooner rather than later. I can't go with you and it's something I won't change my mind about.'

Why was he so adamant that he didn't want to go and see Laura? What had happened between the two of them and what was he hiding?

'And, Esme...'

'Yes?' I didn't know what was coming next.

'Don't get emotionally involved with any of the Richardson family.' He pulled together both sides of his jacket and stood up to leave. 'It won't end well.'

'What is that supposed to mean?' I asked.

'I have seen many women over the years be hurt by the men in that family, including Arthur. They are charming, good-looking and wealthy, intelligent men. What is there not to fall for? But, they are bad news— you don't want to get caught up in all their fiascos.' He turned to walk away. At least this time, I knew he was going and hadn't just disappeared.

'Why do you care?' I walked after him towards the door. I didn't want an argument, I just wanted him to tell me how he really felt.

David quickly turned to face me. 'Esme, you have no idea how much I care for you. I loved you more than I have loved anyone in my entire life, including my wife, but for that reason, I want you to have the best in life. I can't give you children or a young and happy life. You need to find someone you deserve to settle down with. I would hate to see you caught up in that family.' He leaned in to kiss me. I fell for it but he quickly withdrew. 'I must go. It was a bad idea for me to come here.'

'I don't understand. Stay here tonight?' I gave him a pleading look.

'I can't. Call me if you need me.' He walked towards the door, grabbed the handle and opened it. Before he went, he paused, turned around and looked me straight in the eyes. 'I'll always love you.'

I had no words. My eyes filled with tears but I didn't cry. His face was sad. He closed the door behind him and was gone.

I still had so many questions I wanted to ask him about the rest of the family, about Oscar, Emily and the others, but I wasn't in any frame of mind to continue the conversation. I needed closure with David, instead, every time I saw him, it was like going back to the first chapter and re-reading it, each time with a new emotion.

I went to bed feeling solemn, like a part of me was missing and had been for the past three years. I needed to get over him. Maybe that last kiss was the sign I needed. He had walked out for the last time and there was no turning back.

After a turbulent sleep, I woke abruptly at 7 am. The sun was shining in the room, and I felt positive. I needed to focus on the case and a fresh outlook on life after David's visit last night. My window was slightly ajar, and I could smell the aroma of freshly cooked pastry and bread from the coffee shop on the ground floor.

I had a plan of action. Get up, go downstairs and get a coffee as soon as they open. Yes, I had my own coffee machine, but you couldn't beat the taste of a freshly made cup accompanied by a cinnamon swirl and a busy shop to set you up for the day. It was almost like a ritual for me, it started my day off the right way. I would then give the hospital a call and see if I could pay a visit to see Laura Richardson.

I wanted David to come with me, but after his comment last night, I wanted to prove him wrong and to show him that I was more than capable of solving this case on my own. They opened at 8 am, that was enough time to get showered, changed, grab a coffee and make my way there.

Making sure that my phone was fully charged. I had every intention of recording the conversation with Laura so that I could replay it repeatedly to get the information I needed. If she was willing to divulge it, of course.

The coffee shop was buzzing with people for a Saturday morning.

'Morning, Scott.' I smiled and greeted my most favourite barista in the world. He knew how I liked my coffee and always had a story to tell.

'Morning, Esme. The usual? You're a little earlier this morning, couldn't sleep?' Scott was in his early 20s, very handsome, extremely talkative and you could tell he worked out. The branded t-shirt he wore was pulled tight against his muscular biceps. He was single. I knew that because, most mornings, he would tell me about his dates from the previous night. If there was anyone failing more miserably than myself at relationships, it was him. Or perhaps he wasn't failing, he just chose not to settle down and preferred the young, free and single lifestyle.

'Pretty much. I have a lot to get done though so it has done me a favour,' I replied. 'How was last night?'

'Ugh, not for me, Esme.' He laughed to himself. 'We had dinner, a few drinks. I said something I shouldn't have, and she got a cab home. I can't for the life of me remember what I said, but clearly, she was offended. I was in bed by midnight. Safe escape if you ask me.' Scott was busy crashing around on the coffee machine making my latte. He turned to me and we both laughed.

'Women, eh?' I shrugged my shoulders.

'Oh, before I forget, Esme. There was a guy in here yesterday looking for you... he asked if I knew you.' He lifted the tongs from the side and placed a cinnamon swirl on a small white plate, handing it to me over the counter.

'A man looking for me?' I asked, taken aback. 'What did he look like?' I immediately thought of David but he knew where I lived and would know where to find me, so it wouldn't be him.

'Erm... he was quite a tall man, I would say just over 6ft and smart dressed. 6ft 2 or maybe 6ft 3. Dark hair, well-spoken. He had a picture of you on his phone. He knew your name.' Scott passed me my latte, being careful not to spill it. 'It's on the house this morning for my most favourite customer.' He smiled as I gulped in panic.

Why would someone be looking for me? Who was it? I racked my brains trying to think of anyone that could be trying to find me. P*erhaps the Richardsons were on to me and they had kidnappers out to drag me into their car.*

I had to call the hospital quickly before my mind ran away with all sorts of scenarios.

'Thanks, Scott, you are amazing. Free coffee served by my favourite barista will taste all the better.' I pulled up a chair next to a small table at the window of the shop. It was placed in the corner, a small alcove that meant my call would be as private as possible without people listening in and no one would try joining me or making conversation.

I had previously searched for the number of the hospital and saved it. All I needed to do was call and ask for opening hours. I held the phone up to my ear and listened for the dialling tone. I swallowed, nervous as to what questions they may want to ask me.

'Good morning, Pashen Hospital, how may I help you?' a lady answered.

'Oh, good morning. I was hoping to visit one of your patients and wondered what time visiting hours are today please?' I paused and waited for her to answer, taking the opportunity to blow and then sip my drink.

'Visiting hours are between 9 am and 11 am. Can I ask your name please as we will need to add it to the register for when you arrive? Also, which patient are you coming to see please?'

'Sure, my name is Esmeralda King, and I am coming to see Laura Richardson.' I took another sip and waited for her to reply but it went quiet. I gave it a few moments more, but she still didn't say anything. 'Hello?'

'Sorry... hello. Can I ask how you are related to the patient please?' the lady finally spoke.

'Yes, I am a family friend. I haven't seen her in a while and wanted to see how she was doing if that's okay?' I stared down at my pastry, hoping that I had said the right thing.

'That's fine. I would recommend coming after 9.30 am once she has had her medication.' Without waiting for my response, she hung up the phone.

Well, that was strange. I thought to myself. *She didn't seem to like the fact that I'm visiting Laura. I wonder if she normally has many visitors. Surely Oscar goes there regularly?*

I glanced at the time—it was already close to 9 am. I had enough time to finish my coffee, eat my breakfast and get a cab to the hospital and hopefully be there just after 9.30 am.

'See you later, Scott. Have a good weekend. See you Monday,' I said, pushing my mug and plate to the centre of the table and leaving the shop to hail a cab.

'You too!' he called after me. I could hear his reply as I left and began walking down the street.

The nice part about living in London was that a cab was never too far away. I walked like a crab sideways along the curb, watching the traffic as I went with my arm in the air. A few passed, already carrying passengers, but I waited until the next one indicated and pulled over.

I asked him for Pashen Hospital, which was only a few miles away. I could have walked but it was easier and quicker to get a cab.

In less than 15 minutes, the driver took a left turn into a set of iron gates with security guards on standby at the entrance. A short winding driveway with plush trees on either side lined the way to the impressive old house. It seemed strange, a beautiful mansion with gardens right in the heart of the city.

I thanked him for the journey, paid and looked up at the house as I climbed out. Maybe this wasn't such a bad place after all. I always imagined mental health hospitals to look daunting. Perhaps Laura liked being here more than she liked being at home, with the specialist care that she needed. It seemed peaceful and the birds were singing. It was only February, but I noticed the pretty start to bulbs shooting from the flower beds either side of reception.

I didn't know what to expect today. Would she be willing to talk to me? Would she be reluctant or hostile towards me?

I approached the main stone steps and pressed the buzzer for reception. I heard a beep.

'Esmeralda King to see Laura Richardson.' I heard the door buzz again and then the sound of the mechanism opening the lock. I pushed, leaning on the solid wooden door with all my weight and it opened.

The inside was stunning. A large, elegant twisting staircase led to the upper floors. Reception was lit by a huge glass window in the roof and the décor looked like it dated back to a picturesque country mansion from the 1970s. There was something sinister about the place. I had captured images in my mind from past horror films that could have been filmed here and the thought sent shivers down my spine.

Focus on why you are here, Esmeralda, and not how scary this place is. I tried talking some sense into myself. *Speak to Laura, get the recording and get the hell out of there.*

A frail elderly lady came to greet me from one of the side rooms. 'Hello, dear. I understand you are here to see Ms Richardson. I'll walk you to where she is.' She smiled and started walking towards the right-hand corridor and alongside a pretty orangery. There were plenty of people sitting in armchairs chatting amongst themselves. I could hear the distant sound of gentle piano music playing in the background.

'Have you worked here long?' I tried to make conversation.

'Oh, a very long time, dear... since I was a young lady in my early 20s, just like yourself. But many moons ago.' She chuckled gently. 'I've seen so many people stay and leave in my time.'

'I bet you have. It's a beautiful place though.' I loved her compliment comparing me to a lady in her early 20s. It, too, seemed like many moons ago.

'It is to those who visit.' She hobbled along to the end of the corridor and pushed open a creaky door into a carpeted stairwell. It was a little quieter here as the music faded. 'So, you are here to see Ms Richardson as well. Quite the celebrity she is this week.'

'I'm sorry?' I didn't really understand what she was trying to say.

'Well, she hasn't had a single visitor for a good few months, then suddenly, her son visited yesterday. A family friend came to see her at 9 am this morning, in fact, you have just missed him, and now yourself. It's not her birthday, is it?' She turned to me and smiled curiously.

So, Oscar has been to see her. I wonder what he wanted. He could have just come to say hello but why after so many months if had he not seen her? Especially before or after the death of his father. Surely, he would have wanted to speak to his mother. Who was the other man who came this morning? I pondered.

'I don't think it is her birthday. After the death of her husband, I just thought I would see how she was. You don't happen to know who was here this morning, do you?' I asked, hoping that she would be able to tell me something.

'Her husband... dead? Oh no, dear he was here a few weeks ago, he's not dead. Although, he did refuse to put his name in the book. I'm quite sure she speaks to him daily on the phone. What's the day today?' she asked.

'Saturday,' I quickly answered.

'That's right, Saturday. Then she spoke to him last on Thursday. Sorry, dear, my memory isn't as good as it once was. It was her brother.' She led me up the stairs to the next floor and onto a landing area looking out onto the main gardens at the back of the house and two big wooden doors in front of us.

'Are you sure it was her brother? Who she spoke to on Thursday?' I questioned.

'No, no. That was her husband. She spoke to her husband on Thursday. Her brother visited this morning.' She knocked as loud as she could, rapping her old and fragile knuckles on the panels and then pushed the left-hand door as wide as possible. 'Ms Richardson. I have a visitor for you. Miss Esmeralda King. Please buzz when you are finished and ask for Edna.' She smiled politely at me, allowing me to step inside the room and then closed the door with a bang.

I looked around the room, blinking profusely, trying to make sense of the conversation I'd just had with the old lady.

Brother? I didn't even know she had a brother... I thought she was an only child, and speaking to her husband on Thursday, she must have been mistaken.

He's been dead for nearly a month. The poor old lady must have been confused.

I stood in what looked like a well-decorated five-star hotel suite. A large, four-poster bed to one side and two material armchairs, both facing the large floor-to-ceiling windows that also looked out onto the landscaped rear gardens. The room had a pleasant smell to it—fresh linen and an aroma of sweet perfume.

I wasn't sure whether I should take a seat or stay standing. I swallowed, took a deep breath in and went for it.

'Good afternoon, Laura. Are you well?' I asked, searching around the room for clues as to where she may be.

I didn't hear a sound, just a quick glimpse of a hand moving from within the armchair and a shift of movement from that direction. I took a few steps forward and managed to see the back of a woman's head and her medium-length blonde hair sitting in the chair, staring out at the view.

'Hi, Laura, do you mind if I join you?' I slowly tried to make my way to the chair opposite her and perched myself precariously on the edge. My hands resting gently on my lap. 'I'll turn my phone on silent so we aren't disturbed.' But instead of turning it to silent, I reached inside my bag and quickly flipped the microphone button onto record and slowly placed my bag back on the floor, hoping it would be able to hear everything.

I looked at Laura. Her eyes looked tired, in fact, her whole body looked fatigued. She barely blinked, maintaining her stare on the horizon the whole time.

'Well, it's lovely to meet you, Laura.' I didn't know what else to say. 'My name is Esmeralda. I'm a friend of Sarah's, your sister-in-law. I'm sorry to hear about your husband, it must have been a terrible shock.' She blinked a couple of times and gently swallowed. I wondered if I had touched a nerve.

I looked down at the table—there was a small plastic tray and two yellow pills within it, and next to the tray was a small glass of water. I wasn't sure if she was supposed to take them or if they were there for later.

'It must have been nice to see your brother earlier?' I asked. 'I'm very close to my brother, you know.'

Laura turned her face to look at me. Her black eyes frostily stuck on mine, staring me straight in the pupils. I had never been in a room with someone so empty. It was as if she had no soul. Her eyes just a dark circle of torment looking straight back at me.

'Why have you come here, Esmeralda? What do you *really* want?' she said softly.

'I'm sorry. I didn't want to bother you, but I had a few questions to ask about your husband's death. I...' I felt bad, as if I was intruding into her space. She was in a private hospital recovering from a problem with her health and here I was questioning her personal life and a recent bereavement.

'What questions?' She returned to looking out of the window. I probably would have had more luck getting information from Edna than I would have had from Laura.

'It was just erm... did Michael say or do anything suspicious before his death? I mean, do you think that he had any enemies? Anyone that would have wanted him dead?' I asked, hoping she would give me something—anything at all.

Laura lifted her head and rolled her eyes to the ceiling, giggling quietly to herself as she did so.

What is so funny?

'Can't you ask your boyfriend, David?' she quietly spoke.

'I'm sorry, what?' *How does she know I was speaking to David or even knew him?*

'You should be careful getting involved in other people's business. Especially the Richardsons. A mighty, mighty mess you may find yourself in.' She suddenly looked sad and empty. Her laughter immediately shut down and her face turned solemn. Her eyes looked watery in the reflection of the glass window.

'Laura. Is everything alright?' She started sobbing. I didn't know whether to hug her, console her or get some help.

'I'm not the evil one... she is. She did this to me.' Laura changed her tone, her quiet and calm voice changed to a scolded, dark and pained tone. 'She did. Go and find her, she's the answer to all your questions.'

Just as she stood up and started waving her arms around in chaos, the doors swung open and a younger lady stormed in. 'What on earth? Who are you and why are you here? Can't you see she is distressed and hasn't had her medication yet?

I was in shock. W*hat did I do?*

'I... I'm sorry... I didn't realise she...' I stood back in shock while two other nurses came charging in to help calm Laura.

'Who let you in here?' the other nurse screamed at me.

'Edna. Laura said...' Before I could finish explaining, the two nurses looked at each other in shock as if they had seen a ghost.

'What?' I didn't understand what the problem was.

'She must by lying,' one nurse said to the other.

'I'm not lying.' Laura laughed at the top of her voice—it was a shrill, wicked laugh. My eyebrows frowned as they all turned to look at me. *What is happening?*

'Edna hasn't worked here in ten years. She died in 2019. The only one that says they have seen her since is Laura.' The youngest nurse's words sent shivers down my spine. What were they trying to say?

As soon as I spoke about Edna, Laura seemed to look at me in a different way. *What was she thinking?*

'I'll go, I'm sorry I upset you, Laura. That wasn't my intention.' I apologised as I began to leave the room. I had almost reached the door on the way out when Laura called out to me.

'Esmeralda Sophia King.' I froze instantly but stood still without turning around. Not many people knew my full name... how did she know my middle name? No one ever called me by that, not even the girls or Hunter.

'You know he wanted to leave Jane for you, but it was her dying wish and he felt so guilty for what happened to her.' My heart pounded, the panic in my veins flushed through my body like a powerful torrent.

How does she know all of this?

'He poured his heart out to me, Esmeralda. If you want answers so bad, go and speak to the evil witch herself'. I turned around to find Laura standing there, surrounded by nurses holding her wrists and the small pot of tablets. She had a cursed smile on her face.

'And that is?' I replied.

'Emma knows the truth. Go and ask her.' No sooner had she said that, she smacked the pot of tablets clean out of the nurse's hand. It flipped high into the air and sent the tablets onto the carpet. Laura tried frantically to break free from their tight restraints, screaming as she did so, but it was no use—their grips only became stronger.

'Leave, just leave please and make your way back to reception!' the nurses shouted after me.

I felt so helpless, but I didn't need to be told twice. I began walking so fast back to reception that I practically could have run all the way. Trying to remember the way, I followed the cold and eerie corridor that I had previously walked with someone that didn't exist until I reached the main reception, waiting for someone to let me back out. My whole body was shaking in panic.

I looked all around but no one appeared to be on duty. I hadn't even called a cab to get me back home. Even if it was raining, I wanted to walk alone. *I'll put my headphones on and try to make sense of what the hell just happened in there.*

Who is Emma? And more importantly, how on earth is she connected to David? They clearly spoke about a lot of things. Why? That's how David managed to know so much about her when he came over yesterday. He knew far more than he said he did. That's why he wouldn't visit her with me. I had to find out who her brother was and why Oscar was there yesterday, even if it was just to see how she was.

I guess I should sign out of the book if I was leaving. I picked up the pen from beside the pad of paper and started to complete the columns with my name. *Should I put my real name or a pretend one?* The nurses knew who I was, and by the sounds of it, Oscar had already been.

'What? Wait just a minute...' I said out loud as I read the name of the previous visitor from the list. I ran my finger along the column to the date and time that they checked in and out, just to make sure I wasn't reading it wrong.

But it didn't make sense. Could it be another strange coincidence?

D. Roberts stood out in bold writing as clear as day. He signed in at 09.02 am this morning and checked out at 09.25 am—15 minutes earlier than I arrived.

I stopped and threw my hand over my mouth in shock.

If her brother had visited her this morning and she knew so much about David... she is his sister. David and Laura are brother and sister.

That's why he didn't want to visit her with me. He didn't want me to know. Had anyone else from the Richardson family found out they were related?

Chapter 6
An Old Acquaintance

I felt cheated.

That afternoon after returning home from visiting Laura, I sat on the sofa, staring down into the bustling London Street below my apartment. David never told me he had a sister, he said last night that she was an only child. Why would he say that?

I wondered how he knew so much about Laura. Just when I thought I knew everything about him, was this another lie that David had fed me and I didn't know him at all? Why wasn't he honest? Was he ashamed that Laura was his sister?

I can't help but think it was just another reason as to why David felt obligated to cover up the Richardson family files—he was protecting his sister and brother-in-law as well as his best friend. So, technically, that made Oscar his nephew. Everything was starting to make sense to me now. He was involved in this way more than I first anticipated.

The more submerged I was in this case, the more scared I became. Maybe I should have taken David's advice and stayed well away, but it was too late now. I was caught up in a tangled spider web of Richardson family misfortunes.

I needed to sit down with Hunter and the girls and go through everything, hoping to make some sense of it. I plumped up the cushions, placed my laptop on crossed legs, but just as I was about to update the case notes, my phone began to vibrate—David was calling.

I looked at the screen and put it face-down on the sofa next to me. I didn't want to speak to him, I wasn't sure I could even believe the words coming out of his mouth anyway but before it rang out to answerphone, something inside of me was telling me to pick it up. Something wasn't quite right, and I didn't know what. I had a nagging feeling in the back of my head. I needed to trust my gut instinct from time to time and now was that time.

I flipped it over and swiped to answer quickly before I lost him.

I didn't answer, I didn't say a word. I wanted David to do all the talking. After all, he was in the wrong.

'Esme... thank goodness you answered.' He sounded out of breath. 'I have some information for you.'

'Uh huh.' I tried to act blasé like I didn't care that he was calling, and I wanted him to get the message that I wasn't interested anymore. I was onto his lies.

'She's not who you think she is. Be careful... be very careful. I knew I had seen her somewhere before, just a lot older than I remember but it is definitely her.' His heavy breathing was muffling the speaker and his words kept cutting in and out, making it extremely difficult to make out exactly what he was saying. 'But she's being controlled.' His voice broke again and all I could hear was 'Gaslighting.'

What on earth is he talking about, what is gaslighting?

'Laura confirmed it. Check her records, her background. It will give you all the answers you've been searching for. She...' David's line went quiet again as if he was travelling through a tunnel.

'When were you going to tell me how you were connected to Laura? You lied to me.' I wasn't listening to what he was telling me, I was more concerned about what he didn't tell me.

'Esmeralda. Listen.' He sounded serious. I had never heard him like this before. I heard a door slam, something made of glass shattered, then it went quiet and the busy background turned to silence. David whispered. 'Oscar, he's on to you. Emily. She isn't...

Sarah is...' There was a loud bang, almost as though he had dropped the phone, then nothing. The line went dead.

'David. Emily isn't what?' I asked, hoping he would repeat himself. 'David, what do you mean Oscar is onto me?' Nothing but silence returned. 'David, answer me! Are you there, David?'

I was almost screaming at my phone for him to answer. It beeped in my ear then nothing. I tried calling back several times, but his number just went to voicemail.

'What was he trying to say?' I paced up and down the living room talking to myself. It made better sense that way. 'Emily isn't what? Sarah is what? Gaslighting?' None of it made any sense. I had to search the word gaslighting—it means a form of psychological abuse; it causes a person to question their sanity or their perception of reality. *Who was he referring to? Laura? Sarah? Emily?*

I held my phone in my hand as I made my way to the kitchen to make another cup of coffee with the recording of Laura and our conversation from earlier playing on loudspeaker for me to digest. She made no sense either—who was Emma in all of this?

I needed to do some digging on social media profiles around Laura and Emily. I had tried previously but not much came up. I think I needed to go back further on timelines, to look at pictures, connections, familiar faces or anything that would give me a clue as to what David and Laura were talking about.

I had Emily's full name, but I couldn't find anything on social media, on internet searches, pictures or anything. It was as if she didn't exist.

I turned to Laura's pages instead. She also didn't have that much on her, but she did feature in a couple of newspaper articles where she appeared in a photograph that the paparazzi had taken while she wasn't looking. There were no family pictures at all. I found a couple of medical journals referencing her qualifications and some of the practices that she had previously worked at, but they were both leading to dead ends.

Finally, I turned to Oscar's pages. Most of them were private but there were a few pictures online. One of his graduation that showed all the family, including his grandparents and parents, and the other at a charity fundraising event in London, which featured Arthur next to Emily, Oscar and his parents.

I stared and stared at the photograph, but I couldn't see anything obvious. What wasn't I getting? What was hidden in this picture that I wasn't seeing?

If I couldn't get hold of David... maybe I needed to try another route and get closer to the family.

That night, I tossed and turned. I had the same crazy nightmare that I had been having for the past couple of days. I had gone to pay David a visit at his home, I rang the bell and knocked on the door, but it went unanswered. I knew he was in because his car was in the driveway, so I walked around the back to see if he was in the garden. There was a crash and I noticed David lying on the ground surrounded by a pool of blood. I woke up in a hot and sweaty panic. It was strange and it affected me in such a way that I had never experienced from a nightmare before—it had seemed so real.

Monday morning arrived and I was sitting at my desk, pretending to carry out work for my undercover job at the office. Sitting in a daydream, I scanned the office full of busy co-workers and wondered what was really going on behind the scenes at a seemingly normal place of work.

ATR & Partners was a highly successful and well-respected investment company trading on the London Stock Exchange. Arthur Richardson had done an incredible job of building a family-run empire. To some degree, I could understand the struggle between family members to inherit such an asset, if only I could piece together the truth for Sarah.

David still wasn't answering his phone—it went to voicemail every time I tried. *That's strange,* I thought.

I pushed my pile of papers on my desk into a neat pile and placed my keyboard strategically over the top of them so I would know if anyone had moved them or interfered with any of it before picking up my empty mug and heading to the kitchen for a coffee refill. I needed a well-earned smoke break, but I wanted to get a few things done first so I could leave the office early and head home that afternoon.

The kitchen was more of a communal gossip area, and as expected, I turned the corner to the open plan area of small white modern-looking tables and chairs, sporadically placed around a long worktop and a side display of cupboards, a sink, fridge and microwave. Four women were huddled around a neat tray of tea bags, coffee, sugar and sweetener sachets and small spoons. They appeared to be whispering amongst themselves, but I caught the odd word or two as I pretended to quietly reach for a clean mug from the furthest cupboard, trying not to disturb them or distract them from their conversation.

The kitchen smelt like warm porridge that someone had heated up in the microwave for a late breakfast.

'I know, it's strange, isn't it? I don't believe that Michael drowned at all.' The tall brunette shook her head as she spoke and looked tearful, the others, in turn, did the same, looking sad and solemn as if they were missing an old friend, but there was something about the way she appeared closer to him than just a work colleague.

'But surely Oscar would have realised that he... surely, he wouldn't... I mean...' a petite blonde replied before realising that I was in the kitchen with them and glaring at the other girls to stop talking.

It felt like they had been caught out and equally pretended that they were just going about their normal routine and looking completely off guard.

'Morning, ladies,' I chirped in, banging my mug on the side and helping myself to the coffee and other condiments.

'Oh, morning, Esmeralda. How are you?' the petite blonde asked. Her name was Kristin, I had been introduced to her previously and spoken to her several times since I had started. She seemed nice enough, but I was yet to know any of them well enough.

'Great, thanks. You?' I needed to fit in as much as I could.

'The girls and I were saying this morning that you should come out for a drink or two with us after work if you fancy it? We all get on really well and thought, since you are fairly new to the team, you could do with the company?' She smiled pleasantly at me, waiting for my response.

This would be the perfect way to break into the team and find out what was really going on behind the scenes. It may be gossip but there could be a few things they let slip that would be vital to me knowing.

'That would be lovely if you don't mind. I would really like that,' I beamed back at her.

'Great, tomorrow after work, Ye Old Watling on Watling Street, it's just around the corner from here. We will all be there. The landlord knows us well. See you then.' With that, she grabbed her mug from the side and waltzed out of the kitchen. One by one, the others followed their leader out and I was left stirring my coffee on my own once again.

So, everyone is talking about Michael... they all think that something is up, but what? They don't believe he drowned either. Did they also have reservations about Oscar?

Chinking the side of my mug with a teaspoon, I plopped it into the sink along with all the other spoons and made my way back to my desk. Hidden behind large, freestanding screen dividers, my desk was one of many in the huge building. I had enough privacy to be able to sit and concentrate on hacking the Richardson family work files and email accounts without being disturbed.

The first accounts that I needed to check were the work accounts. Normally, the first reason that everyone gets a little protective over a business is when money is missing or things go wrong. From there, I could then start to check individual files and email accounts.

I already had a domain login, but I needed to break into the accounting system. The business didn't have very good security controls in place, so it wasn't too difficult for me to steal credentials for those in the accounts department.

This type of work never failed to get my adrenaline pumping. It was like running a race for me, the energy behind each 100 metres, jumping a hurdle and then onto the next stretch of track, uncovering data as I went.

I started with the first full set of accounts from last year—money in, money out. All seemed to be fairly normal. Tax, VAT and salary payments, it was all quite standard practice.

Hmmm, I pondered. N*ot much is going on. Let's go back another year.*

I noticed a few transactions that were frequently occurring, accounting firms, banks and employees. I scanned, line by line, transaction by transaction. The green glare from the screen reflected off of my glasses as my eyes flickered.

Then, as if it stood out like a sore thumb, a big transaction to a firm, Harper & Leavesden—£500,000. Two weeks later, another payment to the same firm of the same amount. I searched for the company on the internet. They were a business that sold funds and shares. The owner and CEO was a gentleman called Robert Ferguson.

Okay, nothing too abnormal, but that's a big investment, I thought and noted it down to be further investigated.

I noticed a payment to Michael Richardson for £10,000, and it was referenced 'dividend'. This in itself didn't seem strange, but the fact that there were no other dividend payments to Sarah, Samuel or Arthur seemed odd. The same payment to Michael was repeated every month for the whole year as well as his regular salary.

Why was Michael getting a regular dividend from the business but no one else was? I sighed, resting my heavy head on my left hand as I used my right hand to glide the mouse down over the screen in front of me. This could have been completely innocent, but I always noted down everything slightly out of the ordinary and disqualified them against evidence at a later date.

Just as I was about to flick to the previous years' set of accounts and start the whole process again, my eyes were quickly drawn to two transactions on the last day of the financial year. One said £50,000 to Oscar Richardson for 'services rendered' and the other just had a cash withdrawal for the same amount.

In the scheme of things, and to the Richardson family, that probably wasn't a lot of money, but in my eyes, that seemed like a large sum... and what did services rendered mean? More importantly, £50,000 in cash would have needed to have been ordered and withdrawn in person. *Where did this go? To who? For what? Why cash?*

'Esmeralda,' a man called out my name, making me instantly jump. I panicked and closed the accounts tab I was searching on and looked up to find a familiar face peering over the screen around my desk.

'Sorry, I didn't mean to make you jump. I just thought I would say hi.' He smiled and stood there patiently.

'Oh, hi. I... um... you didn't make me jump.' I didn't know whether to stay seated, stand up or walk around to greet him.

'Fancy lunch sometime?' Samuel asked. I hadn't seen him since the funeral but there was something about his dark, charming looks that attracted me to him. I heard David's voice in the back of my mind warning me against him, but the more someone told me not to do something, the more I did the opposite.

'Erm... yes, that would be lovely.'

Goddammit, Esme, why didn't you say no? I kicked myself.

'I'm a bit busy this week but next week could be good. How are you settling in by the way? I didn't realise you had transferred from the US office. I thought you said that you previously worked with Michael.' He hung his head to one side and looked at me as if to study my quivering face. 'Sarah was filling me in yesterday when I spoke with her.'

'Yes... I have... I...' I wasn't sure quite what to say before he rescued me. I messed up the part about knowing Michael, if I had been invited by Sarah to the funeral, I wouldn't have had to lie. I was hoping he would change the subject.

'Anyway, must dash, I have a meeting that I'm late for. Nice to meet you again. I'll be in touch,' he said before turning and continuing along the walkway. Thank goodness for that, I was saved by his meeting. Halfway up, he looked back and caught me looking after him. He winked as I awkwardly looked away.

I was never very good at conversations or personal situations with men where I was supposed to respond or take compliments. Why did he want to go to lunch with me? Was he already on to me as well as Oscar and that's why he mentioned me not knowing Michael at all?

Samuel was the least of my worries. I had to get to the bottom of Emily, Oscar and this mysterious Emma. My biggest worry of all was why David wasn't answering... maybe he was choosing to ignore me and I would hear from him in another three years' time.

Ensuring the coast was clear and no one else was about to disturb my investigations, I opened back up the page and ran through the list of files one by one.

'Let's have a look through the equity file.' I quite often spoke to myself. It wasn't that I was expecting a response but more a case of sanity-checking my actions with someone that wasn't able to argue back.

I found a combination of private investors and family shareholders were listed. That seemed normal but the rate at which shares were traded was odd. The Richardson family had held varying quantities for years but there was a flurry of private investors selling their equity.

I quickly checked the dates and amounts and noticed that it was last year. A similar time to the large investments sent to Harper & Leavesden.

'Hmmm,' *I said* again, questioning what I was seeing. 'Who had access to the accounts? Arthur only or did Michael have access too?'

I reached for my phone and sent Sarah a text.

'HEY, SARAH, WHO HAD ACCESS TO THE BUSINESS ACCOUNTS LAST YEAR?' I asked.

Waiting for Sarah to reply, I continued scrolling through the list of shareholders and noticed L

Richardson & Co. This must be Laura Richardson, right? The same Laura, that I visited on Saturday and managed to say very few words. Why was her business buying up shares of ATR & Partners? Surely, she was entitled to dividends if she was married to Michael?

My phone buzzed—it was Sarah.

'IN THE UK – MICHAEL AND MY FATHER. MICHAEL COULD ONLY AUTHORISE TRANSACTIONS UP TO £50K. IN THE US – ME. NOW OSCAR HAS ACCESS AND CONTROL OVER EVERYTHING. S.'

'THANKS, SARAH.' I was brief as I didn't have time for idle chit-chat.

That would explain the transactions for that amount, but surely Arthur would notice those amounts going out if he was checking the accounts. These were all transactions from last year, most of which were whilst Arthur was still alive.

It wasn't my business and none of it should make the blindest bit of difference but Sarah telling me that Oscar had full control of all UK accounts made me feel apprehensive. Why didn't I trust that incredibly good-looking man and his charming demeanour? What experience did he have to control over the whole company and its bank accounts?

Something didn't quite add up.

'Wow, don't tell me you have had your head stuck in the same acquisitions project this whole time.' It was the second time today that Samuel had made me jump whilst I was engrossed in figuring out this messed-up family's secrets.

I looked up into his dark brown eyes for a moment, wondering just how much he was hiding and how much of it he was completely oblivious to. I didn't believe for one minute that he was completely innocent but there was something about a bad boy that attracted me to them. The more I wanted to say no, the more I was tempted to say yes.

'Dinner?' he asked again before I had a chance to speak.

'Um...' Did I come across as shocked, lost for words or just plain ignorant? He caught me off guard for the second time today. I glanced at my watch. I had been sitting there staring at the confidential files of his family's business for hours and the afternoon had crept away with me.

'I'll pick you up at 7.30 pm.' He seemed sure of himself and grinned.

'Don't you need to know where I live for that?' I asked.

'I'll text you,' he almost shouted back at me as he walked off in the opposite direction than he had done earlier.

Just as I was about to log out of my system and start powering everything down, an email flashed into my inbox. The sender was Samuel Richardson. No content, completely blank. Just the header with numbers.

'I'm guessing that is his mobile number,' I muttered. *Oh, he's smooth. He's very smooth.*

I sat there for a moment, wondering what to do. I was always overcautious when it came to dating men, especially when there was a work-related connection. After being burned in the past, I didn't want it to happen again. But this time, I could use it to my advantage. There didn't need to be any love or emotion in going to dinner with someone. I had questions to ask, things I needed to find out... what harm could going for dinner with a man do? All I had to do was keep it platonic and make sure he knew I wasn't down for anything more. Things didn't need to get complicated, right?

I typed his number into my phone and began compiling a message.

'HI, SAMUEL, IT'S ESMERALDA.' I paused, then deleted it. Of course, it was me, he gave me his number.

'HI, SAMUEL, MY ADDRESS IS...' I paused again and pressed the delete button several times—too direct.

'HI, SORRY, I WAS IN THE MIDDLE OF SOMETHING EARLIER, I WOULD LOVE DINNER, MY ADDRESS IS...'

Nope, too needy. I couldn't decide on the best way to text him my details. I deleted it and started again.

'HEY, SAMUEL, THANKS FOR SENDING ME YOUR NUMBER. MY ADDRESS IS 267F CLAYMORE STREET. SEE YOU AT 7.30. ESME.' Perfect—direct and straight to the point, starting just as I meant to go on. I pressed send and placed my phone back on the desk.

He instantly replied but with just a thumbs-up. I wasn't sure how to take it. Do *I just leave it there? I don't think there is anything to go back to that with.*

Ugh. I'm no good at this. I sighed.

At least with the girls, I knew how to read their texts, and with David, he didn't text, he always called so it was easy to hear his tone and read his body language.

Speaking of David... where the hell was he? Would it be another three years before I would see him again? I tried one last time to call him before I got the same immediate transfer to voicemail as I did previously, so I finished what I was doing and packed everything away, leaving the office slightly earlier than I normally did. My highest priority was thinking about getting ready for this evening.

Without knowing where we were heading, it was difficult to dress for the occasion. Did I dress casually, anticipating a bar that served snacks or should I go dressed to impress in a figure-hugging number that he would be attracted to and give me the answers to any questions I directed at him?

I opted for an in-between. Tight black trousers, black heels and a nicely fitted top and jacket. This way, I could fit into most venues and not look too out of place. The great thing about owning your own cocktail bar was that we got to see what all our clientele were wearing. What was in fashion, what was on the high street and what looked good, so I went with what I had seen recently being worn.

For once, my hair was down and blow-dried and I had a face full of makeup.

I had to get a move on, he would be here in less than 15 minutes and I was nowhere near ready.

My apartment looked an absolute mess where I had pulled every item of clothing from my cupboard and used it as a catwalk and changing area to make sure I chose the right outfit. I needed to remind myself constantly that this was not a date, this was a business dinner and I needed him to co-operate.

I paced back and forth a couple of times, muttering away to myself as I did so, practicing lines that I could say to him in the car on the way to the restaurant. I was nervous. *Why am I so nervous?*

Glancing out of the window, I saw a dark car pull up below my apartment and park against the pavement. His lights dimmed. I couldn't see if it was Samuel or not, but it was 7.29 pm so I decided to make my way downstairs anyway.

Checking around the room like I always did when I left to make sure I had switched everything off, I reached for my phone, keys and small clutch bag and left, slamming the door behind me.

My phone vibrated in my bag. Just as I pressed the lift button, I peered at the small screen in my hand and saw a message from Samuel.

'OUTSIDE. BLACK ASTON MARTIN.'

I went to reply. S*hit, wait, what? A black Aston Martin. That is my favourite car of all time. I just need to act calm and not be at all impressed by what he is driving.*

'OKAY. JUST HEADING DOWN. BE 5 MINS.'

I made every attempt not to be impressed just as I told myself to behave but you could have captured the expression on my face with a camera by the way I looked at his car. It was beautiful and it made all the other cars parked within a short parameter look dull. I hadn't been this excited about a date in years—no, wait, I mean ever. Oh, and it wasn't a date either.

I took a deep breath and approached the passenger side. It opened as if by magic. Samuel had reached over and was holding it just ajar enough for me to open and climb in.

'Evening, Esmeralda. You look incredible,' he complimented me as soon as I sat in and clicked the door closed.

'Thank you,' I returned, checking out his expensive-looking attire. 'You too.' I smiled nervously as he sped away and up the street. My body thrust against the figure-hugging sports seats.

'I hope you don't mind but I took the liberty of booking a nice bistro restaurant a bit further into town. They serve incredible food, and the house wine is nice too. As it is not a date, I thought we would go for something a bit more casual, then perhaps something a bit more formal next time?' He looked at me and smiled, revealing his almost perfect set of teeth. His brown eyes glistened magically as we sped past the streetlights.

'Of course, I don't mind, Samuel. That's lovely of you to have booked something. I really don't mind where we go. Thank you for picking me up.' I kept my eyes on the road as I didn't want to look into his luring eyes any more than was necessary. 'You must be busy quite a lot of the time with work?' I asked.

'If you don't mind, Esmeralda. I'd rather not talk about work this evening. I spend enough of my time during the day and with family talking about pointless work politics that I don't want it to ruin my personal life as well.' Well, he shot that down pretty quickly, I was so disappointed that this was the whole point of us going out tonight. Well, in my eyes it was anyway.

'Oh, I'm sorry. I didn't mean to...'

'No, I'm sorry. I didn't want you to think I was rude then. I just wanted to make it clear from the beginning that you might not always want to believe what you read in the papers or online about our family. Don't let that spoil your perception of me as a person.' He seemed quite genuine so far. Why was this man single when all he had been so far was polite, apologetic and courteous?

'So, Esmeralda, let me start by asking you a question. What do you like to do in your spare time?'

That should be a simple question, but the fact is, I don't have any spare time as it is taken up working on cases like this one for your sister.

'I love a good workout. Yoga in Hyde Park is lovely in springtime or a nice walk along the river.' That was a complete lie, but he didn't know that.

'Me too, I'm into cycling and quite often take a cycle route out of London and into the countryside. You should come with me.' I could see him looking at me out of the corner of his eye to check my reaction.

'That would be great. I'd like that.' I wasn't completely lying. It wasn't something I would normally do but it did sound quite enjoyable.

Samuel indicated and pulled alongside the kerb of a swanky-looking restaurant and turned off the engine. It had fire heaters on either side of the main doors.

'I really hope you like this place, it's one of my favourites. He turned to me and smiled endearingly.

'I'm sure I will, it looks really nice.' He seemed to have gone to a lot of trouble for just dinner and all I had done was get ready and look pretty. I followed him as he got out of the car and waited on the steps for me to join.

'Good evening, Mr Richardson, we have our finest table ready for you, if you would like to follow me.' A smartly-dressed gentleman greeted us and walked us to where we were to be seated—a nice cosy round table with enough room for four people in the corner, the quietest part of the establishment.

The restaurant was very rustic and antique-looking. Dark wooden floorboards, cracked leather chairs and low ambient lighting from the flickering wall lights and candles. If I hadn't been so adamant about it not being a date, I would say it was almost romantic.

The staff seemed to know Samuel well as they all nodded their heads as we passed and quietly said, 'Mr Richardson,' smiling at me in turn.

The food was exquisite, the company was surprisingly pleasant, and I really enjoyed the evening. Samuel was charming, polite and a complete gentleman. For the first time in so many years, I had found myself warm inside. Being the woman that I was—independent and proud—I offered to pay the bill, but he refused.

As soon as we settled the bill and were getting ready to leave, I could hear my phone vibrating in my handbag. I ignored the annoying sound and waited for it to go to voicemail. *It's probably Hunter,* I presumed. I didn't want it to spoil my evening, despite me originally not wanting to be here.

There it was again, and again and again. Someone was either persistent or there was something wrong.

'Did you want to get that?' Samuel asked.

'No, it's okay, they can wait.' I continued to act like I wasn't that bothered, but deep down inside, I was itching to find out who it was. I couldn't answer it in front of Samuel—what if it was his sister calling about the case.

'Hey, honestly, I'm fine with you answering it. It sounds like they are desperate to speak to you,' he insisted.

'I'll just have a quick look at who it is. If it's my brother, then he can wait till I'm home.' I picked up my handbag and peered at the screen, but as I gazed down at the illuminated screen, I noticed six missed calls—all numbers that I didn't recognise.

I almost switched it off and placed it back in my bag, but a text briefly flashed on the screen and gripped my attention. I tried to hide the look of fear on my face.

'IT'S JOSH, DAVID'S SON. CALL ME... IT'S URGENT!'

Samuel noticed my reaction instantly.

'Hey, if you need to get that, you are more than welcome to. I will grab our coats and meet you outside if you prefer to take it in private?' He seemed so understanding but this was a conversation I needed to have in private, completely out of earshot of anyone.

I gulped, trying to hide the tension in my body.

'No, honestly, it's fine. It can wait.'

Chapter 7
A Secret Message

After what felt like a breath of fresh air and enjoying dinner with a man that I was told not to get too close to, I spent the entire journey home completely distracted by the text message from David's son.

I couldn't answer it and call him back because it would attract so many questions from Samuel that I didn't want him involved in. I was panic-stricken. *Why on earth is he calling me? How did he get hold of my number and why on earth isn't David calling me back?*

I felt so rude. If I was Samuel, I wouldn't talk to me again and I most definitely wouldn't treat myself to another night out after behaving the way I did. I looked out of the window, contemplating all the scenarios in my head until we reached my apartment.

Samuel pulled up alongside the kerb and turned off the engine, leaving the dull light of the headlights lighting the way ahead. Small droplets of rain were beginning to fall in the cold February air.

'Well, thank you for an incredible night, Esmeralda. I'd like to say that I want to see you again, but I feel that you have other things on your mind and may not want to see me. Did you want to talk about it?' He turned in his seat to face me. His large muscular legs restricted in movement.

'I'm so sorry, Samuel, I feel like I have ruined the evening. Up until that phone call, I had such a good night and I can't thank you enough. My brother can be quite persistent at times, I just need to call him once I am home and all will be fine.' I had a sense that he knew I was lying but I went with that story anyway.

'If you are sure everything's okay, you know if you are ever in trouble, you can always come to me,' he said as he put his large, warm hand on my shoulder. I thought I would move away if he touched me, but I didn't, I just stayed still. It felt nice, reassuring and somewhat comforting ahead of what I felt I was just about to walk into.

I looked straight into his eyes. 'Thank you, Samuel, that is so nice of you, I may take you up on your offer.' And I meant it. I felt something, I'm not sure what but I definitely felt at ease whilst being with him. I didn't want to leave.

Two drunk girls suddenly and loudly passed the car window, staggering all over the place, a bottle of wine in their hands. That was my cue to bring myself back to reality and get myself out of the car and into my apartment where I could call Josh back.

I pulled at the car handle as it released the lock and got out. I felt bad for not inviting him up for a coffee or a nightcap, but I had no choice. I had to deal with this first. As I walked to the building entrance, his eyes following me every step of the way, I waved to say thank you and goodnight.

He wound down the window and gently said, 'Same time tomorrow night?

'I'm sorry, Samuel, I can't tomorrow night as I'm out with the girls from the office. I can another night though?' I shrugged my shoulders, hoping he would pick another day.

'Sure, I will message you,' he said as the window started to close again. 'Oh... and, Esmeralda.'

'Yes?' I turned back around.

'It's Sam. Call me Sam.' The window closed and he disappeared. The loud sound of his Aston Martin engine purred and echoed along the street as he sped away.

I couldn't wait till I reached my apartment before I called Josh back. I quickly snatched my phone from my handbag and checked my messages. One after the other, they appeared on the screen. At first, they were urgent but calm, then they turned frantic. He must have sent me more than 20 messages.

I took the stairs instead of the lift, so my call wasn't interrupted, but the lights were out, it was pitch black. Only the light from my phone lit the stairwell. *That's strange,* I thought, then I felt the broken glass beneath my heels shatter and crack.

What the... I looked up to find that the lightbulbs had all been smashed. 'Who would...' I mumbled under my breath the whole way up the flight of stairs to my floor and turned right to reach my door.

That's when I noticed...

My door was wide open.

My heart was pounding in my chest, something was wrong. Just as I reached the doorway, Joshua answered.

'Oh my god. What took you so long to call me back?' He was hysterical.

'Look, Josh, I was—' He cut me off instantly.

'I don't know who you are or what connection you have to my father, but I received a brown letter addressed to you and your number on the front of it. As soon as I got it, I called him to ask what on earth it was for, but he didn't answer, so I went to his house. I can't believe he's gone.' He was choked, he stopped talking and I could hear the pained tears of a young man crying.

'What do you mean he's gone?' I knew the answer, but I couldn't bring myself to believe it until I heard him confirm it.

'He's dead, Esmeralda. Someone has killed my father.' My knees buckled and I fell to the floor. I heard the dreaded words, but to add to that, I caught a glimpse of the inside of my apartment. My home was upside down and ransacked. I had been burgled.

'Are you listening to me?' Josh said quite angrily. 'Who would want to kill my father? I don't understand. I need to find the person who did this.'

'I'm sorry, Josh. Yes, I'm here. I'm still here. Have you opened the envelope? What is inside it?' I asked, quickly scanning the room to see the extent of the chaos.

'No, I haven't. I didn't know... I... do you want me to open it?' he asked.

'Yes, open it quickly. Tell me what's inside.' I was still sitting on the floor with the door wide open.

'I don't understand. There are pictures—some of a girl, some of a woman and newspaper cuttings. And school photographs. What has this got to do with my father?'

Poor Josh. I was sure that he didn't know David's real profession, he had been fed lies about where he worked from a young age.

He always wanted them to think that he worked in IT for the government but not on special cases or investigations. Yet another lie that he told his family as well as the lies he'd been feeding me. I guess to protect those that he cared about, but sometimes it was easier than explaining what we actually did. I know for sure that David didn't tell his children about me, I didn't expect him to, and I had never met them.

'What happened? Were you the one to find your father? Have you called the police? Where are you now?' I quickly asked him so many questions.

'He sent me a strange message saying he had sent me a brown package and that I must get it to you if anything happened. I found it hidden in a box in his old garden shed. It has your name and number scribbled on the front. He said you would know what to do with it, but when I couldn't get hold of him, I thought it was strange. I knocked on the front door. There was no answer, his car was on the driveway, so I went around the back and that's when I saw him...' I could hear his devastated tears. 'He was on the floor, there was blood everywhere. He...' He stopped, unable to continue.

I couldn't quite believe it. The nightmare I had last night and the previous night was exactly as Josh was describing. Nothing was making sense...

'Josh, do you want me to come over?' I didn't know him, and he didn't know me, but I felt like we had been thrown together in a mutually catastrophic moment for us both. David would have wanted me to go and see him, especially as his mother had passed away in the last few years.

'Yes, please.' His response came from a scared, lost and distraught little boy. He gave me his address and I told him to give me an hour as I needed to work out what had happened to my apartment in the meantime.

The concept of David being dead hadn't even hit me yet, it hadn't sunk in. I was still emotionally attached to him, but everything had happened in such a short space of time.

I knew it would hit at some point, but until then, I had to figure out what was going on. I called the only person I always did when I was in trouble—Hunter.

It rang less than twice before he picked it up.

'Esme.' He yawned.

'Hunter, I need you. My apartment has been burgled, my stuff is everywhere, and David...' I couldn't bring myself to say the words.

'David what?'

'He's... I... um...' My voice was broken, the tears streaming down my cheeks and my whole body shaking with both fear and shock.' I tried again, but it was so difficult to say. 'He's gone... murdered...'

'Are you okay?' He suddenly seemed attentive. 'I'll be over in ten minutes—I'll bring the squad and call into the control room to see what I can find out for you regarding David. Do you know when police were dispatched there?'

'I don't know.' I wiped the tears from my face. I could speak but there was still a painful lump in my throat that I couldn't get to clear. 'I got a call from his son saying he found him and that they had been called but I don't know if they are still there or have left. I'm not sure if they have taken anything from my apartment or if it was just to scare me. Even my laptop and computer are still here.' I scanned the room again, trying to remember where everything was and if I could envisage anything that was missing but I wasn't thinking straight.

Even if they had taken my laptop or computer, everything was stored in the cloud so they would have had to break into my accounts and they could do that from anywhere.

Was the Richardson family trying to send me a message? Quite a coincidence that Samuel had taken me to dinner—one of the unusual occasions where I had left my apartment. Is he in on it as well? David warned me about their charming and charismatic ways —maybe he was right and this was a sign? I had so many alarm bells ringing around my head that I didn't know what to think.

I spent the next 15 minutes pacing around my apartment trying to figure out if they had taken anything until my brother turned up, in a full police uniform and with two of his colleagues. They stepped over the upturned furniture, bits of broken glass and china, with my belongings strewn across the floor.

'You sure you are okay, Esme? Do you have any idea who could have done this?' He winked at me as he spoke. It was a sign for *play the game, don't say anything you shouldn't and let them carry out their work.*

'Erm... no, I don't know who this could have possibly been.' I shrugged my shoulders. His two colleagues walked around each room taking pictures and swabbing several areas.

Hunter stood beside me and leaned in to whisper so the others couldn't hear. 'They will do a fingerprint check to see if they can find any and run it through the database, it could give us an idea of who was behind this. We saw the broken lights in the stairwell as we came in. You don't think it could be the Richardson family, do you?' He raised his eyebrows.

'I don't know, but if they did, I think they also have something to do with David's murder. I guess it is a good sign.' I turned around to face Hunter.

'Why is this mess a good sign?'

'It means we are getting closer to the case, and we are obviously onto something. Why else would they be warning us to stay away? David's son, Josh, said that he had been sent a brown envelop with pictures of girls and women in it along with some newspaper cuttings. I haven't seen them yet, but I am going to head there and find out what David was trying to send me. I just don't want his children caught up in all of this, it's not fair.'

'Be careful, Esme. Do you want me to come with you? I'm concerned that this is getting too dangerous.' He gave me a worrying look.

'No, not just yet. If I appear to be a caring friend of David's, it won't raise suspicion. Which, I am, may I add. However, if a police officer turns up, that could set alarm bells ringing. I'll call you if I need you.' I gave him a hug and left the three of them in my apartment checking everything over as I went to see Josh.

It felt a little strange going to see the son of my ex-lover in his ex-wife's house, but I had to push that past me and do the right thing. I couldn't imagine what Josh and his siblings were going through.

I could have called a cab... it would have been easier, but instead, I walked down to the underground car park beneath my apartment building and chose to drive. The lights turned on, column by column, as I approached my car parked in the underground bay. I noticed a man sat on his motorbike in the corner, his helmet closed and full leather protective clothing so I couldn't see his face. He looked up and glanced in my direction, but I just kept my head down, clicked the key fob in my hand and continued to my car.

As soon as I was in, I locked it behind me. Taking a deep breath before starting the engine and heading off.

Just as I approached the ramp and waited for the barriers to open, I looked back in my wing mirrors, noticing that the motorbike rider was following me, waiting behind my car. I tried reading the number plate, but the numbers and letters were too blurry—I didn't have my glasses on. Maybe it was just a coincidence that he was leaving at the same time as I was.

Come on, hurry up, barriers. Open, please.

They slowly rose, I indicated, took a right and continued down the street. The motorbike was close behind me. I contemplated pulling over so he could overtake me, but he seemed to be looking down one of the side streets as another motorbike pulled out behind me and swung in beside him.

That's odd. Are they riding together?

I picked up the pace, but they only went faster to keep up with me.

I slowed, so did they. I indicated, so did they. I felt a sudden wave of fear. *Are they following me? How did they know I would be getting in my car? Were they waiting for me? Were they the culprits that burgled my apartment?*

I tried taking a photograph from my phone but the lights ahead of me changed to red and I needed to break suddenly. They pulled in behind me, either side of the back of the car but in my blind spot.

Hunter—I needed to speak to him! I asked my car system to dial his number, it dialled but he didn't pick up. My heart was racing and the adrenaline was pumping through my veins. I had to just keep driving to lose them.

A text message popped up.

'BE CAREFUL WHAT YOU UNCOVER, YOU MAY NOT LIKE THE OUTCOME'. It read from an unknown number. It couldn't be them as they were riding. Who was it? Then another one.

'DAVID SNOOPED MORE THAN HE SHOULD HAVE.'

Who is this? Hunter, where are you? Call me back goddammit!

As the lights turned green, I put my foot to the metal and pushed as hard as I could on the accelerator, my car sped away. It didn't seem to make the slightest bit of difference, in fact, they seemed to enjoy the race. Both motorbikes pulled up beside me—one on my left and one on my right.

They couldn't have been closer if they tried. Another car was coming in the opposite direction, so I tried moving over as close to the middle of the road so there was no room between us and the other car. They swerved. The car on the other side slowed and looked at me like I was a mad woman who had lost her mind. They didn't know what was really going on.

I was only three miles away from Josh's location, but I didn't really want to lead these men straight to his home. I spotted a petrol station in the distance and thought that if I could just catch them on CCTV there, I would find out who they were.

I pulled in, screeched to a halt and looked all around me. The two motorbikes swung in behind me then quickly sped past and out of the exit. I pressed the button for the handbrake, sunk my head into the headrest and took a big deep breath. My heart still racing heavily.

Had they really gone or were they just waiting around the corner to continue the chase? At least they had now been caught on camera and I could get Hunter to ask them for a copy.

It took me less than ten minutes to reach Josh, looking all around me as I went to make sure they weren't following. Hunter called just as I pulled up on the driveway.

'Hey, are you okay?' he said just as I answered.

'Oh, Hunter. Two men on motorbikes were in pursuit of me right up until about a mile away. I had to pull into the petrol station to shake them off. Do you think we could trace their plates to see who they were?' I asked.

'Do you know which station it was or what model of bike they were riding?' I could hear voices in the background.

'Erm, let me look. It was the one on Turner Road.' I had to quickly look it up on my maps. 'I recognised that they were Ducatis, but I couldn't tell you what model. The motorbikes were both black.'

'Okay, got it. I'll head there now and see if we can check their CCTV and run it through the system for matches. Are you sure you're okay? I will come and meet you if you like. We've left your apartment... I don't think there were any prints though. We will see what we can do.' He sighed.

'Just a little shaken, I wasn't expecting them to be following. I'll text you when I leave as I don't know how late I will be.'

'Stay Safe, Esme.' He paused for a moment and then hung up.

I stood on the doorstep of a beautiful mid-terrace London home. I hoped I had the right house and rang the doorbell. I could see movement inside followed by a young man who answered. He was the image of David. Immediately throwing his arms around me, I could feel the young man sobbing, his whole body shaking. I was a stranger to him, but I guessed that since his father trusted me, he did too.

His hug eased as we stopped our embrace. I stood on the doorstep, studying his features for the first time.

'Josh?' I asked.

He nodded.

Two other young men joined behind him, equally as tall and slender. I could see they resembled some of their father's features but not as much as Josh. Perhaps they were more like their mother.

'What if she has something to do with it?' one of the boys said.

'Don't be stupid. If she was, our father wouldn't be asking us to send this to her.' Josh held up the brown envelope in his hand.

'You had better come in then.' The three of them turned around and walked into the room with the first door on the right-hand side of the hallway. I walked in, shutting the front door behind me. Just to be careful, I took one last look around outside to make sure there was no one else there.

The front room was beautifully decorated but with an older generation's taste in furniture. There were empty glasses and plates across the coffee table and drying washing on the radiators. The curtains were drawn and the lamps at either end barely lit the room. They needed a cleaner, more importantly, they needed carers. I felt sorry for them having lost both parents within such a short space of time, but they were legally able to look after themselves.

David would have made sure that they were financially stable. At *least they have each other,* I thought.

'I'm so sorry for your loss.' The truth suddenly hit home as I saw family pictures across the walls and in frames. I was choked. I felt a hard ball in my dry throat, it was pushing me to cry. I had tears in my eyes but I had to stay composed.

'Do you have any idea who could have done this to him?' the eldest son asked. 'Why would anyone want to kill our father?'

'And what do those pictures have to do with him?' the middle son demanded.

'I... um...' I was worried about how much I should or should not say.

'This is James,' Josh said, pointing to the eldest of his brothers. 'And that is Jonny.' He pointed to his other brother.

'Nice to meet you all. I wish it was under better circumstances. I am so sorry for your loss. All of you,' I replied, looking at each of them in turn.

Josh handed me the brown envelope. I took the liberty of sitting down on the sofa, emptying out the contents onto my lap as all three looked on, confused.

The first picture appeared to be an old school photograph, the name of the school in gold pictures engraved onto the card frame read 'Lower Compton School.' It meant nothing to me yet.

The second picture was a little less quality, but again, it was a school photograph. *Why did David want me to have these pictures so desperately?* I thought. I continued picture after picture, then I noticed two of the girls in all the pictures. *Who are they? What is he trying to tell me?*

The next photograph was one of the Richardson family. I looked at each of the faces, calling them out in turn— Arthur, Emily, Michael, Laura, Samuel, Sarah, Oscar. I still couldn't see what the connection was.

Another couple of pictures of Michael looking an awful lot younger than he was in the picture from his coffin, but he didn't look like he was with Laura.

Who is the woman in the photograph? I wondered. I flipped it over to find handwritten notes on the back saying 'Michael and Emma, Greyview Gardens.'

It was a newspaper article, a bit faded in areas, but it looked like David had printed it onto an A4 piece of paper. It had a group of girls and the headline 'Lower Compton School Wins Again.' The same school as in the photograph, a small article about an interschool sports competition, listing all the girls' names underneath; Sarah Smith, Jane Kemp, Emma Campbell, Joanne Lane, Elizabeth Mistry, Pauline Jacobs, Libby Connelly and Laura Roberts.

The last piece of paper was handwritten—I knew that writing well... it was David's.

'Esme, I did a few background checks on people connected to the Richardson family and looked at my sister's pictures from school (I'll explain that piece later). Have a look at the government database for Emma Campbell, date of birth 14th April 1970 and the same with Emily Carter, same date of birth. Look at her criminal history. Don't share this with anyone else. D. Roberts x'

I looked up at the brothers, still studying me like I was about to reveal all.

So, he was admitting that his sister was, in fact, Laura Roberts, now known as Laura Richardson, but who was

Emma Campbell? Did his sons know who their Aunty Laura was?

Chapter 8
Smoke And Mirrors

I didn't stay long at David's son's house. It didn't feel right... I felt like I was intruding. I gave my condolences, told them that I was always there if they needed anything and that I was an old work colleague and friend of his, leaving it at that. It didn't make sense to muddy the waters or to create any unwanted tension.

I said I needed to do some work on the photographs as I couldn't quite work out the connection. I had to do as David told me and check the central government files and any criminal background for the family.

As much as it seemed totally surreal, I had to go and see David and speak to him. I needed to see his face, to get the closure I needed and somehow put things to rest. I had so many things I wanted to say. Even though he wasn't there anymore, it only felt right.

Hunter managed to call the hospital that his body had been taken to on my behalf and obtain special police force clearance for me to see him. I had worked previously on a few sensitive cases such as this for the government, but it was mainly photographs and images, not face to face. This would be the first time that I would be seeing a dead body in the flesh.

I had an image in my head that a mortuary would be a dark old house, all the bodies would be kept in a dingy, low-lit basement and metal storage cabinets. They would be dressed in hospital gowns with a tag on their big toe.

David's body was currently at the hospital he was taken to soon after he was found. I sat in a long empty corridor on one of the plastic chairs wondering what he was going to look like. Would I be shocked, empty, sad or upset? Maybe all of those together, only time would tell. They didn't keep me waiting long. The leading pathologist greeted me, said sorry for my losses and offered to stay with me whilst he took me to where David was resting. It was appreciated but there were so many things I wanted to say that I wouldn't have been able to in front of a stranger.

I was taken to the room that he was in. It was a large space that resembled an operating theatre. Only one small window that let in the most peaceful rays of natural light. It felt cold and empty and I shivered as the quietness of the room closed in. A hospital was normally a busy place, people rushing around and chaos, except this room was the opposite—calm, quiet and strangely still.

I found it hard to believe that the table in the middle of the room had a dead body on it, and more sobering was the thought that the body was that of David's. The once full of life man that I had shared a coffee, a work relationship and a bed with was now gone. I edged slowly forwards.

Most of his body was covered with a white sheet. Only his head was on show.

'I'll leave you two alone. I will be back in 15 minutes. Is that enough time?' He was a short, plump, balding man wearing thick-rimmed glasses. 'Unless you would like me to stay with you?'

I glanced back to see him by the doors. It was as if he was leaving me in the room with a dangerous caged animal. 'No, no, that will be fine. Thank you,' I answered softly.

The door gently closed behind him. It was just David and I.

I pulled up a chair beside the table and sat down. He didn't look dead, he looked peaceful like he was in a deep sleep. I wanted to hold his hand just one last time and talk to him, to tell him how I really felt but I didn't dare touch him. I felt as if he could hear me.

'Oh, David, I am so sorry.' I broke down. 'What were you trying to tell me? What did you uncover that was so bad that someone had to cover it up?' I leaned forward in my chair, wiping my eyes full of tears as they ran down my cheeks and dropped onto my blouse below. 'I will solve this case and bring the person who did this to justice if it's the last thing I do.' I sniffed, holding my head up and tried to compose myself.

Struggling to focus, I looked at the sheet draped across his grey, stiff body, noticing a line down his chest that was raised. It must have been from the autopsy. I knew what they did to bodies to carry out their cause of death, but it didn't bear thinking about what they had done to his. I needed to remember him the way he was.

I spoke to David for the next ten minutes, reminiscing about memories, all the fun times we had together, laughing gently to myself as I remembered, half-hoping that he would open his eyes and laugh with me. My first day at work, the trips we went on, and most important of all, everything he taught me.

The pathologist knocked and then popped his head around the door, so the 15 minutes must have been up.

'I'm sorry to disturb you, are you okay or would you like additional time? I can come back if you want me to.'

'No, no, it's okay. I've said everything I wanted to. Besides, he isn't very conversational.' I smiled. He smiled back, knowing what I meant.

'Esmeralda?' he said as he walked over to me.

'Yes.' I looked up, wondering what he was about to say.

'Normally, we only allow the next of kin to come and see the bodies before they are sent to the funeral directors, we get some really odd people who just want to look, if you know what I mean.' He gave me a forced wink. 'But I did it as a favour to your brother, Hunter, as he is a very old friend of mine.' He stood beside me, both of us looking at the corpse with our heads to the side.

'Oh, thank you, it was really appreciated and very kind of you,' I said in a whisper.

'I didn't want you to thank me. I was only saying this because I know you are investigating a possible connected death and I'm sure that you want the person who did this to pay, but there is something happening here that I really think you should be careful of,' he began in a quiet voice.

'Whatever do you mean?' I looked at his worried face.

'I think this is a lot bigger than you could possibly imagine. It might not be safe.' He stared at me in a way that made me concerned. He was trying to tell me something, just like David had been... and now look where he was.

'Go on,' I pushed for more.

'I thought that something was strange the morning that Michael Richardson was bought in. It was the early hours, and I was about to finish my shift, so it was passed onto my colleague to finish the paperwork and autopsy.' He shuffled nervously from foot to foot and looked flushed. 'I've seen a lot of dead bodies in my years here.'

'What was strange?' I asked.

'The man that came in was battered and bruised from having been in the sea, but that wasn't what killed him... nor did he drown. His body was seriously malnourished, his teeth had decayed from years of extensive alcohol and drug abuse, we also found synthetic opioids in his system.' He turned to the worktop behind him and looked as though he was carrying out his duties whilst telling me things he shouldn't be.

'Synthetic opioids,' I repeated after him. They weren't something I was familiar with.

''Yes, they are drugs that are chemically processed. Heroin is a semi-synthetic drug. Highly addictive but becoming increasingly popular on the streets across the UK. Now, correct me if I am wrong here, but the dental records of Michael Richardson that were brought in several weeks ago didn't match the dental records of Michael Richardson that we had on file, and I've seen him in the media. He didn't look to me like a man that was seriously malnourished or a drug addict.' He turned around to face me and returned to whispering.

'I asked to see the files from my colleague, but he was extremely cagey about them. He said they had already been completed and sent off as his son was chasing the examination results for the purpose of claims according to his will. Sometimes it can take weeks or months to get a copy of these. In the meantime, my colleague, Steffan, didn't return to work the week after this was submitted and no one has seen or heard from him since.'

I had been sitting attentively listening to this man so closely that I'd fully forgotten that there was a dead body lying here next to us the whole time.

'So, what are you saying?' I questioned.

'I'm saying that the body that came in was not the body of Michael Richardson, and it was covered up. Quickly too. His body was recovered, brought in to us with the funeral directors, and in the ground in less than ten days. Normally, it is two to three weeks, at least.' He turned around and looked busy again but remained quiet.

'Despite the fact that his body was malnourished, he had drugs in his system and his dental and medical records didn't match. I put down that the cause of his death was a broken neck, consistent with someone who had suffered a neck trauma whilst still alive.' He stood still, looking straight into my eyes.

'You mean...' I knew what he was alluding to, but I wanted him to spell it out for me.

'I mean, his neck was broken.'

'As in he fell?' I clarified.

'No, I mean someone had hold of his neck and twisted it, aggressively and deliberately to end his life.' The pathologist couldn't have been clearer.

I held my hand over my mouth in shock. My mind guessing who was to blame.

'I've seen it before. I am confident that was his cause of death and what was on the report... only, it was removed.'

I sat still, motionless, thinking about the information he had given me and what I needed to do with it. *If it wasn't Michael Richardson. Who was it?*

I felt my watch vibrate. A text notification popped up on the screen as I lifted my wrist and read it.

'CALL ME. IT'S URGENT.' It was Mollie.

I desperately wanted to find out what she had to tell me, but I needed to finish here first, and I wouldn't be able to talk confidentially with her.

'CAN'T TALK RIGHT NOW. GIVE ME FIVE MINUTES.' I wanted to keep her by her phone so I could call her straight back, but I needed to get outside.

'I must go now but thank you for the information. This will help me with the case. Can I come back to you if I have more questions?' I asked. He seemed the type of person that wanted to help. Someone that couldn't leave things to go unnoticed or let the wrong thing happen. It was a rarity—most others would turn a blind eye.

'Sure.' His chubby face seemed genuine.

I said my goodbyes to David, knowing that it was the last time I would ever see him, and made my way through the many corridors and lifts until I reached the main reception. I tried to smile politely as I passed people, but you could see the sadness in people's faces as most of them were there because they were sick, poorly, injured or a loved one was. I was desperate to get back to Mollie and find out what it was she needed to speak to me about.

I stepped inside the busy lift with a doctor and a nurse pushing a child on a hospital bed, so I apologised before reaching beside them and quickly pressed the ground floor button.

The doors closed as I pressed my back against the cold glass panels and lifted my head up, staring at the ceiling and waiting for it to gently drop to reception. In a matter of a few minutes, it stopped, there was a faint ping and the doors re-opened to the first floor where I waited patiently for them to leave. The same happened again as I reached the ground floor to be greeted by the bright and airy main entrance of the hospital.

I quickly hurried towards the revolving doors and took a deep breath of fresh air from outside. I pulled out a cigarette packet from my coat pocket, shaking. I plucked one from the pack and popped it gently between my lips, holding the lighter towards the end and sparked to light it. I took one quick deep breath to inhale the nicotine and felt it flow down into my lungs before dialling Mollie from my phone and holding it to my ear, patiently waiting for her to answer.

'Hey!' she answered immediately.

'Hi. Sorry, I had to leave the building. What's up? I was eager to hear what she had to say.

'So, I've been doing a little digging on the Richardson family's medical records.' She paused.

'Come on, Mollie, don't keep me hanging. What have you found?' I was intrigued and impatient.

'So, originally, I was looking up Laura Richardson and I found some out some fascinating facts, but then I went on to the rest of the family, Arthur and Michael, and it looks like all of them need further investigation.' She cleared her throat.

'So, what does that mean?' I asked.

'You're right. Laura had a history of mental health problems—schizophrenia was the biggest culprit in a lot of her issues but that was soon brought under control with the correct medication. The part that I found the most interesting was a private medical record that I found from an IVF clinic in London. It looks like her and Michael were having major issues conceiving. They ran multiple tests for both her and him.'

'Oh, that's interesting.' I continued to listen to what she had found out.

'What's even more interesting is that her tests came back completely normal. Good quality eggs, hormone levels fine, but Michael, on the other hand...' She stopped as if to build up the suspense. 'According to the records, there was no way that he would be able to father a child, almost non-existent sperm count results.'

'So, what are you saying?'

'I'm saying that Laura was told they couldn't have children and there was the option of a sperm donor. The records show no sign of them pursuing a donor or going through that process with that clinic or any other for that matter. Fast forward to a year later and she is pregnant.'

'So, they were wrong and she conceived naturally?'

'Nope. As soon as the baby was born, a paternity test was done, and the results are also on record. For that to happen, the presumed biological father would need to provide consent.' If I was sitting down at this moment, Mollie would have had me on the edge of my seat.

'So... drum roll please, the father is...' I was aching for the answer.

'Samuel. Samuel Richardson!' She erupted with his name.

'What?' I hollered down the phone so that passers-by turned to look at me. 'As in Michael's brother... Samuel Richardson?'

Of course, it is, that's where Oscar got his good looks from, I thought to myself.

'Crazy, huh?' Mollie almost sniggered. 'So, Samuel isn't Oscar's uncle, he is his father, and he knows as the paternity test results were shared with him at the time. What I can't see is whether they were shared with Michael and whether he knew.'

I gasped.

'Do you think the rest of the family know? Or even Oscar? He kept referring to Michael as his father at the funeral. What if it was all one big facade?' I don't think Mollie had any more of an idea than I did but it was more of a rhetorical question.

'Who knows,' she replied.

'Wow.' I needed to sit down. I walked over to a raised planter a short distance from the office and sat down.

'This is one fucked up little family, Esme. And there's more.' She sniggered again down the line.

'Really? I don't know if I am ready to hear this, Mollie. I'm still trying to come to terms with Samuel being Oscar's father.' Mollie was unaware that I'd had dinner with Samuel last night.

'Well, the thing is, it looks like Arthur had been going back and forth to the doctors for about six months before he died. As he had private medical cover, he was referred to several specialists, each of which sent a copy of the test results to his email address.' She coughed to clear her throat.

'And...' I listened in.

'Well, it appeared that Arthur had suffered for many years with chronic kidney disease, known as CKD, and he had previously been treated for kidney stones. It is actually quite common, but over the last few months, there appears to be more frequent visits to specialists due to him complaining about intractable hiccups, insomnia and stomach pains.' Mollie was talking to me as if she was reading a page of notes from a medical journal.

'So, Arthur went to the doctors because he had hiccups and couldn't sleep?' I asked

'No, quite the opposite. Tests revealed that he had developed an acute kidney injury. He seemed to be suffering from nephrotoxicity, a toxic effect caused by medications or chemicals, but he didn't appear to be on any medications according to his records.' Mollie paused again briefly before continuing. 'A number of tests were conducted after he was admitted for nausea and gastrointestinal pains but the most interesting one was a renal biopsy. Some of the tubules showed evidence of regeneration and oxalate crystals associated with acute tubular epithelial injury. Patchy tubular atrophy and high interstitial fibrosis was discovered. He was given a diagnosis of induced oxalate nephropathy and required haemodialysis.'

I had no idea what Mollie was talking about, understanding none of her medical terms or references.

'Esme? Are you listening to me?'

'I am, Mollie, but if I'm honest, that makes no sense to me whatsoever. In plain English for idiots, what was wrong with him?' I asked.

'He was either taking something or being given something that was affecting his kidneys. There is no other explanation as to why he went downhill so rapidly. Something was causing oxalate crystals and I can't find anything else on his records to explain it. According to his files, the medical professionals were just as confused. You need to check his emails from a Mr Peter Anderson at Parker Medical Centre, London.' Mollie sounded concerned.

'So, what you are saying is, he was poisoned?' I took the last inhale of my cigarette, throwing it on the floor and stamping it out as I thought seriously about the information Mollie was giving me and trying to remember the consultant's name from Parker Medical Centre so I could search archived emails.

'I'm not saying anything, Esme, I just think it doesn't add up. I can try reaching out to Mr Anderson but he's going to ask why I need that information. Check his emails first if you can and I will then do what I can on my side. I'll ask my colleagues for their opinion, but I must be careful.'

'I wonder if that's why he called David. He knew something was up. But who would...' I kept jumping to conclusions in my head. *What if he was poisoned just as Sarah had suspected? But why?*

'Who knows, Esme. We may need to have more of a look into why and who, and in the meantime, I can see if I can find any more medical evidence. I'll give you a shout as soon as I know more.' I could hear her sigh from all the information she had just unloaded.

'Thanks, Mollie, you're amazing. Love you.' I hung up and made my way back up to the office, passing reception with a smile, knowing what I now knew.

That evening, I was out with the ladies from the office. They were so lovely and welcoming, but I didn't bond instantly with them like I had done with Casey, Mollie, Amie and Tilly.

The usual characters of the group were out this evening—the wild one that drank too much and was told to calm down by her office colleagues. She was funny to laugh at and great for a good night out but was always carried home by the others, regretting whatever she had done in the morning—that was Jade.

The one that always had an agenda and snitched on you the minute you turned your back just so that she had something to talk to people about. She lured you into a false sense of being able to confide in her so you would tell her your darkest, dirtiest secrets, then she would tell the world, the snitch as I called them— that was Claire.

Then there was the annoying one that either moaned about everything not being right or things weren't up to their expectations and the rest of the group spoke about them behind their back, yet they were invited out time and time again, either because the group felt guilty if they didn't or because they always got a free meal or drinks as a result of said moaning—that was Andrea.

And finally, there was the wild one that always caused a drama, deliberately causing a scene or an argument with others outside of the group, making the night so much more entertaining. It normally resulted in being asked to leave. Why? Well... because they can—that was Abigail.

At first, we grabbed a few proseccos, some nibbles and engaged in general chit-chat about the office. A little bit of gossip followed by some shots of tequila. That's when it started to get interesting.

I managed to find out that Michael wasn't as innocent as everyone had made out. They all knew he was the son of the CEO, but they used it to their advantage. Apparently, Michael was a ladies' man, despite being married to Laura. They would sleep with him and then blackmail him into promotions or perks in the office. The sad thing was, all the girls were talking about him, about what they had managed to get out of him and the fact that he hadn't learned. Time and time again, he fell for it.

From what I could gather, Michael wasn't as smart as I thought he was. Arthur was the real mastermind, the hard-working businessman that liked a side-hustle. He did what he did to get what he wanted. Almost like the gangsters you read about. He was a lovely man, but get on the wrong side of him and you knew about it.

Sarah had learned that from her father, but she was having to prove her worth to him and Samuel was the only semi-innocent party because his mother had kept him away from most of the sagas.

I found it interesting that not many people liked Emily and didn't trust her. The ladies said she had tried to be part of their group several times, but they didn't feel comfortable being around her.

Oscar came up in a few conversations but only because they were talking about how arrogant he was and none of them stood a chance. He was hunting for a supermodel girlfriend with very wealthy parents. Something he wouldn't find in the office at work.

Other than that, I hadn't managed to find out a huge amount about Arthur's or Michael's deaths and the mysterious circumstances. They all found it odd but had no more information around it than I did.

I didn't stay long, I made my excuses and started to walk home. Back to the drawing board and relying on the team and Hunter for the answers to the case.

Chapter 9
Gathering Evidence

I needed to make progress on the case and achieve a breakthrough of some kind. That was going to take a lot of focus and a few days without interruption.

As a private investigator, sometimes it was necessary to capture moments on camera as well as documented evidence.

I decided to start with Oscar first. To figure out where he went during the day, what he was up to and whether he had any connections. Maybe if I knew a little more about him as a person and what he was up to, I would be able to solve some of the questions I had so far.

As I was in the corporate directory as a member of staff, I had full access to the calendars of most of my colleagues. Senior management, however, was a different story. Most of them had private and locked diaries, but by using my hacking techniques, I managed to gain access and find out exactly where Oscar's appointments were during the day and with who.

The most interesting of them all was the lunch scheduled today with a private member of staff at The Ivy in Covent Garden. The location was perfect for following someone and being able to take pictures. It was extremely busy, and due to the high amounts of tourists, there was always someone taking photographs and trying to obtain the ultimate background for social media purposes.

I decided to wear unsuspecting clothes, something that I wouldn't normally wear (well, not outside of the house anyway), so I put on a pair of jogging bottoms, trainers, a hoodie that matched my baseball cap and glasses just so it was more difficult to recognise my facial features.

My outfit was well and truly comfortable. I looked myself up and down in the tall mirror that I had resting against my bedroom wall. Maybe I had been dressing wrong this whole time and casual was the way to go. I laughed comically at my reflection.

Right, I need to get a move on if I stand any chance of being anywhere near The Ivy for when Oscar arrives to greet his mysterious date.

I didn't have time to get stuck in traffic, so I pulled my hat down as far as it would go to the brim of my glasses and left my apartment. I ensured that my phone had enough memory to be able to capture all the images I wanted to take from today's events.

The worst-case scenario was that Oscar cancelled and it was a wasted journey, but that was a risk I was willing to take.

I jumped on the tube as quickly as I possibly could, shoving past everyone as the train hurled out of the station. I worked my way up the northern line and changed onto the Piccadilly for one stop until I reached Covent Garden station.

I had been here a million times at weekends in the sunshine. So many places to eat and drink and a great part of London to enjoy with friends. This time was different though, I wasn't here for lunch, I was here purely to be a stalker and see if I could spot Oscar.

February was freezing in the UK, so sitting outside for lunch was only on the proviso that a heater was on, and the restaurant gave you an optional blanket or two to stop you getting frostbite.

The Ivy was right on the corner of Henrietta Street— the ideal spot for me to hang around the entrance of the indoor mall directly opposite or sit in the cafeteria across from it and take some unsuspecting pictures on my phone.

A short walking distance from the tube station entrance, I walked around the corner hesitantly. I watched from the darkness of my sunglasses each and every person that was near me. Although it was a cold winter's morning, the sun was on full display, so my glasses didn't look too out of place.

I approached the cobbled courtyard, joining the hundreds of people all flitting about the streets, and found a secluded corner to stand and wait. I looked over at The Ivy but couldn't see Oscar yet. No familiar faces and no guests outside waiting to be seated.

The time was only just before 12, so I was early.

I loved people-watching. Their behaviours, their habits, personalities and characters all on display for all to see. It distracted my focus, I had to concentrate on the restaurant just in case I missed them, even for a moment. What if they sat indoors? I wouldn't be able to take as many pictures as I had hoped for.

The Ivy was pretty. It had delicious food and was famous for its authentic décor dating back to 1917. Standing here staring at all the restaurants in close proximity, waiting for Oscar to arrive, was making me feel hungry. I could visually imagine the menu in my mind, I knew what I would have ordered too.

Dressed Dorset Crab for starter and the Roasted Iberico pork chop for my main dish. I was salivating thinking about its taste just as the handsome Oscar Richardson ventured into my line of sight. He gently jumped out of the black London cab that had pulled onto the corner of the courtyard, and as suave as could be, walked over to the main doors of The Ivy.

I watched as he chatted to the maître d' for a few minutes. He was then taken indoors.

Dammit, I cursed under my breath. Now I wouldn't be able to see the conversation he was about to have. Less than two minutes later, the next star of the show arrived—Emily Carter.

I was surprised to see her here with Oscar, but it gave me the opportunity to see what they were both doing together.

Emily did the same and spoke to the maître d'. Minutes later, she made her way inside the restaurant and they had both disappointingly disappeared from sight. I did manage to take a couple of shots, but they weren't the ones I was hoping for.

I tapped the side of the wall behind my back impatiently as I stood perched against the pillar of the building. I could be waiting here for hours waiting for them to come back out again. How long did I leave it before calling it a day? I glanced at my watch, noting the entry time of Oscar and Emily. I would wait 30 minutes, and if they didn't reappear, I would make a move.

No sooner had I dropped my wrist back by my side. Oscar appeared in the doorway, he was followed closely behind by Emily and had a white envelope in his hand. He looked happy, she did too. Maybe they were both there just to deliver something?

What were they up to? I pretended to take a picture of the architecture but with them in the background, followed by a couple of panoramic photographs whilst doing a complete turn on the spot.

Oscar handed the envelope to Emily, kissed her on the cheek and then left. She placed the small white envelope into her handbag and spoke to the maître d' yet again. This time, she was seated out the front of the restaurant. The waiter walked around, turned on the heater above her, giving her an orange glow, and handed her a menu. He placed another menu on the other side of her table. I presumed it was for her guest.

I was torn. *Do I follow Oscar or do I stay here and watch Emily?* Oscar seemed the most obvious, but for some reason, I was compelled to find out what Emily was up to.

Less than five minutes later, a smartly dressed gentleman approached The Ivy.

Could this be her guest? My eyes followed him all the way to her table where he stopped. Emily looked up, smiled and got to her feet. They air kissed, then both of them sat back down together.

He looked like a tough man, he had a shaved head, dark stubble covered his chin and a very masculine jaw line. His neck was thick set, you could tell he was extremely muscular and worked out. Various tattoos on his hands and fingers, although I couldn't quite make out what they were from this distance. He wore a grey jumper covered by an expensive-looking black overcoat, dark blue jeans and a pair of Chelsea boots.

I would never be one to judge a book by its cover but he definitely fit the stereotypical image for a hard man —a very scary man, in fact.

What is Emily doing in the company of such a person?

I turned to face the mall and pretended to take a picture of myself with them in the background. I zoomed in heavily so I could capture as much detail as possible.

I noticed that Emily was sliding pieces of paper with writing on and tapping them on the table as if to draw his attention to them. They were deep in conversation before he collected them from the table, folded them in half and inserted them into his deep overcoat pockets. The man looked all around, checking to see if anyone was watching. Little did he know that I was lurking in the crowds.

I held my phone awkwardly in my hand and snapped away. If anything, maybe I could get a facial recognition on his face and find out who he was.

I studied their body language... the way they interacted together. During my time working for the government, we had been on a lot of courses that taught us certain traits and how to read common types of body language. It was extremely useful. Based on this, I had come to the conclusion that this was not a lunch between friends. This was purely a business transaction.

No laughter or touching, just what looked like an exchange of documents or information, or perhaps both, and that was that.

He looked to be putting an envelope, similar to what Oscar had handed Emily, into the middle of the menu, closed it and handed it to Emily. The perfect exchange of something he didn't want anyone else to see.

The man then held out his hand across the table. Emily shook it as they both stood up, nodding in agreement between each other and he left in the same direction as Oscar had. Emily checked her watch, grabbed the envelope from the menu, pushed it to the middle of the table, not having ordered anything at all, and slotted it into her handbag with the other one. She checked all around her and began walking out towards the other end of the courtyard.

If anyone other than myself had been watching, she made that transaction appear extremely suspicious in nature.

There was nothing for me to do than make my way back to my apartment with the evidence on my phone.

Within the hour and without being spotted, I made it back home after grabbing a quick sandwich and getting through the crowds on the underground. I opened my front door, kicked off my trainers, slammed it closed behind me and threw my mobile down on my desk.

Still eating the sandwich I purchased, I was just about to grab a bottle of water from my fridge in the kitchen, I heard a voice call out to me.

'Good day?' It startled me. I almost spat my food onto the floor and screamed.

'Hunter, will you please stop letting yourself into my apartment and helping yourself to my stuff.' He was sitting on my sofa eating a bag of crisps and drinking one of my cans of drink.

'Oh, sorry, Esme, I finished my shift early and thought I would run through the case with you. I should have called first but thought you would be in.' He continued crunching the food in his mouth.

'Or tried knocking perhaps?' I mumbled under my breath.

'So, where have you been all afternoon? The gym?' He looked my outfit up and down.

'No, this was supposed to be my disguise.' I laughed to myself. It wasn't much of an outfit.

'Nice,' was all he returned with.

'So, basically, I was stalking Oscar but then Emily turned up and was giving something to a man in Covent Garden. It all looked a little shady so I thought I would run an identity check on him.' I sat down at my desk, turning on my computer as I did so.

This suddenly seemed appealing to Hunter as he got up to join me.

'Let's have a look.' He reached for my phone as I opened the pictures. Hunter began flicking through them one by one.

'Hmmm. This guy here looks very familiar.' He tapped the screen and frowned as he studied the man's features.

'Really, do you recognise him?'

'Yes, but I can't think why.' He scratched his head.

'Well, we will soon figure out why,' I said.

First of all, I ran a criminal check. I still had access to the government's central database for criminals, and so did Hunter. He was familiar with the system, so we uploaded the pictures one by one and let it search. It came back with no results.

So, I then decided to run an internet search. I had access to a software package that checks for similar facial images to the one I had. It was quite good at matching but sometimes it threw up some images that weren't even remotely similar.

I would run that first, then some manual intervention may be required.

It took a moment to search. I saw the screen flickering through millions upon millions of images. It was too fast for the human eye to see each one that it checked, so Hunter and I let it run the process whilst we talked between us for a moment.

The subject of our parents came up and how we hadn't seen them for a while. We needed to plan a family visit at some point in the near future. Perhaps when the chaos of this trial was over and things began to calm themselves a little.

Just as we began to look at dates, the screen froze and showcased a few possibilities for us to choose from.

'Interesting,' I said. My eyes blinking at the image on the screen. I'd never seen him before in my life.

Hunter, on the other hand, slapped the desk and said, 'I knew I had seen him somewhere.'

'Where?' I asked. 'Who is he?'

'He is a famous social media and newspaper journalist. He covers most of the rich and famous stories. He is a paparazzi menace.' Hunter clapped his hands together as if he had guessed the right answer to a pub quiz.

'Really?' I moved closer to the screen and read his name out loud. 'Marcus Jaffar.'

'That's it.' Hunter looked excited. 'Search for his name. I guarantee it will come back with lots of search results. Lots of celebrities have been snapped by him.'

I did as I was told and entered his name. Hunter was right, there were so many stories and articles using his images.

'It doesn't quite make sense.' I looked at him confused.

'What doesn't?' he asked.

'If he is a journalist and a paparazzi. What was he doing with Emily and what was she feeding him? And more to the point, what did he give her in exchange?' My eyes narrowed, thinking hard and clicking through the pictures that I had taken earlier.

'If you ask me, Emily is feeding the media information about the Richardson family.'

'But isn't that a little risky, considering Oscar was there minutes before?' I asked.

'Not if you are paying the media to publish what you want them to.' He cast me a malicious smile.

'You mean paying the papers to print false information?'

'Exactly.' Hunter and I had a lot more work to do if we were to get to the bottom of this, but Emily was quickly becoming my number one suspect in this case.

Chapter 10
No Turning Back

'LUNCH?'

The following day, a text message from Hunter popped up on the screen of my phone as I was busy brushing my teeth. It was already 08.02 am and I was late leaving the apartment for work.

Although I'd like to think that the reason I was late was because I'd had a lay in, it wasn't. It was because I had been lying in bed thinking about the case. I couldn't seem to get the evidence from Mollie and the company records to fit together. I was missing something in the middle, but what was it? Emily was chief suspect but it was as if she didn't exist. I needed much more than I already had.

The only way of tracing her would be through her human resources files at work, listing her national insurance numbers, next of kin details and any banking documents I could source. I didn't believe that in today's modern world, someone could be impossible to find. There would be an online trace somewhere that I would be able to obtain.

Then there was the information that the pathologist at the mortuary gave me. Who did the dead body belong to if it wasn't Michael Richardson, and if it did belong to another person, where was Michael?

I knew there was an ulterior motive with Hunter—he never just wanted lunch. He either had something to tell me or wanted to ask a favour.

'SURE. WHEN, WHERE?' I texted back.

'12.30. I'LL MEET YOU OUTSIDE ATR. WE CAN WALK AND TALK.' Although Hunter and I were very close, we would speak and see each other frequently and I would like to think that I knew most things about him, but we still kept some things close to our chest. I think it was more protection than anything else or perhaps not wanting to disappoint the other. For me, I didn't want Hunter to be put in any awkward situations that would affect his work, and he was equally as careful that he didn't mention anything he thought I might act on.

'SEE YOU THEN.' I hit send, running back and forth to gather all my belongings and left the apartment, slamming the front door behind me.

I stood in the lift for a brief moment thinking about Oscar. None of the family had a good word to say about him, but was he such a bad person that would have had anything to do with his father's or even grandfather's death? The whole scenario just didn't make sense. I didn't have one single example of why the family were pointing all their fingers at him.

I spent the morning reading through archived emails from the past two years. In particular, ones that had been sent back and forth between Michael, Samuel, Arthur, Oscar and Emily. It was difficult in some scenarios to understand what they were talking about but there were a few that had raised concern.

Michael had requested access to certain files and folders, requesting IT to delete some confidential information and other worrying emails from Arthur asking IT to restrict Michael's access to certain areas within the business.

I searched through multiple expense receipts and took copies of file movements. I used intelligent cyber security software that allowed me to search keywords, terms or phrases but you had to know what you were looking for to get the results you wanted. For example, I found folders called 'Family Photos' when, in fact, they were screenshots of stock and share dashboards and equity transactions.

If I were an auditor and found these, I would be investigating this further. Why were they naming folders incorrectly and hiding certain files or emails? The trouble with the Richardson family was that they had the luxury of paying back handers to people who audited them or, in Emily's case, legally advised them what they could and couldn't do.

My alarm buzzed on my watch. I had set it five minutes earlier than I was supposed to meet Hunter so that I had enough time to log out of the system, grab my belongings and meet him outside.

I made my way through the corridors, taking the lift down to the first floor, but as I hit reception, I saw Samuel. *Do I avoid him and pretend I haven't seen him, or do I openly walk past and expect him to say something?* Here I was reasoning with my feelings again. *Why couldn't I just act on the spot rather than analysing what I should or shouldn't do?*

'Hey, Esme.' He looked me up and down first then back to my eyes. 'Are you free this evening?

'Sure,' I said, caught off guard.

'Same time? I'll meet you outside, same place as before? Wear something casual, I'm taking you somewhere fun. Did you manage to resolve things with your brother?' He smiled but all I could see was an older version of Oscar. The resemblance now that I knew was uncanny.

'My brother?' I looked at him, confused. 'Oh, Hunter. Yes, from the other night. Of course. Apologies, yes, all resolved and fine now. I'm sorry again for letting that put a damper on our evening.' I suddenly realised what he was talking about—the call from Josh.

Samuel seemed to look at me in an unnerving way. It was almost as if he knew who really was calling and that I was lying. I could see Hunter waiting for me outside from the corner of my eye so I hurriedly continued about my business.

'See you at 7.30 tonight, Samuel.' I quickly ended the conversation and left him standing at reception.

'Yes, and it's Sam,' he called after me.

'Who was he?' Hunter asked as soon as I reached him. No 'How are you,' or, 'Nice to see you, Esme.' Hunter— ever the protector. He needed a girlfriend so that he could focus on her instead of me.

'Okay, so what do we have, Hunter?' I changed the subject of the conversation. He looked at me with a raised expression. I wasn't about to divulge who Samuel was, I didn't want him to think that I was getting too close to the case or the suspects.

'Look, he's still looking after you. I think that man has a sweet spot for you, Esmeralda.' Hunter nodded in Samuel's direction.

'Come on,' I said, pulling him away from the main glass entrance and along the road.

'I don't know where to start... I have so much to fill you in on.' He seemed excited.

'Well, that sounds ominous. After everything that Mollie shared with me regarding the medical records, why am I not surprised about this family doing anything underhand or suspicious?'

I shrugged, looking at all the food places as we walked past them. 'I'm starving, Hunter, are you eating?'

'No, I'm okay, thank you. My shift starts in an hour, and I need to get back home and changed before then.' He sighed. I could tell he wanted to. 'So, we had an anonymous tip off two days ago from someone that lives in the homeless encampment in Anne Street Park, Blackfriars. I say anonymous but we know who he is. It isn't my case so I had to do a little snooping around to get access to the files and listen to the interview recordings to get the information. The man in question said that he and a couple of his friends had been approached by a middle-aged woman offering them a sum of money in exchange for someone they were trying to find.' Hunter appeared to look on edge.

'Okay?' I asked, confused.

'Normally, I wouldn't have paid much attention but there were a few things surrounding this case that felt odd and could be connected to the Richardson family case,' he confessed.

'So, why did this man report it?' I asked, my head tilted to one side.

'He is scared for his life, Esme, and so are the others in the camp. He suspects that something has happened to his friend as he hasn't been seen since this woman appeared. He said she hadn't kept to her side of the agreement to pay the remaining money that was promised in exchange for delivering him to her. Since his disappearance, their camp has been set on fire and they received threatening visits from a group of men. They had no choice but to break up the camp and all go their separate ways. This poor chap doesn't know what else to do, he is scared for his life, so now so we have him in protected custody until we can figure this whole thing out.' Hunter looked concerned.

'Do we know who the woman is? Would he testify and be able to identify her? Why do you think this is connected to the Richardson family?' It didn't make sense but I could tell Hunter hadn't finished.

'It appears that his friend, Brian Ferguson, has gone missing after leaving with said woman. He was suffering from drug addiction at the time, a regular at the local hospital's accident and emergency department on suspected overdoses. The man told us that Brian had been quite an affluent gentleman until a few years back when he lost his family, his home and all his money, and as a result, ended up on the streets.

They found him lying on a park bench and took him in to their camp about two years or so ago.'

Hunter scratched his head with a pained look. 'I must say, Esme, it is difficult. Homeless people go missing all the time. It's hard for the police to trace them as they could be anywhere, and they aren't reported missing immediately. However, this time, I think there is something not quite right with Brian Ferguson and I'm drawn to it.' He pursed his lips together, stopped walking and turned sideways to look at me.

'This mysterious lady had approached the camp looking for Brian Ferguson and offered the others £25,000 if they could deliver him to them along with a small bag of his personal belongings. The man looked remorseful but said it seemed like easy money—he didn't expect him to disappear.' Hunters' voice got quieter as he got into the detail.

'That's a lot of money,' I said quietly.

'Brian never returned... he thought it was strange as he had no contact with any friends or family and nowhere to go, they don't believe that he just left like that. They reported him missing originally but the police took no interest. I found the file, it was never followed up. The man gave us some of the cash that she had given him, hoping that her fingerprints were on it.' Hunter paused, leaning in to whisper to me.

'And?' I pushed him to continue.

'We ran a check on the system. It's quite difficult to trace fingerprints, especially on banking notes, they do hold prints well, but because they exchange hands so frequently, there can be multiple individuals that they belong to. In this instance, there were two names that I had previously heard of.' Hunter stopped. He bit nervously down on his lip before revealing them.

'Let me guess, Emily Carter?' I froze, waiting for his confirmation.

'No, not at all—an Emma Campbell and Michael Richardson.'

'What the...' I had no words.

'Emma Campbell?' *There that name was again, the ex-fiancé of Michael... were they in it together? David had said that Emma turned psychotic after Michael finished things with her and she had been arrested, but I wondered if there was more to her criminal record than I was aware of.*

'You mentioned her name the other day and the pictures from David? She has quite an extensive criminal record it appears.' Hunter was running out of time to explain things as he needed to get ready for his shift.

'Really?' I was fascinated to find out more.

'The man who was reported missing was Brian Ferguson, except he's not missing. I checked passport and identity scans globally. Where is the one place that you would open an offshore bank account to be accessed from the US if you wanted to stay under the radar?' he asked.

'Switzerland,' I responded.

'Exactly.' Hunter nodded in agreement. 'A bank account was created just weeks before Brian's disappearance, using his identification, with an opening balance of £50,000. That's not small change for most people. His passport had been used to gain access to the USA, so I then checked with the customs and immigration staff across the country. To officially enter the USA, you must first apply for a full visa if visiting for more than 90 days or a visa waiver scheme if staying for less. There is a visa application for Brian Ferguson, and he entered American airspace in Florida on the same night that Michael disappeared by private yacht.' I instantly felt sick, we were onto something way bigger than I could have imagined.

'Now how and why would a homeless man suddenly set up a bank account in Switzerland, deposit £50,000 and fly to Florida of all places? To hide?' Hunter suggested. I felt like he was onto the truth here.

'So, why would Emma offer money in exchange of a homeless person, and why him of all people? Why would Michael's prints be on the same notes? It seems strange that they are in contact with each other again after all these years, he was responsible for breaking her heart and now they are tied to the mystery disappearance of a man called Brian Ferguson.' Even Hunter found it all odd.

'Hmm.' I had no words.

'So, I'm guessing Emma was the one who offered the homeless camp money?'

'Potentially correct,' Hunter confirmed. 'But without the man giving evidence, we can't be sure, with or without the fingerprints.'

'So, what we need to find out is why Emma Campbell is helping a homeless man escape to Florida? Exactly who is she?' I asked. 'Finally, have you managed to find out more about Michael's death?'

'Yes, according to the records, Michael was aboard his private yacht, he had named it Lillian after his late mother, just the two of them... him and Oscar. It was moored at Lymington Yacht Haven. I understand it is a quiet marina. I read the notes, the report says it can be very dark at night, no busy and bustling restaurants or bars, so the perfect location for a yacht to sail without raising too many concerns. They apparently left at 8 pm, Oscar reported his father having fallen overboard the vessel at 1 am the following morning. They should have reached Northwest France by that time, but when the coastguards reached him, they were still only midway through the UK and France channel!' Hunter exclaimed.

'I don't know what that means, Hunter, I'm not very good with yachts,' I explained.

'Michael owned a 75ft Sunseeker, on a full tank, that should have been doing around 25 knots per hour, so in five hours, they should have been around 125 miles away from the UK. They were nowhere near that. Now you could have argued that they were cruising but it seems highly unlikely.'

'The body was also found just off the coast of Cornwall, an area where the rocks and elements would have badly damaged and bashed the body against its rough coastline. Quite appropriate for trying to disguise a body, don't you think?' Hunter had an accusing smile on his face.

'So, what are you saying exactly?' I asked.

'What if the man that was washed ashore wasn't Michael... it was, in fact, Brian Ferguson. A man that could quite easily disappear, especially if money was involved, and Michael was still, in fact, alive and well. It was all a cover-up and this Emma Campbell was involved?' Hunter suggested. He quickly looked at his watch to check how much time he had left. 'I need to shoot but I thought I would tell you where we were at and if you thought it was relevant or not.'

'Wait, you can't leave it like that. If Emma Campbell is involved, then Oscar must be involved too!' I exclaimed. 'Who identified the body at the mortuary when it was found?'

'Precisely—Oscar.'

'What? And no one has challenged this? Has anyone interviewed or called her in for questioning? Is this not a missing person's case?'

'No, because he's not missing, he is in Florida somewhere. We have alerted officials out there to find him, but until now, we have yet to identify his whereabouts and it is not a priority in their eyes. I'm trying to formally identify Emma Campbell but it's proving difficult.'

'Esme, we need to find this Emma Campbell and fast. I could have taken two and two and got five, but I'm certain she could be the key to this whole Richardson case. Why did David send you those photographs of Laura and Emma together? He knew the truth and that was potentially why he was murdered.' Hunter swallowed heavily.

'The pathologist said he was concerned when the body of Michael came in as it didn't match the records they held. He also said that the cause of death had been changed from his death certificate. What if...' I stood as still as a concrete statue.

Hunter did the same, our brains were working too quickly for us to talk at the same time.

'That reminds me... on the subject of David's death, are they any further forward with who they think did it? Any prints there? Clues? Anything?' I asked.

'No, nothing. No prints. They have said that the cause of death was trauma to the skull but nothing other than that. They are keeping it very close to their chests. I will do some more searching this afternoon and see if I can find anything out, but nothing as yet.' Hunter leaned in and gave me a hug, squeezing me tightly. I could tell he was concerned but I was fine. I knew what I was doing.

I also needed to get back to the office as I only had a couple of hours to access some files before getting ready to meet Samuel again.

Later that evening, just as he did before, Samuel turned up, beeped his horn as he patiently waited alongside the kerb below my apartment.

As I climbed into his super sexy Aston Martin, I felt underdressed in my black jeans, plain white trainers and a blouse. There was something about Samuel that I liked this evening. He had a branded polo shirt, the top buttons undone, exposing his dark hairy chest, designer jeans and trainers. He smelt so incredible that even my nose was attracted to him.

He turned to me and smiled. 'Are you ready?'

'For what?' I asked, intrigued by his secrecy.

'You will have to wait and see.' Samuel put his foot down hard on the accelerator and we sped for as far as we could before being stopped by a set of traffic lights.

'I hope you don't mind losing because I am incredibly competitive.' He laughed.

'Where on earth are we going?' I laughed back. He indicated left and pulled up alongside an old dockside building in Canary Wharf. There were neon signs above the main doors and a group of people in their early 20s outside smoking and vaping.

'This, Miss King, is our destination.' Samuel sniggered, turning off the engine to the car and started to get out. I did the same and followed.

We reached the large glass doors that were held open by a large security guard.

'Have you booked?' he asked.

'We have. I've paid for two games for both of us.' Samuel showed the confirmation email on the screen of his phone as the man allowed us past, showing us the way to the main reception area.

Samuel and I were led into a brightly decorated warehouse. The smell of loaded fries, wings and pizza filled the air. A fully stocked bar stood right in the middle of the warehouse serving what looked like the most incredible cocktails I had ever seen.

Looking at the man I had met at his brother's funeral several weeks ago, the multi-millionaire and shareholder of ATR & Partners, he had taken me to an indoor amusement arcade for a date. And I loved the thought of it.

Around the outside of the warehouse were a variety of games, you scored points for how fast or how well you played, and at the end, there was a leaderboard.

At a quick glance, I could see basketball hoops, shooting games, throw the bean bags, whack the mole and other childish games that adults loved.

Samuel and I spent the next couple of hours laughing, shoving and trying to put each other off winning the games as we had a go at each of them in turn, but it was no use. He won hands down on every single one. I tried not to, but I watched his masculine arms and physically fit body exert themselves.

'I am quite impressed, Esmeralda,' he said.

'With what?' I asked, my face red and my body wet from the heat of the activities.

'For coming second.' He laughed and threw a playful arm around my shoulders.

I didn't know what to say—it didn't feel awkward or uncomfortable, it felt nice, and it also felt so good not having to hide our relationship from the world. The only time I was with David outside my apartment or his house was at work. The rest of the time, I had to act like my feelings for him didn't matter.

We stayed for food and a few drinks, but we couldn't have too many as he was driving. I didn't want to be that embarrassing date that had drunk way too much and had to be put to bed, so I stopped with him.

'Thank you, Samuel. I had a really great time tonight. Probably the best date I have ever been on,' I said appreciatively as I got back into his car.

'Oh, so you acknowledge that it is a date now?' He cast me a side glance.

Oh no, Esmeralda, you have blown it now.

'Oh... I... um...' I was lost for words.

'Well, it's good that I thought it was the best date I had ever been on too.' He laughed as he got behind the wheel.

Chapter 11
Miami

My suitcase packing wasn't the best. Most women would have their entire wardrobe laid out on their bed beforehand and a strategic plan as to what to wear on what days along with a few extras in case plans change. I, on the other hand, was more of a tactical planner. I'm going for ten days so I will take ten pairs of underwear, swimwear, jeans, tops, blouses and a few dinner dresses just in case I go anywhere nice. A selection of shoes to suit all occasions, including trainers, heels, a pair of boots and a pair of flats. Perfect—just my washbag, makeup bag and hairdryer to go in and I was done.

I also didn't iron any of my clothes before I placed them in, it was a case of throw them in roughly because by the time I get there, they would be crumpled anyway. They would have an iron at the hotel, so I'd iron them there.

Sarah called me yesterday and informed me that she had seen on the corporate travel system that Oscar had booked flights to Miami and was leaving today. He had booked a return flight, business class the following week, and Sarah wondered why he was going. Everything that happened in the US was agreed to fall under Sarah's jurisdiction, so why Oscar was travelling there without making her aware worried her enormously. Naturally, she wanted me to go too and see if I could follow him, find out what he was up to and if it was anything to do with business or just a holiday.

It gave me next to no time to organise everything and leave. My flights and accommodation were booked immediately by her and an itinerary of times and travel had been scheduled. A cab would collect me from outside my apartment tomorrow afternoon at 1 pm—my flight was at 5 pm. Oscar was on the earlier flight, so hopefully I wouldn't bump into him at the airport, but I knew what hotel he was staying at and had to stay close.

I wondered if he was going with Emily or whether he was going on his own.

I struggled to sleep that night, wondering what Oscar would do if he found out I was following or indeed if he knew I was working for Sarah. The more I was finding out, the more I wondered what his involvement was in this case and just how dangerous he was.

I tossed and turned, a mixture of thoughts running through my head until the sun began to rise and it was time to get up. I could hear the rain outside pouring down and the harsh winter wind gushing against the windows. At least I would be pleased to escape the dreary English weather and head to somewhere warmer.

There were a few things I needed to get done before finally being collected and whisked away to the airport. I uploaded a few updates to the case files online, spoke to Hunter who had a spare set of keys for my apartment and warned me to be safe. One by one, all the girls had told me to be careful out there on my own. I wasn't on my own—I could reach out to Sarah if anything went horribly wrong. What could possibly happen? if Oscar bumped into me, I would just say it was a coincidence.

The driver beeped his horn from downstairs. Slamming the door closed, I wrapped my handbag around the handle of my suitcase and pulled it along to the lift. Hurriedly, I got in before I bumped into my neighbours and had to make polite conversation. I made my way to the Addison Lee car parked outside the front entrance.

Smartly dressed in a dark suit and a black chauffeurs' hat, he nodded to note my arrival and got out of the car, popping the boot open as he did so and collected my suitcase from me.

I could get used to this, I thought to myself. It's quite nice being collected and waited on. I hadn't experienced it before, being the independent woman that I was.

'Afternoon, madam. Would you like to keep your hand luggage or prefer it in the back?' he asked, taking them both from me.

'Erm. I think I'll keep hold of my bag please but the suitcase is okay in there.' I smiled appreciatively.

He seemed quite a shy and quiet man, his short blonde hair gently poking out in places from underneath his cap. He opened the car door for me and proceeded to put my bags in. As soon as I got in, he ran back around and shut my door, then getting in himself.

'Wow, I can't wait to get away from this weather.' I nervously made conversation with him but he looked at me from the rear-view mirror and nodded.

'Yes, it's not nice, is it?' That was all he returned with. No continued conversation or pleasantries, he indicated, pulled away and concentrated on the road. A local radio station played quietly in the background.

I looked out of the windows miserably, watching the droplets run down the glass.

What was I going to find out in Miami? Perhaps nothing but I had a bad feeling about where I was heading, despite me telling the others that I would be absolutely fine. My work left me feeling completely lonely at times, no real friends that I could bond with or spend time with. One case after another and I was on to the next, leaving everything and everyone behind.

The 35-minute journey was quiet. As soon as we approached the busy lanes of traffic joining the arrival and departure queues, I shuffled in my seat and got ready to get out.

'I'll just pull up on the side here to let you out and I will be on my way if that's okay?' he said.

Not quite the chatty London cab drivers that I was used to but it gave me a chance to go through a couple of emails and run a few checks that I wanted to do on the way.

The airport was heaving—everyone in their own sense of chaos and confusion as to where to go and what to do.

Looking up at the boards above me as I entered the large glass box of a building, attempting to find the desk that I needed to head for, I instantly froze. Standing to one side of the security gates was Oscar. He was pacing back and forth on a call, looking extremely agitated.

What is here doing here? I quickly turned my head so my face wasn't visible to him and tried to skirt around the side of the crowds of people and out of the way. He should have boarded hours ago.

Thousands of people fly every single day from this same airport and I bump into the one person I didn't want to.

Winding my way through the masses of people, I ducked quickly behind the closest pillar I could find, pulling my bag in behind me and checking the screens above. I scanned through all the destinations trying to find Miami.

Oh, great... all the flights are delayed. No wonder Oscar was hanging around. I wondered if he was irate about that or something else. Maybe it was an important business meeting after all, and I was on a wild goose chase for no real reason.

Firstly, I needed to get in the queue for bag drop without him seeing. Secondly, I needed to get through security with an equal amount of stealth. I peered around the pillar gently to check on his whereabouts, but he was gone. I tried to search around for him without drawing attention to myself but I couldn't see him anywhere.

An hour and a lot of tactical manoeuvres later and I was passed check-in, through security and sat in the private lounge. Heading for the furthest, most concealed area of the room, I sighed heavily in relief, only another hour to wait until boarding. A nine-and-a-half-hour flight to Miami and I was home free.

Making the best use of my time, I logged onto the airport's Wi-Fi and continued working on my laptop. What was it about personal space that every time you wanted a bit of quiet time or to focus on work in a public place, people seemed to take that as a free pass to sit right next to you and start chatting.

'Don't mind if I sit here, do you?' An elderly woman casually approached, placing her handbag on the chair and smiled endearingly. 'I need a good strong cup of coffee after getting through security, would you like one?' she asked.

'Erm, feel free, and I'm okay for coffee at the moment, thanks.' I did mind and I really needed a coffee, but instead, I smiled back, dropped my head back into my laptop and tapped away.

Ignoring all the workers in the background loading all the planes and carrying out their safety checks, I failed to notice Oscar waltz into the same private lounge that I was in and sat just a few tables in front of me until the old lady came back to remove her handbag from the chair, place it neatly on the floor and sit opposite me, sipping as loud as she could.

Wow, how is this even possible? I caught a quick glimpse of his handsome face. *Who is following who?*

229

Shuffling in my chair to hide behind the laptop screen, he turned around and took a double take at me. I couldn't help it, but as I looked up, he looked straight at me.

Oh no, oh no, no, no. Now what? I shrank back in the chair like a mouse caught in a trap. There was no way of leaving now, and to make matters worse, he got to his feet and started to make his way over.

I gulped. I had to greet him. I stood up and gulped again.

Act normal, Esmeralda, for goodness sake.

'Mr Richardson.' I nodded.

He didn't attempt to shake my hand, instead, he came closer to me and with one hand on my shoulder, kissed me on the side of the cheek, then proceeded to kiss the other.

'Ms King, right? We meet again. How peculiar... where are you off to?' he asked.

'Erm...' I tried not to swallow so heavily that he could see but I could hear the sound in my ears as clear as day. 'Miami, I'm going to meet with some old friends...' It was the best lie I could think of.

His face dropped the minute I said Miami as if I had pierced his heart with a knife and he was in excruciating pain.

'You?' I quickly asked.

'Miami on business. Family business,' he quickly added.

'Ah, nice.' I couldn't think of anything else to say. I could have said, *'Great, I'm here to follow you,'* but maybe he already knew and was deliberately following me in retaliation.

Oh, my goodness, I suddenly thought in a panic. *What if he does know that I am indeed following him, and he is trying to play me at my own game? At least it would make the flight easier knowing that he had already spotted me, and I didn't have to hide anymore. I could relax until I was on the other side.*

I wished at times that my mind would switch off from overthinking, it would make my life so much easier.

'Whereabouts in Miami are you staying?' He threw me a crafty smile as if trying to catch me out.

'Not far from South Beach. You?' I wasn't lying.

Just as he was about to answer, the tannoy echoed around the room, announcing that our flight was boarding and that we needed to make our way to the gate. Of course, I already knew where he was staying but the announcement gave him the break he needed to finish our conversation.

I had a quick idea that would make my life so much easier out in Miami and the ability to track his every move.

I fumbled in the clear plastic bag from within my handbag that I had emptied my makeup into at the security checkpoint and grabbed a foil-sealed packet of tablets that Mollie managed to get for me on prescription. She knew that flying caused me so much stress and anxiety, even though I would travel quite frequently, so she told me to try these tablets to ease my nerves.

A six-pack of diazepam and strict instructions on when to take it would help me relax a little on the long journey. I was thinking that if I gave Oscar more than the prescribed dose, it would put him into a heavier sleep, giving me the chance to try and track him without him even noticing.

'Well, Esmeralda. If you and your friends fancy meeting up whilst you are about, let me know. I am quite familiar with club and restaurant owners in The Ocean Drive area.' He reached inside his expensive-looking jacket, pulled out a business card and tried to hand it to me, but as he did so, I deliberately delayed taking it. Instead, he watched me take a tablet out and gulp it down with a sip from my bottled water.

'Thanks, Oscar, I will definitely give you a ring,' I said, glancing at his card briefly and acting completely blasé about the tablets, hoping he would acknowledge them. 'Just something to settle the nerves a little on the flight.'

Looking at him and staring deep into his dark eyes, it was as if he had no soul—there were a million stories waiting to escape but I didn't know how to get close enough to him to figure out what they were.

'Settle the nerves? What are they?' He threw me an inquisitive smile and waited for me to reply.

'Diazepam.' I paused. 'Would you like one or two? They work wonders. Just take one now before you board, then another two with a glass of wine or two on the plane and you should sleep for a couple of hours. I don't go on a plane journey without them now.' I popped out three small tablets and held out my hand for him to take them.

Oscar didn't even seem to question them—it was like giving a child candy, his eyes lit up instantly. He took one in his hand and swallowed it without a sip of water and placed the other two in his pocket. He fell for it, just as I hoped he would. I had to hope now that he would take the other two once we had boarded... it would then be a case of executing my next plan.

He patted me on the shoulder like an old school friend. 'Thanks, Esmeralda. Safe flight.' He swaggered off to the lounge exit and out of the door.

It took me a while to compose myself, especially as I had been trying to avoid him for the past couple of hours. At least I had managed to achieve the first stage.

The second part of the plan would be to trace his every move so that I could follow him out in Miami. I always carried around a few gadgets with me, just in case. Things that could be untraceable to general security or to the public, but I knew they existed and so did the government.

Just on the inside of my eyebrow brush kit was a micro GPRS tracker, this tiny little sticker was less than a millimetre in diameter. All I needed to do was get this on his mobile phone and I would be able to locate Oscar to within 100 yards. It all sounded quite easy really—except it wasn't. How would I get hold of his phone and how would I do it without him noticing? Let's just hope he takes those sleeping tablets and I can get access.

I wheeled out my belongings from the airport lounge, said goodbye to the sweet but incredibly annoying lady, and made my way to the gate. I could see the large aircraft parked outside the huge glass windows like a car in a car park. It scared me just looking at the sheer size of it and how modern technology was able to keep something that size in the air for so many hours.

One by one, we all shuffled to the front of the queue, holding up our passports and boarding passes as we were greeted by the wonderfully beautiful air stewardesses on either side of the gate. Always so pristine and made up in their smart and elegant uniforms.

All I could think about was how I needed to keep an eye on Oscar, but how would I be able to without sitting in first class?

Hmm. I wonder if...

It was my turn at the front of the queue. I smiled patiently as both my hands leaned on the desk in front of me. I used my lips to purse together and let out a gentle breath of fresh air, blowing the hair out of my face.

The lady looked at me, but I returned a pained look.

'Are you okay, madam?' she asked. 'You look a little pale.'

'Oh, I'm sorry. I... actually, I don't really feel...' Bringing my hand up towards my forehead like a well-staged theatrical production, I appeared to touch my head as if it was a smouldering, sweating mess and then juddered forwards, making out I was going to faint.

'Oh no.' The lady tried to run around the desk to my aid. Another air stewardess who had seen the commotion suddenly came running from the side, and the man standing directly behind me ran in to catch me as I pretended to fall backwards. I closed my eyes and listened to everyone's panic around me.

I felt cold air blow on my face. As I opened my eyes, she was wafting my passport to help me regain consciousness.

'Oh goodness, are you okay?' she asked as I pretended again to come around.

'I'm very sorry. I don't know what happened. It must have been the stress of it all.' As I looked up, I was surrounded by four of the air stewardesses and two of the flight attendants.

'Here, take a sip of this,' one of them said, handing me a glass of water. I took it in my hands and thanked him.

'I'm feeling much better now, thank you. It must have been the stress of the flight, I do apologise. I get a little claustrophobic.' I tried looking up like a lost puppy.

'Oh, you poor thing. I know what... let's see if we can get you into first class and comfortable. We can't have you fainting again.' She stood up at the desk and began tapping away, checking to see if there were any seats available for me. 'Ah hah. Please bear with me a second... if I just move this around... and... here we go, let's just print off your boarding pass and you are good to go.' She pulled the card from the printer in front of her and handed it to me.

'Thank you so much, that is so kind of you to move me around. I have never been in first class before, I'm sure it will make me a lot calmer.' I tried my best to hide the smile inside of me—my plan had worked, and I was hopefully in the same class as Oscar would be. Now for the next part of my plan and how to get as close to Oscar as possible.

I followed the normal hustle and bustle of the people queuing to board the plane. The queue was normally a lot longer, but as I had wasted the past 20 minutes pretending to faint, there were only a few people in front of me.

The whirring engines and security checks were all happening around me and I could still smell the fuel filtering through the air.

I just wanted to be able to sit on the flight for a few hours and not panic at every amount of turbulence. I was fine with the take-off and landing, but for some reason, the minute the plane shook and juddered between the sky's air pockets, my heart raced, my palms became sweaty, and I wanted to escape. I knew it was the safest mode of transportation, but in my head, I had other ideas.

As I neared the front of the queue, the two women on either side of the door were smiling and greeting everyone as they made their way to their seats. That's when the first diazepam hit me. My eyelids felt heavier than normal and my heart rate slowed. Noticing that my body was more chilled than it normally was and the panic that normally set in by the time I clicked my seatbelt around me seemed to ease away.

I couldn't believe how much roomier first class was, including incredible booths with a bigger personal screen than those in economy. A thicker blanket, an eye mask, and just as I moved to where my seat was, a male flight attendant was bringing around glasses of champagne as a treat. I was sat in 15D, right at the front of the Boeing 787 Dreamliner.

The crisp bubbles made me want to taste them but I knew that if I did, coupled with the tablet, I would be asleep for a fair few hours, and although that may have been quite a good thing, I couldn't help but think that if I did, I wouldn't be able to place that little GPRS chip on the back of Oscar's phone. It would be a challenge in itself.

Placing it on the table in front of me, I suddenly spotted Oscar's jet-black hair and shoulders, only a couple of seats in front of me on the left-hand side of the plane in seat 11A. Of course, it was one of the most spacious areas of first class. The first row behind the cockpit and pole position at the front.

Perfect, I thought.

The challenge was whether he would have his phone out or hidden away. He was already typing away on his screen. If I leant gently to one side, I could just about see what he was doing, but I had to make sure I remained unnoticed.

I watched the air stewards and stewardesses pacing the cabin, checking all the overhead lockers were snapped shut, everyone's bags were stowed away or under their booth seats. Final checks to ensure all seatbelts were securely fastened and we were onto the safety briefing. Not only did we have to watch their display of hand signals and prompts, but there was also a cartoon safety video playing.

I couldn't help but think, and I did this at the beginning of every flight, that if the plane was crashing and we were heading for a disaster, a life jacket and a whistle would not help my chances of survival. I listened anyway whilst everyone around me fidgeted and organised themselves.

As I looked out the window, the plane began to gently make its way to the runway, I almost admired the way a plane glided along the runway and through the air until it landed with a thump at the other end.

With its wings all lined up and ready for take-off, full throttle was underway, and we lifted off the tarmac below us. I looked up at the ceiling, my hands gripping at the armrests as we went.

The large buildings, cars and landscape gradually became smaller and smaller until it looked like a miniature model railway scene. I could feel the full force of the plane as we climbed higher and higher into the sky, the monitor in front of me that showed our altitude was increasing rapidly until I could no longer see the ground. We entered the first blanket of grey rain clouds, followed by white fluffy clouds and, finally, beaming sunshine and pure blue skies.

It was at this point that I quite enjoyed the fight, no turbulence as yet, thrilled at the fact that the engines hadn't failed, and we were just steadily climbing. After a few minutes, the seatbelt signs dinged and were unilluminated.

I had been so engrossed in the flight to realise that Oscar's head was nodded and he appeared to be asleep.

Brilliant, I thought to myself. B*ut for how long and where is his phone?*

I tried shuffling on my seat, using my arms to hold me a little higher but I couldn't see it on his lap or on the table.

Dammit, how will I get that tracker on his device now?

As we were able to unclip our seatbelts and move around, I stood to stretch my legs, standing in the aisle, deliberately looking in the direction of Oscar. I moved a little further and then noticed the edge of his phone down the side of the chair, next to his thigh.

If I could just get it without anyone seeing and quickly flip the cover off, it would take me a couple of minutes... less than that... seconds in fact.

But how?

I made my way towards the toilet door directly in front of him, but just before I reached it and just beside his seat, I pretended to drop my own phone, but instead of picking up mine, I would pick up his and take it to the toilet. On the way out, I would simply place it back and all would be done—simple!

I did as I planned. Coughing, I dropped my phone. I then gently pulled his from his seat without anyone noticing and pushed the door open to the toilet, locking it abruptly behind me. I placed the lid down and perched sitting down. Popping my eyebrow case quickly open, I flipped the back of his protective case off from around his phone and collected the tiniest GPRS chip between my fingernails like a pair of tweezers and removed the sticky back cover. Time was ticking away in my mind.

I stuck it right in the bottom corner, so it was difficult to see, ran my fingers over it to ensure it had firmly stuck and replaced the cover.

I took a deep breath and composed myself.

Quick, Esmeralda, flush the toilet, get the hell out of here and replace his phone before he wakes up.

As I flicked the lock open and pushed the accordion-style door open, I panicked. Oscar had woken whilst I was in there and was frantically searching around for his phone.

Now what? My heart went from 80 beats per minute to over 200 in an instant. B*reathe, Esmeralda, breathe.*

'Oh, let me help you with that, it's on the floor.' Before Oscar could look down, I had bent over and pretended to reach it from underneath his seat and present it to him like a magician. He looked a combination of sleepy and angry all at the same time.

'Ugh, thank you.' I'm not sure he even realised it was me. He snatched it from my hands, leaned back against the seat and pushed it firmly inside his pocket before turning away from me and going back to sleep.

'You're welcome,' I muttered as I made my way back to my seat and calmed down.

Phew! I need that drink now. I might as well take the other diazepam tablet that I have now that the flight is fully underway. Plucking the silver foiled packet that I had earlier popped open in the airport lounge when I was with Oscar, I picked up the flute, but instead of taking a gentle ladylike sip, I gulped the entire contents down and placed the glass back on the table.

I knew I needed to check that the GPRS device was still tracking and I was able to trace it, but both the chip and the access to log in would need a signal that we wouldn't get up here. I would have to wait until we landed. The plane did have Wi-Fi that I could pay for, but it still wasn't the most reliable. The best option was to check everything once we had landed. Fingers crossed, it worked.

I spent the next 15 minutes flicking through the numerous entertainment channels, games and media that was on the screen in front of me. Undecided in terms of what to watch, I clicked on a film that I had already seen but loved and reclined back. The blanket pulled up over my lap and arms and earphones clamped completely over my ears as loud as I could to drown out the noisy sound of the aircraft's humming. My eyelids became heavier and heavier as I drifted off.

I'm not sure if it was the clanging of the trolley or the loud sound of the airplane adjusting its wings as my headphones slipped off the side of my head and startled me. I half-expected it to be an hour or two into the flight, but as I checked the flight tracker, it said we had 55 minutes remaining.

I quickly sat up in my seat. This should be a nine-hour flight, I couldn't possibly have less than an hour left?

'Ladies and gentlemen, cabin crew will shortly be serving your last meal of the flight and ensuring that all items are stowed back away in the overhead lockers. We will be starting our descent down into Miami Airport. The air temperature on land is approximately 27 degrees centigrade or 81 degrees Fahrenheit, quite a warm and pleasant evening. The local time when we land will be 10 pm. We hope you have enjoyed the flight so far and will keep you informed of our progress,' the captain announced.

I looked over at Oscar, but he wasn't in his seat. I wrapped the blanket up into a small bundle and placed it back on my lap, stretching as I did so.

I hoped that he hadn't realised what I'd done to his phone and that the tracking would work. There was no reason why it shouldn't, but I was being over cautious as per usual.

The plane pulled into its parking bay. The seatbelt signs were turned off and there was a mad dash to get off, just as there always was from everyone around me. I sat in my chair, watching the chaos of people desperately collecting their belongings.

Oscar still hadn't returned to his seat...

That's odd.

He couldn't have vanished from a closed aeroplane, there was nowhere for him to go. I looked up at the locker above his seat. It was open and empty.

What was it about Oscar that made me feel like he was playing with me?

My phone began vibrating angrily in my pocket. Notifications from carriers buzzing their way into my message's inbox, I switched to the local carrier and saw everything update. I didn't have time to check everything, but the one thing I was eager to find out was whether Oscar's phone was tracking.

I pressed to open the application—it took a few moments to load but I patiently waited for it to register. The GPRS began scanning and located Oscar's phone.

That's strange, I frowned.

It is saying that he is either in or near the cockpit. *But he can't be?* I stood up and took a complete U-turn on my feet, making sure that the tracker was working correctly, but it didn't move. Only in exceptional circumstances were airline staff allowed into the cockpit.

Before long, the plane was empty and I was the last person, pretending to unpack and re-pack my bags to waste time until two of the air stewardesses approached me.

'Apologies, madam, we are going to have to ask you to hurry along. We need to turn the plane around and you appear to be the last person.' She smiled at me with her bright red lipstick still immaculately applied to her lips.

I looked all around hoping that Oscar would appear, but he didn't.

I had no choice but to collect all my items and make my way to baggage collection.

Feeling slightly groggy and frosty from the flight, I retrieved my luggage and headed for the taxi rank outside of the building. The hot, humid Miami air hit me as soon as the exit doors automatically slid sideways.

Still no sign of Oscar. It was as if he had just disappeared.

The moment I didn't want to see him at Heathrow Airport, there he was, yet when I wanted to see him, he was nowhere to be seen.

I panicked. *What if those tablets had affected him? Maybe he has realised I am tracking him.*

I got in the next cab in line and asked the driver to take me to my hotel. Maybe after I had unpacked, checked in and freshened up, I would be able to think straight and work out where Oscar was and what he was up to.

Chapter 12
Deception

I had just finished dinner in the hotel lobby when my phone began to vibrate. I was hoping it meant that Oscar was on the move again.

Leaning forward, I collected my phone from the table and checked the settings. His location was heading to downtown Miami. Maybe he was joining friends for a casual dinner or perhaps it was a business meeting and Sarah's presumptions were correct. I had to find out.

Quickly wiping the remains of any food from the corners of my mouth onto a perfectly white linen napkin, I made a gesture to the waiter for the bill. He nodded, understanding my hand movements and casually made his way to the register.

One thing was for certain here in Miami... the food was expensive. I needed an expenses bill just for the food and drink out here.

He walked over with a debonair smile, a pen and small leather wallet containing the paper receipt in his hands. I wasn't surprised as I opened it that a small mortgage was needed to cover it, but I paid anyway in dollars and handed it back to him.

I didn't feel unsafe walking the streets of Miami, but I did feel a little lost not speaking Spanish. The city was full of multicultural languages, making it a fantastic place to visit and be, but having dark skin with dark eyes and hair, I had quite frequently been mistaken for another nationality.

I had learned to say 'lo siento soy Ingles' and I had used it several times since being here.

This time, I didn't want to bump into Oscar, not after the airport fiasco. I needed to get close enough to be able to see him and potentially what he was up to but far enough away that he didn't spot me watching.

I made my move and followed the pulsing directions on my phone. With every step, I was closer and closer to his location. 0.9 miles and closing in.

Wouldn't it look a little odd, me being on my own? No, I'm sure half of Miami are out alone, having a stroll at night, or sitting in bars and clubs by themselves. Of course, they aren't... who am I kidding? I looked as suspicious as hell, but I needed to do this. The paranoia in my mind was setting in.

0.4 miles and he had stopped. I had to keep going.

I wonder who he is with?

0.1 miles and I was almost on top of him. According to my phone, I should be able to get within 100 yards but, when you are inside a busy restaurant or bar, it becomes difficult to pinpoint the exact person in a crowd full of people. This was the bit where I needed to be extremely careful.

I had reached Ocean Drive—one of the busiest strips of entertainment areas in Miami. The music was playing so loud that the pavement felt like it was vibrating. Cars lined the sidewalks and cruised up and down the street. I watched copious amounts of people enjoying drinks, spilling out from inside each of the bars and onto the walkways.

About halfway down the long road, there was a park separating it from the beach. A police car was parked up on one side, tucked in underneath the palm trees. Its lights were off, but as I passed, I could see two police officers sat in the front seats just watching in case there was trouble. I had recognised Ocean Drive from featuring in a few famous films but it was so much more vibrant in real life. A small concrete hut next to the police car stood home to male toilets on one side and female on the other. A long, white curved wall surrounded it along with a park bench.

If I sat here for long enough, I could keep an eye on each of the places, watching out for Oscar and monitoring any movement from my phone.

I took a long hard look at myself wearing a pair of dark jeans and a pair of black leather ankle boots. I thought it would be chilly, especially after the spring sun went down, so I threw a comfy cardigan over a simple black blouse with thin straps. I then looked at all the women and what they were wearing—small miniskirts, short designer dresses, strappy heels and clutch bags as accessories. I couldn't see one woman who was dressed the way that I was, sticking out like a sore thumb.

As for the men, well, they were all matching as if there was a dress code for each of the establishments in Miami—dinner jackets, smart, expensive-looking shoes, well-groomed and most of them looked notably toned and muscular. I didn't fit in here at all. Not one little bit.

The most elegantly dressed of all of them were the socialites queuing to enter a rather beautiful building with a series of stone steps leading up to the main entrance. I couldn't make out what it said on the front door, so I looked on maps.

'Casa Casuarina, otherwise known as the Versace Mansion,' I read.

I raised my eyebrows as I read its description and history and why so many people were queuing to gain entry.

No wonder they were so wonderfully dressed. I had seen several Ferraris and other super cars arrive just outside, dropping off their guests in turn at this exclusive venue. Although it was described as a boutique hotel, the guests looked to be partying in the front two rooms and beyond, but I couldn't quite see inside very far, but what I could see was an exclusive venue that only the rich and famous had access to.

Just as I had been reading and studying the attraction to this place, I spotted a familiar face. From the sight of his shoes, all the way up his stocky legs and thighs, I had seen those before. I recognised him instantly.

Oscar. I gasped. *There he is.*

Recently, he had been the feature of my dreams, nightmares and premonitions. His face imprinted on my mind. He was standing in the middle of the queue and seemed to know quite a few of the people surrounding him, chatting away in his usual suave, charming and sophisticated manner.

Maybe Oscar was here to dine with friends and had a whole other life out in America that both Sarah and I weren't aware of.

I was slightly disappointed. I was looking for more mystery, more answers to conclude some parts of the case. I took a few pictures on my phone, but just as I was trying to zoom in, I recognised yet another familiar face.

But it can't be?

It is.

I clicked a few shots and then enlarged the screen again. Standing right next to Oscar, her arm holding on to his, was no other than Emily. Seeing Oscar and Emily together was becoming a regular occurrence. They looked thick as thieves. Slightly intimate, in fact.

Why on earth is she out here with Oscar? On business or pleasure? I questioned.

And would Oscar really have anything more than a business relationship with someone who had been dating his grandfather? It seemed slightly peculiar in my eyes. I sat thinking about the two of them from across the street.

I didn't see her on the same flight as us or at the airport. I wondered when she travelled out.

Multiple people joined Oscar and Emily and greeted them with a faire la bise—a kiss on each cheek—and an air kiss sound. I wondered who they were. Acquaintances, friends, family... who knew?

Just about to reach the front doors, they were greeted by the maître d' and security guard, and within a few minutes, were shown through and into the main building, out of my sight and my ability to see what they were doing once again.

There was no way that I would be able to get access to that building. Even if I did, Oscar and Emily would find it extremely coincidental.

I could have sat here on this bench all night, waiting for them to re-appear, but I couldn't tell whether it would be one hour or the early hours of the following morning, so I chose to head back to my hotel and wait for their next movement.

Like a lonely tourist, I followed the maps on my phone for several blocks until I reached my hotel. Although Miami was a busy city that never slept, the walk back gave me a chance to clear my head, to think about everything I had uncovered and all the parts I was yet to discover.

Each time I reached the traffic lights at the end of the street, I checked all around me. The trouble with my job was that I was constantly looking over my shoulder. Was anyone following me or stalking my whereabouts? I could never be too careful. Everyone looked suspicious to me.

As I reached the main doors of the hotel, I noticed that the bar was still open. The round, cosy armchairs looked inviting and there were a few people sat perched on the edge of bar stools enjoying a drink or two. It looked so tempting, I had to almost talk myself into going back to my hotel room and out the way of being seen by anyone from the Richardson family.

Instead, I walked to the bar man and asked him for a bottle of wine and a glass that I could take up to my room and charge to my tab. That way, I could drink in my room and wait for Oscar's next steps.

The rooms in Miami were bigger, bolder and comfier than any hotel I had stayed at in the UK. I threw off my shoes, placing the cold, silver wine cooler on the bedside table and filled my glass half full, sipping the dry tones and began savouring its taste. I lay back, three pillows stacked behind me, staring up at the ceiling.

I knew I was onto something big—I had a bad feeling that Oscar and Emily were up to no good being out here in Miami, but exactly what it was, I had no idea.

An hour later, I looked at my tracker. They were still at the venue in Ocean Drive. Slight movement, room to room perhaps or to the toilet and back, but still in that location.

I finished the rest of the bottle, took the last sip and drifted off to sleep.

It wasn't until 2 am that they left and got in a taxi to their hotel that they were staying at, across the street from me.

I decided to wake up early the following morning. I had a slightly hazy hangover from the bottle of wine but I was feeling positive. Today was the day that I would find out what Oscar was really up to. Looking at my phone, I was surprised to see that he was already on the move.

07.02 am, only five hours after they were partying, and their location was moving. The pin was heading out of Miami and across Florida. They must have been in a car as I zoomed in and could see that they were on US Highway 41 heading east to west. *Where are they going? Is it just Oscar, or is Emily still with him?* I had to follow... I had to find out.

I got showered, changed and quickly headed downstairs to reception and reached the main desk.

'Erm... can you please order me a cab and quickly?' I asked impatiently.

'Good morning, ma'am, and where would you like to go today?' If there was one thing that Americans were, it was happy. Always cheerful, trying to be helpful and in an over friendly tone.

'I'm not quite sure, I would like to head along US Highway 41 to the west coast of Florida please.'

The lady looked confused.

'And your destination?' she questioned.

'I don't know.' I picked up my phone, scanning the locations on the West Coast and picked a destination, hoping that it was where Oscar was going too. 'Marco Island?' I looked up to see her reaction.

'Sure. I can order you a cab, but it may be cheaper and easier to use Uber.' I think that was my cue to order my own taxi. At least that way I could change the destination according to where Oscar was heading.

'Okay, no problems. Thanks, I will do that instead.' I left the desk, opened the application on my phone and typed in Marco Island as the destination from my current location and pressed enter. It thought for a few moments, confirming that it was going to be five minutes and a driver was pending. I waited for it to change to confirmed whilst quickly grabbing a few pastries, a bottle of water and an apple from the restaurant and stuffed it all into my handbag like a packed lunch, ready for my journey.

According to the details, it would take me more than an hour to reach his current location. Fingers crossed he would stay there, otherwise, I could be riding around in an Uber all day.

It felt like a wild goose chase. I was travelling halfway across Florida just to find out what this man was doing, when he and Emily could be simply on a minibreak.

The cab driver was outside waiting for me. I grabbed my belongings, checked it was the right vehicle and climbed in. I had Hunter on speed dial if I needed him. There wasn't a huge amount he would have been able to do that far away but it made me feel more at ease that I could call someone if I needed to.

The driver tried to make pleasantries to start the journey but soon trailed off as my answers were delayed and non-engaging. I was more focused on tracking Oscar's route, making sure he wasn't making any sudden changes in his direction.

I looked out of the window occasionally as he drove, but the landscape very rarely changed. For miles and miles, there was the same landscape displaying of swamp land, the tallest of trees and smooth straight roads. The side gullies were strewn with alligators, stealthily hiding in the shade of the woodland as we entered the vast acres of the US's famous everglades.

'What happens if I need to change the location of my destination?' I asked the driver.

'I'm sorry, what do you mean?' he returned.

'I mean, if I change my mind on where I am heading from Marco Island to somewhere else. Is that possible?' I asked again.

'Of course,' he replied. 'Simply go back into the application and change it. Where are you wanting to go now?'

As I studied the location, it looked like Oscar was heading towards Naples—a city on the west coast of Florida on the Gulf of Mexico. My location tracker had him currently pinpointed in the centre of the town and wasn't moving.

What is he doing there?

I quickly searched Naples. Other than being known for its high-priced houses, long white sandy beaches and various shopping outlets, I couldn't see why Oscar would be attracted to visiting this place, but we continued along the route, closer and closer to reaching him. I couldn't find any tourist attractions there or famous landmarks, just a quiet town that was home to multi-millionaires.

Oscar's location hadn't moved for at least 30 minutes, but it was still a further 30 minutes before I would reach him. Hoping that he would be remaining where he was and I had a chance to catch up, I checked my phone every few minutes, refreshing the application to make sure I was as up to date as possible.

We finally reached the sleeping city of Naples. Expensive-looking yachts lined the canals as we reached the bridge into the city. Luxurious cars surrounded us as we queued to reach his precise location.

I looked all around for signs of why he would be here, or perhaps something that would trigger a reaction. An office building that he might be attending, an event that he had been invited to or a particular monument that he wanted to visit but there was nothing except boutique shops and restaurants.

I hoped that this wasn't a wasted journey.

As we entered Naples, I was almost on top of Oscar's location. To avoid him seeing me, I asked the driver if he could drop me off in a park opposite the central streets. From there, I would find my way to a place that was within close proximity of him to catch a glimpse. I thanked the driver, grabbed my belongings and got out of the car.

After zooming in on the map, he appeared to be in a local coffee shop—The Narrative Coffee Roasters, to be precise, on Central Avenue. He didn't stop for long. Perhaps he was grabbing a freshly roasted latte, and started making his way down 1st Avenue South, in the direction of the main beach.

As I started along the same road, keeping a distance behind him, close enough that I could track him but far enough away so that he couldn't see me, I noticed how enchanting this city truly was. The houses weren't houses—they were mansions. Neat, cobbled driveways edged with the most perfectly trimmed box hedges. Expensive trucks and cars parked outside their grand front doors. It was so clean, pathways were swept, the grass verges so neat they looked like artificial turf. The streets looked historical—1950s, 1960s perhaps—with tall palm trees strategically planted at several intervals.

I had never heard of Naples before, but after seeing only two or three avenues, I wanted to explore more of this elegant and sleepy city.

Oscar kept walking straight, as far as he could to the end of 1st Avenue South, and stopped. I could finally see his familiar swagger in the distance, so I held back a little, disguising my body behind one of the large palm tree trunks and stood there for a moment.

The night before, as I was walking back to my hotel, I had purchased a natural coloured, downturned sun hat and a new pair of sunglasses, making it difficult for anyone to recognise me with my hat pulled over my head and glasses covering half of my face.

It was quiet. I couldn't see any other people out walking or passing by, so I pretended occasionally to look at my phone in case anyone looked out their window to find me hovering and watching Oscar's every move.

He wasn't with Emily—he was on his own. Why was he standing still, what was he doing?

My eyes were drawn to the end of the street where the road met a line of mangrove trees and the houses stopped. A rustic wooden bridge in the clearing was the start of a boardwalk but I couldn't see much after that except the clear blue sky. I presumed that the beach lay in between in the distance.

I continued to lean slightly to one side of the palm tree for visibility and noticed that Oscar was looking around shortly before a gentleman walked towards him. I couldn't see his face, only his thick black hair from the back. He was casual, wearing chino shorts, sandals and a polo shirt. A pair of what looked like designer sunglasses were covering most of his sun-kissed complexion.

Who is he?

The mystery man held up both arms and placed them around Oscar, who did the same by return as they patted each other on the back before releasing. They clearly knew each other and well.

Were they friends? Family? Acquaintances?

I walked forwards a little to the next palm tree and pulled back in behind it. I tried to conceal my phone as I took a few pictures to analyse later.

The pair turned with their backs to me and made their way towards the bridge and disappeared along the boardwalk. I had to see where they were going. I had to find out who this man was and what they were discussing.

At the end of the boardwalk, they turned right, both moving their sunglasses from their heads to cover their eyes from the bright sunshine. This was my cue to start walking on again and make my way over the same bridge.

The day was beginning to warm. The late morning sunshine edged closer to the highest point in the sky so there was little shade except the shadows of the palm trees. It was only spring, but in Florida, the weather was similar to a warm summer's day in England. Not quite as humid as their summer and beautifully pleasant. I rolled up the sleeves of my cotton dress and exhaled, blowing the hair from around my face as I kept up the pace behind Oscar.

I neared the bridge, just about to head over the top and onto the boardwalk, but I stopped before doing so. On either side of the bridge, looking out onto a crystal-clear ocean and the whitest sand I have ever seen were two stunning beach homes. Modern by design, floor-to-ceiling windows that must give the most admirable view for as far as the eye can see. Open gardens with infinity pools and landscaped surrounds.

If I had all the money in the world, this is where I would want to live. Imagine opening your bedroom doors onto the most picturesque beach in Florida. It felt like a dream. I wanted to share the moment with someone, anyone, but here I was on my own, stalking Oscar Richardson instead.

I didn't have time to admire this place more than I was. I had to keep walking, but its beauty stopped me in my tracks. Even the birds flitting in the trees had the most incredible song.

Turning to my right but keeping along the tree line, I could still see the two men walking side by side along the glistening sand dunes. Both had removed their shoes and sandals and were carrying them in their hands.

I held onto my hat with one hand so that the wind didn't tussle it away and tried to get a little closer, but as they reached the next block and access route for Central Avenue, they paused.

Should I pause too or continue? They both looked behind as if looking directly at me but then turned and sat down on the wooden steps staring out into the horizon.

If only I was close enough to hear their conversation, to be a fly on the wall. The other man lifted his glasses and rubbed his eyes. I still couldn't see his face clearly.

Would they notice me if I walked past? Was I confident enough that my hat and glasses would shield my true identity? Was I reading too much into it and that they were way too engrossed in their discussion to even notice me walking past?

I went for it and continued confidently, step by step, closer and closer to them.

That's when it hit me. Around 200 yards away, with my sunglasses blocking the direction of my eyes, I looked straight at his face. I knew exactly who that man was and what connection he had to Oscar.

Michael.

It was Michael Richardson—larger than life. I had never met or seen him before, but I recognised him instantly from the picture on his coffin and all the research I had done online.

He wasn't dead, he was here in Florida. Oscar had come to see his father. Only, it wasn't his father. Samuel was his father. But did either of them know that?

I was stunned but I had to remain calm, breathing in and out of my nose to gain composure, I kept my head down and headed for the next block along—1st Avenue North. From there, I would head back up the street and into a restaurant or bar. I needed a drink to steady myself. My whole body was shaking with the thought of them realising who I was and why I was following them. I would be blowing Michael's cover for sure. His secret life out in Florida would be over.

So, if Michael wasn't dead... who did the body in the mortuary belong to? The pathologist was right all along. I wanted to confront them both, but at the same time, I wanted to run far away from here and catch the next flight back to London.

My pace picked up. I didn't dare look back in case they realised who I was. Each step now seemed to drag and the turning for 1st Avenue North felt so far away.

Finally, I reached the turning, keeping to my right to make my way along the street, but before I did so, I took hold of the start of the rails to steady myself and used my hands to brush as much of the sand from the bottom of my feet as I could. I glanced in their direction carefully to find that they were gone. I slipped my right shoe back on and did the same to my left, looking in the other direction in case they had walked behind me and along the remainder of the beach, but they were nowhere to be seen.

The only place they could have gone was Central Avenue. I quickly rustled in my bag for my phone and opened the tracker. It wouldn't load—his location wasn't displaying. I couldn't tell where Oscar or Michael was or even if they were still together.

I felt uneasy. I had a horrible feeling in the pit of my stomach.

I began making my way back to the point I was dropped off at, but directions were never my strong point. I had no idea where I was going, and my phone was completely dead. I held it up, trying desperately to turn it on but it was no good. Lifeless and useless.

How did people function before the invention of phones?

Maybe it was better to go to a crowded place, where I was safe, get some food and a coffee and then head back when my phone was back up and running.

Halfway along Central Avenue, I noticed a few more people out walking but they seemed to all be heading in the same direction. I chose to follow them, hoping for a busier place to stop, and took a right and headed down 5th Street South.

My senses were heightened as I turned around, expecting someone to be following behind. But each time I did, there was no one there. Had I gone from being a hunter to someone hunting me?

I checked my phone, it turned on but was saying no signal. Was it just me? Was my network down? Why wouldn't it work? This time, I turned it onto flight mode and tried again. Hopefully, it would reset, but just as I did so, I reached the end of 5th Street. I tried stepping out into the road, but a car narrowly missed me, screeching to a halt and shaking their head at me. Panicked, I stood back on the pavement and took a deep breath, composing myself. I needed to concentrate on where I was and where I was going.

I looked up at the signs and it appeared I was now on 5th Avenue South. A bustling strip of upper-class restaurants, coffee shops and boutique outlets. I peered in the glass window next to me and could see a whole display of yachts for sale and their prices. Not one of them was under $1 million. As I looked up, the road was lined with expensive cars and what looked like very wealthy individuals elegantly sitting outside dining establishments, surrounded by designer bags. All were sipping wine and enjoying the afternoon sun. I felt like I had walked into a millionaire's playground—no wonder Michael and Oscar were here.

Feeling very out of place and uncomfortable, I wiped the sweat from my forehead, pulled my hat a little more over my face and pushed up my sunglasses, continuing along the street to find a place to rest. It wasn't easy. It was mid-week but yet it felt like a Saturday afternoon. Didn't these people all have businesses to run or empires to build? They sat there, not a care in the world.

Finally, I found a small round table for two. I smiled at the waiter before placing my bag on one chair and sat on the other, crossing my legs confidently and picking up a menu from the table. I could only just about read the writing with my glasses on, but I was too scared to take them off.

The waiter was a young well-dressed gentleman, slim, tall and had a welcoming face. He clutched a large, round, silver tray and a small notepad.

'Good afternoon, madam, what can I get for you this afternoon?' he asked, eager to take my order, standing before me with his pen poised.

I was too preoccupied to look at the prices. I simply chose a glass of the house wine to steady my nerves and the tagliatelle, then handed him back the menu.

Frustrated with my phone not working, I switched off flight mode and waited for everything to turn back to normal. Without a phone, I was lost, it was my only connection to the rest of the world, to safety, to everyone back in the UK. I took a moment to pause and study everything around me.

Small birds were flitting tree to tree, the gentle purr of the cars that cost more than my apartment cruised down the street and the chink of glasses and cutlery of everyone enjoying their afternoon. It was almost too perfect—except I still couldn't relax. I felt eyes on me, the strangest of feelings, like a burning hole in the side of me.

The waiter returned carrying a glass of blush wine in a thin glass and a bottle of sparkling water.

'Thank you,' I said, about to take a sip, but he stopped me.

'I won't bring the bill over at the end, I believe the wine and pasta are complimentary from the gentleman,' he said and placed the sparkling water on the table.

'I'm sorry?' I looked at him confused.

'Yes, the gentleman said he would cover the bill. Apparently, you earned it.' The waiter gestured directly across the street from me.

I looked up and followed my attention to where he was pointing. It wasn't just a feeling of someone looking at me. Someone *had* been watching me.

Oscar and Michael were sat in the opposite restaurant and raised their glasses to me as I stared them straight in the eyes. They looked at each other and deceitfully laughed, returning their stares back to me.

I felt overwhelmed with fear. How long had they been on to me? Was it the beach? Had they followed me back here or had I stupidly picked the restaurant opposite them and they had spotted me instantly? Did they both know why I was there and did Michael realise that I knew who he was and was on to him?

I didn't know whether to raise my glass in return or get up and walk away. I felt like doing the latter, but I calmly raised my glass in return and smiled appreciatively.

'I'm sorry, I can't accept him paying for my bill, sir,' I said to the waiter.

'I'm afraid it's too late, he has already settled it,' he replied and walked off back into the restaurant.

This was the most awkward I had felt in a long time. I suddenly wasn't hungry and didn't want to eat like it was my last meal. I was an animal in a cage with the Richardsons teasing and tormenting my existence.

My phone suddenly vibrated and was back in action. A burst of missed call notifications, text messages and voicemails buzzed one by one as it shot to life.

Thank goodness for that. I sighed in relief. I should never have come here on my own, I should have been here with Hunter or the girls, but I knew deep down that what I had to do was outsmart Oscar. I had to get clever and be one step ahead of him and his associated Richardson family members.

I am going to sit here, sip my wine, enjoy my lunch and act like they don't concern me at all. The more he knows that he's not getting to me, the more I will have the upper hand.

My lunch was served shortly after, and it was the nicest tagliatelle I had ever tasted. I wanted another wine, but I needed to finish and get out of here and book a meeting with Sarah. There were so many things we needed to cover before I flew back home to London.

Out of principle, I didn't want to eat a meal that Oscar had paid for, but I was here to play a game and that's what I was going to do. Placing my knife and fork together, I slid the plate slowly towards the middle of the table. I took the last sip of wine from the glass and placed it together with my napkin and the leftover sparkling water.

I wanted to look over at Oscar and Michael and give them one last satisfied acknowledgement, but as I lifted my head in their direction, the table and chairs that they had sat at earlier were now empty.

Where had they gone? I looked up and down the street, but they were nowhere to be seen. I had lost them again. Frantically, I started to check my location tracker. Everything else was working on my phone except that application.

'Brilliant!' I said out loud. *That's all I need. It had to be that one didn't it! You don't think...*

That was my trouble, I thought too much. I had a suspicion that maybe Oscar had realised he was being tracked but there was nothing I could do, and how would he know that it was me who did it?

In all fairness, I had come to Miami to find out why Oscar was here and who he was meeting. I had managed to find out who he was meeting but not why.

There was only one thing left and that was for me to gather my belongings, book my Uber back to Miami, meet Sarah and get the next flight home.

It took a while, but I managed to allocate a cab and confirmed the pickup point for the end of the Avenue. The afternoon sun had turned the pleasant warmth into a hot and humid sun trap. As I waited for him to arrive, I noticed his arrival point changing.

That's strange, I thought, desperately trying to change it back to its original location but it was no use. He had parked around the corner and alongside Cambier Park. I followed the flashing circle before it altogether stopped, and I received a notification saying that my Uber had been cancelled.

I didn't understand what was happening.

The park was empty, not a single person walking—no children playing on the slide or swings and no cars parked in the bays. The large, thick trunked trees in the middle gave it an eerie feeling.

I'd just order another one and wait for it to arrive. I sat down on one of the long, curvy, close to the ground branches and tried again. I heard a twig snap in the distance that startled me. Turning around, there was no one there so I continued.

There it was again, but I chose to ignore it this time. The wind was whistling in my ears in the cool shade of its leaves.

'We need to stop meeting like this.' I felt a hard object pressing into my back and a voice that I knew only too well. The same dreaded feeling from the restaurant earlier had returned. I didn't dare look anywhere other than down. Oscar was standing behind me. 'Scream or draw attention to yourself and I won't be afraid to use it.' He meant business.

I couldn't tell whether he had a real gun pressing into my rib cage, but I wasn't about to risk finding out. My whole-body quivered with fear.

'What do you want from me?' I said in a panic.

'Some things are better left alone, Esmeralda. I think you know what I want and why I am here,' he whispered into my ear.

I stood as still as I possibly could, too afraid to even blink.

'I don't know what you are doing here or what you are trying to achieve but it is better that you leave Michael out of this.' He paused. 'His new life is here now and doesn't need you dragging things up. Give me one good reason why I shouldn't just kill you now and cover it up, just like Michael's?'

He called him Michael and not his father. That's strange.

'I won't say a word. Michael who?' I pretended like I hadn't seen him, but I wasn't so sure that he would trust me to keep such a secret, especially with a policeman for a brother. I had to convince him and quick.

'Why are you following me?' Oscar asked. 'I thought you seemed on edge when I met you at the funeral for the first time, but then the airport, the same flight, and now here in Naples. It's clearly not just a coincidence. Who are you working for?' His voice was getting louder and angrier.

Do I tell him the truth, or do I quickly make something up? I had to be fast, my life depended on it.

He shoved the gun harder into my back. 'I'm waiting,' he said.

'Sarah. I was asked by Sarah to investigate. She suspected something was wrong with her father's death and wanted me to investigate it. I'll say I haven't seen you, that I want nothing further to do with the case and leave you both alone,' I panicked and told the truth. No amount of money was worth dying for.

'Sarah?' He sounded confused. 'As in Sarah Richardson? My Aunty? Why would she...' Oscar's voice trailed off and he genuinely seemed shocked.

I nodded to confirm but sat waiting for him to make the next move. My body was heating up, and I could feel a thick layer of perspiration on my forehead. Never had I been so scared in my entire life. I had no thoughts on what I could do to escape. This was it... I was going to die in a park in Naples, Florida. On my own, without anyone I knew or loved. My whole existence flashing before my eyes.

'You see, the thing is, Esmeralda, Michael doesn't want to be found. He has done a lot of naughty things that he shouldn't have done and now his slate is clean. Free to start over. He is living his best life in paradise without a care in the world, whilst I run everything for him.' His explanation almost seemed to be understandable.

I wonder what naughty things he was referring to.

I managed to find the courage to say a few words, but inside, I just wanted to break down. *Come on, Esmeralda, you have got this.*

'I understand, Oscar. I'll tell Sarah that I don't want to continue with the case and that will be the last of it. You will never hear from or see me again.'

'How do I know you will keep to your side of the agreement?' He leaned forward and almost had his chin on my shoulder.

'You have my word. I swear it,' I promised him in fear of my life.

'Well, Esmeralda, I know I have your word because, if you don't keep your promise, I can tell the officials all about your little cash heist where you stole money from an investment bank a few years back and used the currency to buy your cute little club in London. Cinco Chicas. Isn't that what it's called?' He paused briefly. 'I'd say we are talking a few years in prison for that, sweetheart.' Oscar instantly sent shivers down my spine, the way he phrased it in such a threatening manner. The force of his gun on my back felt like it was piercing my skin and entering my body.

How on earth does he know about Cinco Chicas? No one knows about that. He is smart, very smart.

'In fact, I could probably do with someone like you to hack into a few investment firms and steal money on my behalf, but I can wait until the time is right for that.' He laughed in such a way that crushed me. 'So, how about... if you leave Michael and I alone, we will do the same for you.'

The pressure of the gun in my back eased slightly, enabling me to breathe more freely.

'I completely understand, Oscar,' I mumbled a response. A small tear rolled down my cheek. I could hear my trembling heartbeat thumping in my chest and ears.

'I'm sure we will see each other again soon. Have a safe flight back to London.' I could no longer feel anything in my back or Oscar's presence behind me. He had vanished as quickly as he had appeared, but I still didn't raise my head or look around. I sat painstakingly still. Too scared to move a muscle or do anything.

Chapter 13

Two-Faced

I needed to get back to the safety of my hotel and quickly. I couldn't sit in the park forever. I wanted to curl up in a little ball on the ground and wait for it to swallow me.

I had tried repeatedly to order an Uber but my phone wouldn't work, and I was desperate to get the hell out of here. Maybe it was better that I walked back to the bustling comfort of the main street rather than this secluded park, so I got up, brushed myself down along with my bruised confidence and started making my way to the main strip of Naples.

Three minutes away and the pickup point was on the corner section of where I was originally dropped off earlier today.

I couldn't have walked much faster unless I sprinted, holding my phone up in my hand, my eyes glued to the moving map as I got closer to the vehicle that would be collecting me and taking me all the way back to Miami.

As I neared the corner, I could see the dark blue Toyota Corolla indicate and pull alongside the kerb ahead of me.

Perfect, I thought, clicking my phone off and slotting it back into my handbag.

All I could think about was sitting in the back in the comfort and safety of the car and drifting off whilst he drove me all the way back to Miami. I wasn't watching anything else.

I checked the number plate of the car—it matched the description of what I had been sent. My fingers gripped the plastic handle and lifted as it clicked open. I pulled the door towards me. The driver turned his head slightly but not fully, so I didn't really catch a glimpse of his face. He was wearing a dark pair of sunglasses and I noticed the designer branded badge on his arm.

'Miss King,' he said briefly, checking my identity.

'Yes, Miami please.' The driver had my exact location, but I just wanted to make sure.

'Sure.' The car jolted forwards as we left the side of the pavement and joined the queues of passing traffic from the side streets to the main roads heading back towards east Florida.

I had every intention of sitting back, my head tilted against the cushion of the headrest behind me and closing my eyes, but I noticed that his satellite navigation system wasn't following the route.

How did he know where we were heading unless he knew the route like the back of his hand? Maybe he lived in Miami and did this route regularly.

I looked up at all the road signs as they swung precariously above us, but we seemed to be driving in the opposite direction to where we needed to go to.

The cab driver indicated right and headed in that direction instead. My head turned from left to right, checking as we went. I reached for my phone and tapped to open the maps, tracing the route of the car as he drove. My face frowning with confusion.

Now what? I thought, panicking yet again.

'So, Miss King,' he finally said in a chilled undertone. 'I'm sorry if Oscar scared you somewhat, he has a tendency to be a little hot-headed at times.'

I was looking out of the small back window as he spoke, but as soon as he did, I didn't recognise his voice but I still gulped with pure fear, anticipating the compromised situation that I now found myself in.

If he knows about Oscar scaring me, there is only one person that this driver could be. I panicked, reaching quickly for the door handle but it was too late, he pressed the button located on his driver's door, instantly locking the whole car so I couldn't get out. I was trapped in a vehicle with Michael Richardson. The man who had supposedly died over a month ago.

I looked up in alarm. If he was worried about Oscar scaring me in the park, what on earth did he think that locking an Uber car mid-drive would do? Excite me?

'Stop the car, Michael,' I tried reasoning with him, hoping that he would tell me what he wanted and then let me out.

'I'm afraid I can't do that, Esmeralda. I need to speak to you first.' Michael raised his glasses up onto the top of his head so I could see his eyes as he looked into the rear-view mirror. He had the characteristic dark brown eyes that the Richardson family carried down through the generations.

'Why not? Oscar has already told me to drop the case. I get it, I understand. You have my word—I won't take it any further.' I tried explaining the conversation with Oscar to him, but he continued to drive.

'You see, the thing is, Esmeralda. There's more to this than you realise and neither of us can afford any fuck ups,' he said in a disturbed way.

Michael's driving became more and more erratic. I was completely in his hands and there was nothing I could do about it. He turned right, then right again, and pulled up behind the back of a row of retail units. The car skidded to an abrupt stop, he pulled up the handbrake and sat breathing heavily in and out.

'Look, Michael,' I quickly said in a calm voice. 'You can trust me. You have my word. I can walk away and pretend I never met the Richardson family before. I can make it all go away.'

I unclipped my seatbelt and edged forwards in my seat, trying to reach a point where I could see his face and understand what he was going through. I was still too far to be able to unlock the car, so I had to rely on my bargaining tactics.

'Michael?' I tried him again, hoping he would at least listen to me.

'You don't understand why I need to be here,' he finally said.

'Try me?' I replied. 'What happened, Michael? Why was everything so bad that you need to be out here hiding?' I wanted him to open up to me. To help me understand what had really happened back in England.

Michael didn't say a word, he dropped his head and sat looking down at his lap. He wasn't dangerous. You could tell that from a person's eyes. I didn't believe for one moment that he was about to take me to a quiet place in Naples, kill me and dump me somewhere that no one could find me—even though that is what I had imagined my fate to be 30 seconds earlier. He was just a scared middle-aged man that needed to disappear, and I was the only person in his way.

'Michael, I have a lot at stake too. It's not just you. The files that I access and the people that help me do it are breaking the law, it's not legal searching for confidential files or information. We can both walk away from this and pretend it never even happened.' I clutched at the passenger seat head rest, hoping that he would look up and I could finally see his face.

He sat back in his chair and looked out of the dusky windscreen ahead.

What is a multi-millionaire doing in a beaten-up Toyota Corolla posing as an Uber driver? I thought to myself.

'She is not well, Esmeralda. She never has been.' His gaze turned to a deep stare at a point in the distance.

'Who isn't well?' I asked.

'Laura,' he said her name so lovingly.

'I know, I went to see her in hospital,' I explained.

'How was she?' He quickly spun his head around to me as if I had awoken his attention.

'She was fine. A little distant perhaps, but fine other than that.' I hoped that it would reassure him.

'We used to be so happy, but then when I realised it was only the money she was after, it broke my heart. I had everything—the house, the wife, the perfect son.' He sighed, bringing back memories of how his life had been. 'But then I woke up one morning and everything had turned to dust.'

Michael looked at me in a way that made me feel sorry for him.

'I would have done anything for her.' His eyes were crushed. 'Anything.'

'I'm sure you would have.' I put my hand on his shoulder.

'Sarah got into her head. She was like a puppet on strings. I just wanted my father to be proud of me, you know.' Michael had an uncanny resemblance to Samuel—they were more like twins than brothers. The same use of expressions and the same deep and meaningful brown eyes. I had a weakness for Samuel, maybe that was why I felt like Michael wasn't dangerous either.

I took a moment just to sit and look at him. Many thoughts ran through my mind as to what kind of a life Michael had lived along with Samuel and Sarah. The high expectations of a multi-millionaire father would have caused so much pressure growing up.

'I'm sure he was proud, Michael.'

'Sarah has never forgiven me for what happened. She changed that day. And, well, Samuel just doesn't talk about it, I think he was too young to remember.' A small tear trickled down his face and into the dark stubble that freckled the lower part of his cheeks and chin.

'What day, Michael. What happened?' I sat nervously on the edge of my seat, hoping he was going to tell me what had happened to the Richardson family all those years ago.

'Sarah was a twin.' The words dropped out of his mouth like he had spilled them unintentionally.

I tried to hide the shock on my face but I couldn't help it. I gulped. Attentively listening to what he was saying. Michael seemed to squirm in his seat uncomfortably recalling the fateful day.

'The three of us would quite often play in the woods at the bottom of the garden. The biggest oak tree that stood on the banks of a small stream was our favourite.' His face lit up for a small second before returning to his solemn demeanour.

'Sophie and I were inseparable, even though her and Sarah were twins and we weren't. She was always so jealous and wanted Sophie to herself.' He stopped talking and took a deep breath, sighing loudly as he exhaled.

'What happened, Michael? You can tell me.' I urged him to keep talking. A stranger walked past the car, rudely looking in but soon continued passing. 'It's okay.' I gently squeezed his shoulder, half of me imagining it was Samuel instead of Michael and wanting to re-live his childhood trauma with him.

'Sarah was sulking as per usual below us. She was sitting up against the trunk making daisy chains. The morning sunshine was set in the most perfect blue sky, not a cloud to be seen. The grass still had a little dew on it and had left the top of our socks slightly damp as we ran through it to the tree.' Michael reached down to his right ankle and touched it as if he could still feel his damp socks from that day.

'We built a tree swing—my father had given us some strong rope and we found a large branch that was big enough for us to reach right out and fall into the stream. I loved hearing Sophie giggle every time she launched herself into the freezing cold water.' I smiled listening to his story.

'Where was Samuel?' I asked.

'He was quite often with my mother. He is six years younger than me so he would have been four at the time.'

Perhaps that was why Samuel had never mentioned it before. He was too young to remember.

'We were sitting together on the bottom branch but Sarah's moaning was annoying me so I pestered Sophie into climbing higher with me so we couldn't hear. Sarah wouldn't climb the tree without our help. Sophie didn't want to go any higher, she was scared and told me not to, but I kept telling her she was a baby. We managed to reach a couple of the branches above us, but Sophie started to cry and wanted to go back home. The more she cried, the angrier I became. I wanted her to stop and tried putting my hand over her mouth, but it made her worse. She tried hitting me to get me to leave her alone, but I flipped and pushed her in retaliation.' Michael was talking so fast, almost to get it all out in one go. He suddenly stopped and swallowed, struggling to continue.

My face dropped and my heart sank. I knew exactly what the outcome was without Michael finishing what he was saying, but I was more than aware it didn't stop there. With tears in my eyes, I listened as he began again.

'There was silence. I was too scared at first to look down, but when I did, the stream had turned red. Sarah had stopped crying, she was sitting motionless at the bottom of the tree, not even the birds were chirping. I froze. I should have clambered down that tree as quickly as I could, but I couldn't.' Michael began to sob uncontrollably. 'I see her in my dreams every single night. I see the blood in the sink every time I wash my hands and I hear her laughter every time I hear a little girl playing.' Michael wiped away at his face, trying to clear the tears, but each time he did, more fell. He was distraught.

'Sarah and I sat in that tree for over an hour, not moving, not wanting to face the reality of what had just happened. It wasn't until my mother called us for lunch and we didn't answer that she came to find us and it all became a reality. I have never heard anything like it. The shrill scream of a mother finding her daughter lying dead before her still sends shivers down my spine.' Michael looked at me in such a way that he wanted my forgiveness for something I couldn't give.

'Sarah told our parents that she was messing around and just fell. I got told off for being too high, but I think they both knew something else happened. From that day on, everything changed. They struggled to bond with Sarah because she reminded them of Sophie. Sarah resented me for what happened, and I couldn't forgive myself. The guilt is an unbearable burden.' Michael gripped both hands on the steering wheel and shook the car as if he wanted to rip it off in anger.

'I'm so sorry, Michael. It was an accident... you didn't mean to...' My voice trailed off as he stepped in.

'But I did mean to, Esmeralda. My temper got the better of me. I pushed her. It was completely my fault, and I would give anything to take that back.' His face turned to an angry guise.

I sat back in my chair, unable to add any context to the situation he was in.

'When my father announced that he was giving me shares in the business and he wanted me to learn the ropes, Laura had just announced she was pregnant—it was like a new lease of life. We, as a family, had something to look forward to. We even hoped it was a girl. I wanted to prove to my father that I wasn't a lost cause.' Michael turned in his seat to face me. 'When Sarah told me about a business deal that was too good to be true, I jumped at the chance. I didn't realise for one moment that it was a setup. It was Sarah's way of claiming her entitlement, getting her own back on me and showing how clever she was.'

'After all those years?' I exclaimed.

'She has always been the smart one, highly intelligent and independent, but the day Sophie died was almost the day that Sarah died too. Ignored by both our parents, too traumatised by what had happened that Sarah wanted to prove her worth to everyone.' Michael cleared his throat.

That's why she is so cold and unemotional. It all makes so much more sense.

'I withdrew some of the business funds and made an investment. One that I was sure would bring huge gains to the company, but when the deal went wrong, our shares plummeted and we lost millions. My father was enraged. He wanted me off the business. Sarah suddenly stepped in and looked like the saviour for a brief time. It had involved another rival firm, and as a result, we received death threats and the press were in a frenzy. It needed to be cleared up. I did the only thing I knew how to... I killed the head of the rival firm. The Richardson family rose to become one of the most feared investment firms in the industry at the time. When I thought my father would be angry, he instead became my best friend for sorting out the mess. A plan that Sarah had pulled together ended in my father thinking I was the mastermind and Sarah was the outcast once again.' Michael raised his eyebrows as if he couldn't believe what he was telling me.

'So, where does that leave you now?' I asked.

'It all got a bit messy. Sarah wanted ownership of the business, but my father wanted me to run everything. He said I was the only one who had the guts to protect the company. I knew she was plotting to have him removed but I wanted nothing to do with it. Emily arrived on the scene, and when my father died, I wasn't surprised that Sarah had something to do with it. She said that for once in her life, she wanted the limelight that she deserved. The only thing keeping me in England was my wife and my son, but Sarah soon put a stop to that.'

'What do you mean?' I couldn't work out the relevance.

'Finding out that my only son wasn't mine and that I couldn't have children after my wife had lied to me for over 20 years broke my heart in two. Imagine finding that out from your sister.'

'I'm so sorry, Michael,' I said. *So, it was Sarah that told Michael. Why would she do that? Revenge?*

'Just when I thought everything was over, Brian Ferguson appears. He was the son of the owner of the investment firm that crashed following our bad investment. They too lost millions. When the owner disappeared, the son knew full well it was the Richardson family who had wiped out their business and killed his father. He wanted to get his own back and began blackmailing me. When his attempts didn't work, he turned to drugs and alcohol. He lost everything—what was left of his business, his family... everything because of me. I don't know how, but Sarah and Emily managed to find him. He was chained to a chair in one of our warehouses, a dirty, smelly homeless man with his hair and beard overgrown, apologising for the threats that he sent.' Michael wiped away more tears as he continued with his story.

We had been sitting in the car park in the beaming hot sun for nearly an hour and I was beginning to feel dehydrated, unsure of where and when this was all going to end.

'Esmeralda,' he said, suddenly making me jump. 'If you were tied up in a chair, facing the man that destroyed your business and killed your father, would you be begging for forgiveness for blackmailing him?'

'I... um... I don't know... I...' I didn't know how to reply to his question.

'You see, the thing is, he didn't deserve to die. I was the one that deserved to die but he knew too much about the business and his father's murder. He was a homeless man who didn't have anything to lose. I had everything to lose. He had to go...' At this point, after everything that Michael had told me, he didn't seem remorseful for his death.

'I get it,' I said. 'You had no choice.'

I didn't get it at all. Everyone has a choice, and this is how he chose to end it, I thought, but I wasn't in a situation to disagree with Michael at all. I sat patiently still.

'Sarah and I made a further pact. Another life for a life. For what happened all those years ago as a child. For Sophie. For everything I had done. It was her turn now. With the help from a few people, we stole Brian's identity. In exchange for the business, I have everything I need now. Financial freedom and never having to look over my shoulder again.' Michael sat calmly looking into the distance.

'That's why, Esmeralda, I can't have anyone messing that up for me. It's finally over.' He had a look in his eye that made me very afraid. 'And Sarah also has everything she ever wanted.'

Before I had a chance to reply, I heard a muffled mobile phone ringing. Michael quickly reached into his pocket and pulled out his phone.

'Yep,' he said, holding it to his ear. I couldn't hear the words being spoken but I was confident that it was Sarah. Michael tutted a couple of times, followed by, 'Uh huh.' Then he hung up.

'It looks like we need you, so I have been told not to do anything to ruin that.' Michael seemed almost frustrated with any plans that he had for me to be halted. It sounded like Sarah had just saved my life.

'I promise you, Michael, I am on your side. Why would I want to bring the Richardson family down? There would be no benefit in that for me,' I questioned him.

'I thought your brother was a policeman. Hunter... is that correct?' His eyes looked curious.

'Yes, but...' There was a tap at the window and a tall gentleman walked around to Michael's window.

Michael tapped the button and lowered his window. 'Sorry, buddy. I think I'm finished here, just give me two minutes and it's all yours.' He smiled, allowing for the window to raise back to its closed position.

'Right, Esmeralda. Looks like our time is up. This man needs his car back and you need to head back to

Miami I'm guessing.' He watched me for a few moments, testing my reaction.

I nodded in agreement and watched as Michael got out of the car, dropping his sunglasses to cover his eyes once again, then he took a big wad of dollars from his pocket, counting them as he did so and handed them to the gentleman. Michael patted the man on his upper arm, both his hands sunk deep into his trouser pockets, and he calmly walked off to the main street.

I looked at the man and the car.

Now what? I thought. Is *this the real Uber driver? Am I going to make it safely back to Miami in one piece or is this a man that Michael paid to take me somewhere?*

The driver said nothing. I spent two hours in the back of the car without saying a word. I kept my eyes open the whole time for fear of waking up somewhere I shouldn't. A constant check of my phone to ensure we were heading in the right direction.

Chapter 14

Check Mate

By the time we reached my hotel back in Miami, clutching hold of my bag like a comfort blanket, I got out of the car and almost fell to my knees. All I could think about were the warnings from both Michael and Oscar.

I was too far into the case to back out now. The whole family were dangerous and I couldn't afford to jeopardise my life or those of my friends and family. One false move and I could be in the same coffin as Brian Ferguson.

David had warned me about the Richardson family, but I hadn't allowed for how well-connected they were or what they were capable of.

The only positive here was that I wasn't skulking around Miami, trying not to be seen or noticed. In all of this, there was still one thing bothering me more than anything else and that was Emily. What did she have to do with this whole case? I should have asked Michael and Oscar, but whilst a gun is in your back or you are locked in a car with someone capable of murder, you tend to forget important things to ask.

My plan was to call Hunter as soon as I arrived out of earshot of the cab driver and explain the events of the day. I hadn't quite worked out what to say yet and my plans always deviated, but at least I had the evening to piece things together.

It was early evening—the sun was setting and I was tired from such a traumatic day. That would make it the middle of the night back home. I would leave a message, hoping that he would call me first thing in the morning.

'HUNTER, CALL ME, IT'S URGENT.'

I almost ran back to my room. I whizzed past reception without saying hello.

I began desperately making my plans for leaving the following day.

'SARAH, WE NEED TO TALK. CAN YOU MEET FOR LUNCH? I'M CATCHING A FLIGHT HOME TOMORROW NIGHT.' I desperately texted her, hoping that she would pick it up quickly.

'12.30 TOMORROW. LA MAR RESTAURANT AT THE MANDARIN ORIENTAL. 500 BRICKELL KEY DRIVE,

DOWNTOWN MIAMI,' she immediately replied.

'PERFECT. SEE YOU THEN.'

I made my way up to my room via the lift and along the corridor, passing trays of leftover room service that the maids had removed and were waiting for the kitchen staff to collect.

I fished around in my purse for the room key and swiped the door entry system, shoving the door open wide and then letting it slam abruptly behind me. I stood there for a moment, my back up against the wooden panel. My head leaned against it and I closed my eyes.

I wished that David was here with me. As much as I hadn't seen him for years, and I wouldn't again, I realised how much in the past I had confided in him and relied on his advice. He would know what to do right now, much more than Hunter would—he was always swayed about what the police force would do rather than what was right and fighting for justice.

I was scared, and rightly so, but if Oscar had helped to fake Michael's death and Michael had killed Brian Ferguson, I should be going to the police for sure. Justice was seeing them go to prison, but he also knew about what I had done and that meant bringing down my best friends and brother too. I had no choice really.

I was sat on the floor in my hotel room staring at the photographs David had sent me, coupled with the possible connection to the homeless man, Brian Ferguson. It made me sad thinking of him and the memories we shared together, but it also made me more determined to solve this case.

I looked at Emma Campbell and studied her facial features.

What went wrong? A private education, a wealthy family, a wonderful fiancé, to suddenly a life of crime according to Hunter's check on the fingerprints handed in and left on the bank notes in exchange for Brian Ferguson. What was the connection?

I spread out the photographs across the carpet.

I lifted the Richardson family photograph, wondering why Arthur fell for Emily after his beloved wife died. Was it a life crisis? Was it one last fling before he died? Was he attracted to the younger woman that made him turn his head or was she just interested in his money?

Wait a minute...

I studied Emily's facial features just as I had done with Emma Campbell.

Emma had brown eyes and brown hair and Emily had blonde hair and blue eyes, but her features seemed weirdly familiar. Same smile, same lines and same type of nose and lips.

They couldn't possibly be the same person, could they?

Of course, they couldn't. I was being ridiculous. I needed some sleep—my mind was playing tricks on me.

I picked up both the photographs together, side by side, and studied them as if it was a spot the difference between the two.

Why would Emma pretend to be Emily and why would she befriend the father and family of her ex-fiancé? Was it revenge for being dropped by Michael and Laura? Did the family know who she really was?

My mind was running away with me. I needed Hunter to run a check on the database for me and see if he could find anything relating to Emily Carter and whether she existed or not.

'Hey, I'm so pleased to hear your voice,' I said as Hunter called.

'Are you okay? You sound shaken?' he asked. He could read me like a book.

I walked over to the king-sized bed and threw my body backwards onto it. 'Well, Hunter, I'm not going to lie, I've had a bit of a day. I took a cab to the West Coast of Florida.'

'Why?' he asked before I could finish.

'I was following Oscar. But when I got there, he was with Michael.'

'As in Michael Richardson? The deceased Michael Richardson?' Hunter said it as if it was no surprise to him.

'Nope. As alive as me and you. To make it worse, they know I am onto them. My phone had to be reset, so I stopped at one of the restaurants for lunch, but on the way back, Oscar threatened me with a gun and warned me to stay away.' I left out the part about lunch... he didn't really need to know that Oscar was playing games with me.

'He did what?' Hunter instantly sounded defensive. 'You need to come home, Esme, right away. Get the first flight you can back or I'm flying out there.'

'I'm okay.' I sighed. 'He told me to drop the case, Hunter.'

'Then you should, or I will arrange for him to be arrested. I'm not scared of him, Esme.'

'He knows.' I cut Hunter off before he could say any more.

'I don't care if he knows about the case or the stupid Richardson games. Enough is enough.'

'No, Hunter, he knows about the money. He knows about the investment company, and he knows all about Cinco Chicas,' I explained. He went quiet, I couldn't hear a thing. I checked my phone to make sure he was still there. 'Hunter?' I called out.

'Uh huh. I heard you loud and clear. How the hell does he know that?' He almost seemed in a rage.

'I have no idea. No one knows that apart from the six of us. If I don't drop this case, he will hold that against us and I can't do that, Hunter. I just can't.'

'Look, I understand. You don't need to convince me. Tell Sarah you can't continue and fly home. I will have you covered.' I knew he had my back.

'Not only that... I had a conversation with Michael.' I paused, waiting for his reaction.

'What do you mean you spoke to him. What did he say?' Hunter sounded desperate for more information.

'There is so much to tell you. The history of what happened. Why he needs to escape. How the others helped him. It's a whole can of worms, I'm telling you. Oh, and I nearly forgot...'

'Go on,' he replied.

'Emma is Emily...' I paused again.

'What are you talking about?' he asked.

'I've been looking at the photographs that David sent me, and then after seeing her the night before in Miami... she's the same person.'

'She's what?' He couldn't believe what I was telling him.

'I'll tell you more when I get home but I wanted to give you the heads up.'

'This case is getting more and more complicated by the day. What will we find out next?' I could tell Hunter was shocked at this new revelation.

'I'm meeting Sarah at lunchtime tomorrow at a restaurant in downtown Miami. I better go, I really need to get out of these clothes and record everything I have been given before I forget. it's been stressful to say the least.' I wanted to get in a hot steamy shower. I felt stressed and emotionally drained from all the chaos of today. Oscar telling me to drop the case, Hunter telling me to come home and Michael confiding in me. I knew what I had to do—no one had to tell me, I could make the right decisions for myself.

'Okay, if you are sure you're safe. And, Esme...' He paused and waited for me to reply.

'Yes...'

'Call me tomorrow and let me know what flight you are on...' I could imagine the fatherly look on his face and his hand on his hips as he was telling me what to do, but it was all for my own good—I knew that.

'Uh huh. Speak tomorrow.' Hunter hung up.

I walked back over to the door and made sure that the latch was fastened and it was securely locked.

There was always something about standing in a hot steamy shower that made you feel at ease, letting the water run down your body, washing all the stress of the day off and down the plughole, the vapour swirling around the air like a cloud of smoke.

I pulled open the large glass door to the cubicle and turned on the large silver tap so that the water began to flow from the ceiling shower head. Whilst it heated, I began to get undressed, reaching for a white fluffy towel, and placed it on the floor next to me.

I stepped inside, shutting the door firmly behind me. I looked up as the droplets fell and calmly closed my eyes, taking the moment to just think about nothing, but it was no good, I had too many things swirling around all at once.

I had it planned out in my mind exactly what I wanted to say to Sarah. I went over and over it, so by the time I briskly dried myself with the towel, I knew it off by heart. I wouldn't be disclosing all the items that I had discovered from email trails, documents and files, but I was going to tell her about the incident with Oscar and that I had found out Emma was, in fact, Emily. I would mention Michael, but I believe she already knew that.

The Mandarin Oriental wasn't just any hotel... it was a spectacular building. Even during the day, it lit up like a sparkling chandelier. I'm sure it was all the prettier at night. Overlooking the skyline of Biscayne Bay and on the exclusive island of Brickell Key, I felt like a celebrity attending a gala dinner.

Climbing out of the cab and looking up at such beautiful architecture, I hadn't noticed Sarah standing outside the main entrance on the phone. She turned to greet me with an informal hug and a couple of air kisses.

'Great to see you again, Esmeralda. You're looking wonderful today. The Florida sunshine has given you a lovely glow.' She looked at me up and down as if to check I was wearing the right dress code. I couldn't help that she was also being condescending.

'And you. What a beautiful location,' I returned the compliment.

'Come, follow me. Our table is just through reception.' Sarah turned and walked towards the main doors and on to the restaurant, telling me along the way about the exquisite menu we were about to divulge in by the acclaimed chef, Gaston Acurio. It sounded very much like Sarah was a connoisseur of fine dining, so I took her lead, and if she said the food was great here, then I was quietly confident that it would be.

The food wasn't the focus of my evening though. I had to tell Sarah the bad news and I wasn't quite sure how she was going to take it.

The open-air restaurant was on the waterfront. The glittering array of tall buildings lined our view, the reflection of lights from above sat on the water and gently rippled. It was quiet—a few of the other guests were at tables surrounding us, but it wasn't the chaotic and loud environment that I had been used to in other parts of Miami.

'I took the liberty of ordering us one of their finest champagnes, I hope you don't mind,' Sarah said as the waiter pulled her chair backwards for her to sit down on the seat opposite me. I recognised the brand of champagne from our drinks list served at Cinco Chicas, so I was familiar with how expensive it was.

'That's lovely, thank you, Sarah.' I wasn't my usual bubbly and confident self. I hadn't worked out my conversation starters yet, so I let her continue. I also didn't want to drink too much as I needed to catch my flight back later this evening.

'So, how has Miami been so far?' She lifted her menu and began scanning through the options. I felt I should follow and do the same. It may hide my nervousness.

'It's been an eye-opener. I have a lot to run through with you. See, the thing is I—' We were interrupted by the waiter as he returned, standing at the side of the table.

'Good evening, ladies, would you like some water for the table?' he asked, holding his hands close to his chest and clasped together. 'Can I also ask, will you be ordering from the specials menu or from the A La Carte?' He stood there waiting for an answer.

'It will be A La Carte and some sparkling water would be delightful.' I found Sarah quite an awkward person to talk to and I had only met her a couple of times so hadn't had a chance to bond as yet. She tried not to make eye contact wherever possible and took control in every situation. I nodded in agreement with her as it was the easiest thing to do, especially as I was just about to drop a bombshell.

I was also wary of what Michael had told me yesterday. It couldn't have been easy for Sarah to lose her twin, so I tended to make excuses for her arrogant behaviour.

Sarah, like the rest of the Richardson family, had dark straight hair. She wore the front half up in a neat clasp at the back of her head and a thick long fringe that ran down the side of her face. Her makeup was always very well-executed. It wasn't heavy—quite natural, in fact— but it made her look sophisticated. You could tell instantly from the clothes she wore, how she presented herself and her mannerisms that she was highly intelligent, business smart and wealthy. I got the feeling that she didn't care what anyone thought of her, and she always got what she wanted in the end.

The waiter left us to make our decisions from the menu and walked back to the inside of the restaurant.

'I would strongly recommend the Picante De Mani, which is the crispy pork belly, ají panca, papa seca and peanut cream served with white rice and choclo or the Planchaza, that has jumbo tiger shrimps, Spanish octopus grilled with anticuchera sauce, garlic butter, chimichurri, Peruvian yellow potatoes, choclo. In fact, Esmeralda, it is all exquisite.' Sarah looked up at me, studied my face and then returned to her menu. 'I think I will be going with the Picante.' She placed her menu back on the table, sank both arms to her lap and held her hands in a steeple gesture. She meant business.

'I think I will do the same.' I smiled, placing my menu back on the table as well.

'I understand you bumped into my nephew yesterday.' She stared deep into my eyes, no facial expression whatsoever, making it so difficult to read her emotions.

Shit. Shit. Shit. I thought. *Now, what? Is she upset with me? Is she angry?*

'I... um... well, the thing is...' I blabbered like an idiot.

'Esmeralda, let me make this simple for you.' She leaned onto the table and lowered her voice.

'Okay.'

'A few things have come to my attention. In fact, now that Oscar knows I started this investigation, certain happenings now make far more sense than they did before.'

'They do?' I asked. I wasn't completely sure what exactly she was referring to yet.

'Uh huh. I'm sure you are going to fill me in on all the evidence that you have been gathering, but...' Just as she was mid-conversation, I noticed a tall dark gentleman approaching from behind Sarah. I didn't want to seem rude and draw my attention away from what Sarah was saying but I couldn't help looking up to find Oscar making his way to our table.

What on earth is he doing here? The memory of him from yesterday in the park, his threatening words and the thought of him holding a gun against my back made me quiver. *Well, this is going to be interesting.*

'Good evening, Miss King. We meet again.' He confidently pulled up a chair between Sarah and I and sat down.

'Ah, Oscar, you made it.' Sarah smiled and placed her hand on his shoulder.

None of this made any sense. Sarah was the one at the beginning who said that he was up to something and that I needed to investigate. Samuel didn't have a good word to say about him, and after yesterday, I had no idea what was going to happen next. I looked from Sarah to Oscar in a confused manner.

What on earth is going on?

'It's okay, Esmeralda, we will explain everything shortly.'

'I'm sorry about yesterday, Miss King. I get quite protective over Michael, and well, you see, Sarah hadn't quite explained her plan to me until I called her. Now I understand.' His handsome brown eyes and perfect smile beamed back at me like a cunning fox.

'Okay, I'm listening.'

'So, yesterday, Oscar got a little excited and protective over the Richardson family. We both apologise profusely for that.' She glanced at him with an authoritative glare. 'It won't happen again. That is why I asked him to join us this afternoon. We also understand that Oscar told you to drop the case.'

'He did,' I agreed with her.

'However, we both don't want you to drop the case. In fact, we want you to take the case to the authorities and bring the culprit to justice in all of this.'

Before she could continue, the waiter returned to take our food order, but Sarah rudely ushered him away, asking if he could give us a moment and that she would call him over when we were all ready.

'Here is the interesting part, Esmeralda... Oscar has informed me just how clever you are at hacking into corporate networks and previous successful attempts at stealing money from businesses and turning them into your own money laundering empire. I'm very impressed, I can't thank David enough for recommending you.' She smiled. She was smart, very smart, and now they both had the upper hand here. Sarah's eyes glinted in the sunshine as if she had found a golden ticket and wanted to extort my expertise for her own gain.

'We need to find out what happened to my father, who that person was and they need to pay. The Michael situation needs to be buried and forgotten in exchange for your little secret as he doesn't want to be found.' Sarah and Oscar both raised their eyebrows and looked at me.

This was a change from what Sarah wanted me to originally find out for her. I also had some doubts in my mind after what I now knew about Sarah's childhood, growing up and what happened to her twin.

'And David? What about what happened to him?' I asked.

'Yes, and David. Of course. I was upset about Uncle David. He had been a family friend for many years.'

'So, let me get this right... you both don't want me to drop the case? You want me to go to the police and bring forward the case of your father's murder and David's murder, but you want me to forget about Michael's staged death in exchange for keeping my little secret quiet?' I checked.

'I think she's got it right, Sarah.' Oscar almost smirked. He motioned towards the waiter before I could quickly say anything.

I sat for a moment thinking about their ultimatum. *Do I have a choice in all of this?*

The waiter took all three of our orders, placed three champagne flutes on the table, filled them halfway and placed the remains of the bottle in the floor-standing champagne cooler to chill. Leaving me for a few moments to ponder the ramifications of such a deal with the Richardson family.

As soon as the waiter was out of earshot, I asked, 'Does Samuel know about any of this?'

'Nope,' Sarah quickly replied. 'I'm sure he will know soon, especially if you take this to the officials.' She looked at Oscar and shrugged her shoulders. 'So, what do you think?' Sarah asked.

'Do I have a choice? I mean, what is to say that Michael's incident doesn't come out? Who else was involved in this scenario? We have a homeless gentleman who has reported Brian Ferguson missing to the Metropolitan Police and a visual on a woman offering him money who resembles your legal friend, Emily Carter,' I said. 'What does Emily have to do with all of this?'

Sarah and Oscar both looked agitated. I think their poker faces were quite well-practiced but, on this occasion, I felt I had hit a nerve. There was something about Emily that I wasn't being told.

'We need to keep Emily close.' Oscar rubbed his head with frustration. 'We can sort that, the homeless gentleman may have been mistaken, he was probably on drugs or something. Besides, isn't your brother in the police—Hunter? I'm sure he can pull a few strings, right?'

I felt like this case had turned from me being an undercover investigator and working for the Richardson family to now being a part of this case and working with them. This was not the plan by any stretch of the imagination. Oscar was trying desperately to be a gangster and covering up their sloppy mistakes. Sarah was making every attempt to bring things together for the sake of finding out what happened to her father in a bid to prove to everyone that she could protect the Richardson business empire.

'So, Esmeralda. Can I call you Esme?' Sarah asked.

'Yes, of course.'

'Esme, what do we have so far?' They both leaned back, arms folded and waited for me to explain all the evidence I had uncovered to date.

'Okay, I will start from the beginning.' I felt like I was in a counselling session, about to spill my life story. 'We managed to get access to your father's medical records. He did have a history of kidney disease but what seems strange is there was a toxin found in his system that caused major kidney failure, which is ultimately what killed him. I have been searching through emails, files and correspondence to see what this could possibly be and who could be behind it.' Sarah and Oscar both frowned. I had their undivided attention.

'I went to speak to your mother, Oscar, and there were a few things that concerned me.' His face turned from focused to pained.

'And...' He pushed me to continue.

'She kept mentioning Emma and I couldn't understand who she was or why she had anything to do with this. Then when David was murdered and he sent me the photographs connecting Emma Campbell to Emily Carter, I soon realised what the connection was.'

'Emma Campbell?' I could tell from Oscar's face that he had no idea who Emma was, but it seemed strange that Sarah didn't look surprised at all.

'Yes, Emma Campbell was originally engaged to your father before he and your mother met. I did a little digging around and found that Emma took this rather badly—your father was the love of her life and wouldn't let it drop that your father and mother were now together. Emma changed her name to Emily Carter, she wears contact lenses and has died her hair, and up until a few years ago, she remained distant to the family. For some reason, she managed to get back in contact with the family, acting as a legal adviser, charming Arthur and befriending you all. There is a lot of evidence connecting Emily to the death of your father and David, but what I can't understand is what was in it for her in helping with the disappearance of Michael.' I looked at Oscar, who appeared genuinely shocked by me revealing Emily's true identity.

Had he really not known about her or her history with the Richardson family? Sarah, on the other hand, sat there still with a very cold look on her face.

The waiter arrived with our dishes and placed them all one by one on the table in front of us. I don't know about the other two, but I had definitely lost my appetite. It felt awkward enjoying a pleasant meal when there was so much happening around us.

'So, you think Emily is the culprit in all of this?' Sarah asked as the waiter disappeared back inside.

'I'm almost certain. All the documentation and evidence point to her.' I picked up my knife and fork but waited for Sarah and Oscar to begin first, but instead, Oscar stared at his plate frowning. He slammed down his cutlery and stood up.

'If you will excuse me for a second, please, ladies.' He stormed inside the restaurant, reaching for his phone, pressing his screen and raising it to his ear.

Is he calling Emily?

'I don't think he has taken that too well.' Sarah, still smirking, began to eat. Clearing her first mouthful, she continued. 'So, do you think you have enough evidence to bring a case together against Emily? I understand you have a legal friend that is very good.'

'Casey?' I presumed that was who she was referring to. 'Erm, yes, she is very good.'

'Great, well, she is going to need to be, although I have never liked Emily. She knows the legal system very well and it will be tough to take her down, but with the right evidence, I think we could do it.'

Why did I feel like Sarah already had this planned out? *Am I just here to execute her own devious plan?* I was just a porn in a game of chess and Sarah had just called Check Mate.

Oscar never returned to lunch. Sarah and I gave up waiting for him. I didn't want to ask what the relationship was between him and Emily, but I felt like he had been hurt and was now vulnerable. Had she played him as well as Arthur? Or perhaps she knew a lot more about the family than Sarah realised and Oscar was the one spilling the details.

Chapter 15
All Tied Up

Miami was a flying visit. I didn't get to see much of the city, only from a distance as I worked the case. Despite Naples being at the centre of two threats from two very dangerous men, it was a place that I would love to visit again, but this time, for pleasure. Its picturesque traditional American homes lining the streets, the expensive boutique shops and restaurants and the most stunning beach I had ever seen. Naples was the best-hidden secret in all of Florida, no wonder multi-millionaires chose it for their homes.

Although I had managed to find out a lot and the case had taken a complete U-turn after meeting with Oscar and Sarah, I was still apprehensive and confused. Yes, all the evidence pointed to Emily, but Sarah was pushing for her to be taken down immediately. If it was down to me, I would have liked to spend a little more time filtering through the details. I had a few doubts in my mind, and someone's life was at stake, so I had to be sure.

The plan was for the six of us to meet at Cinco Chicas and run through everything we had so far. I would de-brief them on the meeting with Sarah and Oscar. The next step would be to take the details to the police and legal advisers to arrest Emily, bring forward the charges and take it to trial.

I had to be careful with mentioning anything about Michael, and I had to speak to Hunter about burying the records regarding Brian Ferguson. As far as everyone was concerned, Brian was out in Florida, enjoying the sunshine and that was that. I didn't like putting Hunter in an awkward position but there was nothing I could do. He was in it just as much as I was.

The only question I had in my mind was Emily raising it. If she was to get the blame for everything to do with Arthur and David, would she mention Michael and risk being given an additional sentence? Did Emily know about Michael or was she just fed information? She gave the homeless the money and helped deliver Brian to the Richardsons, but I didn't know whether she was aware he was in Naples.

I needed time with her before we bought about her case.

The flight back seemed so much less stressful. No drugging of co-passengers or tracking of people on the way home. I just needed to sit back, relax and enjoy the nine hours of peace and quiet before the madness really began when I touched down.

The minute the plane hit the runway, my phone lit up like a Christmas tree in December.

What on earth? I couldn't make sense of the messages. One by one, they popped up, text after text. I couldn't see how many missed calls I'd had because my phone didn't have signal and I wasn't paying for Wi-Fi during the journey. I thought people could wait until I had arrived home—how wrong was I? I did have 12 voicemails though.

'Esme, you need to call me right now, we have a situation.' That was Hunter

'Erm. Darling, you are needed here. We are at the club, what time do you land?' Casey.

'It's all happening here, Esme. Cinco Chicas is about to blow up.' Mollie

'I have everything under control, but we really need you. Call me.' Hugo's voicemail seemed really interesting. I'm not sure whether it was the screaming and shouting in the background or the sound of smashing glasses and furniture.

I tried desperately to get off the plane as quickly as I could, but everyone was just as eager as I was. Scrambling for our luggage, checking we hadn't left anything behind and pushing and shoving past people who were too slow to make it to the jetway and back through security and customs.

I arrived at the main entrance hall where the lines of people zig-zagged back and forth. The horrid stench of body odour and sweaty people who had sat on the flight for nearly ten hours shuffled along, yawning as they went. EU and Europe arrivals to the left, all the other countries to the right. I queued again, passport and belongings in hand, waiting for my turn. I finally arrived at the barriers.

Biometric scanners and facial recognition-controlled access whilst the odd security guard patrolled those who couldn't make it through. I placed my passport on the top of the steel barrier and looked into the camera. I stood patiently as the scanner moved up and down, then flashed red.

'Come on, goddammit!' I complained as I shoved the passport out of the placement area and rammed it back in again. I tried to smile as I looked into the display, but it did the same thing again. Flashing red like an alarming beacon and saying 'Unable to verify.'

'Bloody technology,' I moaned, waving my passport at the security guard to get his attention. I *haven't got time for this. I* was frustrated and had to find out what on earth was going on at Cinco Chicas.

The security guard ushered me to follow him to a desk where an immigration professional ran further checks.

'Thank you, madam, if you would like to look into the camera for me.' She pointed at the small screen to her left while taking my passport from my grasp and studying it. 'I can see you have returned from The United States, was it business or pleasure?'

'Business—a meeting with a client.'

'Okay, and which hotel did you stay at?'

'Erm. The National Hotel.' *Am I in trouble?* I panicked slightly. T*his is all I need right now.* I looked at her, but I couldn't hide my concern. She must have noticed and looked up at the other security guard behind me and nodded.

'Okay, if you would like to follow the gentleman behind you to the passport control office, just beside the desks.' She handed me back my passport and continued to the next person.

I was being treated like a criminal—a suspect. W*hy?*

'Excuse me, why am I being taken to the passport office?' I asked him as he led me to a small office with blinds and a heavily damaged door. It looked like a police interrogation room.

'Just a routine check, it is only precautionary. I'm sure they won't be long.' His face didn't change, he looked stern, scary and completely uncompromising.

'It's just that I have somewhere I need to be...' I tried reasoning.

'Don't we all, that's what everyone says.' He held out a hand, showing me into the room. 'Take a seat, someone will be with you in a minute.' No sooner had he done that, he walked off leaving me staring at the plain white walls and my phone that was still going crazy.

'Miss King, right?' A smartly dressed middle-aged lady entered the room.

'Yes, that's me.' I looked up at her nervously.

'We have a strange situation. It looks like there was a marker placed on your passport. I'm not sure why, but after checking it, I don't see what the issue is here.' She raised her eyes to look at the paperwork she had in her hand.

'A marker?' I queried.

'Yes, it's normally a check due to an anomaly but I can't seem to find anything wrong. You've been in Miami for five nights, is that correct? And you stayed at The National Hotel, correct?' She asked.

'Correct to both, yes.' I couldn't see what the problem was.

'Hmm, strange,' she replied. 'And you're not a government official?'

'I used to be up until 2022.'

'Uh huh. I think you are free to go. I will walk you past the barriers, if you can make your way to baggage reclaim.' She smiled and opened the door for me to leave.

Just as I left the room. Oscar was standing at the security barrier having his passport and face scanned. He clocked me as soon as I emerged, taking a double check, but instead of a nice greeting smile, he returned an evil and calculated expression.

Was it him? Was he up to this? How had he managed to get a marker on my passport? I hadn't seen him or Emily on the flight or at Miami Airport. Was it a coincidence that he was at the security gates at the same time as me when there were hundreds of thousands of people arriving here daily? This was no coincidence to me.

I hurried as quickly as I could to the baggage reclaim area and waited for my suitcase to present itself on the conveyer belt. I stood as close as possible to big crowds so that Oscar couldn't see me or follow me.

While the same numerous amounts of bags shunted around and around the black rubber conveyor belts, I picked up my phone and read yet more messages. I needed to call Hunter and find out what on earth was going on.

I dialled his number—it rang and rang but he didn't pick up. I tried Hugo next. If he was at Cinco Chicas, he would be able to tell me the situation and if the others were there.

It rang and he answered almost straight away.

'Hugo?' I'm not sure who I was expecting.

'Finally. Haven't you heard of Wi-Fi on planes nowadays?' he said in his cute Spanish accent.

'I'm sorry I... I didn't think I would be needed for nine hours. What's going on?' I asked.

'Well, it's a long story but we have a friend of yours here and he is in a bit of bother.' Hugo was making no sense whatsoever.

'A friend? Who? What bother?'

'I believe he is one of the Richardson Gang.' Hugo went quiet but I could hear my name being shouted in the background. I knew that voice, I knew exactly who that was.

'What is he doing there?' I was puzzled.

'He said he was looking for you, but we caught him snooping around in the back room. The Albanians had him at first, so you might not recognise him.' Hugo laughed a little. Sometimes he laughed at the most inappropriate of times and wasn't fazed by anyone or anything. I think that's half the reason why we hired him and his connections to the Albanians.

'Oh no, what have you done to him?' I caught a glimpse of Oscar arriving on the other side of the trail of bags whirring past us. I *could do without this right now.*

'He needed to be taught a little lesson.'

'Are the others there with you?' I asked.

'Yes, everyone is here, you are the only one missing from the party.' He chuckled again.

'Right, I will be about 40 minutes. I need to get the Heathrow Express and the tube from Paddington to there. Just don't do anything else till I get there. Okay?' I hung up just as I spotted my suitcase bundle its way before me. I hoisted it up and placed it on the floor, ready to drag it along behind me as I made my way to the train exit.

I felt a little more comfortable getting the train to London rather than a cab as I didn't want to get stuck in traffic and I also didn't think that Oscar would catch the tube. It was an easy way to lose him.

In less than 40 minutes, I was outside the main doors to Cinco Chicas, smelly, sweaty and heavily exhausted. All I wanted was to have a shower and freshen up but I was worried about what had happened in my absence.

'Hey, Amar,' I said as I approached my favourite 6ft, 7in security guard, standing on duty at the front of our London club.

'Hey, Miss King. Let me get that for you,' he said with his deep, broken English voice as he pulled at the long steel bar on the front door and opened it up for me. 'Shall I take your case for you?'

'Why thank you.' I smiled courteously.

'Oh, Miss King?' he said after me. 'I'm sorry if I broke him.' He shrugged his shoulders in a bullish way.

'That's okay, Amar, I know you were only doing your job. Thank you.' I patted him on the shoulder and walked through the doorway. I couldn't help but laugh at the way he said he had broken him but was nervous to find out if he was okay.

It was a bit of a walk from the main doors, up the stairs, past the bar and up to the back room. The club seemed quiet—everyone must be up there together, but it was hard to tell as it was all dark and shut down.

I pushed the heavy doors open but I wasn't quite expecting the chaos that I was greeted with.

The girls were all together sitting on the sofas in the corner, side by side, drinking, chatting and laughing as if nothing was going on around them. Hugo was standing to one side with a wooden baseball bat in his hand and Hunter was standing next to him talking. They looked serious and in deep conversation.

Right in the middle of the room, muffled with what looked like a tea towel tied around his lower face and mouth. He had been thrown in a chair, both arms tied around his back and both legs tied to each leg of the chair, blood pouring from his nose and across his entire body. His head drooped to one side from lack of energy enabling him to hold it up. Both of his eyes were bruised, swollen and closed.

What on earth have they done to him?

I didn't want to say that he didn't deserve it for snooping, but I couldn't help feeling that he didn't deserve that.

I stormed over to him and untied the rag from around his face.

'What on earth were you thinking?' I shouted at Samuel.

'About bloody time, where the hell have you been?' Hunter shouted back and joined me, standing in front of his broken body.

'It wasn't anything he didn't deserve,' Hugo added.

'Let the man speak and explain himself!' I demanded.

'Hey, Esme, there's a drink here for you,' Casey shouted out.

'Samuel, go on.' I tried to resume some sense into the room. A drink was the last thing I wanted at this precise moment.

'Hey, look, I tried to explain but it's not what you think. I didn't even realise that you owned this club.' He looked around the room. 'It's quite nice, by the way, from what I can still see,' Samuel said as he tried to look up at me.

'Get to the point.' I ignored his complimentary remark and tried to act serious.

'So, I received a call from Oscar a few days back saying that a club manager in London had some evidence about my father and brother's death and that there was a money deal arrangement taking place. I had to find out, wouldn't you?' He looked at each of us in turn.

I could see his point, but I couldn't help but feel that it was a bit shady, and judging by the rest of the family, I struggled to believe that was all he was up to. I also knew way more than the others about Samuel. If there was one good egg in this whole family, it was him, but from experience, I didn't trust anyone.

'You believe me, don't you, Esme?' He had a pained look in his bloodshot eyes.

'How did you get past Amar out the front in the first place? He is a big guy to get past,' I questioned his story. 'You must have had help to distract him.'

'Not at all, I said I was the drinks license inspector and needed to check your documents. Amar came up with me, but when I met Hugo and asked to use the toilet, I waited for the opportunity when their backs were turned with deliveries downstairs to quickly slip in here. I knew I only had a few minutes, but they were quick.'

'So, what else did Oscar say?' I asked. There must have been more to the conversation. 'And how did he know to come here? You didn't know about this place, how did he?

The only way I could think that they knew about this place was if Oscar had been following me. Just like the time they knew that I would be in that underground car park, and I would be driving to David's son's house.

'I don't know how he knew. That was all he said. He told me that he was away in Miami and needed me to check something out to do with his father and grandfather.' He gulped heavily. 'He missed out the part about you owning it. Oscar's words were something along the lines of a money laundering establishment that had answers to the questions we have been asking.'

We both knew that Michael wasn't Oscar's father, but we went along with it anyway and kept it quiet for the sake of the others in the room asking questions.

'So, what did you find here?' I asked. 'Anything?'

'Nothing. Absolutely nothing,' he replied.

'Do you know who your brother was with in Miami?' I tested his knowledge and his reaction to what I was about to say to him.

'No, he said he was going to see Sarah and was on a business deal. He was quite cagey, but I presumed it was an acquisitions deal that he was trying to muscle in on and left it at that.' Samuel looked at the three of us in turn.

'Then he didn't tell you that he was with Michael?' I frowned, staring into his deep eyes.

'Michael who?' he replied as if it was a trick question.

'Your dead brother Michael, that's who.'

Samuel looked genuinely shocked.

The girls behind me suddenly became quiet. There was silence in the room as if I had just dropped the biggest bombshell of the case so far.

'I don't understand.' He twisted his arms in the chair, they were beginning to turn white through lack of circulation. I looked all around the room to find something sharp to cut the ropes from around them but I couldn't see anything.

'I'll get a knife from the kitchen, Esme,' Hugo said as he walked out of the room. I think everyone was starting to see that Samuel was, in fact, not like the other Richardsons in the family, he was more like Arthur. Still a businessman at heart but he knew right from wrong.

'Neither do I, Samuel, but I'm starting to pull things together. I'm starting to realise that you and Arthur are or were the only decent ones in the family. Did you know that Emily was also with him?' I revealed.

'Emily? What was she doing with him?' He frowned again as Hugo appeared with a kitchen knife.

'Or should I call her Emma Campbell from now on.'

'Esme, you aren't making any sense.' As Hugo cut the rope from around his wrists, Samuel pulled each one in turn and rubbed at the marks, clenching his fists and releasing them one by one.

'Did she not look or appear familiar to you?' I asked.

'You mean Emma as in Michael's ex, Emma? She couldn't possibly be Emily. I mean, she was crazy, but she looks nothing like her.

I think it was time that Samuel got the reality check that he needed. I took the girls up on the drink that they offered, released Samuel from the chair and explained a lot of things about the case that he didn't already know.

Chapter 16
Golden Boy

That night, Samuel and I left the club together. I felt bad that he had gone to Cinco Chicas on the presumption of finding answers as to his brother's death but instead got beaten black and blue by my club manager and his security team.

He shouldn't have been snooping around and he could have come away with a lot worse had he been caught red-handed, but that was beside the point. He was lucky that I was on his side. You could tell the girls and Hunter had been looking at me rather suspiciously when I defended him on several occasions.

I hailed down a black cab from just outside the club and helped Samuel into it. He clenched hold of his ribs the whole time and hung his head low so that the driver couldn't see too much of his bruised and blood-soaked face.

I noticed the disappointed look on Hunter, Mollie and Amie's faces as we both left. Casey was Casey and never attempted to take the moral high ground with me. She understood.

'Are you okay there, mister?' the driver asked through the screen. 'Do you need me to take him to a hospital at all?' He nodded in Samuel's direction. He must have caught a glimpse as we passed the light from the lampposts.

'Erm, no, he should be okay, thanks.' I smiled but didn't want to draw any more attention to him than there already was.

'Where are we heading?' the driver asked.

I looked at Samuel, ready for him to disclose his home address. I was half-expecting Kensington, Chelsea or perhaps Mayfair but his response surprised me somewhat.

'Arlian House, Wentworth, please.' He looked up to ensure that the driver had acknowledged his request.

'Wentworth as in *the* Wentworth?' The driver looked astonished.

'Yes, that's correct. It'll give you directions once you hit the main entrance.'

The driver's face was full of excitement and nodded like a nervous child. I'm sure he would be telling the next ten passengers that he had driven there for a customer.

The more I got to know Samuel, the more I realised that he wasn't like the rest of the family. He was such a breath of fresh air.

Michael seemed to be the black sheep of the family. The eldest that was supposed to have been the strongest, the leader and the heir to the business empire, but instead, he appeared to be the one that had messed up the accounts, caused the family heartache and the one who couldn't be trusted. He had a rage inside him that he clearly couldn't control.

Sarah seemed to me to be the strong one, the leader, the one who took control and fought for everything she believed in, got things done that needed doing, but equally, she felt shunned by the family. Lacking in confidence and never really got over the death of her twin sister.

Samuel was the youngest—the baby of the family. The one that perhaps his mother fussed over because he was the baby. He was too young to experience the pain that everyone else did and probably wasn't as close to Sophie as all the others. He followed his heart more than his head and knew right from wrong.

Well, that was my take on the family anyway, whether it was right or wrong was anyone's guess.

I told Hunter that I was taking him home and then leaving but that wasn't how the evening ended.

'Esmeralda?' Samuel looked up at me.

'It's Esme, and yes.' I had my arm around his shoulders and was holding his jacket into him, he had broken ribs for sure.

'You can say no if you like but I wondered if you would be able to come back to my home with me and stay. What with everything that has happened this afternoon, it would be nice to have a little company this evening if you don't mind. I'm always on my own.' He looked at me in a way that made me feel guilty for the second time this evening. How could I leave him on his own? I would be thinking about him all night if I didn't stay.

'Err...' I didn't know what to say. I wasn't sure it was such a good idea. David's words rang out in my mind over and over again. *'Don't get too close,'* he had said. *'The Richardson family are bad news.'*

But what did David know? All he had ever done was set my expectations high and then drop me like an unloved and outgrown toy.

I wasn't looking for answers from the Richardson family anymore, but it would be interesting to find out where Samuel lived and a little more about his personal life. I was intrigued, fascinated and charmed perhaps.

What makes this man tick? What is he truly like behind closed doors? Maybe everyone has got him wrong and I know the real Samuel.

He turned away and looked out of the cab window as if he was hurt—broken that I hadn't instantly responded with a yes like most other women probably did. I'm sure that they jumped at the chance of spending the night with a multi-millionaire, but that wasn't me and I didn't want the complications of what would follow.

'Okay, I'll come in, just to make sure you're okay,' I said.

Samuel turned his head to face me and smiled before switching his expression quickly back to a pained look. It must have hurt him to move.

'Thanks, it's appreciated.' When Samuel spoke, he looked in a way that I felt he meant every word he said. I didn't get that from Sarah, Michael or Oscar. I was normally a good judge of character and trusted my instincts.

'Why are we heading back to Surrey when you live in London?' I asked him.

'I have an apartment in London that I tend to use during the week. It is closer to the office and it's convenient, but my father left me the family home when he passed away. It's my go-to when I want to relax, feel comfortable and just be me.' Despite being hurt, Samuel did appear different this evening. He was more at ease, less rigid and professional than he normally was. He had dropped his bravado that I experienced the first night we went out for dinner.

'I see. So, almost your weekend home and your weekday residence.' I chuckled internally.

'Esme—' Samuel went to speak and it had sounded like the start of something deep and meaningful, but the driver cut him off instantly.

'Just about to arrive. Should I just continue through the main gates?' he asked politely.

'Yes, that's right, just past the country club and swing a left. You will reach a set of security gates, but we can get out from there.'

As we approached the main gates to his home, the driver slowed and we got ready to get out. I tried paying but Samuel reached up and stopped my hands in their tracks.

I wondered what he was about to say to me, but I was too distracted with our arrival to ask.

'I will get this, after all, it is some distance from London. I will organise a return journey for you in the morning.' He attempted another painful smile but stopped and continued to pay.

It was quite dark so I couldn't really see much except the lights from the house filtering above the thick metal gates that stood towering above us. Samuel limped towards the keypad and started entering the code to let us in. The gates began to slowly open.

To say I was impressed was an understatement. I hadn't heard of the Wentworth Golf estate as I wasn't keen on the sport, but Samuel explained to me that it was world-renowned and it was an exclusive place to join. Those sorts of things didn't impress me, but what did was the building that stood at the end of the long gravel driveway in front of us as we made our way onwards to the entrance.

It was a building of beauty—an architectural masterpiece.

A large white curved frontage the size of a car showroom greeted us. A circular glass structure at its centre, featuring a swirling grand stair from within, the light of the chandelier glistening through the windowpanes. There weren't many windows, the only ones were small and surrounded with black frames.

The clean white walls of the house extended either side to what I guessed were the acres of land that he also owned. To the right-hand side, a garage or small outhouse, still the size of my London apartment, was sheltered below the tall oak trees.

No wonder Samuel felt at home and comfortable here. If I owned a house this elegant, I wouldn't want to leave either. I would quite happily move from the busy and bustling city of London and escape to this country retreat.

'Do you like it?' Samuel looked at my reaction.

'I don't like it, I love it. This is beautiful.' I beamed at him. 'Your parents had great taste. Wow!'

'They sure did. Wait till you see it in the morning light, it's even better. My mother chose it. Designed and built back in 1935 by a famous architect. She fell in love with it the minute she saw it. My father didn't have the heart to sell it when she passed away and he made sure that Emily didn't get her hands on it either. I'm lucky to have inherited it and I plan to keep it in the family for my children and grandchildren.' Samuel sounded like an estate agent as he told me all about the history of his home.

'Your children.' I almost frowned, looking at him. I couldn't help but think about Oscar. Is that who he was referring to?

'And no, I don't mean Oscar.' Samuel reached for the front door and held out his hand. It had a biometric reader. I heard the catch release as soon as it scanned his fingertips. Samuel took the words right out of my mouth and mind for that matter.

'I...' I wanted to ask how he knew but it was too late.

'It's okay, Esme, I know you know. We can have a chat about that in a moment.'

I followed Samuel into the main entrance. It felt like a hotel reception. Marble floors, the most beautiful artwork and ornaments. So many doors leading in multiple directions all from this point.

I swallowed hard and took in all the sights and smells of this astonishing home, yet the thing I noticed more than anything else was the quietness and emptiness of such a place. You could hear a pin drop, an eerie stillness. Samuel must be lonely here, all by himself. It was a house, not a home.

'Drink?' Samuel walked off in the direction of one of the rooms to the right and disappeared.

I followed.

I found him in one of his many rooms, cream leather sofas that looked like they had never been sat in, a beautifully oiled oak parquet floor, white walls and a series of dark wood beading effect displays. Once again, it felt more like a hotel lounge than a home. Expensive artwork and ornaments littered the room.

He was standing in front of a glass wall, a row of bottles of alcohol and a neatly displayed bar.

'What can I get you?' He looked up as I entered the room. 'I have a bottle of champagne chilling if you would like that?' He was busy pouring himself a glass of rum in a small crystal tumbler. The smell as I approached was the memory of David and his love of rum, I had to block that part of my mind out this evening.

The look of pure release from Samuel as the glass met his lips for the first time and he took a sip. He held his head back and sighed. I was drawn to finding out what was going on inside his head.

'That would be lovely, yes, please.' I pulled back one of the brass metal bar stools and took a seat on the brushed velvet cushion. 'I'm so very sorry, Samuel, that's why we hired them so that they would be our protection should any trouble break out at Cinco Chicas. We weren't expecting it to be you.'

'It's fine. I shouldn't have been snooping around in the first place, only Oscar told me...' He pulled from the wine fridge a new bottle of unopened champagne and popped the cork. The bottle hissed and a small string of smoke filtered from the top. I watched as he slanted the flute to one side and poured it like he was a suave bartender.

Samuel placed the glass on a copper coaster and rested both hands on the bar, staring at me.

'The question is how a beautiful young lady such as yourself came to own a swanky London club like Cinco Chicas. I mean—' I needed to cut him off before I gave him too much information on me. Oscar already knew too much.

'It's a long story,' I said bluntly.

'I have all evening.' He looked further into my eyes. 'So, why did Sarah choose you out of everyone to take on our family case?' Was now the right time to tell him everything? Should I really let my guard down? Maybe this was his plan all along. To lure me into a false sense of security, obtain as much information and then be able to hold it against me forever more.

'I was recommended by David.' I took a sip of champagne, letting the bubbles flow down my dry throat, hoping that his questions would stop. I hated the confrontation between us, but I equally needed to interrogate him for as much information as I could.

'As in my father's best friend David?' He seemed taken aback. 'How did you know him?'

'He was a work colleague... David was my manager and mentor for many years.' I circled the rim of the elegant champagne glass with my finger, allowing my eyes to focus on its detail rather than looking Samuel in the eyes.

'Why do I sense there's something more to it than that?' I could feel his eyes burning a hole in me, I wanted to get up and walk away. 'You slept with him, didn't you?'

How do I answer that? How does he know? We hadn't known each other that long but, already, he could read my body language and knew I was keeping something from him.

Why does he want to know? Is Samuel jealous of my relationship with David?

'I don't really want to talk about it,' I immediately shot an answer to him on the defensive.

There was silence in the room, both of us with thoughts running through our heads about each other.

'Look, Esme, there are a lot of things I'm not proud of, but equally, I'm not the person you think I am.' His comment made me look up.

'And that is?'

'The media always portray us as bad villains, the Richardson family—notorious wrongdoers. They don't show all the good things that we do and how hard we work.' Samuel swirled his drink, crashing together the remains of his unmelted ice cubes. 'There are a lot of things that I keep close to my chest.'

'Like Oscar?' the comment shot out of my mouth before I'd had a chance to think about how it would affect Samuel. His face changed to expressionless. There was silence once again.

'You don't know the full story, Esme. There is a lot that we haven't told you and for deliberate reasons.'

Samuel removed his large and muscular hands from the bar and walked over to take a seat on the comfortable armchairs behind us, his glass in one hand, clutching the bottles of champagne and rum by the neck in the other hand, and placed them on the glass table in the middle.

I followed, sitting directly beside him, hoping to hear what he had to say.

'Try me,' I said, falling back into the plush armchair. 'Does Oscar know you are his father?'

'I was young and credulous, especially when it came to women.' Samuel leant back in the chair, his legs stretched out, one foot on top of the other and his arms cuddling the glass on his stomach. 'Michael loved Emma, but he wasn't *in love* with her. She, on the other hand, was besotted by him. She tried making plans, settling down with him, getting married, having children, the whole thing. Michael was feeling overwhelmed at such a young age, but he didn't know how to break from the relationship.' Samuel was finally beginning to open up to me, I could feel the emotion in his tone.

'Emma had been on at Michael to get engaged but he didn't want to. This one night, they had been out at a friend's party and her jealousy and rage caused a blazing row between the two of them. Michael had disappeared and couldn't be found... or didn't want to be found. I returned home from a night out to find

343

Emma in tears on my doorstep in the pouring rain.' Samuel looked up at me like a child that had been caught red-handed.

'What happened?' I prompted him.

'I don't remember much, Esme, but she spent the night. Michael met Laura... they had met before, a long time ago as Emma and Laura were school friends, but when he had a sports injury and Laura was treating him, they became inseparable. He tried telling Emma, but she said she was pregnant and Michael was torn between the two. Our father told him he had to do the right thing and stand by her, but it wasn't where his heart was. He was miserable, and after a month or so, he ended it.'

'How did she take it?' I asked.

'She was possessed. I had never seen anything or anyone like it before. She was uncontrollable, smashing all the lights, scratching Laura's car, turning up outside the house at night, saying she was going to hurt the baby.' Samuel rubbed his forehead painfully.

'It wasn't Michael's baby, was it?' I carefully looked at Samuel, unsure what his reaction would be.

He sat there motionless for a moment, staring at the tumbler on his stomach and then looked at me.

'No, it wasn't.' He looked hurt. 'Emma told me that it wasn't his and that they hadn't slept together for about six months as he never wanted to. She lied and told him that the night they conceived was the following night after she stayed with me, Emma said he was drunk but Michael couldn't remember so she left him believing that it was his so that they could be together. She was never interested in me—it was her way of keeping hold of him.' Samuel gave me a side look that felt meaningful. Checking whether I was listening to his story.

I smiled reassuringly. I didn't know what else to say.

'But then she lost it?'

'Yes.' He slowly nodded. 'Laura had a visit from Emma at work, it was the last straw. Emma's tantrums were affecting Laura's patients at the hospital. There were complaints but she wouldn't leave. Emma was warning Laura to step away from Michael, that he belonged to her. Eventually, Laura called the police and got a restraining order, but before they could arrest her, she became violent, throwing equipment and hitting out at the officers. She ran out into the busy road, the poor man on his motorbike couldn't break in time and knocked her unconscious. When she awoke in the hospital bed the following morning, they told her the news.' Samuel frowned, recalling the memory.

'I went to visit Emma. Michael doesn't know... no one knows. I felt sorry for her, even though I knew she was dangerous, but she was a broken and empty mess. And, she was carrying my child. Emma had lost everything, and she knew it.' Samuel looked upset, his eyes a watery brown, staring into oblivion. 'I gave her my number and told her to call if she needed anything, but I never heard from her again.'

'Didn't she have any family?' I asked.

'I believe she was an only child and her parents died when she was young. Michael and our family were the only people she had in her life.'

Samuel paused and thought for a moment.

'I love my brother, Esme, but for some reason, he is attracted to psychopaths, or they are attracted to him. I still haven't worked out which one it is.'

I laughed gently at his remark.

'Then Michael and Laura happened. At first, they were a match made in heaven, they were so in love. Anyone in the same room as them could tell. After Emma was no longer bothering them, Laura became more and more infatuated. She wanted the same—to settle down, have a family and get married. They tried and tried but it was no use. I think my father felt sorry for them after what had happened to Emma, he gave them the money to try privately and went to a London clinic for IVF. That's when it happened again.' Samuel hung his head low like a heavy weight was pulling from his chin.

'When what happened again?' I looked at Samuel confused.

'Laura was in tears and couldn't speak. She wanted to come over and speak to me... she said it was about Michael and that she needed my help. I had no idea what she was talking about. I answered the door and she was distraught, clutching a set of paper files in her hand.' Samuel leaned forward, refilling his glass full of rum, this time with no ice, ready to continue with his story.

'Laura said the clinic had told her that it was practically impossible that Michael would be able to father a child. I don't know how or when, but Emma must have told her that it was my baby she was carrying as Laura left me with an ultimatum. Either I gave her a child, or she would tell my brother about Emma. I thought it was done and buried, that I would never have to tell him, and I didn't want shame from Michael or my father, so I gave in. We both agreed never to talk about it. Not even to tell Oscar.' Samuel took a large gulp and leaned back.

'So, how did he find out?' I leaned into him, wanting to know more.

'He wouldn't tell me at first. I presumed it was his mother as we were the only two people who knew, but something wasn't right after my father died, and to some degree, I took out all my hatred and sorrow from losing my father on Emily. She told me that she knew Michael couldn't have children, that Laura had confided in her, but I never believed it. Now it all fits together. Emily, being Emma, knows all about what happened between us, would have told Laura and she would have been the one to tell Oscar.' Samuel stood up like a shock to his system. 'I need to use the bathroom, I'll be back in a moment. Help yourself to the champagne.'

I think it was an excuse for Samuel to remove himself from the room and the bad memories at the same time. He left me feeling exhausted just listening to it all. So much to take in. The Richardsons were one troubled family.

I half-presumed that Oscar came about because of a quiet love affair between the two of them, but it turns out that Samuel was emotionally blackmailed by both Laura and Emma into something they wanted more than anything in the world—his brother, Michael.

'The truth is, Esmeralda, I've never trusted women after that,' Samuel said as he re-entered the room. 'Only after what they want, and they will do anything to get it. Money, children, men. That is until I met you. You seem different.' He had unbuttoned his shirt slightly to reveal his dark, hairy chest and his sleeves rolled up. It was nice to see him so relaxed and at ease.

'Maybe I'm not different to them.' I poured the bottle to fill my glass half full and sat back in my chair, crossing my legs.

'What, you like my brother?' Samuel had a smile on his face for the first time this evening. 'Nope, I think you are very different, especially from Emma and Laura.' He raised his eyebrows and pointed his little finger in my direction in appreciation.

'So, how is it now between you and Oscar?' I wanted to change the subject away from his attitude towards women—me, in particular.

'It was strange at first. We agreed that it was Michael who had raised him and been there every day and night. He cared for him and that was how it was going to stay. He still sees me as an uncle rather than a father and that's fine with me.' His lips pursed together. I couldn't help but feel that maybe that wasn't the case and that wasn't how he really felt. 'Besides it would have broken Michael if he found out.'

'What if Michael did know?' I nervously asked.

'All hell would break loose... he would never speak to me again and I would be dead and buried in the ground. Michael has a rage.' Something stopped Samuel from talking, he looked at me in panic. 'He knows, doesn't he?'

'I'm sorry, Samuel. I...' I felt so sorry for him.

'Is he angry with me?'

'I think he realised that it wasn't you, it was Laura, but I can't comment for sure.' I needed to change the subject. The air suddenly filled with tension and unease.

'What about more children?' I quickly asked.

'I would love children of my own, Esme, but up until now, I've not met the right person.' Samuel looked at me in a way that I didn't understand.

What was he trying to say? Was he referring to me? I felt uncomfortable in a way, but I also felt slightly flattered. I looked at my watch to check the time.

'Erm... it's quite late, do you mind if I make a move?' My watch read 2 am.

'Of course. I'll show you to the spare room. I'll be up early and in the gym in the basement, so if you fancy some breakfast, just let me know in advance and I'll cook us something.' Samuel started to walk to the winding staircase as I followed.

It felt strange that I was being walked by a man that I had only known a few weeks to his spare room, and although I tried my hardest to deny that I was even remotely attracted to him, I wondered why he didn't make a move or why he made subtle comments about me but didn't directly say that he liked me.

We reached the top of the landing where small, expensive-looking lamps on side tables lit the way as we stood at the beginning of one of the prettiest and biggest hallways I had ever seen.

'I will leave you here, Esme. The second door on the right is yours. Help yourself to anything, there are fresh towels in the en suite.' Samuel was standing still, just looking directly into my eyes, searching for something but I just returned the stare. Neither of us spoke or made a move. It didn't feel awkward, we were both comfortable in the silence.

'Goodnight, Esme,' he finally said.

'Goodnight, Sam.' It was the first time I had called him that.

We both smiled and I turned to walk to the door, he did the same and made his way back down the staircase.

I reached for the brushed metal handle and opened the door, stepping inside. I gently felt around for the light switch just beside the frame and slowly closed it behind me. I moved so my back was firmly against the door, my head back against the wood and my eyes closed, breathing heavily in and out.

What even was that? I asked myself. *What on earth am I doing here?*

I'm in the spare room of Samuel Richardson's house, a multi-millionaire who I think likes me but hasn't made a move, and I am about to present a case in court related to the murder of his father.

I wondered what Samuel was doing right now... had he gone back down for a drink?

I heard a tap at the door followed by my name. It made me jump. Quickly, I spun around but froze before opening the door.

Gripping the handle, I opened it slowly, standing curiously in the doorway.

'I wondered if you wanted company?' Samuel stood opposite me and shrugged.

I didn't answer, instead, I opened the door wider so he could walk in. Both of us smiled.

That night, Samuel restored the feelings I had for any intimate relationship since David left me all those years ago. Neither of us were looking for a whirlwind romance or anything intense but he made me feel like an attractive woman again.

I didn't want to put my trust in someone so soon, but I felt like I had a friend as well as a lover in Samuel and he was good. He was very good.

Only one thing was certain—there was no way that I would be telling Hunter or any of the girls that I had spent the night with Samuel Richardson.

It was 07.32 am and I woke to the smell of bacon filtering into the room. I looked at the bed beside me and Oscar wasn't there.

Was he too good to be true? An amazing lover, an intelligent and caring man that wanted nothing more than company and a good woman.

I stepped out of the bed and walked towards the wardrobe, hoping to find something that I could wear to walk downstairs. As I opened the cupboard, I found rows of neatly ironed shirts arranged by colour from white to dark blue. I picked one, pulling it on over my naked body, hoping that he wouldn't mind me wearing it. It barely covered my bottom but it was just enough that I could speak to him and work out plans for me getting back home.

I tiptoed out of the room and along the hallway, approaching the same spiral staircase from last night and followed the breakfast smell to his kitchen.

Everything that I wanted to say disappeared from my mind. Instead, I was drawn to the large, floor-to-ceiling glass panels that distanced the kitchen from outdoors.

Samuel looked up as I entered the room.

'Good morning, beautiful. Bacon, avocado and scrambled eggs?' he asked.

I couldn't quite believe what I was seeing. I was more amazed by the garden than answering his question. I stood before the most beautifully landscaped garden I had ever seen. A stunning porcelain patio ran the entire length of the house. Next to this was an infinity pool, the water gently rippling over the edge... so tempting that I just wanted to jump in. Then there was the greenest of grass with the neatest of lines running as far into the distance as I could see.

What happens next? I thought. *Will this all be over the minute the case finishes and Samuel won't want to see me again? What if this is just the start of something beautiful? Telling Hunter and the girls won't be easy.*

Today was not the day for me to make that decision...

Chapter 17
Behind Bars

'ESMERALDA, WE ARE GOING IN, ARE YOU READY?'
Hunter texted me late the following night. The
evidence had been presented to the police. Casey was
on standby as a legal advisor to the Richardson family,
and it was the day when Emily was about to be
arrested.

I breathed a big sigh. There was no turning back now.
I couldn't believe what was about to happen.

Had I done the right thing? I wasn't sure if I was on
the right or the wrong side anymore, so many mixed
emotions all bubbling away under the surface about to
implode.

'I THINK SO.' I texted back but felt the need to
call him.

'Hunter?' I said as soon as he answered.

'Yeah.' There was a lot of commotion in the background, so I knew he was at the station with the team.

'Have I done the right thing? Why do I feel like such a traitor? This is Emily's life we are ruining.'

'It's too late now, Esme. She knew what she was doing and what she was getting involved in. You said yourself at the beginning, the Richardson family are a force to be reckoned with. The evidence is substantial. Besides, we have a lot to lose as well. I've got to go—everyone is on standby.'

'Oh, okay. You'll keep me informed, won't you?' That was a rhetorical question.

'Uh huh.' He hung up.

'GIRLS, I NEED A DRINK. HEADING TO CINCO CHICAS.' I put in the group chat, hoping that everyone would join me. If none of the others did, at least Hugo would be there.

I gathered my belongings from my apartment, laced up my boots and decided to walk to the club. It gave me a few moments to collect my thoughts and pull myself together.

As I walked along the road, I had visions of the Metropolitan Police force arriving at Emily Carter's house and arresting her. They would be in full force. Flashing undercover police cars arriving on her doorstep at any second. I could imagine her face as they knocked on her front door, reading out her rights as a citizen, handcuffing her petite wrists and taking her in the back seat to the station for questioning.

I had never been in that situation before, but I could sense the angst and apprehension she would feel. Unless, of course, she lacked empathy, guilt and any connection to the consequences of her actions just like a true murderer—just as David said she would.

The end of this case wasn't in sight just yet, not by a long shot but what was about to happen was important. We all had to play our part in showcasing the evidence to Casey so that she could defend the Richardson family in court. Emily would have to either defend herself or hire a good lawyer, in which case it would be expensive. We already knew that she had no access to funds without the Richardson family and she had no other form of income.

'Hey, Amar,' I said as I approached the club.

'Good evening, Miss King. Nice to see you,' he said in his deep accent.

'You too,' I said, almost running up to the bar to see Hugo. There was nothing in this world I needed more than to sit with my friends and have a drink in my second home.

'Vodka, blackcurrant and lemonade is it, Esme?' Hugo asked. 'Single or a double?'

'Oh, a double, please. What a day.' I placed my handbag under the bar and pulled up a stool.

'Is today the day?' Hugo reached for a highball glass, held it up to one of the bar butlers behind him and dispensed me two measures of grey goose vodka and a few cubes of ice. He then added a splash of blackcurrant cordial and a spray of lemonade from the bar gun, swirling it around to mix it with a swizzle stick, finally passing it to me like a well-earned prize.

The first sip was always the best, but it tasted so much better because of where I was.

'It sure is.' I took another sip and placed the glass back down, smiling from ear to ear.

'You look tired. You need a break.' Despite the overly large size of Hugo and sometimes the way he conducted himself towards women, he was the gentlest man you would ever meet. He was caring, loving and would do anything for you. Cross him and that was another matter... just as Samuel had recently found out.

He cared for us girls, just as Hunter cared for me as a big brother. We were lucky to have this team and I think Hugo felt we were like his second family.

'I am, Hugo, I am. Where should we go?' We both laughed.

'Somewhere sunny.' He chuckled as he worked his way around the bar, tidying and setting up for the night ahead when our doors would be open to the public.

One by one, all the girls started to arrive. Like sisters, we hugged one another. It had been a while since we'd all caught up properly without commotion or something happening in the background. We spoke all the time on the phone and messaged, but it wasn't the same as face to face or a good drink together.

Casey was nervous about the arrest, she had spoken to the Richardson family, and based on the evidence supplied by me and Hunter, agreed to take the case against Emily Carter. It would be a great experience as well as a high-profile case that would see her in the media. It wasn't certain but there was a strong chance that she would win too.

Mollie had gathered some fantastic evidence around medical records that would be presented as part of the case in court and had been promoted at work.

Amie was working with the Richardson family on stabilising Laura and was asked to see her on a regular basis as her psychiatrist. Casey would be calling on Amie to make a professional judgement on whether Emily was in a reasonable state of mind to be prosecuted for the murders of Arthur and David.

Tilly had also been hired to take over as the head of acquisitions by Samuel and Oscar at ATR & Partners.

Her vast knowledge of business and her ability to make smart and informed business decisions made her an ideal candidate.

We all had a reason to celebrate this evening but there was still so much that was up in the air and needed to be concluded, so we were far away from closing drinks.

That left me to finalise this case with Casey and move onto the next one.

For the first time in what seemed like many months, it was an enjoyable evening with the girls and Hugo. We all took our drinks through to the back room and drank like we used to back in the university days. I laughed so much that my sides hurt, and although it was only for a couple of hours, I felt like a weight had been lifted from my shoulders. Not a care in the world.

I was missing Hunter but I knew that he would be joining us as soon as his shift was over.

Mollie came sauntering into the backroom from having visited the toilets, but she made a loud entrance.

'Esmeralda, your boyfriend is here.' Samuel appeared from behind her, and for the first time, looked embarrassed. Just to clarify, Mollie never called me Esmeralda unless I had done something wrong, or she was angry with me, and Samuel was not my boyfriend. Not even close to it.

'Thanks, Mollie.' I laughed and pushed past her to greet Samuel. 'Have you heard?'

'If you are referring to Emily's arrest, then yes. Oscar just called me. He said he was there when the arrest happened. Apparently, she was devastated, begging him to do something to stop them but he was only there to make sure that it went through. She asked him to go to the station with her, but he declined. According to insider knowledge, she has been in questioning ever since.' I loved how the Richardsons had insider knowledge everywhere.

'Hunter should be here shortly. He said he would head over as soon as his shift finished.' I glanced at the time on my watch, which read 10.30 pm. He should have been here by now.

Just as I looked up again at Samuel, Hunter walked in. He hadn't even changed, complete in his full uniform, except his hat was under his arm. I think he did it because he liked the attention from the public in the main bar watching him, thinking there was something happening, and Casey liked his full uniform too.

She noticed the minute he appeared and walked over to greet him, snatching his hat from under his arm and placing it on her ruffled hair instead.

'Good evening, officer, what brings you here on this occasion?' Casey winked and tugged at the front of the hat above her eyes. She had a low-cut, revealing black dress on. Hunter's eyes didn't know whether to look there or straight at her giggling face.

'Well, that was interesting,' Hunter said, snatching his hat playfully back from Casey.

'Drink?' she asked.

'Yes, please, now that I am not on duty. I need to get changed quickly and will explain everything that happened.'

'That sounds ominous,' Samuel said, raising his eyebrows, and pulled up a seat next to the others.

We all gathered around the corner sofas and glass table like a board meeting. All eager to hear what was going on.

Hunter appeared like the star of the show in a more casual-looking outfit. Dark jeans, a polo shirt and white trainers. His hair flattened from having worn his hat all afternoon.

Casey passed him his usual, Jack Daniel's and Coke with a few ice cubes in a small tumbler and sat back down.

'Where do I begin?' He sighed, took a seat and sat back, finally relaxed.

'At the beginning, maybe,' I said, wanting him to hurry up.

'As soon as we arrived at the house, she was in disbelief. Two cars and an armed response vehicle, just in case there were any problems. She didn't resist arrest, but she kept quoting her rights as a citizen and that we had no evidence against her. Oscar was there too. She begged him to do something, but he almost seemed to laugh as they took her away.' Hunter looked at Samuel who was sitting there with his head in his hands listening to the unfolding events of Emily's arrest.

'We got to the station and she was really fired up... like a caged animal had been unleashed. She changed from the upset lady that we arrested to an angry and malicious woman,' he explained.

'Hell hath no fury like a woman scorned,' Amie said and laughed.

'She said she wouldn't answer any questions without a legal representative. We introduced her to our on-duty legal aid, but she still refused, answering everything with *no comment*. The evidence was compelling. In my eyes, she has no leg to stand on, but without her confirming or denying anything, she will be sent for trial. We have up to 96 hours to hold her in custody without charging her and we seized her mobile phone. They are running more checks as we speak.' Hunter scratched his head as if in disarray.

'The part I'm mostly shocked about is the lack of compassion shown by her.'

'What do you mean?' I asked.

'The questioning officer asked for her full name. She wouldn't give it. He then asked if her name was Emma Jane Campbell, to which she confirmed. She didn't even argue that it was Emily Carter. We also confiscated three passports, all with different names—Emma Campbell, Emily Carter and an Ella Curtis. Graphic photographs were shown of David's murder to which she didn't even flinch, nor the deceased picture of Arthur Richardson.' Hunter turned to Samuel. 'I'm sorry, I know he was your father and it must be difficult hearing this. I shouldn't really be disclosing this, it should be kept confidential, but we are all in this together, right?'

He didn't need confirmation from us. We trusted one another implicitly.

'So, when do you think her case will be heard?' I asked. Hunter turned to Casey to answer.

'There are normally two parts to every criminal trial here in the UK. This will consist of the prosecution and the defence case. The first will be about us providing the evidence in the courtroom to members of the jury and the judge, proving the charge against the defendant. The second will contain the defence case for Emma to prove her innocence. If there is any. This can take anywhere from a few months to over a year, but generally speaking, the time between being charged and the first hearing is 34 days. Between the first and second hearing, around nine days, and the time between sending the case to the crown court and the start of the trial approx. 119.' Casey confidently explained. I had no reservation in her legal skills, knowledge or ability.

'I NEED YOU HERE IN THE UK FOR THE TRIAL,' I texted Sarah, letting her know. 'THE ARREST HAS BEEN MADE. SHE IS IN CUSTODY.'

'THAT'S GREAT NEWS,' she replied instantly.

It was now a waiting game until the case.

The following day, Hunter returned to the station where Emma was being held in custody. She had been charged pending a trial date. I got a call from Hunter at the request of Emma.

'Esme.' Hunter's voice sounded cagey yet professional.

'Yes,' I answered.

'You have been requested by Emma Campbell to come in and speak to her,' he explained.

'Why? What does she want?'

'She says she needs to speak with you. It's important but won't say why. Emma will be transferred to a secure prison now that she has been charged. She will be transferred later this afternoon pending her trial date. At this point, she will be given a few visiting orders, which she will need to leave at the reception gate area for you to collect. Do you want to visit her? I can discuss this later with you.' He paused.

'Do you know which prison she is being transferred to?' I asked, my heart rate increasing rapidly.

'Probably His Majesty's Prison Bronzefield in Ashford, Surrey. It's a category A, high-security female-only prison,' he added.

I swallowed heavily and wanted a moment to contemplate but I had to go. There was so much I needed to speak to her about, I had a bad feeling about what she wanted from me.

'I had better go. I just wanted to let you know, Esme. I'll speak to you later.' He hung up.

'Okay, thank you.' I looked at the screen on my phone and just stared at the background display. I took on this case not anticipating the aftermath of uncovering the details and the consequences of what would happen to everyone involved. I know that Emma had a colourful past, but the reality soon hits home when someone is charged and sent to a high-security prison. This would be years of her life spent behind bars. Emma would be an old woman by the time she would be released.

My mind wasn't on anything else other than the pending visit to see the notorious Emma Campbell at Bronzefield Prison.

Hunter had given me all the instructions I needed. He offered to drive and I willingly accepted as I wanted to talk about the pending court case on the way.

The journey was quiet, both of us staring out of the front windscreen in a daydream. The occasional conversation but it didn't include Emma Campbell. We were only about a mile away and Hunter checked in.

'Are you sure about this?' he asked. 'I don't know what she will be like. She could be upset, angry, threatening or many other mixed emotions.' Hunter looked at me to gauge my state of mind.

'It will be fine. I need to do this. If it wasn't for my evidence, she wouldn't be behind bars in the first place.' I looked back at him with a blameworthy expression.

'What are you going to ask her?'

'I have so many things that I want to ask, but it depends on time, how responsive she is and what she wants from me. I would like to know why she did what she did. Why the name change? Is there anything I don't know about the Richardson family? I have been going over and over them in my head a million times the past couple of days.'

'Remember, the warden will be with you the whole time. If you are worried at any point, just tell him, you want to leave and I will be right outside. It's best I don't go in. Having a policeman accompany you may affect the hearing.'

As we approached the main gates for the estate, a separate building stood on the left-hand side of us. A tall female security guard approached the car as I slowly pressed the window release button to speak to her.

'Visitors?' she simply asked.

'Yes, we are here to see Emma Campbell, I believe she was only sent here 48 hours ago.' I looked out of the window nervously at her serious face. My palms were sweaty and my heart was racing.

'Okay, if you pull up into a space and walk around the side of the building to the main entrance, they should have a visitor's order for you to collect and look after you from there.' She stepped back from the car and waved us on, following our car as we pulled up into one of only a couple of spaces left.

'I'll wait in the car... I don't think you will be longer than an hour. They will enforce a restriction on times.' Hunter placed his hand on my shoulder for reassurance.

I took a long deep breath to regain composure, gaining all the strength and courage I had to walk in there. I was also mindful that this was not a nice place to visit. I had done a little research the night before, Bronzefield had the capacity for over 500 inmates and the majority of those already there were dangerous. I had to keep my wits about me and remain calm.

'Okay, thanks, Hunter. I've got this,' I said, pulling the door handle and slowly getting out of the car.

I looked up at the enormity of the building before me, surrounded by a large white wall. It looked more like a school than a prison—quite modern in design, large glass windows at the entrance with smaller square windows above and a floor-standing silver sign with the words HMP/YOI Bronzefield engraved.

The weather was miserable to match how I was feeling today, thick dark clouds were brewing in the sky above me and a few spatters of rain started to mark the pavement. I looked back at Hunter in the car park and finally started to walk in.

My hands were shaking. I wanted to turn around and walk out but I had to get this over and done with.

I stood at the desk, waiting for the woman behind the counter to finish her telephone conversation. I smiled patiently as she looked up at me, gesturing that she would only be a minute and was just finishing. I stepped back, allowing her some space.

As I looked around, the building appeared empty and clinical. I felt as though I was in a hospital waiting area. A smell of fresh paint lingering in the air. I had a reality check... it was time for Esmeralda King to hold her head up, be brave and get on with it.

The lady placed the receiver down and looked up once again. 'How can I help you?'

'I'm here to see Emma Campbell. I believe there should be a visiting order here for me, my name is Esmeralda King.' I stood confidently.

'Bear with me a second,' she replied, tapping away at her keyboard and checking her computer screen.

'Ah, yes. Let me just message the warden. Can I see photographic identification please?' she asked.

I ruffled in my bag, pulling out my purse and extracted my driver's license for her to see. She took a quick glance and thanked me for showing her.

'Just a couple of house rules,' she said. 'You will be taken to the visitors' hall. You can purchase teas and coffees in there but please do not take more than ten pounds with you. The rest of your belongings must be placed in the locker room and a member of staff will carry out a quick search before you enter. Is that clear?'

'Absolutely.' I nodded in acknowledgement.

'Okay, if you would like to follow my colleague.' She raised her hand in the direction of another female security guard that had appeared behind me.

'Your name?' she asked. 'You are here to see Emma Campbell, is that correct?'

'Esmeralda King. That is correct, yes,' I replied, walking after her.

She walked me through the next set of security doors, showed me the locker room to place my handbag in and checked my pockets, quickly spot-checked the rest of my body in case I was bringing anything in and then walked me in the direction of what appeared to be similar to a large canteen area. Rows and rows of plastic tables and chairs. I glanced around, there were a few people already seated having conversations, but when I was taken to where Emma Campbell was seated, I almost stepped back with shock.

The lady that I had originally met at Michael's funeral all those weeks ago had been replaced with a plain-looking, broken woman hanging her head in shame. I had to hide the look of dismay on my face as I approached her table.

'You have 30 minutes. I will be standing right here until your time is up.' The security lady stood with her arms crossed about ten feet away from us, watching the whole time like a hawk.

I felt uncomfortable, afraid and emotional all at the same time. It wasn't right what she had done but I was the one who brought her to justice. There was a large part of me that felt I had betrayed her.

'Miss Esmeralda King,' Emma said, looking up and directly into my soul.

'I wanted to call you Emily, but I understand your name is really Emma?' I opened the conversation.

'Well done for figuring that part out.' She gave me a devious smile.

It was like talking to a different person. Emily at the funeral was meek, mild and polite, someone that you would want to be friends with. Emma, who was now sitting directly before me, appeared evil and calculating with a dark look in her eyes.

'What happened, Emma? Talk to me. Tell me about you and Michael, how you first met.' I clasped my hands together for strength, hoping she would open up.

She didn't.

'I don't want to go there, thanks. Why don't you ask Laura?' She sat back in her chair but looked hurt. I felt that was a memory she didn't want to visit.

'Why Arthur? I thought you loved him?' I tried again.

'Oh, Arthur. Kind, sweet Arthur.' She smiled, this time with a pleasurable smile. 'I did love Arthur—I think, but he didn't love me. He did at first, but then he only wanted to protect his business and money. He wouldn't give me a penny. He only cared about his precious children. It was greed that killed him, Esmeralda. Not me, just plain awful greed.'

'Greed, why was he greedy?' I questioned her words.

'Everyone thought he was a warm and generous man, but I knew the real Arthur. He was into so many illegal business transactions. He was heartless when it came to business deals. He would have killed for money. He did kill for money, but it was covered up time and time again. How does that make him any different to me?' She angrily leaned forward towards me and raised her voice.

'That's enough, Ms Campbell,' the security guard warned her.

'He only wanted me in the end to cover up his sloppy deals that had gone wrong.' She sat back again after her outburst.

'So, that's the reason you poisoned him?' I prompted her.

'I don't know what you mean.' That same cunning smile returned as she dismissed my comment.

'What about Brian Ferguson. Who was he?'

'Who was he? Don't you mean who *is* he? He's living his best life in Florida at the moment. In Naples to be precise.' She gave out a low crackling laugh, it was chilling to hear. She was playing games with me—she was referring to Michael and I knew it. Sarah and Oscar said she didn't know but she clearly did. What if she let it slip during the case? Was that a risk they were willing to take?

'What about David?' I finally asked. This pained me more than anything else as I had an emotional attachment to him. I didn't know Michael or Arthur, so it felt slightly less relevant. I still had visions of seeing him cold and motionless on the table at the mortuary.

'Oh, well, now... David. He came digging into things that didn't concern him. He was Arthur's trusted advisor before I came along.' *Is she admitting to it?* I looked up at the security guard, with her arms folded, standing to attention like a guard of honour.

'Did you kill him, Emma?' I asked.

'No comment,' she spoke sarcastically.

'Emma, did you kill David?' I asked again.

'Are you deaf? I said no comment.' Emma was extremely angry, I could hear it in her brash tone.

'Why did you ask me to come here?'

'You can only hit a dog so many times before they turn, Esmeralda. None of this was my fault.' She crossed her arms stubbornly as if to deny any wrongdoing.

'What do you mean?' I needed an explanation.

'Laura ruined my life. Michael didn't love her, he loved me.' Her voice turned into a hurt, broken woman.

'She lied to him—he couldn't have children. Oscar is not his son.' She had tears in her eyes, her throat was cracking and she swallowed heavily.

'I know, Emma. We found that out, but you lied too.'

Her face suddenly turned, giving a shocked expression.

'Oh, I see. Fallen for Samuel, have we? He's a bit of a suave character that one. Did he give you the old sob story about Laura and I seducing him or did he give you the real story...' Her voice trailed off.

'I'm sorry, what are you talking about?'

'The real story that Samuel just can't keep his hands to himself. A complete womaniser, always jealous of Michael's ability to attract women so he just steals them when he isn't looking. Quite a charmer if you know what I mean?' I didn't want to believe what she was saying. Surely, she couldn't be telling the truth. It was a lie. All lies.

'That's enough, Emma. I'm leaving.' I immediately shut her down.

'They ruined my life. She ruined my life, he was mine. I lost my job, my home, my baby... everything. We were so happy together until she came along.' She looked down and away from me.

'You have two minutes left,' the security guard called out to us both.

I glanced at my watch, surely our time can't be over yet.

'We have only been here for...' I tried arguing with the security guard as we had only been talking for 15 minutes but she bellowed out the same words again, telling us we only had two minutes left. I wasn't going to argue the point in case I wanted to come back.

'Then if it was such a hard memory, why the name change? Why come back to the family that ruined your life?' I tried getting an answer from Emma, but the security guard stepped forward and asked me to return to the locker room to retrieve my belongings.

I was confused, I didn't understand. Why the urgency to get me out of the room? It was as if she didn't want me to get the answers from Emma and had been under instruction.

'I didn't want to, Esmeralda,' Emma shouted as she was turned around and asked by a warden to head back to her cell. 'If Sarah hadn't asked... I...'

Before Emma could continue, the warden pushed her and made her trip. She fell instantly to the floor with a yell. I stood there in shock. What was happening? What were the security guards and wardens trying to cover up? Why wasn't Emma allowed to speak?

There was nothing I could do. I could hear her cries and screams as she was walked out of the room and down the corridor. The security guard asked me to leave immediately but every time I tried asking what was happening, they said that she didn't know what she was saying. That she would do anything to get her sentence lifted and not believe anything that was spoken about today.

I left the prison feeling more confused than when I went in. I knew that Emily was guilty, and she had a history, but I couldn't help feeling that there was something to what she was saying.

Why would someone want to be involved with a family that had caused her so much pain and distress unless there was something in it for her? Something to gain? The promise of money... shares?

Was it true what she was saying about Samuel being a ladies' man and jealous of Michael? So many questions were still unanswered and I was no closer to the truth. In fact, I had more questions now than when I went in.

Chapter 18
Chaos In Court

The morning had a spring feel to it. The skies were partly cloudy, the temperature surprisingly pleasant and everywhere you looked, the trees were beginning to regain their leaves.

All six of us gathered outside the Old Bailey dressed in black as if we were at a family funeral. I hadn't been this nervous in a long time and I'm almost certain that this was the first time that everyone had been together since our university graduation all those years ago.

The outcome didn't affect us in so many ways, but I still felt like it did. I felt strangely connected to this one. Despite David telling me not to, I had grown to know the Richardson family in a comforting way. Samuel was now more than a close friend—maybe more than he should be. Oscar and Sarah needed my help and wanted me to work on projects in the future (how legal they were, I didn't know).

The one thing still festering away in the back of my mind was Emma Campbell and some of the things that she shouted at me when I went to visit her. Something had sat uncomfortably inside me since that day at Bronzefield and I couldn't figure out what it was. I hadn't been allowed back since I was told that she was not mentally stable enough for visitors. I was confident that officials were distancing Emma from the rest of the world.

Today would be the first time I would see her, and she would be questioned by Casey in front of the judge and jury.

'Are you okay with everything, Casey?' I asked.

She was pacing awkwardly back and forth along the main steps of the building, muttering under her breath all the things that she needed to remember and the points of the case.

'I think so. Too late now, I guess. As long as I don't mess this up for the Richardson family then I think we should be fine.' She glanced up and towards Samuel who was standing by my side. He was the only good thing to come out of this case.

'What about you, are you nervous?' Samuel asked, touching my shoulder.

'Hell yes. I'm very nervous about the case. Whether we are doing the right thing. Is there anything that we don't know? Whether her lawyer is any good, and the fact that Emma herself knows the legal system herself inside and out could be a huge advantage. She will know how to get around it, I'm sure.'

'Let's remain positive. I've got this.' Casey turned to face me and smiled lovingly. I admired her in so many ways, she was beautiful, smart, intelligent and confident. So many traits that I wish I had. Her desirable figure snuggly fit into a dark grey pencil skirt and suit jacket. Her hair neatly pulled backwards into a claw clip and a long fringe of blonde hair brushed along the side of her face.

A black London cab pulled up along the side of the entrance, inches from the kerb, and stopped. The door swung violently open and out stepped Sarah and Oscar together. Thick as thieves. Oscar nodded firmly at Samuel—no handshake or hug, just an assertive face gesture that meant hello. Sarah, on the other hand, walked around shaking our hands in turn and giving Samuel an uncomfortable hug.

For the first time since we had met, Sarah seemed slightly on edge, pending the verdict of the trial.

'I trust that we have everything in order?' She threw her stare towards Casey, impatiently waiting for a response.

'I do.' Casey nodded at her optimistically.

Hunter joined me on the other side of Samuel, his hand on my shoulder.

'We are nearly there, Esme. Nearly there and then it will all be over.' He shrugged.

Why do I get the feeling this will never be over? I grinned back at him and watched as everyone started to make their way to the courtroom.

Small pockets of people hovered in the main entrance of the building. I had never been inside the Old Bailey before, but I could instantly see why it was so well-known and regarded as such a majestic building. It compared only to an architectural masterpiece, the resemblance of an old art gallery and a historical wonder. As I looked up, I could see gold-clad glass domes above me, elegant paintings on the ceiling, ornate mosaic arches and stone statues on every corner. The floor was paved with bold Sicilian black and white marble.

My heart was racing, the adrenaline kicking in, enabling me to cope through the next couple of hours. The public gallery entrance was on the other side of the building so it would be interesting to see if anyone else was attending outside of those directly involved in this case.

The large courtroom wooden doors swung open and we filtered through. Dark wooden panels lined every inch of the room, except the large Sword of State that hung on the wall above where the judge would soon be seated.

Hunter, Samuel, Mollie, Amie, Tilly and I sat in the large balcony area of the room. Casey, Sarah and Oscar took pole positions to the right of us, just as Emma Campbell was led into the room. A prison guard and her lawyer in tandem. The judge was seated to the left of us, leaving the court clerks and barristers in the middle. Opposite us were a growing number of jurors entering the room and taking their seats.

You could cut the tension in the air with a knife. Quiet murmurs of people shuffling around and whispering questions to one another. I sat up straight, my hands on my lap, patiently waiting for the hearing to unfold.

I glanced over at Casey, who was sat like a pretty ornament in between Sarah and Oscar. She looked calm and collected, shuffling the papers on the desk in front of the three of them.

The female judge was seated and ready to speak. She appeared to be casting an eye around the room, settling in, checking everyone was in place, finding her bearings and clearing her throat.

I couldn't help but admire the traditional wardrobe that the judge was exhibiting, from the neat and well-kept peruke positioned on top of her head to the black gown and white jabot, otherwise known as a court bib or neck doily.

I could feel Hunter breathing heavily beside me and Samuel, nervously chewing the lateral nail folds on several of his fingers as he watched anxiously.

The judge banged ferociously on the table with her gavel, instantly bringing silence to the room, only the occasional sniffle or cough could be heard. She approached Casey first as she was the plaintiff and asked for her opening statement. This was her chance to bring the case forward and to talk about any evidence she would be presenting. Casey would then turn to the jurors and explain how she would like the jurors to rule based on said evidence. It was her time to tell the story and to call on any witnesses or statements to prove Emma Campbell guilty of murder.

It would then be the turn of Emma's lawyer—the defendant lawyer or respondent would cross-examine any witnesses as well as being allowed to testify to her innocence and provide any evidence to the contrary.

I sat on the bench, fascinated by how Casey confidently stood and addressed the courtroom. It was as if she was on stage in the spotlight and was performing a theatrical production.

Emma Campbell sat in the docks, her solemn head down, staring at the floor. She began to sniffle as Casey read out the case against her. I felt empathy for her. The further Casey began to read, the more Emma's sniffles turned into shoulder-shaking tears. She seemed remorseful, she showed regret, and in a way, my heart pained for her. A woman that loved someone so much would have done anything for him.

But was she acting? I couldn't tell. Was she really the sweet innocent woman that I met at the funeral or was she the malicious, lying and deceitful lady that hated me at the prison?

Emma was on trial for two counts of murder—Arthur Richardson and David Roberts. My eyes narrowed as they said his name. Never did I think all those years ago when we were working together that I would be sat giving evidence at his murder trial. I kept silent and listened, watching all the unfolding that was happening around me.

'And how does the defendant plead?' the judge asked Emma Campbell's lawyer.

A small plump man with brown hair and spectacles at the end of his nose was representing Emma. He must be good as I wondered why she had chosen him out of everyone from her network of lawyers.

'Not guilty, My Lady,' he said in a slightly squeaky, monotone voice.

There was a gasp in the room.

How is she pleading not guilty when the evidence was so compelling? I shook my head in disbelief, my eyes wandered briefly in her direction as she looked up and shot me an eerie stare. I didn't know how to take it.

Did she do it or didn't she? If she didn't, then who did? My mind mumbled away to itself.

Casey began the case with Arthur's medical records. First up to the stand was Mollie so that she could explain what they meant and why they were essential to the trial.

Mollie proceeded to describe Arthur's health and the condition of his kidneys as she pulled up examples of his scans and x-rays. Samuel looked down, too upset to hear some of the truths that Mollie was uncovering.

'So, can you confirm the cause of death on the coroner's report for the interest of the jury please?' the judge asked.

'Well...' Mollie continued. 'The cause of death was kidney and multiple organ failure. However, it is what caused this failure that we need to focus our attention on.'

'Please continue.' The judge accepted there was more.

'At first, the tests showed a toxic build-up, but we couldn't work out what was causing the toxicity. After further diagnosis and something unusual that appeared on Ms Campbell's receipts caused a red flag, we investigated further.' Mollie coughed, holding a fist up to her mouth as she did so. 'Star fruit is quite a rare choice of fruit, and it isn't the easiest item to obtain.' She looked directly up to the judge.

'I'm sorry, I don't understand the relevance of this fact, please explain or dismiss.' The judge held her face in contempt as Mollie carried on.

'For someone with kidney problems, the consumption of star fruit can have a harmful and toxic effect on a person, and in some cases, fatal consequences.' I could see the faces of the jurors turning to one another with concern as Mollie spoke about the first piece of evidence. 'It wasn't until Ms Campbell's mobile phone was confiscated by police when arrested on the suspicion of Mr Roberts' death that we found online shopping receipts for a substantial amount of star fruit and search terms referring to the effects on health for such an item. Please see article A.' Mollie displayed on the screen that stood at the front of the courtroom, for everyone to see, evidence of her purchases and her internet browser history.

All eyes were on Emma as she remained seated with her head down.

'Now, you could argue that Ms Campbell was unaware of the effects of star fruit on someone's health, but a further message to a Ms Richardson is more concerning.' Casey picked up the first piece of paper in her pile and began to read. 'That dithering old fool is getting worse. Those smoothies seem to be working, although the smell is making me feel nauseous.'

Our eyes turned to Sarah when her name was mentioned. Samuel, in particular, seemed disturbed by what was revealed—this was all news to him.

'Just to confirm with the court. When I refer to Ms Richardson, I mean Mrs Richardson. Mrs Laura Richardson was the recipient of said message.' Casey paused.

'Objection, My Lady. The evidence is misleading. Laura Richardson is unable to testify as she is currently being treated for several medical issues in hospital,' Emma's lawyer called out, but before the judge could sustain or overrule the objection, her sobs became louder and louder till she reached an outburst.

'It wasn't meant to kill him... it was simply meant to make him complacent and confused. I didn't realise he...' Her voice trailed off as her lawyer tried silencing her. At this point, Emma seemed afraid. She looked directly at Sarah in an almost scared fashion after what she had just said. Sarah returned with a very cold and hostile stare.

What's going on?

By this point, Samuel looked angry and I didn't blame him.

'Objection overruled. Plaintiff, please continue.'

'In conclusion, My Lady. The dates tie up with the consumption of star fruit. Arthur did, indeed, have kidney problems, but up until the point at which the star fruit had been ingested, they were mild and being monitored. As soon as he was given the fruit in copious quantities, he was admitted to hospital with complaints of vomiting, neurological complications and seizures, mainly caused by the fruit's high oxalate content.' Casey paused, observing her audience.

'One final piece of evidence was an email from Ms Campbell to Ms Sarah Richardson two months prior to his death. It read as follows...' Casey began to read from the second piece of paper. 'At the point of Arthur's death, what will my class A shares be worth?'

'Objection, My Lady. Evidence taken out of context,' her lawyer spoke up again.

'Objection sustained.' The judge looked angry at his outbursts. Emma sat with her head in her hands, shaking in disbelief. 'Why would the defendant be asking about shares upon the death of the deceased if not for financial gain?'

'That is all, My Lady. Next, I would like to present the case for David Roberts.' Casey waited for the judge to respond. It seemed only a short piece of evidence given for Arthur's death, but it was fairly straightforward. Casey and Mollie had multiple pieces of evidence in addition to this that they had submitted beforehand such as lab reports, medical evidence, forensics and pathology results.

Members of the jury flicked through their case files like a book that they were reading while the court was in progress.

This case was like a boxing match, of which Casey had won the first couple of rounds, but how would the next few turn out and what would the defence case look like?'

Hunter placed his hand on my shoulder. 'I feel like this is about to heat up a notch or two.' He sat like he was watching a television show and was drawn into the confusion of the room.

'Mr Roberts was found by his son, who immediately notified the police and reported a break-in. When police arrived, they found the body of a middle-aged man on the floor of his front room with several wounds to the head. I would like to bring his son, Josh Roberts, to the witness stand.' The room was silent as all eyes followed the upset young man that I had visited the night of his death.

I could see Samuel staring at me from the corner of my eye, watching my reaction.

'Mr Joshua Roberts, can you please tell me in your own words how you found your father that night and the actions you carried out following it.' Casey remained standing before him.

'Yes, I was worried as I hadn't heard from him in a couple of days. That is unusual as he normally calls or texts me most days. The last time I saw him, he was acting very distant, not quite himself... like something was on his mind.' His sad eyes kept building up with tears and he stalled his recall of the event a couple of times to hold his voice.

'Have you ever seen your father in this state previously?' Casey prompted him.

'Only twice before, once when my mother was diagnosed with liver failure and we knew there was nothing that could be done. The second time was when my mother...' His head dropped and he paused, choked.

Liver failure? I frowned dramatically as Samuel turned to face me. D*avid told me that she died from cancer. I just presumed that it was breast cancer. I don't know why.*

'It's okay, Mr Roberts. I understand that you lost both your mother and father recently. I'm very sorry for your loss,' Casey tried reassuring him, bringing him back on track to answer further questions.

'So, you were aware that there was something troubling your father. What was the first thing you did when you found him?' She pushed Joshua for more information.

'He wasn't answering the door, but his car was on the drive. He never walked anywhere so I decided to go around the back in case he hadn't heard, but when I did, I found...' He paused again.

'It's okay, take your time.'

'The patio doors were smashed, the curtains were blowing, and as I stepped inside, I could see his legs. He was lying on the floor. There was blood everywhere.' Joshua broke down, wiping the tears from his eyes. His two siblings were watching from the same balcony that we were sitting in a few rows back. They too had tears rolling down their cheeks that they periodically wiped away.

'Did you notice anything else unusual about that night, Joshua?' Casey asked.

'Yes, there were a few things that were missing from front room—he was quite a tidy man and he liked things to be in their place.'

'Can you describe those objects for me please?' she asked.

'Yes, one was a thick glass vase, it had thin daisy flowers painted on the side. It was special to him because he gave it to my mother on their last anniversary together.' A few tears rolled down my face, as I thought about the pain and trouble I must have caused sleeping with a married man. They were already in the process of getting a divorce when we spent our first night together, but I felt for Josh as he recalled the memory of finding his father.

'Is this the same vase you remember?' Casey pointed to a vase that had been placed in a plastic evidence bag and was rested on the table in the middle of the courtroom.

He nodded at Casey.

'Can you please confirm with a yes or no for the courtroom,' the judge called out to him.

'Yes, it is,' he replied.

'Thank you. Mr Roberts.' Casey then held up a second piece of evidence, again from within a plastic bag with a number on it. 'Secondly, do you recognise this item?'

'I do, yes. It is my father's paperweight.'

The shock hit my stomach with full force. I recognised that item—it was a glass paperweight. I had given it to him as a gift after a weekend in Poland. We visited the glass-blowing factory in the city of Jelenia Gora, he said how beautiful they were and I wanted to give him something to remember us by. Never in a million years did I expect to see that again.

Casey turned towards the judge and began to speak from her third piece of paper.

'My Lady. The two belongings were seized from the home of Ms Campbell, both have fingerprints matching those of the accused and traces of blood belonging to the deceased. The second exhibit matches the coroner's report of the item that caused the fatal blow to Mr Roberts' skull. I apologise if this is disturbing for you.' Casey turned to address Joshua in case he wanted to look away.

Pictures were shown to the jury of David's head and skull.

I felt a stabbing in my heart and an urge to cry that I couldn't control. Hunter knew how much David meant to me at one point in time, but Samuel looked at me confused—he had no idea. To him, he was a family friend, a man so close to his father that they called him uncle and the brother of his sister-in-law.

I pulled out a new tissue from my trouser pocket and dabbed my eyes so that my mascara wouldn't smear across the rest of my face. It was hard seeing David like that. It must have been even harder for his three sons. I wanted to leave the room but I knew that I would miss crucial moments. I broke through it, pushing aside any more of my emotions till the unthinkable happened.

'It's all a lie. A big setup. I've been framed, I have never seen those items before in my life. She is the one who did it. She is behind it all.' Emma stood up hysterically shouting at the judge and turning, screaming at the jury, pointing desperately at Sarah Richardson who sat there amid it all with a big smile on her face like a Cheshire cat, attempting to humiliate Emma.

'I'm innocent, you hear me! I have done nothing wrong. Oscar, tell them... tell them I am innocent,' she pleaded with him, but despite her cries for help, Oscar couldn't even look her in the eye.

Her lawyer was pleading for her to remain seated and calm down. The judge was losing her patience. I looked all around to see the chaos unfolding around me. There were gasps from the members of the jury as Emma was causing such a scene.

'Ms Campbell, I won't tell you again. Any more of these outbursts and I will have you in contempt of court.' The judges' words made no difference at all. Emma was frantic and out of control.

While all of this was happening, my eyes were drawn to Sarah and Oscar. Casey was enjoying the aftermath of her evidence reveal and seemed to be writhing in the onslaught. Sarah, on the other hand, was looking at the judge, who, in turn, was looking at her. Something felt uneasy with me and the way their exchange was a little longer than most. It was as if they were communicating with each other that only they knew what it meant.

I was expecting calm to be restored in the courtroom once the judge had given her orders, but Emma was still agitated.

'It is all a big conspiracy. Ask them about Brian Ferguson. Where is Michael Richardson now?' She continued screaming at Sarah and Oscar, but the more she continued, the more the jury and their chatter became louder and louder.

'That's enough.' The judge banged her gavel on the desk and everything stopped. 'You have had more than your fair share of my patience today, Ms Campbell, and I have warned you on numerous occasions. I am suspending court proceedings today based on disruptive conduct. I will not tolerate behaviour in the courtroom that substantially interferes with the dignity and decorum of judicial proceedings. I am also suspending today's hearing because of non-compos mentis. Ms Campbell, I understand that this can be a very traumatic time for you, but this has given me reason to believe that you need further medical and psychological examinations to stand further trial. Do you understand?' The judge was stern and affirmative.

'No, no, no, no. This isn't fair!' she cried. 'She is the guilty one here, not me.' Emma lunged forward to attack Sarah, but she stood instantly to her defence. Two large security guards rushed in and took hold of Emma's wrists, holding them behind her back, attempting to restrain her in handcuffs but she repeatedly wriggled free from them.

The front row of attendees, including Hunter, Samuel and I stood up, watching helplessly.

Finally, her arms were bound, the handcuffs were twisted closed, and Emma stopped moving. Her wails and cries were heard for quite a while as she was marched out of the courtroom, her lawyer in close proximity the whole time.

'Oh my god,' I said, clasping a hand over my mouth, gawping at Casey. She turned around to face me and held her hands up in dismay.

'Members of the jury, the case is adjourned, you will be notified of the pending court date for the continuation of this trial.' The judge stood angrily; she also made her way out of the room, leaving the remainder of us in complete disarray.

'Now what happens?' Samuel asked.

'The jury will give their feedback based on the evidence so far and the judge will give recommendations on whether she thinks Emma Campbell is fit to stand trial again or whether the case will be settled out of court,' Hunter explained.

'Can they really do that?' Samuel took a hand to his head and held it like he was in angst.

I just raised my eyebrows in response. I had no words to follow what a commotion we had all just experienced. I wasn't expecting it in the slightest.

Why was Emma Campbell so adamant about Sarah Richardson being the guilty party here when all the evidence clearly pointed to her?

Neither of us wanted Brian Ferguson or Michael's staged death mentioned in the courtroom for fear of bringing up other hidden secrets... the worry was how much Emma knew and how much she was prepared to keep quiet about. She had nothing left to lose, so what was stopping her? I had no idea whether she knew about my agreement with the Richardsons or the secret that they were hiding for me in exchange for theirs.

We all left the courtroom feeling broken and disorientated. The only two that seemed chirpy were Sarah and Casey, who were excitedly talking between the two of them about how well it was going so far. Poor Oscar looked like a rabbit in headlights.

Chapter 19
Pleading Guilty

A few weeks, but what felt like eternity, saw the return of the Richardson and Roberts murder case. This time, however, everyone except Casey seemed a little more confident of how court cases were run and the familiarities of the proceedings. For Casey, this was a daily or weekly occurrence and her normal work routine.

From the seemingly obvious sentencing that I had expected from the first hearing to the outbreak of Emma Campbell and how it had all ended last time, this time, I went in with a clear mind and open to anything that may occur. Everyone else, on the other hand, was adamant that Emma Campbell was guilty.

I wanted to see what her lawyer had in store for Casey.

Just as before, we were herded like cattle into the dark wooden courtroom. Everyone took their places in the same positions.

I had an overwhelming sense of déjà vu as I sat between Hunter and Samuel, overlooking the rest of the room like a theatre production about to begin.

Casey gave her opening statement and recapped the progress and evidence given from last time. The judge nodded in agreement.

'The defence, for clarity, how do you plead? We will continue with the defending case.' The judge had her head lowered and seemed to be writing away on paperwork, anticipating the answer from the defence lawyer to be the same as last time.

'Guilty, My Lady.' Another gasp of confusion rippled through the courtroom.

Guilty? I wasn't expecting that. Why? What has changed? I contemplated.

'Now what?' Samuel whispered in my ear, expecting me to know the answers.

'I don't know,' I replied, shrugging.

Sarah and Oscar sat in the centre of the courtroom like two smug individuals.

'A reduced sentence for good behaviour, perhaps? Intelligence against your family in exchange, perhaps?'

I whispered back to Samuel. 'Or a threat from people in prison, maybe?'

The jury were chatting away quietly to one another.

'Guilty. Okay, and how would you like to proceed?' Even the judge herself looked quite shocked.

'My Lady, I would like to call the first witness to the stand,' he addressed the court.

'Please proceed.' The judge nodded to confirm his request.

Laura Richardson appeared from the back of the courtroom—she must have snuck in at the last minute when we were all seated as I hadn't noticed her standing outside the room prior to it starting.

She looked strangely well. Her hair brushed and washed, a small amount of makeup and a smart dress with heels. Nervously, she took the witness stand, staring at Sarah with the darkest of eyes. Was this another family feud that I was unaware of?

Oscar looked up to her lovingly, despite his cold personality. This was the first time that I had seen him look at something other than himself with even the tiniest shred of love.

Between Laura and Emma, I felt the two of them were playing games. Two people with split personalities involved with the same family.

'I'd like to ask you a few questions, if I may?' Emma's lawyer began introducing her to the witness stand.

I was intrigued by why he called upon her, of all people. Could she really be classed as a reliable witness? Maybe these were all the witnesses Emma had.

'Yes.' Laura nodded in agreement.

'How long have you known Ms Campbell?' he asked.

'I have known her ever since primary school, we were in the same class.' The lawyer held up a photograph—first to the jury, then the wider courtroom, and finally for Laura. 'Please can you point out the same Emma that you see here in the courtroom in that picture.'

'That is her and that is me. Next to each other.' She smiled at the judge.

'Okay, great, thank you. May I ask what you were doing on the night of February 15th at around 8pm.' He stood looking at the courtroom like he was about to perform a magic trick. The suspense was growing as Laura carefully considered his question and then answered.

'Yes, I was in my room talking to Emma. She had paid me a visit,' Laura said matter-of-factly.

'And what time did Ms Campbell leave your room?' he asked.

'Not till gone 9 pm, she stayed for about an hour, but the rules are that visitors must be gone by 9.30 pm as lights out are 10 pm,' Laura explained.

'My Lady. I believe the time of death of Mr Roberts was estimated at around 8 pm, so the accused couldn't have been in two places at once. It takes approximately 20 minutes by car between the home of Mr Roberts and Laura's location. We also checked the street cameras and there appeared to be no vehicle matching Ms Campbell's that entered or left the street at that time. In fact, there were no camera recordings at all. Not one single door or street camera on the night of his murder.' Emma's lawyer, Mr Edward Darkin, who I had briefly been introduced to before entering the court, turned to face everyone with a look of revelation.

Casey seemed to take that as a threat, she detested losing with a passion, so being a lawyer was perfect for her.

'My Lady. I would like to cross-examine the witness, if I may?' She stood up and made her way over to where Laura was standing.

'You say that Emma came to visit you on the 15th at 8 pm?' Casey began repeating the details that Mr Darkin had quoted a few minutes earlier.

'That's right,' Laura replied with a slight smile.

'And you are certain about this?' Casey asked again.

'Yes.'

'Could you also confirm where you currently reside for me, Laura?' Casey asked a rhetorical question. She knew exactly where Laura lived.

'At Pashen House,' Laura said in a quiet tone of voice.

'And for the members of the jury, Pashen House is a hospital well-known for its excellent care facilities for mental health and wellbeing, is that correct? Can I ask, Laura, are you currently on any medication for your mental health?'

Casey walked closer to Laura, but her voice grew so that everyone could hear her, loud and clear.

'I, um, don't see that this has anything to do with—' Casey cut her off before she could talk her way out of it.

'This has everything to do with your evidence. Could you please confirm if you are on any medication and what for?' she repeated her question.

'I am on medication for schizophrenia.' Laura hung her head low as if she was ashamed as the whispering amongst the jury became gradually louder.

'I have one further question for you, Laura. Have you and Emma always been friends?' I felt that Casey was being crafty here. She was getting to the heart of the issue that we all knew existed between her and Emma.

'I don't erm... I...' Laura's face suddenly seemed to fade from her originally happy self when she first took the stand to a sad and fragile expression.

'Has there ever been any issues between the two of you that you think the court should be aware of? Any history of you both falling out with each other?' Casey worded it in such a way that Laura had no choice but to confess.

'Yes, we do have a history together. Many years ago, though.' Laura kept her face down and her voice low.

'Did you have a restraining order against Emma?' Casey asked. 'Now, for someone that caused you so many issues previously that you needed a restraining order, why on earth would she be visiting you and why would you be covering for her whereabouts? What is in it for you, Laura? What do you stand to gain?' Casey was trying her utmost to place words in Laura's mouth.

'No, that's not right. I'm not covering for her.' Laura seemed distraught, she was shaking her head vigorously, disagreeing with everything that Casey was saying. She held her hands up to her ears as though she was trying to block everything around her and began to cry heavily. 'No, no, no. Make it stop, tell them to stop talking to me, I can't take it all at once.'

Oscar called out, 'Stop it, she can't cope. Leave her alone. It's too much.'

Casey turned around to find Oscar's look of panic as his mother melted before all our eyes. The questioning had pushed her too far.

'I'm so sorry, Laura. I only wanted to ask a couple of questions... I didn't mean you any harm.' Casey tried to calm her down and reassure her, but her hands remained firmly across her ears.

'I think that is enough for this witness. Ms Richardson, you are excused. If you would like to leave the witness stand, thank you for your time.' The judge ushered for her to be removed.

'Mr Darkin, do you have any further witnesses that you would like to call upon?' the judge asked.

'I would like to ask the defendant to approach the witness stand, if I may? Emma's lawyer received the nod of approval from the judge and held out his arm, showing her the way to what felt like the main stage.

Emma stepped out from her chair and walked over to the stand. She looked about two stone lighter than when I had met with her a few weeks ago. Her thin body looked emaciated and a shadow of her former self from when I first met her at the funeral.

'Ms Emma Campbell. Can I ask if you would like to take an oath or make an affirmation that your evidence is true?' Mr Darkin asked.

'I do. I swear to tell the truth, the whole truth and nothing but the truth, so help me God.' She placed one of her hands on the shelf of the pillar she was standing in.

'Thank you. Do you admit to the lawful killing of Arthur Richardson and David Roberts?' he asked in a precious voice.

Emma stood still and didn't speak. Her eyes locked onto Sarah's, not a blink or a movement was made.

'Ms Campbell, did you hear my question?' Mr Darkin repeated, this time louder.

'I do. I agree to the manslaughter of Arthur Richardson. I meant it when I said I never meant to kill him, only to inflict confusion and slight illness. I—' Mr Darkin cut across her like a knife before she could reveal anything she didn't need to.

'And Mr Roberts?' he tried to clarify

'Yes. I killed him at his home on the night of February 15th. The noise grew louder in the courtroom as Emma admitted to everything. She admitted to it in such a calm and collected manner that it was almost not believable.

Mr Darkin threw his hands from his side and into his suit trouser pockets. He stood facing her for a few moments before speaking.

I imagined that this was not how he envisaged it planning out and Emma was digging an even bigger hole for herself.

'My Lady. I have one quick question for the defendant that we have yet to confirm,' Casey butted in whilst Emma was at her most vulnerable.

'Granted,' the judge waved her hand as if for Casey to hurry up and get on with it.

'Emma, can I ask why you changed your name to Miss Emily Carter? The decision to change the colour of your hair and eyes also... was this to confuse and distract the Richardson family?' Casey was good. The courtroom was still, everyone's eyes glued on Emma for a response but not a word was spoken. She simply stared back at Casey in a daze.

'Could you please respond to the questions,' the judge prompted.

'Look, I didn't ask to be a part of the Richardson family again. It's not easy you know—you have to do what they say. If she hadn't...' Emma paused, looking directly at Sarah. Sarah was staring directly back at her, not blinking, not moving, just locked on her features. There was a tension there that I had never seen before but I couldn't work out why the judge wasn't picking up on it.

'If you could just stick to the questions, please. We don't want a repeat of the last hearing, Ms Campbell.

Did you use the name and identity of a Ms Emily Carter, yes or no?' The judge's hands were clasped together on top of her bench, her patience tested.

'Yes. Yes, I did.' Emma kept her eyes on the floor and away from Sarah.

The whispering between the jury picked up again—they clearly didn't like that Emma was concealing her identity.

'Thank you, My Lady. I have a further question, if I may?' Casey took a couple of paces backwards so that she could address the whole court.

'Did you or did you not attempt to give Mr Arthur Richardson star fruit in an attempt to kill him and personally gain from shares and assets?' Casey swung her arms behind her back and held them there, her hands white from the pressure.

'I was told to... I was told that...' She looked painfully at Casey, unable to continue and too scared to tell the truth.

'Yes, Emma... you were told to what?' Casey edged forward. 'Remember, you are in a court of law and must be honest.'

'I was told that it would just make him a little dizzy or disorientated perhaps. That we could then persuade him to step down from the business and hand it down to the family. I didn't know he suffered from kidney issues. He never told me.' Emma nervously shuffled in her chair.

'And if you were told to jump off of a cliff, would you do it?' Casey turned her head and almost chuckled to the jury. I watched how she played a game with all those seated before her.

'No.' Emma frowned.

'Then why would you give someone something potentially lethal because someone told you to?' I was surprised that Casey wasn't asking who.

'The evidence is clear... you purchased the fruit, you searched the side effects, you knowingly chopped it up and put it in his smoothie every morning, didn't you?' Casey kept on and on, pushing and pushing her to admit to it.

'Yes, okay. I did and he got worse, but I just thought the sickness was the worst it would get. I had no idea he would... that he would... I mean, it was so quick... I...' Emma clearly looked distressed. Her eyes narrowed and began to well up. You could hear the sorrow in her voice. 'She...'

Emma looked again at Sarah and looked like she was about to start the same angry episode that she did last time, but Casey shut her down instantly. Turning her back and walking to her seat, she called back, 'Thank you, Emma, and thank you, My Lady. That will be all.' She smiled to herself, but just as she was about to sit down, she stopped herself and stood back up.

'Oh, I'm sorry... there is just one more thing, My Lady.' Casey turned to face the judge.

'Go on.' The judge was pensive.

'Well, you see, there is one thing that I just can't seem to figure out and it is frustrating me thinking about it.' Casey spoke as if she was the character Agatha Christie's Poirot.

'And that is?' The judge looked confused.

'Laura said that Emma had visited her around 8 pm on the 15th of February. We checked the sign-in book in reception and it did indeed say that she attended at 8 pm and left at just after 9 pm. We checked with the on-duty nurses from that day, and they don't recall Laura having any visitors at that time, so we decided to check the CCTV cameras.' Casey was pacing back and forth before us all, watching the neat line of her heels as she did so.

The whole courtroom was on the edge of their seats, desperate for Casey to reveal all.

'I was surprised to see that Emma's car did, in fact, drive all the way up to the hospital on that day and I checked that it was definitely her driving and not someone else.' Just as we thought that Emma had lied about visiting Laura and that her alibi was false, we all sank back into our seats.

'But I was also surprised to see that as Emma arrived at the main gates and drove to the entrance, the sky was dusk, almost dark but not quite. I checked the time of sundown in February in London, and it is approximately between 5.57 pm and 5.58 pm.' Casey turned to the jury and watched as each of their faces turned to shock.

My eyes widened and my ears pricked to listen to the next part of what she had to say.

'So, it can't have been 8 pm that Emma visited Mrs Richardson because, by that time, it would have been pitch black, not dusk. Why would someone lie about the time unless they were attempting to be in two places at once?' Casey was cut short.

'Objection, My Lady!' Mr Darkin shouted.

'Objection overruled. The data is valid. Please continue.' The judge looked at Casey and nodded in a frantic and impatient manner.

'Thank you, My Lady. Furthermore, I would like to draw attention to the fact that Mr Darkin earlier mentioned that cameras were either not working or didn't capture any footage along Mr Roberts' street. This in itself seems highly unusual, given that not one single door or street camera was working the night of David Roberts' break-in and murder. So, we did a few further checks and had a look at the cameras a few streets along for signs of any unusual activity.' Casey paused.

We were all on the edge of our seats. What had she found?

Even the judge's usual serious and grave expression had turned to one of suspense. She leaned forward, both elbows on the desk before her, almost looking over her bench to the witness stand beneath.

'Ms Campbell, can you please confirm if this is your vehicle registration number.' Casey held up a further piece of paper and read aloud the numbers and letters to the courtroom.

This was the first time that Emma Campbell looked guilty. She slumped in the stand. Her eyes red and tearful, her lips quivered as if they were to burst at any moment.

She nodded. A tear rolled down her cheek and she blinked.

'Please answer yes or no.' The judge jolted forwards with her demands.

That's when Emma Campbell broke, erupting with tears. She tried to speak and say the word 'yes' but her voice was fragmented.

Casey didn't wait for her to regain composure—she began playing a video in slow motion on the large screen in the courtroom. Everyone's eyes were clinging onto what she was about to play. No one said a word, no whispers or chatter, you would have been able to hear a pin drop.

She held the remote up, pointing towards the screen and pressed play. The time and duration were featured at the bottom. It read 7.59 pm, the counter was running.

The whole courtroom watched as we saw what looked like Emma Campbell's car pull up into the end of a cul-de-sac, a few streets down from where David lived. To one side was a quiet road, but to the other was a bank of grass, and in the distance, a thick forest full of tall oak and pine trees. It seemed to be a quiet road, but I could have been wrong.

Casey started with the commentary.

'Ms Campbell. Is this your car and is this you getting out of your car?' Of course, Casey knew it was, but it needed confirming to the court.

'Yes...' Emma's voice still crushed from her aching tears.

'The woods that you can see here just in the distance are the same woods that back onto Mr Roberts' house. No wonder no one saw her arrive—she arrived from the back gate. But my question to you, Ms Campbell, is if you were the one who gave the fatal blows to David's head, why did you tell the police when you were arrested that it wasn't you who killed him, and you deny murdering him?' Casey pressed pause and listened to what she had to respond with.

'I wanted to speak to him. To tell him that he had it all wrong,' she whimpered.

'Just to speak to him?' Casey sniggered before the courtroom. 'What did he have wrong, Emma? Couldn't you have called him?'

'He was going to go to the police about me, he suspected things weren't right with Arthur. He was his best friend and I just wanted to tell him the truth. That I didn't mean Arthur any harm, but...' Emma stopped and hung her head. Droplets of tears fell from her eyes onto her lap.

'But what, Ms Campbell?' Casey needed her to continue with her story.

'But, he was already dead on the floor. I panicked. I didn't know what to do, so I glanced around quickly in case someone was still in the house and then ran back to the car.' She took several quick, short breaths in.

Casey fast-forwarded the video in the courtroom, then paused it again.

'Ms Campbell, 18 minutes is quite a long time for you to quickly run through the woods, half a mile from his home, find him lying there dead, look around and run back.'

Emma sat unresponsive.

'What happened in those 18 minutes, Emma?' Casey prompted her but she still sat looking down.

'Do you have anything further to say?' The judge gave her a final chance.

'No comment.' Her tiny words were only just about heard.

Casey shook her head at Sarah and Oscar as she paced back to her desk. This time, she was finished with the cross-examination.

'No further questions, My Lady.' Casey sat down like the grand finale was over.

Samuel stretched both arms above his head as if he was losing the will to continue. Both Hunter and I stared into the ether, nothing to say, struck with the tension in the room, just as it had been when we first entered.

The banging of the gavel echoed, ringing like a gunshot in our ears. The judge scanned the courtroom from left to right, ensuring she had attention from each and every one of us.

'Ladies and gentlemen, I would like to invite the members of the jury to retire and consider their verdict.' One by one, all 12 people of the jury got to their feet and shuffled to leave the room.

So did the judge. The large wooden doors creaked open, and a refreshing waft of fresh air blew like smoke into the room. I sighed and slumped back onto the bench. The room was stuffy and humid.

'I think I need a cigarette.' I looked at Hunter and Samuel in turn, signalling that I wanted to leave the room and stretch my legs.

Carrying a mixed bag of emotions, we all stood up and filtered out of the warmth of the courtroom.

'Well, that was a rollercoaster of a hearing,' Hunter said as we made our way to the main entrance and stood outside. It was as if someone had switched on the lights. The bright sunshine made us all squint as we enjoyed a few moments of freedom.

'You're quiet,' Samuel said as I took out a cigarette from my handbag and lit the end.

'I still have reservations.' I inhaled, letting my body feel the effects of the tobacco as it entered my lungs. I sighed, watching the passersby outside the Old Bailey.

'Reservations about what? The evidence is compelling. She is as guilty as hell. And her stories don't add up.' Samuel almost seemed frustrated with how I felt but I couldn't help it.

'I know, I know. It's just...' I stopped. My mind distracted from Casey, Sarah and Oscar joining us.

'Even the forensics, the murder weapon. The fingerprints. I must say, I think it's going well so far.'

Casey's facial expression was the most elated I had ever seen her before.

'I'm happy for you. This is such a great case to present for your professional career.' Sarah touched her arm and smiled at her supportively, stroking her ego as she did so.

I watched the way she acted, then onto Oscar and his mannerisms. He seemed a million miles away, another planet perhaps, but not in the same vicinity as us. He fumbled nervously on his phone, his hands shaking and unable to stand still.

Ten minutes had passed and the longer we stood waiting, the longer I wasn't sure what the verdict would be. If it was not guilty, how would the Richardson family feel towards me and Casey? If it was guilty, how long would Emma be sentenced to?

Out of the whole case, this was by far the worst part. The threatening behaviours, the gun scenario in the park with Oscar, the car conversation with Michael and everything else that had happened along the way, didn't compare to the draining episode I was currently trapped in.

Another 15 minutes had passed and the crowds of people that gathered inside the main entrance were becoming petulant.

'Ladies and gentlemen, if you would care to take your seats, the hearing is about to proceed.' A large, burly man addressed the room and ushered us all back in.

There was silence. No one had any words. It was uncomfortable. The room had changed to a cold and chilling atmosphere and was filled with the smell of damp wood.

I took a deep breath in and waited impatiently for the judge to take her seat and announce Emma Campbell's fate.

'Ladies and gentlemen, the jury would like to address the court.' Ensuring everyone was quiet and there were no interruptions, she shuffled her attention to the spokesperson for the jury.

A petite man, not much taller than 5ft and a slender frame, stood up. He had neat, combed back greying hair, wearing classic thick-rimmed glasses. His voice was meek and mild.

'Thank you, My Lady,' he began.

'Can you speak up a little so the entire courtroom can hear,' the judge corrected him.

'We have studied the evidence carefully.' His voice was a little louder this time. 'The members of the jury have reached a unanimous decision.' He turned to check with the elderly lady who sat on his right-hand side for moral support but paused before continuing.

She nodded with encouragement.

'How do you find the defendant on the grounds of the murder of Mr Arthur Richardson?' the judge asked.

'Guilty,' he bellowed.

'And for the murder of Mr David Roberts, how do you find the defendant?'

'Guilty.' He quickly shot a look over at Emma Campbell as he shouted out their decision. She instantly fell to her knees, her hands grasping onto the chair beside her, sobbing uncontrollably.

Multiple people around the room had their hands over their astounded mouths.

Casey, Sarah and Oscar were hugging with celebration.

'Order in the courtroom, please,' the judge called out. 'Ms Campbell, please take your seat whilst I read out your sentencing terms.' Mr Darkin helped her up from a crumpled mess on the floor and into her seat. He looked up at the judge, disappointed that he had lost the case. I think, deep down, he knew he had lost it from the minute he agreed to represent her.

'On the basis that the jury find you guilty on two counts of murder, I am sentencing you to life for both cases. They will run in tandem where you will remain at HMP Bronzefield. Court is dismissed.' As quickly as it had started, the hearing was over.

I watched painfully as Emma Campbell was handcuffed again and dragged back to prison. With her tear-stained face and dishevelled hair, she looked back, trembling. Her eyes met mine—we were both locked in a stare with each other. I felt guilty *for* her. The stabbing in my heart that it was my fault she was here. My evidence, my crime-solving that resulted in the rest of her life behind bars.

Samuel squeezed and hugged me the tightest he had ever done before till I couldn't breathe.

'Amazing news, well done, Esmeralda. She is finally behind bars where she belongs. My father would be so proud of you for everything you have done, and the rest of the family are too.' With his hands firmly gripping my shoulders, he gave me the most doting smile.

I forced a deceptive look back at him, but deep down inside, I was tormented with the outcome.

I was in shock.

Chapter 20
Clever Intentions

That was the last time I ever saw Emma. I should have gone to see her, to visit her, but what would I say? And I don't think I would have been welcomed anyway. I think Emma partly blamed me for everything that happened because I was the one who uncovered all the evidence and gave it to Hunter.

I couldn't take away the success of the case from Casey. She had done a sterling job, highly professional and executed perfectly the evidence and the timing of each showcase.

What better way to celebrate than all of us, including Sarah and Oscar, reconvening at Cinco Chicas.

They had never been there before, so it was a tour of the club as well as drinks and cocktails. As soon as we arrived, we occupied the main bar area on the first floor. Hugo was his usual accommodating self, being the host that he was, pouring and making us a variety of alcohol concoctions as he went—of course, he was the main source of entertainment.

He and Samuel had now made amends after what happened the last time he visited the club. I watched the two of them as they spoke admiringly about sport and cars. Samuel had promised Hugo a trip to his home where I had seen his vast collection of luxury cars and a drive of his Ferrari—his pride and joy.

He was easily pleased.

Hunter and Casey were inseparable, just as they always were. He had been praising her for her sterling efforts as a top-notch lawyer and they both laughed about her featuring in newspapers and on social media for the hearing's coverage. Emma Campbell's arrest had featured on many media channels and made big news, so the outcome was sure to be a headliner in the morning.

Mollie, Tilly and Amie were at the end of the bar. They had been a little less vocal during the case because, although they wanted Casey to win, the result didn't really affect them too much in their day to day lives.

The remaining money that Sarah would be paying us would be split equally between all of us anyway.

That left Sarah and Oscar together. She was busy on her phone—I presumed it was work because that is all she ever did. She didn't seem to have much of a life outside of that and she didn't seem to be a well-liked person. Business deal after business deal, everything else was secondary.

Oscar, on the other hand, made eye and body language motions at a group of women who were clearly here for a special occasion—a hen do, possibly. The loudest of them all, a stunningly attractive young lady with long legs stretching out from her short skirt, boldly walked over to where Oscar was sitting on one of the bar stools.

I truly believe that a lot of women could smell money a mile away and were initially attracted to that instead of love at first sight, second were Oscar's good looks, and third was his personality. It definitely wasn't his charm or sophistication as he lacked in that area.

I sat for a moment people-watching, just taking everything in around me. A few minutes just to appreciate the end of all the madness that had taken place over the past few months.

A few deep breaths in and a few sips of my strawberry rhubarb gin and tonic water.

'Esmeralda, my dear.' I felt an abrupt tap on my shoulder from Sarah. Even her tone was condescending like a head teacher to a naughty pupil.

I jumped, turning around quickly to find her standing within my personal space.

'Sorry, yes?' I questioned what she wanted from me, and it wasn't very clear what she was saying as the music was so loud, the heavy thud of the bass banging in our ears.

'Sorry, darling. Do you have Wi-Fi here? I have no signal... and possibly somewhere a little quieter? I just need to, um...' She gestured to her ears and shouted.

'Erm... yes. Come with me.' I waved my hand for her to follow my lead.

I wanted to make sure that I was with her. Despite our relationship growing, I still didn't have one ounce of trust towards that woman and Cinco Chicas was our second home. I didn't want her snooping around. Not that I had anything to hide, of course.

Sarah walked after me. I could see out of the corner of my eye that she was taking note of all her surroundings. I felt like she was intruding.

What is she up to?

Dmitri was standing against the door, guarding our back room. He smiled and opened the door for us both.

'Ah. That's much better, I can hear myself think now,' Sarah said as the doors gently slammed shut and she took another 360-view of our room. 'I don't want to be adding more zeroes than there should be on your final payment, isn't that right, Esmeralda?' She looked at me like a woman possessed.

'Well, feel free if you want to add another zero to the end, Sarah.' I played along with her pointless comments, thinking that working with her would soon be over.

'I'm transferring to the same conspicuous account as last time, right?' I wasn't sure what she meant by conspicuous, but if it she meant the same untraceable, cryptocurrency account as last time, then yes.

'Yep, same account as last time please, Sarah.' I smiled pleasantly when, deep down, I wanted to get back to the bar with everyone else.

I watched her carefully, standing in silence as she tapped away on her keypad, transferring the remaining amount to me for our services. Any minute now, our agreement would be complete and I would be free from the Richardson family... except Samuel, of course, I had grown fond of him and our relationship. Who knew where we were going in the future together.

'I must say, Esmeralda, you did a sterling effort of uncovering all the evidence for me, and if it wasn't for your introduction to the rest of your team—Casey, Hunter, the wider police force, etc.—the case would have taken a lot longer to come to fruition.' She finished what she was doing on her phone and placed it inside her large, black designer handbag and began fishing for something else from within it.

'Although Judge Parker would have never let her be found not guilty, she had her strict instructions.' Sarah paused but kept looking into her bag. I couldn't see her face or make out her expression, but she stopped and froze.

I had a sneaking suspicion that she had just slipped up and said something she shouldn't have.

'I'm sorry, Sarah, what do you mean she had her instructions?' I prompted her to clarify.

'Oh, come on, Esmeralda. You don't really think that I was going to let Emma blab the truth about us all? She knew the consequences if she stuck with a not guilty plea... why do you think she changed her mind? She will be living the life of Riley behind bars now.' Sarah had the face of someone who was playing a game, a comical one at that.

'I'm sorry... I...' I was lost for words at what Sarah was saying.

'I have responsibilities to protect the Richardson family name. No one else will. Oscar is wet behind the ears and Samuel needs to grow a backbone. He's too nice, in my opinion.' *What is Sarah getting at?*

'So, you influenced the judge's decision. You gave her money?' I felt naïve... how did I not see any of this? I had my doubts during the hearing that it was slightly biased, but I didn't see this.

I said I didn't trust Sarah before, but this was on another level. I started to see her in a completely different light, from the minute we had dinner together in Miami to now, she was ruthless.

I stood glaring at her unremorseful expression in silence. I couldn't think of anything to say and the thoughts going through my mind were too strong to repeat.

'Esmeralda, my darling. Don't take the moral high ground with me. Just look around you, if you were so innocent, you wouldn't have a beautiful club like this, would you?' She threw both her arms in the air and rotated on the spot as if to showcase Cinco Chicas to me.

'It is hardly the same thing. We are talking about someone's life here, not stealing money from a business.' My voice raised in frustration.

She sniggered. 'What, hacking into a business account, stealing more than £1 million, embezzling the funds into a cryptocurrency account, sharing it with friends and then using the money to buy a chic London club that you then use further to launder your dirty investigation money?' Sarah walked closer towards me —she meant business.

Now, when you say it like that, it does sound a little worse than how I had made it appear insignificant in my own head over the years.

'Okay, agreed, it was a mistake. I was young and stupid. But I haven't killed anyone.' I tried to calm the situation down between us. 'So, what did Emma do and not do? Or was the whole hearing a complete sham?'

'Oh, well, Miss King. That was what I paid you to find out.' Sarah sneered at me. Her glare was thrilling, looking right through my soul.

'But I—' She instantly interrupted me.

'Did you really think she was that stupid that she got caught and happened to leave the evidence lying around for you to find? No, she was stupid enough to think that we would have ever given her any business shares, assets or equity. She was played from the very beginning. Even my father, who knew she was only after the money, played her for the idiot that she was. We all knew who she was.' Sarah gave an evil and calculated cackle.

I felt like I had been played too. David was right all along... the Richardson family were one to stay away from, but was Sarah that evil that she planned for Emma to kill her father just to gain the business and estates?

Thinking back to it all now, I could replay it over a million times in my head. Sarah led me straight to each piece of evidence and planted it right in front of my nose to find it. All she needed was someone to find it and deliver it into the hands of the police and law enforcement. *Clever, very clever.*

Regardless of her telling me not to, I acted on a strong wave of moral injustice ripping right through me and aimed it at Sarah.

'Do you not feel guilty that she is now rotting in prison for the next 15 years or so?' I shouted angrily.

'Esmeralda. She caused my brother and our entire family, including my late mother, a living hell while I was growing up. I remember it like it was yesterday. She stalked Michael, lost him his job, she would wait outside the house at night like a psychopath, she killed our dog and threatened Laura on numerous occasions. I hope she does rot in hell.' I had hit a nerve—it was the first time that Sarah had shared anything about how she felt or what happened between them all.

'If it wasn't for him inviting her back in exchange for shares and money, I don't know who we would have pinned the blame on.' Sarah raised her eyebrows as if it was a big inconvenience to them.

'Him?' I said, confused. 'Who do you mean?'

'Samuel, of course. Who else do you think kept in contact with her over the years? It wouldn't have been Michael, and Oscar didn't know her.' Sarah had a bemused look on her face.

I couldn't believe it. I couldn't breathe. The room felt small, dark and was closing in. I wanted to drop to the floor. Sarah's words were like a knife straight into my heart and twisted. The one man I thought I could trust other than Hunter. The man who I finally felt comfortable with had lied to me the whole time.

Why would he stay in contact? Why would he call her back in? None of it made sense. Was it more lies from Sarah?

Once again, I had discovered that the only people I could trust were my family and the girls—Casey, Mollie, Tilly and Amie.

The more Sarah spoke, the more I could feel my blood boiling deep inside my veins, my whole body building with pressure, ready to explode.

'But, Esmeralda, don't forget, we all have our secrets and need someone to blame, don't we?' She continued. 'You should know that more than anyone else. You killed David's wife, didn't you?' The pile of papers, encased in a folder that Sarah had been attempting to pull out minutes before our conversation, were neatly placed on the side next to her handbag. She patted them and looked at me.

'I'm sorry I don't understand... what—' I couldn't get a word out before she went on.

'Poor young Esmeralda thinks she has met the married man of her dreams. That is until he suddenly leaves in the middle of the night without saying a word. She is heartbroken and doesn't know why. Then she gets a call from me years later, mentioning his name, only to find out that he felt guilty because his wife was dying. She drank herself into an early grave because her husband fell into the arms of a younger woman. David's wife died of a broken heart, caused by you!' Sarah pointed her finger with full force in my face.

'No, no, no. That's lies. That is not what happened. She died of cancer. How dare you.' I was seething with her accusations. My body was shaking, I was at breaking point, but it raised the point that Josh said his mother died of liver failure in court and I thought it strange.

'Keep telling yourself that, Esmeralda, that you had nothing to do with it, and you will feel so much better. That's exactly what I tell myself, but the truth of it is...' She paused, clearing her throat. 'He told you that to protect you because he felt just as bad as how you are feeling right now.'

'I remember hearing and seeing him in my father's study all those years ago, he was telling him that he had fallen in love with someone half his age. Only, it wasn't until we met in Miami that I soon realised it was you he was talking about.'

'What else did he say?' I asked with tears in my eyes.

'He said that his wife knew something was wrong with their relationship, things hadn't been the same since he met you. She had asked him if he loved you and he said yes, so she asked him to leave. David's wife turned to alcohol because he left her for you. She died from organ failure, from years of drinking... because of you.'

'Stop it!' I screamed. I'd had enough of her lies.

'It's here in black and white.' She threw the file at me.

I frantically began flicking through the papers. It was true, she wasn't lying. David was the one who had lied. From the rehabilitation clinic notes to the coroner's report and her health records from the hospice.

Two blows in one night. Sarah saved this all up for after the case had finished.

David may have lied to protect me, but to find out this way hurt harder than anything I had ever been told before.

'See, Esmeralda, we are the same people. We both do things for our own benefit and gain.' She tried walking towards me, but I stopped her in her tracks.

'I am nothing like the monster that you are,' I spat the words right out of my mouth.

'Emma was right, we were only supposed to make my father a little confused and disorientated. It wasn't meant to kill him, but that was a lesson learned for all those years of blocking me out like I didn't exist.' She shrugged like it was nothing. 'Brian Ferguson was wanted by so many people. He owed so much to drug dealers too, we only had to deliver him to Michael and that was that. It was his body and identification we needed to cover up Michael's disappearance. The swapping of dental, medical and other records was simple. David, on the other hand... I was sad about him. I loved him like an uncle, but he knew far too much and wanted to throw me under the bus just for the sake of my father.' She looked at me to test my reaction.

I shook my head, tears of anger and sadness rolling down my face. There was nothing I could do to stop them, and to be honest, I didn't want them to stop. Months of tension and pressure left my body as the tears flowed.

'I'm sorry I did that, Esmeralda. What is the saying? An eye for an eye, a tooth for a tooth. Or whatever it is.' She too shook her head, staring into an open space in the room. 'So, now I have something on you, and you have something on me. Let's call it quits.' She held out a hand to shake mine.

I couldn't hold the rage inside any longer. Sarah knew she had me right where she wanted me and there was absolutely nothing I could do about it.

I threw the file back at her. 'You can screw your papers.' The documents fell on the floor, strewn in a mess as I steamed out of the door. She tried to follow, but I was too fast.

The first person to approach me outside the room was Samuel. The traitor. The person I let my defences down for. The person who had hurt me the most since David did.

'You need to stay well away from me.' My expression and tone of voice were filled with hatred.

Samuel grabbed both of my shoulders in an attempt to calm me down, but it only enraged me further.

'Esmeralda, what the hell is wrong with you?' he asked, confused as to what had ruffled me.

'Esme, are you okay?' Hunter joined Samuel by his side. His head tilted to one side and looked at me in a way that brothers and sisters communicated, trying to find out if he needed to step in or not.

'She is fine. There are no dramas.' Sarah's voice travelled from behind me as she caught up and tried to calm the situation.

'What the fuck have you said to her, you conniving woman?' Samuel had turned on his sister.

'Nothing much.' Sarah's evil laugh made the hairs on the back of my neck stand on end. I broke free from Samuel's hold, snatching my bag from under the bar, passing Hunter and practically running to the main entrance stairs. I cleared the staircase in minutes, bursting through the front doors like I was trying to outrun a panic attack and out into the fresh, cold, outside air as it hit me with full force.

The rain was heavy, the sky was dark, I stood in the street with my head tilted as far back as it would go. I closed my eyes, letting the drops of water soak my face, my makeup washing away like a melting mask. I took a long deep breath in and held out my arms, letting everything go.

Amar stood to one side, watching me like a mad woman.

'Are you okay, Miss King?' he asked.

'I am now,' I replied.

THE ESMERALDA KING COLLECTION

A new series of books featuring Esmeralda King as the main character. Esme, as her friends and family call her is a cyber security private investigator who solves cases on behalf of the rich and famous.

Her co-owned chic London club called Cinco Chicas is at the heart of their investigations.

Esme has her own secrets that she doesn't want divulged...

DECEPTION IN MIAMI

DISDAIN IN LONDON - AUTUMN 2023...

All books are available in paperback, hardback, ebook and audiobook. Collect your copy from all major bookstores including; Waterstones, Foyles, Barnes & Noble and Independent bookstores. Or download via all online platforms - Amazon, Google, Apple, Kobo, Audible and others.

Globally distributed.

About the Author

Kathryn Louise is an emerging author of crime, drama and adult fiction based novels. She is well known for the rebellious female characters in each of her books.

Born in Berkshire in 1980 as Kathryn Louise Murzell, she married in 2007 changing her name to Bennett but used her first and middle as her pen names. She still lives in Berkshire, UK with her family.

English language and literature has always been a passion for Kathryn Louise. She aspired to be an English teacher from a young age but deviated careers to support her family.

Now in 2022, almost twenty five years later, she has emerged with two collections; The Years Young and Esmeralda King.

The first two books have received outstanding reviews, star ratings and incredible feedback.

Social Media: @kathrynlouiseauthor

Website: www.kathrynlouiseauthor.com

 facebook.com/kathrynlouiseauthor

ESMERALDA KING

DISDAIN IN LONDON

KATHRYN LOUISE

FROM THE BEST SELLING AUTHOR OF THE YEARS
YOUNG COLLECTION